HIS DOMINATION

The Absolute Trilogy

Cynthia Dane
BARACHOU PRESS

His Domination

Copyright: Cynthia Dane
Published: 23rd September 2015
Publisher: Barachou Press

This is a work of fiction. Any and all similarities to any characters, settings, or situations are purely coincidental.

Part 1

PURSUED

Almost A Year Ago

The gun shook in Monica's hand. She had never fired one before – she didn't want today to be the day.

"You don't get to play the games anymore." Although her heart thumped in her chest, she had to be steady, cool. For the first time in her life, Monica had to look like she was in complete control in front of her nightmare.

A dozen pairs of eyes were on her. Jasmine, the woman she was trying to protect besides herself, and Jackson Lyle, the awful shit who called himself her boyfriend, her Dom, her *master*… they were the only ones that mattered. Jasmine, scared out of her wits, and Jackson, who didn't believe in a million years his demure submissive would ever actually *shoot him.*

"Now, my pet, that is a dangerous weapon you have there. You should put it down and give it to me."

The bastard actually held his hand out. *He can't be serious.* After so many years together... after all she had given him... after all he had *done* to her... he really thought he could say a few nice words and get her to back down? What kind of broken spine did he think she had?

"Don't you dare call me your pet ever again. You don't deserve to call me that. You lost that privilege when you started hurting me." The gun was hot against her skin. She hadn't even fired it – yet – and she was already anticipating the burn of revenge.

"Hurting you? What are you talking about?"

Monica's lip trembled. *Don't cry in front of him!* How many times had he made her cry? "I don't have to tell you or anyone else here. You know damn well what you have done. I may be submissive, but I'm still a human being. I'm not sure about you anymore. I don't think you're human at all."

"Monica." A few yards away, Ethan, a friend and the man who had come to take his girlfriend Jasmine away from this terrifying situation said. "This isn't necessary. Let's go."

Somehow Ethan coaxed the gun out of her hand, emptying the clip and showing how serious she had been as each bullet clattered on the floor. *I would have done it.* Her lip continued to tremble. *This man stole my life.* He would continue stealing the lives of other women until someone put him down.

Ethan took both women by the hand and drew them toward the front door of Jackson's lavish mansion, the place Monica had called home for years. She also called it her prison.

This wasn't what she had in mind for a jailbreak.

"You both will be nothing but whores for the rest of your lives," Jackson called after them. "You may not be our whores, but girls like you can't help themselves. You will always be somebody's whore."

Monica never expected it, but she was content with Ethan going up and punching the fucker right in the face.

***

"There must be something we can do..."

"He's too powerful. It's their word against his. That lawyer of his will do everything in his power to discredit Ms. Graham, especially. She pulled a gun on him. They'll get her for being mentally ill, at best."

"Do you have any idea what he did to her?"

"I saw the bruises, Mr. Cole. They would claim it's a result of their lifestyle."

"That's not BDSM. That's abuse."

"Even so..."

"I'll testify against him myself."

"I can tell you care for these women very much, Mr. Cole, but I'm afraid it will never be that simple. As your lawyer, this is my advice. Drop it."

***

One day went by. Two days went by. Soon enough a month had gone, and Monica had no idea how to live life on her own.

Funny thing, being in a relationship with a Dom like Jackson for so long. He had controlled every aspect of her life. She liked it, at first. It was welcoming, and suited her wishes from that kind of relationship. Except her prince turned into a dragon over the years. The words, the smacks that were more pain than pleasure, and then the...

Other people would ask why she didn't leave sooner. Wasn't she strong enough? Didn't she know her worth?

Love. I stayed for love. As toxic as Jackson had been, he was her Master... and Monica wanted nothing more from life than to love and serve her Master.

Now she was broken. A sub without a Master. Sure, she could move far away from him. Sure, she could rely on friends with connections for a while. And, sure, she could open her own business and stay busy... but her thoughts would always go back to that man, and her heart would always pine, hope, and dream.

Monica wanted to believe that there was something better out there. A better life, a better love...

Wasn't that the same thing?

Chapter 1

Rose Vines

One rose in the bouquet was crooked. Monica stood in front of the long dining table, the late afternoon sunlight streaming across it and blinding the others while she remained determined to figure out how to make that blasted rose no longer crooked.

"It's hardly noticeable," said Sylvia, one of the girls who worked for her. That evening she wore a black cocktail dress accented with pearls, her makeup bright in the lips and smoky around the eyes. Sylvia fancied herself a 21st Century Flapper. Not that she ever got the terminology down… but she could quote *The Great Gatsby* until her patron rolled over and fell asleep in bed. "Nobody is going to care if a single rose is crooked."

"I'll care." Monica reached for the stem and twisted it, the dewy red petals shifting into their new place. When she dropped her hand, however, one of the thorns nicked her fingertip

"Oh dear." Sylvia shuffled to an antique coffee table at the edge of the dining room. One of the drawers opened. Sylvia pulled out a small first aid kit and fetched the smallest Band-Aid she could find. "Do you need alcohol?"

Yes. Not the kind Sylvia was thinking of, however. What Monica needed was a glass of wine or maybe some brandy to settle her nerves. "No thank you. The bandage is fine."

She let her girl put the bandage on before dismissing her to the kitchen, where Sylvia was to find out the status of their dinner. *One hour.* This was the night Monica hated the most in her business. The night every patron and their invited guests came for a banquet of both the stomach and the loins.

Monica knew what she signed up for when she opened her house of sadomasochistic pleasure, especially when she catered to some of the most elite men in the country, let alone the world. The money was there. The *desire* was there. What was also there was a lot of planning, a lot of stress, and God knew a lot of little things that added up to fray Monica's nerves. Like a damned rose too crooked to be in a bouquet.

None of the patrons would notice, sure. Just like they wouldn't notice that one window had a smudge on it, or that the napkins weren't neatly folded, or that one place setting had the forks on the wrong side. They wouldn't notice because those mistakes were no longer there. From the moment they walked through the doors of Monica's Château, they were treated like kings. Presidents. *Gods*. Everything was just right. Even the five women Monica employed as mistresses were about as perfect as they could get. Oh, they had their physical and emotional flaws like anyone else, but they were trained to give and receive pain of the highest order, depending on what the customer wanted. Every girl had customers she saw once or on a semi-regular basis. They also had patrons. Rich, powerful men who paid for specific privileges that the average man coming through the doors didn't get to have.

All five patrons were coming tonight. Once a month the Château hosted a banquet for all five girls and their patrons. Usually only two or three came. Tonight was the first time since the Château opened its doors that all five decided to grace it with their presence at the same time.

For Monica, that meant more work making sure everything was prepared. The cooks had to be perfect on pain of firing. The maids had their outfits inspected multiple times. Monica even went so far as to hold their nails up to her eyes to make sure they weren't too sharp or too dirty. The patrons weren't allowed to touch them, but they had to look impeccable. These were men who were used to the world kowtowing to them, and Monica would not let them receive anything less.

It was business, but it was also personal. Monica was a sub. A Masterless sub, but a sub nonetheless. After spending the past ten years of her life living the existence of a full time sub, she knew nothing else. So when her last relationship ended, opening such a house of ill repute was all that mattered.

The Château was not a brothel. Everything was legal, although legalities were stretched. Police came by often to inspect the goings-on. Monica was ready for them too. So were some of her girls – as it turned out, most of the officers had some Dom in them.

"Chef says dinner is going as scheduled," Sylvia said, waltzing in as if she were Monica's #2. *She likes to think she is.* The girls were all equal in her eyes, although squabbles over who had the best patron and who would retire the richest happened during downtimes. "Anything else I can do?"

"Prepare for your patron." Sylvia couldn't seriously think she was dressed for success that night. Her patron, Mr. Carlisle, was too used to Sylvia's aesthetic. He probably didn't know it, but he would soon grow tired if Sylvia didn't mix it up once in a while. *It's my job to know that for him.* Men liked it when women anticipated their needs and wants before they even had an inkling of them. Mind reader, they called her. No, Monica was observant, and many men were the same in lots of ways.

The hour passed quickly. In the end Monica was almost the one to embarrass them all when she wasn't immediately there to meet Mr. Carlisle in the foyer. She was busy touching up the last of her makeup in the Ready Room at the top of the stairs. The Château was so large that it was ridiculous to expect any of the girls to run between their rooms and the front of the building. The Ready Room was where they kept backup supplies and could clean up if necessary. When Mr. Carlisle was announced, Monica nearly stabbed herself in the eye with her mascara.

She hurried to smooth out her dress, fluff her hair, and make sure she was steady in her shoes. When she reached the top of the grand staircase, however, she was the goddess of poise and the kind of grace her last Master expected of her. *Don't think of him here.* To conjure that man's image in her mind was to invite death into her heart.

"Mr. Carlisle," she greeted, her hand extending to shake his. "You're early tonight."

"Sorry for the inconvenience." He removed his outer coat and handed it to Sylvia, who took it with a graceful bow and hung it up in the wide closet by the door. "My guest canceled earlier today, so I came when I was ready. Don't mind me, Madam. Sylvia will take good care of me." He wrapped his arm around her midsection when she returned, planting a kiss on her cheek. "She always does."

Still, Monica could not let them go without making sure Mr. Carlisle's needs were tended to. Eventually she passed him to Sylvia's care and escorted them to the Receiving Room adjacent to the dining room. The last thing Monica saw before closing the door was Sylvia pouring her patron a glass of liquor from one of the Château's many wet bars.

"Mr. Witherspoon and Mr. Warren." The doorman's voice was steady. It helped that he was also the primary bouncer should a client get too rough. "Here to receive their salutations."

"Shit," Monica muttered. This is what she hated about them all showing up the same night. She wouldn't rest until they left the next morning... if she got to rest at all. She also had no idea who this Mr. Warren was, and meeting new men in the Château could be risky. However, he was apparently the guest of Mr. Witherspoon, the patron of another girl named Chelsea. Sure enough, Chelsea, with her platinum blond hair and red cocktail dress, was there to take the coats of both her patron and his guest.

Sam Witherspoon was a nondescript man of many, many means. Old money. Stinking rich money that nobody could remember the origins of, but it was probably nefarious, and thus best buried in the annals of history. The man had a balding head but did his best to look presentable in a crisp Italian suit and some of the nicest cologne Monica had the pleasure of smelling.

His guest, on the other hand, was a stark contrast.

"This is my old friend Henry Warren," Mr. Witherspoon said with a flourish to the tall man behind him. "We went to St. Mary's together. I told you about St. Mary's, right, Madam?"

Monica nodded. "Of course. Home of the best lacrosse team this coast has ever seen."

"That's right!" Monica hadn't remembered jack. Mr. Witherspoon was the type of man who lived for his glory days, even if those days were in a private high school for elite sons. Almost all those boys played lacrosse. And every one of those schools had "the best lacrosse team on that coast."

"You were introducing me to Mr. Warren?"

"Oh, of course, forgive me." Mr. Witherspoon clapped his hand on his friend's shoulder, which required an upward stretch to grab. "Henry and I are in similar fields of business.

He was in town this weekend, so I told him he should come and live like a king for a night."

As long as he doesn't expect anything. With all the other patrons there, the girls were booked for the whole night. Usually guests could be relegated to girls whose patrons hadn't shown up, assuming they liked each other enough. The girls worked there willingly, and if they didn't like a prospective client, they were allowed to decline an invitation to rendezvous in her room, a lounge, or the crassly called Dungeon. Of course, a girl who turned down too many clients wasn't any good to Monica. Yet there was one girl, Yvette, who turned down almost everybody except her rich patron who more than paid for her to stay there. *She really should move out.* As much as Monica liked the money, she liked having a thriving business more. A thriving business meant girls seeing many clients for spankings and dirty talk.

"Pleasure to meet you, Mr. Warren. I hope you enjoy your stay here."

"Please. Call me Henry."

His voice surprised her, mostly because she was expecting something lighter from this man. But Mr. Warren's – Henry's – voice was deep and clean, the sort of voice that sounded wonderful to fall asleep to while also giving a vigorous lecture that stirred the hearts of passionate students.

Melting. That was a good way to describe it, as if the tone of his voice melted on the air and nobody could make it solid again. Why would they? It was perfect the way it was.

"Henry. Of course." Monica released his hand and averted her eyes from the blond hair that was so dark it was almost brown, and from the strong jawline that likewise melted in a seamless line to join his face and throat. Truth be told, most of the men who walked through that door weren't much to look at. They were rich, charming, and sweet outside of the bedroom, but Monica would call few of them handsome. Maybe in their own ways, but... this Henry was the first man she met in her Château who made her heart flutter.

"Come this way, please." Monica stepped away and motioned for the guests to follow.

One by one the other patrons and their guests arrived. The only other surprise that night was a female guest – to make it an even bigger surprise, it was the wife of the patron. *Why does this surprise me?* Monica knew which patrons were married. It wasn't her place to judge as long as the men understood the risks, but to have one be open with his wife about a submissive mistress was surprising. To bring her to one of the monthly banquets? Not until they sat the table and she watched this woman of good standing leer into Miss Grace's cleavage did Monica finally understand. *I'll have to consider couples as patrons.* Surely there was even more money in that, if the girl was up for it. Grace was bisexual. She would probably be up for it.

"Gentlemen... and ladies." Monica stood at the head of the table, wineglass in hand as she forced herself to look taller. Yet she was a petite woman in a room full of tall vixens and handsome strangers. Even in her five-inch heels she had to stand on the tips of her toes. *If only I we were 5'11 instead of 5'1.*

"My extreme gratitude for everyone who could make it here tonight. As you are probably aware, this is the first time we've had all five patrons here for one of our festivities. Please, don't be shy. Eat up, drink up, and make plenty of merry." She raised her glass, and most of the guests and girls did as well.

Monica couldn't rest during dinner. Her job was far from over, and she was aware that every time someone turned to her it was to either get her guidance or to ask a question. Of course, few people actually talked to her outside of the maids bringing food in and out. And they only talked to her because she made them tell her everything. They would lean down, whisper into her ear, and then depart again, their pristine uniforms fluttering in the air.

Most of the patrons and guests didn't know one another, but Monica partially arranged these meetings to fix that. Inspiration came from the old courtesan houses of Shanghai and beyond, back in the glory days of the early 20th century when Chinese and Western businessmen alike came together to drink liquor, ogle pretty girls, and talk business. How many professional relationships were forged in those dark and perfumed walls? Monica didn't fancy herself a matchmaker of capitalism, but she *did* fancy herself a fantastic hostess, and one who could make all her guests feel relaxed, even in the presence of strangers.

Sure enough, halfway through the first course, Mr. Carlisle introduced himself to Mr. Witherspoon, and the two of them ignored their girls for the majority of dinner to discover how much they had in common. The only time Chelsea got any attention was when she was asked to cut up Mr. Witherspoon's food and feed it to him. Nobody thought anything of it.

Well, nobody except for the man sitting between him and Monica.

By some happenstance Mr. Warren – *Henry* – sat to her left, politely staring at the spectacle going on while a young woman fed an older man his food. A few other people caught on to his staring, and Monica was prompted to say, "Do you know where you are, Mr. Warren?"

"To tell you the truth, Sam only said that this was where his girlfriend lived and we were invited to a party thrown by her, well…"

"Oh, do tell what he's saying I am." Monica had been told many things. Madam, Mistress, *Pimp*. Those words didn't come from the people one would assume, either. The neighbors called her Madam while the disgruntled clients called her pimp. The police didn't call her anything but "treading on thin ice."

"He said you were like a mother."

Monica's fork clattered on her plate as she held her fingers to her mouth and failed at hiding a chuckle. *Haven't been called that one before.* Strange, since most ancient cultures referred to heads of such houses as one form of mother or another. Hearing it in English, however, was something else entirely. "I'm sorry if you were unprepared for my Château, Mr. Warren."

"I told you to call me Henry."

"Fine. Mr. Henry." What? Monica was the head of this household and business. She had to keep some standards, no matter what guests wanted. *Does he want a girl for the evening?* Monica made a mental note to start hiring part-time girls for weekends and these sorts of gatherings. They lived close enough to the city that girls wouldn't mind coming up the mountain a couple days a week to make nearly a thousand dollars. Monica hadn't thought they were necessary until now. "The Château is for many things. For many fantasies."

He glanced at Mr. Witherspoon talking about stock prices while a pretty young woman fed him bits of steak. "I can see that. Apparently my friend has discerning tastes."

"How nice of you to say so." Monica would take even blanketed compliments about her girls to heart. "All our girls here are trained in various forms of pleasure."

"I see."

Monica put her utensils down and folded her finger beneath her chin. "Do you not care for these sorts of tastes, Mr. Henry? I would have hoped that Mr. Witherspoon informed you as to what goes on here before inviting you."

"Perhaps he did tell me, and I wasn't paying attention. Regardless, it would be rude of me to say anything alarming."

"If you are uncomfortable, I can secure you a ride back to the city."

"That won't be necessary." Henry picked up his knife and stared at his untouched steak – medium rare, as requested. "Also, I can cut my own meat fine."

Suited Monica. She was neither Henry's sub nor his mother. *Been a while since I cut a man's food for him.* In her last relationship, that's all she did some days.

The both of them ate in silence for a few minutes while men chatted and women refilled wine and water glasses. When Monica spoke again, she directed her words right at Henry, who snapped his eyes away from his plate to look at her. "Are you married, Mr. Henry?"

"Hm? No. Afraid not."

"Afraid?"

"That's what I'm supposed to say, right? My family would like to see me married as soon as possible. I'm the only son in my father's line."

"I see. So much pressure." A common story. For whatever reason, the local bigshot families weren't into big families. They also tended to be old fashioned, with daughters marrying into other families while sons strived to take over the family business, even if they weren't suited for it. Monica didn't know anything more about Henry than what he already shared. Maybe he was perfect for his family in every way but his lack of a wife. "And you aren't into the lifestyle?"

"Lifestyle?"

Monica gestured to the way her girls doted on their patrons, making them happy and ensuring they would keep paying their monthly fees to call these girls their girlfriends. "Maybe not exactly like this... but something like it."

"You mean the whole BDSM thing."

"Why, yes, I do."

Henry neither bristled nor smiled as he ate his last piece of steak. "Question for the ages, isn't it? What about you, Miss..."

"Monica. Monica Graham."

"Ms. Monica. You into this sort of thing?"

"Of course I am. Do you think I could run this sort of establishment if I didn't understand the nuances of such relationships?"

"I suppose not. Excuse me for asking."

Monica wasn't ashamed of her tastes. She had been involved in the lifestyle for years. It was second nature to her, and her preference. *Why not run a place like this if I have to run a business? There are far worse ways to make a living.* She gave herself a warm bed, healthy food, and good company most nights. That was more than many women could expect in their whole lives. *I've been through a lot to get here, but I'm here!* She wasn't ashamed. She refused to be ashamed.

Dessert and more drinks were served in the nearby salon. More conversation flowed with the liquor, loosening up more than tongues. Monica finally relaxed a little. *Things are going well.* Soon enough the pairs of lovers would retire to the girls' rooms, or they would go with their guests into other rooms to continue conversations, games, and whatever else they decided to get into that night. It wasn't unusual for a patron to share his girl with a guest... sort of like Grace's patron, who continued to rub his wife's thigh and make her blush behind her glasses of champagne. It didn't take long for the three of them to excuse themselves for the evening and head up to Grace's room for their playtime.

Soon the only three left in the room were the Witherspoon party. *I'm jealous.* She had watched everyone but Chelsea exit the room with men – and women – draped on their bodies, whispering sweet promises to be anything but sweet that night. *It's been too long.* Monica's last relationship ended months ago, and she hadn't touched or been touched since. A woman's heart began to ache a lot longer before that. *Especially when that woman is in love.*

Around ten she got up and excused herself from the party. The trio of revelers bade her goodnight, and Monica finally had time to wash up for the evening and sleep. Or at least that was her plan until she caught a strange look from Henry, who sat on a chaise lounge with an empty glass in his hand. The glimpse he gave her stopped her in her tracks – as if his blue eyes personally bade her farewell.

"Good night, Mr. Henry," Monica said with a slow nod of the head. "Take care here." He did not break his gaze as she left the room, latching the salon door behind her. She waited until she was alone by the grand staircase to shiver. Whether pleasurably or in fright from recent memories, Monica did not know.

Chapter 2

Lock & Key

Perhaps Monica's worst habit was her fixation on current events. No, not politics. No, not the economy – although she had to keep up with that one in order to know what her clients were talking about. No, she liked to read the police reports, the terrible crimes appearing on Page 1, and any sort of atrocity she could get her hands on.

She picked up the habit late into her previous relationship, when things were dark and she wondered if she would make it another day without hurting herself in some way – or if her ex would kill her. *It's nice to know that other people have it worse than me.* What a morbid thought. Monica couldn't help it, however, as she sat at the table early the next morning, eating her breakfast of eggs and a bagel. Page 1 had a story about a man killed during an attempted robbery in his own home. "Was like my son," his neighbor said. "Such a kind, charitable man. I don't understand why something like this happened to him. Who would do such a thing?"

Monsters. Monica put her paper down and stabbed her scrambled eggs topped with spring onion. She would know something about monsters. That last lover – Jackson Lyle, one of the richest and cruelest men in the country – made sure she knew how many terrible people there were in the world. At least he didn't have the chance to kill her. This poor man in the paper was *dead.* Killed by a stranger! What a way to go.

"Ugh, I forgot where I was for a second."

Startled, Monica looked up and caught sight of a disheveled Henry standing in the dining room entryway. His suit was tussled, wrinkled in the wrong places and hardly pressed for an important business meeting. His shoes had smudges on them. His wristwatch – Rolex, of course – was upside down, and his hair... his hair! *Where the hell was he sleeping?* Those dark blond locks, once combed to perfection, now stuck up every which way. If Monica didn't know him, she would guess that Henry was a vagabond lost without direction.

"Mr. Henry!" She leaped from her seat, nearly upending the eggs. The newspaper with the awful story fell to the ground. "Are you all right? What happened?"

He held up his hands before she could get too close. *He reeks.* Sweat. Alcohol. Possibly sex. All three were likely after a weekend night in the Château. "Please, I'm fine. I just need to sit down. I had too much to drink last night."

Hungover Henry sank into one of the dining chairs while Monica summoned a maid from the kitchen. A girl arrived with a fresh towel and a glass of water. Monica sent her back to the kitchen to get some oatmeal, bananas, *something*. "You certainly do not look all right. Did you fall asleep in the salon?"

"I must have. I don't remember it... the last thing I remember is playing charades with Sam and that friend of his... I don't know where they are."

Probably in her room. It wasn't unusual for weekend clients – let alone patrons – to spend the night. Monica had seen Mr. Carlisle slink his way through the Château an hour ago. "I can have someone find him for you."

Henry took the towel and water. "I appreciate it, but that's not necessary. I'll shake this off and be on my way in no time."

Still, Monica insisted that Henry use a guest bathroom to shower and freshen himself up. He was in there for a while, long enough for her to finish her breakfast and fret about the poor man left to pass out intoxicated on a salon sofa.

How had nobody seen him? A maid or somebody should have secured him a proper guest room to sleep in. *Somebody's getting fired!* Monica had that thought as Henry emerged from the guest bathroom, his suit not much better, but his face not as flushed and his hair much more manageable. "Thank you for the concern," he said, sounding like the man Monica met yesterday. Henry joined her for breakfast, where both a grapefruit and oatmeal awaited him. "You're quite the hostess... I'm sorry, what was it again?"

"Monica." Henry didn't seem the type to be into calling her Madam or anything like that. The patrons liked that because it helped fulfill their fantasy. Henry, thus far, was devoid of that. "It's my pleasure to be at your assistance. I don't like the idea of one of my guests being passed out on a couch all night."

"Must be in your nature, huh?"

"Excuse me?"

The man shook his head. "I mean... well... being subservient... never mind."

Monica couldn't help but smile. "You can't offend me, Mr. Henry. Not unless you mean to offend me."

"No, I certainly don't intend to offend you. I find it fascinating, that's all. How does someone get into this line of business?"

She folded up the newspaper and left it on the other side of the table. "Not sure I follow you."

"Just a bit of curiosity. How does a woman as young as you become the proprietress of a place like this?"

"Young? How young do you think I am?"

"I wouldn't dare actually guess your age."

"And you're wise to not do so." Monica was hardly old, but she was no spring chicken when it came to love and romance. Or sex. She definitely wasn't a virgin of any kind. "To answer your question, there were a lot of strange circumstances that led me to this profession. I've been into the lifestyle since I was a girl. Things fell into place naturally after that. Well, that's the short story."

"One of these days I should like to hear the long story."

His Domination

Monica sat back, her eyes never leaving Henry's watchful ones. *He reminds me a lot of Jackson.* It was those handsome good looks and the smell of old money. Oh, and the way he grinned when he thought he was being clever. Jackson's hair was sandier, though. And he didn't have the strong jaw that Henry did. Nor was he as tall. Monica fished for more ways these two men were different... she didn't need reminders of her ex haunting her hallowed halls.

Not like I get out of the house much as it is. It had always been that way. If there was a service she couldn't get to come out to the Château, she didn't use it.

"I don't tell the long story often. Too..." She searched for a neutral word to use. "Long. Much too long."

Monica was a master of manipulating her expressions. Queen Poker Face, an ex-lover used to call her. Most men didn't want to know about her emotions. In truth, she didn't want to share them, either. *They are for me and me alone.* The easier it became to push them down and put on a straight, pleasant face, the easier life became in turn.

And yet, when she put on that poker face now to not betray the terrible memories flooding her mind, Henry Warren still cocked his head to one side, rested his elbow on the table, and said, "Must be a terribly long story."

Perhaps Monica should have let it go. After all, most people would have interpreted Henry's words as being merely supportive. Small talk. A final word before they let things go. *I sense something in those words.* An understanding that she hadn't felt in years. She had just met this man, and God knew their interactions were limited to his innocent questions and being hungover, but in that short amount of time Henry came across as more empathetic than the thousands of men Monica had crossed paths with in her life.

I need to get out more.

They didn't see or hear from Mr. Witherspoon until an hour later, when he sauntered down the grand staircase as hungover as the friend he forgot and left behind. The two men exchanged curt words, Henry admonishing his colleague for being so self-centered, and Mr. Witherspoon insisting that he thought Henry would have found a companion of his own.

"And who would it have been, hm?" Monica heard Henry ask. "All the women here are spoken for. Unless you count Ms. Graham in the dining room."

"Who, her?" Although Mr. Witherspoon lowered his voice, Monica could still hear him. "There's a reason she does so well in this business. She's untouchable. You never touch the madam, sir, especially when the madam is the soiled goods of Jackson Lyle. You know, *the* Jackson Lyle."

"Jackson… wasn't he the man recently bought out of his own business he founded?"

"Certainly. The very one. Absolute smarmy little snot, but he was invaluable to a few investments going around and… well… I heard through my driver who heard from his brother who used to work at Lyle's estate that Ms. Graham pulled a gun on him before leaving with a good chunk of his money."

"You don't say. Well, woman is certainly gutsier than she gives off."

"You have to be to run a business like this, wouldn't you agree?"

Monica retained her poker face as the men entered the dining room, oblivious that she had heard either one of them speak so candidly about her. *Everything they say is true.* From the smarm, to the investments, to the gun... Monica had never shot a soul, and the day she held that gun between her and Jackson was the day she finally freed herself from the tyranny he fronted with compassion.

Mr. Witherspoon stayed for breakfast, although Chelsea never came down to join them. Either he had left her to sleep or requested she stay in her room until he departed. Patrons had a habit of showing up in love with their girls before turning a cheek the next day. As long they paid for the privilege, and as long as the girls didn't come crying to Monica, she didn't mind.

Before the men left, Mr. Witherspoon pulled Monica aside and requested to leave a gift for Chelsea. Of course, such things were encouraged, and Monica held out her hand to take the check on Chelsea's behalf. *Ten-thousand dollars.* Half would go to Chelsea. The other half would be split between Monica and improvements to the Château. There was a vase for the dining table she had her eye on. This would help.

"Thank you for your patronage, Mr. Witherspoon. I will be sure to praise Chelsea for a job well done so she will continue to be happy here... and so you will continue to liven us up with your presence, of course."

"I look forward to my next visit. Perhaps in three weeks or so. I'll let you know."

"And I'll make sure Chelsea is informed."

"Do so. Coming, Henry?"

The taller man remained still even as his friend began for the door. Before Mr. Witherspoon even knew he was alone, Henry extended his hand to Monica and said, "Pleasure meeting you, Monica. I'd still like to hear the long story someday."

She smiled, but she did not confirm she would ever do such a thing. Monica did, however, grasp his hand as an offer of civility... his warm, smooth hand that was twice as big as hers and covered her palm, her fingers, and nearly her wrist with one touch.

Their eyes met in that second. Monica shook hands with and looked at many refined men since opening her business, but this was the first time – perhaps the second, since meeting Henry – that she felt something strange in the pit of her stomach and a flurry in her chest. What was it? She hadn't felt something like that in years. Not even with Jackson had she ever felt such tenderness. That firm, yet gentle handshake was the kind of thing she had always searched for since she knew what this lifestyle was.

For Monica was a woman who wanted it firm and strong, but tender and loving all the same. She dreamed of a man who would not relent, but still heed her wishes and desires. She had long figured that such men did not exist. To be sure, putting that sort of pressure on Henry within one day would be foolhardy, and Monica was not a stupid woman. Jaded, sure, but not...

"Thank you for visiting, Mr. Warren," she said, mastering the blush trying to overcome her cheeks. She dropped her hand from his and turned to the side. "Do take care. I hope to see you again." Monica felt his gaze lingering on her body as she slowly ascended the grand staircase and went to check in on Chelsea and the other girls.

Henry left the premises. He did not leave her mind.

Chapter 3

Her Gilded Cage

The only time smoking was allowed on the premises was when it was done outside or in the one designated lounge on the second floor. Clients didn't like being told they couldn't smoke in the girls' rooms, but they soon learned to be mindful of health and, well, the smell.

Such a smell Monica encountered when she stepped into the Cigar Lounge to take inventory. It was reserved that night by a few businessmen looking to have a private place to discuss their wares and maybe enjoy a show or two by an available girl. *Finally, something for Yvette to do.* Better than watching her sit on the balcony drinking wine because she refused to hang out with any clients. She would, at least, put on a demonstration as long as nobody expected to touch or directly talk to her. *She makes a fantastic domme.*

Grace followed her into the Cigar Lounge to write down notes about what was missing. Ever since the trade embargo with Cuba was lifted, they didn't hurt for those. Still, there was an air of the forbidden around them, and clients tended to dive straight for an old-fashioned Cuban above anything else. Monica made Grace order some anyway.

"Madam Graham!" One of the maids appeared in the doorway, her chest heaving and her voice ragged with thick breaths. "I'm sorry to interrupt, but there's someone here to see you."

Monica turned with the swiftness of a fox. "Who? The police?" It was too early in the afternoon for most clients. The only people who came searching for her in the middle of the day usually had legalities to discuss.

"No, ma'am. A gentleman. Henry Warren."

What? She hadn't seen nor heard from him in a few days. Not since he came as Mr. Witherspoon's guest. *I never thought I would see him again.* He must have forgotten something. Something so important that he couldn't call and ask Monica to ship it to him.

Sure enough, Mr. Warren was standing in the foyer, another maid taking his coat and checking his shoes to make sure he had no mud to track through the premises.

"Mr. Henry," Monica called, stepping down the staircase as fast as she dared. Between her stature and the shoes, it could be an arduous task. "To what do I owe this surprising pleasure?"

He certainly looked more put together than he had the morning she last saw him. A new suit – demure beige that looked cheerful for the season, but still serious enough for a man of his station – clung to his body in such a way that Monica stopped and wondered about what he kept beneath. *Now? At a time like this?*

"Good afternoon. I hope I'm not interrupting your business… or is it a day off for you?"

Wednesdays were an odd day for a visit, but they weren't closed. The girls had their weekends on Monday and Tuesday unless otherwise arranged, but Monica stayed busy with books or work every day. "We are open, if that's what you're asking. We're not used to having such guests at this time. Did you forget something the other day?"

Henry stepped back, as if her words were a club smacking him in the chest. *Did I offend?* "No, no. Everything is fine. If I could talk with you privately?"

Monica shooed away the onlookers and escorted Henry into the front salon, the very one he slept in the other night. He turned down a glass of anything and instead perched on the edge of a chair, large hands folded in his lap. Monica took a seat on the sofa across from him and asked once more what she could do for him.

"I suppose I should get right to it," he said. "I was wondering if you could give me a tour of your premises and perhaps introduce me to some of your girls."

That was it? Why did he come here unannounced for something like that? Nevertheless, Monica would not pry. She didn't want to scare off a new, *rich* client. "I hadn't realized you were into this sort of thing, Mr. Henry."

"Perhaps I have a long story or two of my own, Monica."

Now there was a surprise. Monica retained her demeanor, but inside her brain whirled with images of Mr. Henry Warren tying up a woman and whispering filth into her ear. Monica had these thoughts about most of her clients. She had to, in order to anticipate what they might like and what she could do to ensure their satisfaction so they would keep coming back and paying more. But this was the first time since opening her doors that she felt... aroused?... by the act. These effects Henry had on her were starting to get to her in ways she couldn't afford.

"Upfront I have to be blunt that we currently don't have any girls available to a patron." *I really need to hire more.* There were two bedrooms she could rent out to as many girls. They would have to be cleaned and stripped, and then redone to the girl's tastes, but as their business grew so too must the house. "You can of course patron them on an even regular basis, but only if they are available. And you wouldn't receive any of the bonuses."

"Bonuses? Do I even want to know?"

He knew what she meant, and yet she must deflect. *Sex happens with regular clients too, Mr. Warren.* Completely at the girl's discretion, but it wasn't some sacred act confined to her primary business relationship.

"Taking her out on dates, dominating her time, giving her gifts of a greater value than a thousand dollars... there are many bonuses, but a girl may only have one patron at a time. Plus, even if you can't visit her for a while, you must still pay for the privilege. It's a part of what makes up their primary incomes." Some girls were saving up for their dreams. Others had debt they were paying off and they didn't mind doing it this way. Others liked getting paid to whip and be whipped. *Some are all three* She thought of Sylvia.

"I see," Henry said with a curious smile. "You're intriguing me more and more."

"I'm glad to hear it. We cater to a very discerning and particular crowd. It only seems right to intrigue them."

"Oh? Am I a part of this crowd?"

Monica finally smiled in return. "I pegged you as a member from the moment you walked through that door the other night."

They stood and commenced the formal tour, Monica staying four paces in front of Henry as she showed him around the common areas on the first floor. "Of course you are familiar with the salon and the dining room. We also have a Recreation Room with all the current amenities. We had quite the Super Bowl party earlier this year."

"I'm sure."

"Since we are of course hooked up with the fastest internet available, you may be intrigued to know that we have video game consoles with online play capabilities." Even she couldn't believe how many of the rich fuddy-duddies coming through the room wanted to play *Halo* and *Call of Duty*. Sometimes things got loud when the girls were involved. Of course, the girls being into violent video games made the clients happier. Monica never understood the appeal, but she understood the money in her palm.

"Essentially, we have a space for every man's tastes. We have a beautiful garden out back for relaxing in. Our upstairs balcony is popular on clear summer nights, and occasionally has a stargazing party. One of our girls is somewhat an astronomer." Not that Yvette would do anything with it. *Ah, so that's what she's looking at when she sits out there with the champagne at night.* Looking for her shooting star in the sky.

Henry made empty comments about every room he was shown. Even the two guest rooms downstairs, made especially for guests who had difficulties going up and down the stairs. "Every guest room has its own private bathroom of varying sizes." Henry raised his eyebrows, but did not show much more interest than that.

Monica stopped Grace in the upstairs hallway and asked if her room could be used for the tour. The girl consented, flashing Henry a flirtatious glance. Monica didn't know if that was a reflex from her job or if she was truly interested in the newcomer to the Château. Either way, Monica's business mind was already going through multiple options for her new client.

The jingle of keys enticed Henry's curiosity as Monica pulled out a ring of silver and jiggled a key into Grace's lock. *What? Does he think I don't have access to every room in here?* He would be sorely mistaken.

Grace's room was standard. She was a simple girl with simple tastes, as reflected in the bare canopy bed and smooth, modern pieces around the room. The rugs were colored dark and patternless. The paintings on the wall were hardly whimsical, yet not somber. Her partition to the other side had a forest motif, showing some young maid from a long ago time passing through the woods with a basket on her arm.

Few men cared about the decorations of a young woman's room. These men in particular cared about what was on the other side of the partition.

Whips. Chains. Suspension devices. Sex toys. Every lube from every corner of the world. Costumes and jewelry. Cleaning supplies and first aid kits that nobody but the staff was supposed to know existed… Monica kicked one of the supply boxes behind a sofa before Henry noticed it.

"Well then," he said, not flinching. "I figured as much. Sam was always a bit… eager to please, if you know what I mean."

Monica did. Sam Witherspoon liked to spank his girl but was more interested in being chained to the wall and called a sorry sack of capitalistic shit. There were many theories as to why powerful businessmen liked to be treated like a sexual slave by women. Not as many people had theories as to why those same men might like to have a sexual slave in a woman. *Nature, I'm sure.* Monica didn't believe that. Every man – and woman – had their own story to tell. Their own reasons that they were the way they were. Sure, some of it may be nature… she always had a more submissive personality growing up… but there were also triggers that set off certain fetishes. And certain fears.

Their tour ended on the balcony, which had a lovely view of the manicured gardens in the back. When picking a design, Monica decided to keep the original garden intact and create a small labyrinth out of the topiaries. Some poor soul navigated them now, picking petals off a dandelion. It looked like Sylvia.

This time Henry did not say no to a drink – lemonade, but not hard. "You have quite the establishment, if I do say so myself." Henry sat on a chair but did not relax. "And I do."

"Thank you. It took a while to put together, but I have been pleased with the outcome. It's always nice to fulfill a service that's so sorely needed in an area." They lived close enough to one of the biggest financial centers in the country. Not everyone was a rich mogul, but it was big enough to attract other rich people from all around the world. Those circles were small. Once word got out about the Château after a soft opening, clients busted down the doors until Monica had to turn them away and be more stringent about reservations and appointments. So while a part of her wasn't surprised by Henry's interest, she did admit she didn't think she would see him so soon. "I'm glad you found it to your liking. Now you know what I have to ask."

Henry lowered his drink, dangling between legs. "Certainly. You want to know if I want to whip or be whipped."

She suppressed a laugh, solely because she had no idea he would put it like *that*. "I would say it that way. Except I want you to know that I will not judge you for your tastes. Nobody here will. Everyone is completely at your discretion. We take privacy very seriously, and if one of our girls happens to ever break the NDAs she signs for every client – and none of them ever have, I'll have you know – they do not get a second chance in this house."

"I appreciate it. I may not be married, but…"

"Do you have a girlfriend?"

Monica didn't know why she blurted it out like that. It didn't matter one way or another if Henry Warren was attached to someone. Not Monica's problem. That was all up to his sense of morality – and for all she knew, the girlfriend was in on it like with Grace's patron.

"No, I don't." Henry sat up straight, closing his legs and holding the drink off to the side. "I have no moral qualms with what's going on here or my possible involvement with it. I only have one question, really."

"What is it? There isn't a question I can't answer." Monica made it her mission to know everything about her own business. That was good financial sense. "Go on. Try me."

"It's a boring question, I'm afraid. I only want to know how a man becomes a patron."

That's it? Too bad Monica had some unfortunate news for him. "I told you, Mr. Henry, all of the girls currently have patrons. None of them seem interested in leaving anytime soon, so you may be waiting a while. However…"

"Yes?"

"As I also mentioned, I am thinking of hiring a couple of other girls. In which case I would send out an announcement to regular clients saying they're open to a patronage."

"You still haven't answered my question, Monica. I would like to know how a man becomes a patron. Under usual circumstances, of course."

Monica looked between him and the garden, wondering which specific spiel she should give him. By now the sunlight was descending toward the western hills, and a slight glare reflected off Henry's glass. "First, as soon as you have confirmed that a girl is available to take on a patron, you send her an expensive gift that is in care of the Château. This way you make sure I see it and know your intentions."

"Expensive, huh? How expensive?"

"That I can't say. It's up to you to decide. However much you want to invest in your relationship with this girl, I suppose."

"So it's like a backward dowry."

"I suppose you could look at it that way. This is a business, Mr. Henry. At the end of the day you're securing a service, even if human emotions do happen. You don't want to hurt your bottom line, but you also don't want to risk offending the girl... or me."

"Naturally. I would imagine offending you is the best way to not get what you want."

"To be sure."

Henry finished his drink and placed it on a small table between the two lounge chairs. "So what happens after that? If multiple guys have their eyes on a girl, do you pick the guy with the more expensive dowry? This is getting medieval. Kind of exciting."

Monica shook her head. "The price of the gift factors into it, but it's also the gift itself and how the girl feels about it. Of course, I want to make as much money as possible, but I also want her to be happier doing her job. So if she would much rather be with a different man than I would choose, it's not a big deal as long as he can fulfill his obligations."

"And what obligations are those?"

"First, a monthly payment of $10,000 is to be expected. This gives you as many appointments with her as you want. However, you must keep in mind that this is not a monogamous contract. She still has to work outside of your presence."

"I see. What if I wanted monogamous? I'm a bit of a romantic at heart."

"We've never had a man interested in that, but I would wager a substantial increase to cover the financial loss." She kept thinking of Grace. She really needed to charge her patron more. "We could discuss it, but we're talking a lot of hypotheticals anyway. You wanted to know what happens next?"

"I always want to know what happens next in this world. It's incredibly interesting. Tell me more, if you don't mind."

Monica smiled, but she wasn't sure why.

"After your offer is accepted, well… there isn't much more to say. We will go over the rules, the three of us, and then you sign the contract and make your first payment. After that, it's up to you and the girl."

"So it sounds like the most important thing is getting the gift right."

"You could say that. You'll really impress her if you manage to get her something she will instantly like. Shows that you know something about her. That you're paying attention. Really, it's not that much different from wooing a woman any other way. She wants to know that you will take care of her."

"It doesn't sound the same at all." Henry said that, and yet there was a twinkle in his blue eye that said he liked the idea of the challenge. "I'll keep this all in mind."

They ended their conference not too much later, Monica escorting him back to the salon as someone came in to relay that a guest had reserved it some time that night. *Business as usual.* "You are welcome to stay here, Mr. Henry," she said after the maid left. "Do let me know if you are interested in a girl for the evening. There is…" No, wait. *Chelsea is a conflict of interest with his friend. Sylvia has an appointment with a client. Yvette won't even consider it. Judith… she's gone on vacation this week.* That only left Grace. "I have the perfect girl for you."

Henry unexpectedly stood up from his chair and brushed off the top of his pants. "That won't be necessary. I appreciate the hospitality, but I'm afraid I must be going. I merely stopped by for the chat and the tour. I'm sorry if that was improper of me. Should I make a donation?"

I see. She had not anticipated that. Few men made it all the way up into the mountains for a mere tour and chat. At least they wanted to have a little taste of what they could get in the future. "It's no trouble. I am glad you enjoyed my Château."

"Yes." They walked into the foyer together, where Monica opened the coat closet and pulled out Henry's overcoat for him. It wasn't fur or leather, but it was soft against her skin, and big enough to wrap twice around her if she wanted to snuggle without a blanket. *It's comforting.* The last time she felt like that was a long, long time ago. "Thank you again for the tour. I look forward to seeing you again."

Henry tossed his coat over his arm and extended his hand to Monica. She offered it, fingers out, but instead of shaking it, Henry brought her hand up to his lips and kissed the tops of her knuckles. He wasn't the first man at the Château to do so, but it made something tingle within Monica nonetheless. *What a dangerous man.*

The sunlight behind the door blinded her, almost making her miss his shadow disappearing into a Rolls-Royce parked in the front driveway. There was no driver. Henry Warren got in the driver's seat himself before pulling away, sticking his arm out the window to wave adieu to Monica and the Château.

"What is it?" Sylvia asked, after handing Monica a package a few days later. The girl happened to be there when the deliveryman arrived, but now there were too many questions to ask. Sure, Monica got packages all the time, but those were usually the kind wrapped in plain brown paper or nondescript cardboard boxes. This one was wrapped in black with a red ribbon tied around it. "Is it your birthday? Shit, I had no idea!"

"It's not my birthday." Monica stood at the bottom of the grand staircase with the package in hand. Nothing big about it.

Even in her small palms and between her thinner fingers it was small enough to hide somewhere. Cubed. *Heavy.* Whatever was in it easily weighed more than a couple of pounds. "And I don't know what it could be. You sure it was addressed to me?"

"Yes, the deliveryman said it was for Monica Graham. I heard him say it twice."

"Hm." Monica started up the stairs. "If it's anything interesting, I'll let you know."

Sylvia's mood deflated, but with a rousing "Sure!" she disappeared into the dining room to get her lunch. It was Monday, the Château's weekend, and after a busy Saturday some of the girls were still hungover. Even Monica, as she walked to her quarters with the package, still had yet to catch up on her sleep from helping to entertain a dozen men who wanted more food, more drinks, and more shows.

Her quarters were a total of three rooms: the master bedroom, an adjacent office, and a nice bathroom that had a jetted tub and a sink big enough to wash a dog in. Not that Monica had a dog. *I would like a Pomeranian one day.* She didn't have time to dedicate to a pup right now.

She placed the box on her desk and sat in her leather office chair. *Why not tear into it now?* Monica turned the box over, but didn't see anything but a strand of red ribbon held tightly in place. Her fingers touched the outline, but no hidden tags fell out to tell her who sent it. Why didn't Sylvia find out what company the man was from? Monica sat it upside right again and pulled the ribbon apart.

The lid came off easily enough. Inside was a copious amount of white tissue hiding something large and silver.

Large, silver, and encrusted with tiny, sparkling diamonds.

"What the…" She stood up, peering into the box as her fingers felt the smooth surface of metal. Then links. A chain. She uncoiled it, letting it snake in front of her as one foot, two feet, three feet pulled out of the box and revealed the collar on the other end.

The collar was encrusted with diamonds. Several small, sparkling, but *expensive* diamonds twinkling in and out of the light flashing through Monica's office window. *What is this?* She knew what it was, but her mind refused to believe that anybody had sent her a chain and collar. Monica hadn't owned one since… since… *Jackson.* The one he gave her was gold.

Just because this was silver, however, didn't mean it wasn't insanely expensive! How many diamonds were in it? What grade were they? What cut? Was this pure silver or a coating? Monica dumped the collar and chain on her desk, the thud echoing between wood and leather. *Who is giving this to me?* She emptied the box, tearing apart the tissue in search of a card, a piece of paper, anything to discover what the hell had happened. Was this a prank? If it was, it was an expensive one! *No, no, not a prank…*

A horror hit her heart.

Jackson. It had to be from Jackson.

He was the type of sick snake to send her something like this, to remind her that he existed and once controlled her… once chained and locked her up in his mansion to be used as a plaything for weekends at a time. *Once he tied me to our bed and didn't come back for a whole day.* Monica had starved and nearly messed herself, which was exactly what he wanted. She liked a little humiliation, but that was the beginning of the end between her and him.

It didn't matter how expensive this "gift" was. Jackson had billions to burn and wasn't above wasting his money. Monica grabbed the collar and had half a mind to throw it through the window, to rid herself of the jerk who made her life hell and nearly destroyed her spirit.

She held the collar up in her hand. Sunlight reflected off the inside of the silver, illuminating something engraved inside.

Monica held the collar in front of her face and squinted. She could barely make out the tiny words.

"I want to be your patron."

How long did she stare at those words? How long did she hold off the swelling sense of relief, desire, and that budding monstrosity called love?

How long did Monica pretend that she didn't know who *really* sent this? Even when she slowly turned the collar in her hand, she still did not believe she would see the name that popped up on the other side?

"Henry Warren."

Monica collapsed into her chair. The business side of her brain wanted to grab a pen and paper, write a letter telling Henry that she appreciated the offer, but she was not up for patronage.

The other side of her brain? The one that couldn't think clearly because it was lost in a haze of imagining what a man like that could do to her in the bedroom?

It didn't want to write anything at all. It wanted to cry in relief.

Chapter 4

The Patron's Gift

For some inexplicable reason, Monica did not have any of Henry's contact information. Since he never paid for any services, none of his phone numbers, addresses, or even e-mails were on file. *No way I'm calling Mr. Witherspoon to ask.* Monica would die from horror.

There were a few things they needed to get straight. First of all, Monica was *not* one of the available girls. She didn't work like they did. Her job was to keep the Château running smoothly and making sure they all drowned in dollars. What had given him the idea that she could receive a gift like that?

He did understand that she wasn't available, right?

Monica thought back to their tour multiple times, wondering where she had dropped some hint that Henry

Warren was free to bid for her prolonged services. *He didn't seem interested in any of the other girls.* Why would he come all the way out there to turn around and head home? And then to buy something that cost thousands of dollars and send it to *her,* asking if *she* would like to... to...

Every time Monica's thoughts reached this part, her eyes glazed over and she imagined herself naked, or maybe in her lingerie, shackled to bed with that silver, diamond encrusted collar wrapped around her throat. *Blindfold optional.* She tried to cut the thoughts off before Henry Warren entered in his summery suits... no, dark blue... no, *gray...* his large, masculine hand spanking her on the ass before he whispered what he wanted to do to her. *Fuck me.*

Monica didn't have a lot of crushes, but she was still human. When she fell for someone, she fell hard, usually for the most random reasons she never understood. Her first time with Jackson only happened because she liked the way he charmed her. Her other ex Ethan Cole had a brooding bad boy thing going for him that she liked – especially since he was a total puppy inside. *Wish I ended up with Ethan over Jackson.* It was a ménage arrangement back then, until Ethan decided he didn't want to share anymore. Stupid Monica ended up moving in with Jackson full time... and then ended up where she did. *With a gun in my hand and nothing to live for.*

So why Henry? He was handsome, and charismatic, but so were a lot of the other millionaires and billionaires who came to the Château. They all talked to her. Some even expressed romantic interest in her. Monica was able to rebuff them all.

Why did she care about what they had to offer when she could give it to herself? Then here came Henry, grazing his fingers against her skin, kissing the top of her hand with those soft lips, and giving her a sub's collar in a black box.

He wants to dominate me…

Monica canceled her one appointment that afternoon, told the girls she wasn't feeling well, and sat alone in her office. The sunshine slowly descended behind the garden. By the time it kissed the horizon, she still didn't know what to do. She wanted to call Henry and ask him the meaning of this. Except that was silly. She didn't have his number!

I shouldn't be talking to him anyway. No, she should definitely be obsessing over him and his motives instead. That was a good use of her time, especially when all she did was sit at her desk and watch the day slowly go by.

She made an appearance downstairs for dinner. Then she took a bath, hoping the hot water would soak away the absurdity of it. Yet it was dangerous sitting in that tub by herself. naked. She imagined the collar around her neck, the chain dangling over the side of the claw foot tub as Henry's long fingers walked down her bare chest and pinched her nipple. *"Get clean,"* he would say like a true Dom. *"I want to get you dirty all over again."*

Monica went to bed completely beside herself. *I haven't felt this way in so long.* Not even since before Jackson went off the deep end and started hurting her. Rarely did Monica feel such a sexual attraction to men she barely knew. There was so much trust involved in being a sub! These young girls who worked for her had the fortitude to forego knowing a man for more than ten minutes. Besides, it was a job for them. For Monica, it was her lifestyle.

She wanted a man to take control, both in the bedroom and out. She wanted agency, but she also wanted to be taken care of and never have to worry about things again. She wanted a man to overpower her in the bedroom and make her tear apart at every seam.

The problem was that most men who fit that bill turned out to be assholes.

Next time I talk to him, I'll tell him it's off the table. Until then, Monica was plagued with the images swarming her head. Henry Warren. *Mr. Warren.* Grabbing her from behind and pushing his lips against her skin, tasting the sweat her anxious heart pumped from her body; behind her over the bed and pulling away her clothes; teasing her with his cock until she was forced to beg for it; pulling her hair and trapping her against the bed while he fucked her, hard.

Her eyes opened to the realization that her hand was in her underwear, and that sexual sting she felt wasn't only in her imagination.

Monica didn't touch herself often. Not unless her Dom told her to for both of their pleasure. *And in the end with him, it was always about Jackson's pleasure instead of mine.* His corrupted pleasure that only got off if she was miserable.

Her hand came out and she turned over in bed. *I'm weak. I'm sad. I don't deserve any of that shit.* She knew she didn't deserve it, and yet Monica decided to always blame herself. Because then it felt like she had an ounce of power over her own life.

That settled it. She wasn't actually attracted to Henry Warren. She was attracted to the idea of escaping her past and getting into trouble. Telling him to politely go away it was.

If she could.

"Mr. Henry Warren is here to see you."

Monica's head turned from the statements she read on her desk. "Send him in," she said, turning the top letter over and emblazoning it with her signature. "Tell him that I've been expecting him."

The maid nodded and escorted herself out of Monica's office. It wasn't even a full two days later after she received the box from him. The patron's gift. The ode to her sweet nectar. Monica had rewrapped the gift and put it in one of her drawers. No use for it now.

A knock came on her door, and she waited two seconds before glancing up and catching sight of the man from her deplorable fantasies. *Good God.* Dressed in a dark navy blue suit with a silk black tie and sapphire cufflinks, Henry stood straight and proper in her doorway, dark blond hair neatly combed and his leather shoes recently shined. He gave her no knowing looks, instead choosing to bequeath a neither friendly nor business-like demeanor that Monica couldn't read. She was too busy wondering how quickly she could shove everything off her desk so he could take her right there anyway.

Get a hold of yourself. Monica stood up from her chair. "Have a seat."

Henry's graceful legs brought him closer, and now Monica smelled that musky aftershave emanating from his body. She imagined him, on top of her in bed, that scent overpowering her as he thrust between her legs. *Henry. That would be his scent.* Whenever she was out and smelled it on someone else, she would think of him and all the wonderful ways he...

"I see you saw the news this morning," he interrupted her thoughts with a point to the newspaper on her desk. "Terrible what happened to those people on that plane."

Monica shook out her inappropriate thoughts and glared at the color picture of plane wreckage. "Yes. Terrible." Just that morning she was reading it to feel better about her life. Now here came Henry to take away her Schadenfreude. "Can I help you?"

He took his seat in the chair across from her. Even sitting down he was still a good two heads taller than her. *I have a weakness for tall men.* Jackson had been on the shorter side. Monica could barely remember what it felt like to curl up next to a man over a foot taller than her.

"You know why I am here."

Monica folded her hands on her desk, kept her back straight... but could not keep her lips from thinning. "I'm guessing it's about this." She opened the drawer next to her and pulled out the black box. It landed with a thud on the desk between them.

"I'm glad you received it. Did you take a look inside?"

"Of course I did. The contents were shocking."

"Shocking? I thought nothing could possibly shock you."

"I was shocked by the idea that you would think I was available for patronage."

Finally, a reaction. Henry relaxed in his chair and smiled. Nothing sinister. Nothing... toxic. Not the kind of smile Jackson would have given her before he said something nefarious. No, the words coming out of Henry's mouth were anything but. "I was under no assumption that you were available in that way. You have mistaken me."

Monica opened the box and pulled out the collar. She found the inscription and shoved it in Henry's direction. "And what do you call this?"

"My intentions."

"You either think I'm up for patronage or not."

"Let me put it this way. I know that you don't work like the other young ladies here do. I *know* that. I'm also not interested in any of them. I've only been interested in you since the moment I first saw you."

Monica almost lost her posture. "Excuse me?"

"I can't completely explain my attraction to you yet. When I first laid eyes on you that night, I thought, 'What a beautiful, refined woman. I want to get to know her better.' And when I did, my heart only quickened more. Maybe I'm a fool, Monica, but I'm a fool for you."

This was ridiculous. The man was talking like he came from a pre-War record track. *Spare me.* Nevertheless, Monica liked that kind of talk. She liked it when men sounded sophisticated and flattered her. If Henry could write poetry, that would just be… "You don't know me at all. And you send me this? What is this supposed to mean?" The collar shook in her hand.

Whether he was perturbed by her growing frustration or not, he didn't let on. "You said to impress you by sending you something that you would like. Well? Don't you like it?"

"What would make you think that I like this?"

"Because…" Henry stood up, pulling his jacket closed and weaving a single button through its hole. He leaned across the desk, hands splayed in support above the now empty box. His lips were not too far from Monica's, which parted in surprise as she came so close to kissing this relative stranger, but dared not make a fool of herself. "I know a ready submissive woman when I meet one, Monica."

Breath tore from her throat, her chest, and into the empty air between them. *How dare he*… How dare he what? Want her? Recognize her? *Know* her? Her skin was sweaty, making the collar slip between her fingers. Her nail grazed against a diamond, a lump going down her throat. *Those eyes*… Piercing into hers. Seeing her soul. Picking apart her brain and feasting on the morsels she offered. The only thing keeping her from sitting up and kissing Henry Warren was the blaring alarm going off in the back of her head. *Idiot.*

"You would have to be a submissive woman to run a place like this. I can hear these walls echoing with your need to be touched tenderly and with the determination that only a man like me can provide."

Another swallow. "You are sure of yourself."

"Don't insult me, Monica. Are you telling me that I know who you are, but you don't know me? We're two halves balancing each other out. We're Yin and Yang. And you have so much Yin. You really should find an outlet for it before you're consumed by your own energies. You know what? Same could be said for me. We need harmony."

"Don't insult me... you don't know me...?" He didn't mean from a previous encounter. He meant that knowing notion that they were two halves of the same whole. Yes. Of course Monica had noticed it. Hadn't she been fantasizing about Henry tying her up, spanking her, and pinching her body until she cried? *Because he's one of them.* A Dom. Henry never said he wasn't. *Oh, God.* This was not making her position any easier to bear. *I want you, Henry Warren. I want you to make me feel like I used to.* All the pent up stress and frustration was like a ticking time bomb in her gut. Monica could ignore it as long as no one else was around. From the moment Henry entered her life, she *wanted* him to dominate her until she was harmonious again.

She wondered if he was feeling it too. A mighty desire to take out his power on a ready submissive woman. *Let it be me...*

The collar grew hot in her hand. If she put it on, she could have him. Right here. Right now, in her office. Or the bedroom next door. Monica clutched her chest and averted her eyes so those blues no longer destroyed her. It also kept her from kissing the damn man.

Henry lifted his hand, knuckles hovering next to her cheek. "If there's someone else..."

"No." She spat it too quickly, before her emotions could be purged. "There is no one." Monica had to tell herself that until she finally believed it.

"So then…" Henry did not dare touch her. Monica wanted him to, for two reasons: first, she wanted the man to put his hands all over her. Second, if he touched her without permission, then she would know that he would be no better than a man like Jackson. No boundaries. No love for *her*.

But he didn't touch her. The fact tortured her.

Don't tempt me. Tempt her into something stupid. Monica was too close to her previous relationship to even think of starting up a new one, let alone one hinged on domination and submission. It was what she wanted in her heart, but damnit, she wasn't ready!

"Don't touch me," she said, almost breathless. "Please."

He hesitated, but Henry backed away. For the first time Monica saw disappointment in those eyes. What, did he think she would fold beneath his pressure and give him whatever she wanted? She had her reasons. He didn't need to know them. "My apologies. I read the situation all wrong."

:"Yes, you did." *No, you didn't.* Henry was perceptive. Too perceptive. He had read Monica like the open book she apparently was the first moment they met. A man like that could be dangerous. "I'm sorry, somewhere along the way you got the impression that I can be bought like one of my girls." She slammed the lid back on the box and pushed it toward him. *I don't mean it like that.* Her girls weren't "bought." They were professionals selling a service, yes, but they weren't commodities. Yet did men ever see it that way? Maybe men like Henry Warren needed to know exactly where they all stood. She wasn't to be bought. Or sold. Or controlled in that fashion. Monica was her own woman in this world she created. She had to learn how to live on her own and take care of herself. No man would really do that for her.

"I'm sorry to have offended you." Henry replaced his disappointment with the same poker face Monica used. She knew it well. "Please, forgive me. And don't hold this against any of my friends or colleagues. They have no idea I'm here doing this."

"Wouldn't have assumed so." Even when these men were together, they worked independently. "And apology accepted. I don't think you're a bad man or anything. I just think we got our wires crossed. I am not available."

"No, of course not." He cleared his throat and continued to smooth out his jacket. Every time he did this, he created more wrinkles. "If I may say…"

"Go on."

"This only makes me more interested in you."

Monica showed him out after that. *Men.* She latched the door to her quarters and turned to face her small, private hallway where she likewise kept her secrets, fears, and heartbreak locked away. *Men!* Apparently Henry Warren thought she was playing hard to get.

Maybe she was.

Chapter 5

Clipped Wings

"How much is it worth?" Monica tapped her fingers, her favorite appraiser sitting on the other side of her desk and studying the diamonds in the collar. "I need to know if I should sell it or give it to one of my girls."

The appraiser, aptly named Mr. Jules, looked up with his ocular device still in his eye. He was an old and frail man for only being sixty-five, but he was one of the only qualified men in the city Monica could convince to make house calls. She summoned him every time they received a gift of patronage to confirm what she suspected.

I have no idea what to expect with this. As much as she wished she could be rid of the collar in only a few minutes, she was still a businesswoman and had to keep her coffers in mind. If the collar were worth a nice sum, she could get a better payday. However, if Henry Warren had underestimated her worth, well… she would make sure he returned one night to see another girl wearing that collar. *That's what I think of that.* Any of her girls would be delighted to have it. Such a thing meant nothing other than more status to their clients. It would be an excellent way to embarrass Mr. Warren.

Mr. Jules spent another minute staring at one of the diamonds before sitting up. He removed his instruments and jotted something down on a pad of paper before clearing his throat and telling Monica what she had been waiting to hear. "This is only my professional guess at the moment, but I would estimate this… piece of finery… to be worth about…"

"Yes?'

"Thirty-thousand dollars."

'Thirty…" Monica clapped her mouth shut and summoned the propriety she always needed in these situations. She couldn't tell Mr. Jules the collar was the most expensive patronage gift anyone there received. She couldn't tell him that it was worth more than the solid gold collar she had with Jackson. She couldn't even tell him that it had been for her! While Mr. Jules wasn't the type of man to go blabbing around town about her business, there were some things men didn't need to know. "Thank you. You sure that's a good estimate?"

"In truth, it may be more. I'm assuming all the diamonds have the lowest grade I can confirm. The silver is solid, though. The only thing bringing down the value is the inscription.

That's only if you sold it as is. If you pieced out the diamonds and sold the silver as scrap, you could get a lovely price."

"Naturally." That's what she would do. Not for the better price, but to also... what? Do the professional thing, since Henry's name was on that? "Thank you for your help. This definitely helps me make some decisions."

Mr. Jules saw himself out, leaving Monica to sit with her silver collar and chain. *Thirty-thousand dollars.* She knew Henry was loaded, but most patrons – let alone clients – didn't drop that much money on a gift for one girl. Even Mr. Carlisle, who spoiled Sylvia silly, never went higher than twelve-thousand for a full set of jewelry. These men bled green. That didn't mean they bled for their paid girlfriends and mistresses.

The more Monica let herself think about it, the more she heard Henry's voice echoing in her head. *"We're two halves."* Part of her attraction to the submissive lifestyle was the beautiful binary presented to her. Things were black and white. Roles were clear. She never had to think beyond what she wanted for dinner and what she should wear that day – unless they were chosen for her, of course. She liked it when her Dom picked out a beautiful outfit for her to wear, ordered for her in a restaurant, and told her where they were going. But it only worked if he knew her enough to know she would feel great in that dress, love the meal, and enjoy the sights they saw. Monica was envious of her friends who had such men in their lives.

"I want to be your patron." Monica's nail scratched against the inscription. How had she overlooked the potential inside Henry? When they met, she assumed he was like any other

alpha but polite male. That was until he told her what she had really been thinking – that he was Dom through and through.

Before any man was accepted as patron, Monica did some research. What he did, where he lived, how he made his millions... Henry Warren was a name she hadn't heard before. Either he dropped a good amount of his fortune on this collar and chain, or he was a sleeper businessman who controlled the world from behind the scenes. He wasn't the face of a major company. He wasn't a famous heir that showed up on Page 6. He was old money, but he knew how to use it. Monica's last lover was old money as well. *And look how that turned out for me.*

Old money men were snobbish and out of touch. New money men were reckless and prone to bad decisions. Monica would never find a good balance.

Her phone rang.

The landline on her desk, of course, not her cell phone. Few had access to that. Monica shook her head to clear the cobwebs before snatching up the phone and saying, "You have reached Monica Graham. Speak."

Nothing surprised her anymore. Not even hearing Henry's voice on the other end of the line. "Good to hear you sounding so cheerful today."

The collar was cold. "What can I do for you, Mr. Warren?"

"Please, Henry."

"No, Mr. Warren."

The pause was surely not comforting for either of them. "I was wondering if you would do me the honor of dinner, Ms. Graham." He was going to play her game.

"Dinner? Why on Earth would I have dinner with you?"

"I said dinner, not a date. I want to discuss business."

"I'm sure you do!"

"Not *that* kind of business. Investments."

"Excuse me?"

Henry chuckled, although he must have done it far from his phone for as quiet as it was. "I want to discuss the possibility of investing in your business. Don't tell me you couldn't use some extra money in a place like that. You have a lot of expensive clientele to keep happy."

"We already have investors."

"And you don't want more?"

Either her palm was sweaty or Henry Warren was making her phone burn in her hand. "I'm not sure it would be appropriate for us to have dinner."

"It would be good for you to come down from your mountain and join me for dinner. I'm in town for a few days."

"You don't live in the city?"

"No, but I keep a place here. I'm always looking for new ventures to gauge. Come have dinner with me."

"I'm afraid I don't do that. Go into the city, that is."

"Fine. I'll come there."

Why was he being so stubborn? *Men, men, men!* "While I appreciate your vested interest in my business, Mr. Warren, I'm afraid that I am not open to new investors at this time."

"You know, it could be that I want to get to know you."

Well! She certainly wasn't expecting candor like that. "You made that clear when you gave me your idea of a gift."

"Have I offended you? Please, tell me if I have."

"You haven't offended me." *More like made my imagination run wild.*

"Then you shouldn't have any issue with having dinner with me. Tell me when. I'll bring the drinks."

"That won't be necessary." Monica stared at the collar on her desk. *"I want to be your patron."* She imagined her and Henry sitting in a cozy restaurant, the man fawning over her while she in turn fawned over him. "Thursday. Five. If you're even a minute late, it's over."

Another pause. At this rate he was going to kill her with the waiting. "Thank you for taking a chance on me. By the way…"

"Yes?"

He breathed deeply against the phone, that voice, those breaths burrowing into Monica's ear as she felt a trickle of sweat come down her forehead and down her chest. "Never mind. We can talk about it on Thursday."

Monica said the first thing to come to her mind, although she instantly regretted it. "I look forward to it." No, no, no! What in the world was she doing? *Don't encourage him!* Oh, she would encourage him all right. She let a smile cross her face before leaning against her desk and saying with a smile, "I look forward to how you try to seduce me next."

Cat, mouse… who was who and which was which? Furthermore, how much longer would Monica be able to resist?

Chapter 6

The Wolf's Den

The wine was vintage, sweet, and much more delicious than Monica wanted to give Henry credit for. He had spared no expense on the gifts he brought her, beyond the wine. Truffles, exotic flowers, and a transparent light red shawl that glittered in tiny rubies. Since these were given to her publically in the foyer, Monica had no choice but to accept them graciously. The food stuff was put out for their dinner, the flowers sent to the dining table, and the shawl? She handed it to Sylvia and asked her to leave it in the front hallway of the master suite. *No way am I wearing it outside to our dinner in his presence.*

"I don't want you to think I bought it to impress you," he said, as they walked side by side upstairs and toward a small balcony near the master suite. Monica arranged for a two-person dining table to be set up, complete with a lantern and a silk tablecloth. It shouldn't get too dark while they ate, but Monica understood ambiance like her billionaire clients understood the stock market. *He'll think I'm flirting.* She was. She was flirting so hard the outcome pointed to Henry bending her over the railing and giving her what they both wanted.

"I don't think you did that at all." Monica opened the door and waited for Henry to step through. *Sometimes I get to be a gentlelady.* "Because you know I would not be impressed."

"In truth, I didn't buy it. I found it in my sister's bin of things she wants to get rid of. Asked her if I could give it to someone and she said yes."

"How… well, I don't know what to say to that."

"I thought of you when I saw it." Henry pulled a chair out from the table for Monica to sit in. She accepted, and waited for him to sit adjacent to her, both of their seats offering a view of the sunset as it came for the gardens. "You make me think of the color red. Passionate. Straightforward. Strong."

Only one other man had called her strong before. *Ethan Cole, my ex.* He called her that when she broke down crying in his home shortly after he took her away from that awful prison belonging to Jackson Lyle. *"You're stronger than you give yourself credit for. A weaker woman would have died in there."* "You flatter me, Mr. Warren."

"What is your favorite color, anyway?"

Monica looked right into those blue eyes. "I don't know."

"How can you not know your favorite color?"

"It used to be black."

One of the maids came out with wineglasses and ice water to get them started. She knew what to do. *Bring out the bread. Then the vegetable and soup course. Then the main course. Then dessert.* If the bread wasn't out of the kitchen within ten minutes, someone would get fired.

Henry waited for the maid to go back inside before asking, "Used to be?"

"Yes. Used to be." Monica loved the simplicity of the color black. Yet it was strong, resilient, and so useful and loved by millions around the world. Black was the color of "goes with everything." It represented an innocuous coolness that everyone could relate to.

It also made her think of darker days now. Days that practically ruined her ability to love what the color black had to offer and why she should embrace them all. These days, she gravitated toward the color white to get her mind off it. White was refreshing and as versatile, in a cheerful sort of way. Except Monica's room was still black and red. No wonder she felt chills every time she went to bed. Regardless of how much she tried to distance herself from her past, it was always there, waiting for her.

Henry leaned on his elbows and looked between her and the lamp in the middle of the table. "Black and red go well together."

"Those are the colors of my room."

Monica knew what hand she played, and she was not disappointed to hear him say, "I should like to see it."

"I'm sure you would. I'm an impeccable decorator."

"As stated by this entire mansion."

The maid brought out the bread right on time. Henry insisted on cutting up and buttering it while Monica watched the sun begin its descent behind a grove. *I should be doing that for him.* Every time someone did something for her, Monica felt the compulsion to tell them, "No, no! I will do that.   Please, let me serve you." In a more common life she would be happy to work retail and waitressing. Maybe work up to being a maid like one of the workers in her Château. She loved to make other people happy and fulfill their needs. The day she realized she got off on it was a strange, yet liberating one.

"A part of me is surprised that you agreed to have dinner with me." Henry left the bread on his plate but didn't touch it. "I thought for sure that after my faux pas you would want nothing to do with me."

"That's not true." Monica nibbled the corner of her crust and was grateful that a gentle breeze kicked up and washed away the crumbs. "I rather like you, Mr. Warren. I think you misunderstood the intentions going on."

"Oh? And what were those?"

She glanced at him, coolly, the corner of her mouth teasing her cheek with a smile. "You can't buy my desire. You have to earn it."

The wineglass was at the edge of his lips, It remained there, the white wine still in the glass as he gazed at her over the rim. "And how do I do that?"

Monica shrugged. "Make me trust you. That's not an easy thing to do."

Henry put the wineglass down and licked his lips. "I bet it wouldn't be, considering what I know about you."

"And what do you know?" The shields were up. Monica scooted back in her chair, ready to be angry at him.

"I know that you used to be with Jackson Lyle. After you two broke up, he was bought out of his shares at Jackson-Cole. Something happened."

"Is that it? You want to know what's going on in the business world through me? Because I don't have any insider information. I didn't know anything going on in his life besides what he wanted to do to me."

She feared that Henry would push the issue... maybe ask what he wanted to do to her. *Humiliate me. Hurt me.* Bruises weren't supposed to be a part of her lifestyle.

Henry didn't say anything. All he did was place his hand next to hers on the table, where her fingers clenched a napkin and ignored the bread waiting to be consumed.

Monica did not accept his invitation to be touched. That was reserved for a man she could trust – and as attracted as she was to Henry Warren, she didn't know if she could trust him yet. For all she knew...

"I'm sorry I brought it up," he said. "Whatever you went through, it must have been awful. Nobody really likes that guy in the business world. We deal with him because we have to."

"We?"

The hand disappeared. "Why, yes. I won't say I know him personally, but he does pop up in many of my spheres. I've only met him on a handful of occasions. I never guessed he was into that sort of lifestyle."

"You mean domination and submission."

"It seems to be the sort of life that can easily turn dark. With the wrong person, that is."

You have no idea. How could he, as a man? Men held all the power. That's what Monica liked about the situation, but it didn't save her from the evil that sometimes burst from it. She wanted a man to control her in the bedroom, to tell her what to do sometimes, to make her life easier… but not to rule that life. That's what Jackson ended up doing, and she paid for it.

The maid returned with their soup course. Neither of them picked up their spoons. *I'm being a terrible hostess.* Making it all about her past, failed relationships… "Enough about me, Mr. Warren. Tell me more about yourself."

"I'm terribly boring. My job is boring, my hobbies are boring. My house is boring because I'm too busy to do anything with it."

"What do you do?"

"Mergers. Acquisitions. Buy places. Sell them off. Keep the profits. Time-honored tradition my great-grandfather started a hundred years ago, and now here I am. I may have been born with a silver spoon in my mouth, but I intend to earn the right to keep it."

"That's noble." Sounded like what Jackson and most men of old money did. Either that or they married rich before telling her that their own fortunes were crumbling. Monica looked like a woman of means, but she would hardly say that she was. If she lost the Château, she would have next to nothing. *All the money I personally make goes back into it.* Not the best financial planning, but she wanted her business to succeed before worrying about her own future. "At least you keep yourself busy. I've known men who rest on their laurels and pretend everything is going to continue the way it always has. Life doesn't work out that way. It's good to be prepared and stay busy. What do you do for fun?"

"I told you, my hobbies are boring too."

"I highly doubt that. There must be something." Even reading could be an adventure. Assuming Henry had good tastes, of course.

"Reading is perhaps the only hobby I can regularly indulge in." *Ha! I knew it.* Finally, Henry touched his soup, declared it delicious, but still too hot for him to completely eat at the moment. "I'm fluent in French, so I like to read the original works of authors like Proust. Oh, and the Marquis de Sade. I assume you've heard of him."

Monica's mouth twitched again. "I have. I'm afraid I don't think much of him, though." Of course she knew the word "sadistic" came from that man. She also knew why. Many Doms heralded him as some sort of father of their sexualities, which perturbed Monica, since the Marquis was infamous for coercing his servants. *Jackson admired him way too much.* She hoped Henry wasn't the same way.

"His works are fascinating, but perhaps for all the wrong reasons." That was all Henry said on the matter, and Monica did not press him further.

Over the course of dinner she learned a few more things about him. Henry's parents were alive, but they lived in their favorite vacation home in Montana, where his father had a ranch and his mother made jewelry for a "living," not that she needed to. He currently lived in their main house with his younger sister, who was in grad school getting her MBA. They almost sounded like a normal upper middle class family until Monica remembered that Henry Warren was probably one of the richest men in the country. He could do anything with his life... so why was he spending it with her?

"I also like to paint here and there," he said at the beginning of their final course. "Nothing in particular. Just whatever moves me." Henry pointed to the sunset, now sinking fast behind the trees. "Like that. I would like to paint that if I had the chance. The way the light passes through the branches of those evergreens and illuminates the labyrinth is simply breathtaking." He glanced at her. "Looks nice on you as well."

Flattery would get him nowhere. Monica knew what he was up to. "Thank you." She would take the compliment anyway.

"So what do *you* do for fun?" Henry was on his second glass of wine. Monica was still on her first, but she could see the bottom of her glass. "I have a hard time believing you do this for fun all the time." He motioned to the Château.

"Believe what you will or won't. My work is my life now."

"No movies? No books?"

"I read occasionally, but I've found recently that most of the stories I used to enjoy now only frustrate me." They reminded her of her old relationship. Monica devoured books –

dark and comedic – about alpha males and their unwitting women. She particularly enjoyed the recent trend of billionaires and mafia bosses and, and, and… *Nope. Too much like real life.* Few women could say that!

"I'm sorry to hear that. I hope you can enjoy them again soon."

Henry's voice wasn't empty, nor was it full of sarcasm. When they made eye contact, Monica saw nothing but warmth in his eyes. *It's a ruse. A game.* That's what she had to tell herself in order to survive. No man actually cared that she enjoyed "A Billionaire Love Story" ever again. *Because they're not real.* She thought she had that kind of love once. Perhaps she was too jaded by the heartbreak.

"If I may ask…" Henry's fingered the stem of his glass, leaning back in his chair with one leg over the other and his eyes downcast. "What happened between you and Jackson Lyle? You were a famous couple in our circles, even if only by legend."

What a strange thing to say. "Bad things."

The awkward silence she created was not lost on the man dining with her. Henry continued to stare at the table before finally looking up and gazing at Monica's figure in her chair. The maid came, taking away their empty plates and replacing them with a dessert of key lime pie. Perfect for a warm evening.

Yet Henry continued to gaze at her, those unwavering blues caressing Monica's body as if they truly touched. If she closed her own and also leaned back in her chair, she could pretend that Henry stood right next to her, truly caressing her arm, her cheek, and even her hair as he wrapped each dark strand around his fingers and promised to make her feel better.

I'm tragic. What was even more tragic was how pointless it all felt. Henry Warren couldn't cure her of her heartbreak. She was a stupid girl to even pretend that it was possible, even in her fantasies. *It was those fantasies that made me hang on to him for so long.* When in love, the heart fucked shit up. "He hurt me. In ways you could never imagine."

It was too easy unloading her secrets onto him. Henry was a courteous listener, at least, not once interrupting Monica as she attempted to put into words the horrors she went through.

"Everything started innocent enough. Isn't that how it always goes? One day I was a girl in a lounge looking for a little trouble. I found it. His name was Jackson, and he bought me a drink and told me I was the most beautiful woman in the world. It's young girls like me back then who fall for that shit."

"Long story short, he became my Dom. I was happy to serve him. We were deep into the lifestyle. It's how I wanted it, and he grew accustomed to it. He would come home, I would take off his clothes for him, make sure there was a bath ready, order his favorite foods, and then do whatever he told me to do. Sometimes it was sexual, and sometimes he told me to leave him alone, so I did. I suppose this sounds boring, the way I'm telling it. To those in the lifestyle, it is boring. We were just another sub/Dom domestic pair."

"As the years went by, we went deeper. Maybe it happened naturally. Maybe it was all his machinations. Whatever happened, the next thing I knew he was picking out what I

Cynthia Dane

wore and who else I slept with. You see, sometimes he would bring home another girl and tell me to do things with her. I did them. I wasn't disgusted. It was fun, really. But they weren't things I would have asked for or pursued on my own."

"I called him Master. I didn't leave the house unless he accompanied me. When we were home, I stayed in our room until he invited me elsewhere. I couldn't even go outside for a walk without his permission. That was normal. I trusted him."

"It may have happened on one day. It could have worked its way up to it. All I know is that one night he had me chained up like always. And then he slapped me."

"He never laid a hand like that on me before. Not a violent one. It stung so much, and the glee in his voice as he laughed at my reaction made me feel sick to my stomach. After so many years together, though, I forgave him. It was a one time thing. Then he did it another night. Then another. Then he hit me so hard I had a bruise and no excuse for it."

"One night he nearly broke my arm. He grabbed it so hard and turned me around to throw me on the bed so quickly I could feel a pop. I wish that was the worst thing that happened that night. When he was done with me, I felt like I could barely walk. That's all I'll say about that."

"The final straw – because I was so weak – came when he literally kidnapped another woman and intended to make her his sex slave. I woke up that day. I stole his keys and his gun and got that woman and me out of there. I never looked back."

She let her words dissipate in the sunset, each one harder to dissolve than the last. By the time she realized her key lime pie remained untouched, Henry Warren grabbed her hand, making her fork clatter on the table.

"I'm sorry that happened." His grip on her tightened. Monica stiffened, not out of fear, but out of the sense that this man was too good for his own benefit. "It wasn't right. That man doesn't know how to appreciate what he has."

Yes, that was the problem Monica wanted to roll her eyes, but she was frozen in her seat, reliving those awful memories. Closing her eyes was dangerous. If she did that, her brain would place a scene on the back of her eyelids. Maybe the night Jackson slapped her and called her a whore because she always agreed to whatever he wanted. *Didn't he understand that I wanted that too?* Serving him, making him happy…

"No, what he didn't get was what a submissive is. We're not toys, Mr. Warren. We're not vessels of pleasure to be used however a Dom wants. Our joy and pleasure comes from bringing our Dom happiness. Of course we have our preferences and the lines we draw, but at the end of the day, we'll try anything once if it brings him or her joy of any kind. That's how we become so vulnerable. We bare our souls from the first meeting. If we're put in the wrong hands… men like him knew that. I fear for any woman he cons next. He's handsome and wealthy. There will be someone."

"There are none that I know of."

"That you know of. He keeps that shit private." For good reason. He was the type of man to understand what wasn't socially acceptable. But he did them anyway. "Forgive me. You didn't need to know any of that."

"Correction. I didn't *want* to know any of that." When Monica turned her head toward him, bemusement clouding her countenance, he explained, "I don't get any glee or pleasure in hearing what that callous man did to you. Yet I needed to know it. I needed to know what you've been through, so I understand where you come from."

"Where I came from is obvious to anyone who Googles my name." Monica pulled her hand out of his. "Where I'm going, on the other hand, remains a mystery to most."

"Even to yourself?"

"Perhaps. I take things one week at a time."

"*Perhaps* you will be a little old lady running your Château a good forty years from now."

"And I will be happy to do so."

She knew what that look meant. The one telling her, *"Are you going to hide in your mansion of everyone else having pleasure but you for the rest of your life?"* She would if it meant she was never hurt again. Monica could sustain herself on the ambiance of her insular world and never again be touched by another person. She could die happy that way.

"I won't pretend to understand," Henry said. "Obviously I have never been in your position before. All I know is that the world would be a much lonelier place if you never ventured into it again."

Monica blushed. "The world doesn't know who I am."

"I do."

See, this is what's dangerous about this man. Henry had the influence to sway Monica back into the world of powerful relationships. Powerful within, and powerful on the outside. There was the power they exuded on each other behind closed doors, and then the power they presented when they stood before others as a unified front. *If I go out into the world, then I do nothing but wander around it, looking pathetic.* Dominant men were the accepted norm in the business world. They came, they saw, and they conquered the piss out of everything.

Submissive women, on the other hand, looked lost. People often approached Monica when she sat in cafes by herself, asking if she was all right, if she needed help, etc. And that was when she was in a relationship! When people found out she ran her own business, they were floored. People didn't respect submissives as smart, intelligent people who had a lot of will to get things done. Just because Monica wanted to live a life of submissive love and pleasure didn't mean she couldn't do things on her own.

"You continue to flatter me. The fact of the matter is, Mr. Warren, you don't know me from the mole on your back you've never seen before. Like I keep telling you, I'm a sub, not a naïve girl who believes everything a handsome man tells her."

"So you think I'm handsome?"

That knowing smile could sink ships. Like the one capsizing in Monica's stomach right now. "I think you know you're handsome. Men who are handsome always know that they are."

"Meanwhile, beautiful women need constant affirmation."

"Can you blame them?"

"No. Can you blame me for getting to know you better?"

"Mr. Warren, may I remind you that you sent me a silver and diamond sub collar? That's not getting to know me better. That's…"

"A friendly BDSM way of saying hello there gorgeous, I know."

He said it so flippantly that Monica snorted into the back of her hand before giving herself over to overflowing laughter. Her voice echoed in the gardens below, bouncing off the topiaries and rousing a flock of birds into the air. "And what do you know of BDSM, Mr. Warren? I mean, truly…"

Henry wasn't laughing. "A lot more than you probably figure I do."

Monica stopped guffawing and rested her hands on her stomach. Her pie was still untouched. "Do you practice?"

"No, I don't practice." Henry grabbed the half-empty wine bottle and refilled his glass, then Monica's, a set look of determination flickering in the growing lantern light. "That's definitely not the word I would use."

"And what word would you use?"

This time he did not take her hand. Monica didn't even know what he was doing beneath the table until she felt him touch her knee, his delectably warm palm and fingers curling around her bare skin. Shots of desire, both welcomed and menacing, plotted a wavering course up her skin and straight to her groin. Or maybe those were his fingers, treading dangerously close to her thighs and a warmth she kept there.

She didn't push him away. Nor did she tell him to stop or change his ways. Deep down Monica wanted him to touch her intimately, to know what her body felt like beneath his touch. God knew it felt good on her end.

"Rather experienced."

Monica concentrated her breathing, a practice she hadn't had to use since the days she was driven to the edge of orgasm but forbidden from indulging in it until her Dom said it was okay. Deep breathing meant she could stave off her pleasure… it also meant she could keep a level head. "So you tell me now. And here I thought you were bumbling along."

"No you didn't. You never thought that. I told you, Monica, you know who I am. Do I really have to tell you who and what I am?"

She shook her head, eyes darting between his stern visage and the hand tightening on her thigh. *Just a little farther and I won't be able to resist him anymore.* The closer she let this man get to her intimately, the harder it became to deny him. "I know who you are. What surprises me is that you knew me so quickly. How many subs have you had?"

Henry withdrew his hand and straightened his jacket, probably in lieu of having a tie to adjust. "Trick question. I've dallied with submissives, but I've never found the one for me."

"So you're shopping around, and somehow think I can fulfill your needs."

"I don't assume anything. All I know is that I am intrigued by you and want to get to know you better."

"Until now, I wasn't sure what you meant by 'get to know me.' Now I think I do."

"As long as we're on the same page."

"We're not. As I told you, I'm not really ready for something like that again yet. And you still made the mistake of assuming I was up for patronage. Like a whore."

"Then what are those girls? Are they whores?"

"Excuse you. What they want and what I want are completely different. They aren't lifestyle submissives like I am. This is a job to them. I'm careful to not hire lifestyle women. They get too attached to their clients and cause a mess for me and them."

"That is wise." Henry removed his hand, clenching it on top of the table. Still, neither of them ate their dessert. "You really do have a good head for business. It must help that you have a lot of experience in this line of living."

"If only you knew, Mr. Warren." That was not an invitation. *It is. It truly is.* Monica pushed her plate of pie away. "Come. I want to show you something." She stood up, pushed in her chair, and turned resolutely toward the door.

He attempted to follow, but the look on his face expressed that he had no idea what her intentions were. "You already gave me such a great tour last time."

Monica touched the handle and looked over her shoulder. "Not of my room, I didn't."

That certainly got his attention. Henry moved to hold the door open for her, and the moment Monica stepped back into the Château she told the maid to give the pie to anyone who wanted it, and that she and Henry were not to be disturbed unless it was an emergency.

What Henry thought of these instructions she could only imagine. On one hand she was inviting him into her private quarters, beyond her office, but on another it was not a sexual invitation, as much as she wished it could be. But there was something that she wanted Henry to see, and he could only see it in her chambers.

They weren't too far from the balcony. Just a few steps, and they were there, Monica unlocking the door that led to her private world.

Whatever Henry initially thought of her room, he did not let on. It wasn't anything special. A large canopy bed, some antique dark wood furniture, and erotic art that she collected over the past few months.

"Everything you see in this room," she said, pouring herself a glass of brandy and then offering another to Henry, "was procured in a short amount of time. When I left Jackson, I had only the clothes I wore on my back. I don't know what he did with my old things. Maybe he threw them away. Maybe he created a shrine in which he venerates my image and vows to steal me back from my new life. I don't care, but every time I look at these things, I'm reminded that I once had everything and then had nothing."

"It's still impressive."

"I suppose. Most women couldn't leave with nothing and build something like this up in such a short amount of time, true. I'm not most women. There are many different things about me that don't hold true for other women I've met. 'Normal' women."

"Is there really such a thing?"

He stood by the door, declining the brandy. *Don't act like you don't want into my space.* He would have to be mad otherwise. "There is such a thing as what the public perceives as being normal. I am not it."

"Oh, I'm not sure about that. I think a lot of women feel like you do, they just don't know how to express it."

"There's expressing it, and then there's living the lifestyle."

"Is that what you want to do?"

"What? Live the lifestyle?"

"Naturally."

"As you said. Naturally."

Henry eventually took a glass of brandy from Monica's hand, his fingers lingering on hers. *Keep finding excuses to touch me. I dare you.* "You are right to be cautious. There are a lot of terrible people out there looking to take advantage of women looking for that kind of life. Unfortunately, as you prove."

They stood in front of each other, Monica's head tilted back so she could look up into his stoic face. "Are you a terrible person, Mr. Warren?" There was no whimsy in her voice. However he answered would decide the next thing she said to him.

It took a while for him to answer. During that time he sipped the brandy, murmured that it was a good brand, and stuck his hand in his pocket as if searching for his wallet or phone. "I like to think I'm not a terrible person. But all men are a work in progress."

Damn him again. Monica wanted to hear him say that he was awful, that he was the best man in the whole world. Absolutes. That's what she wanted. That way she could write him off as someone either too self-aware or too haughty to be trifled with. Monica drank her whole glass of brandy in one gulp, letting it burn her on the way down in hopes of washing away the memories bubbling up in her stomach. If they reached her brain, she was in real trouble.

Too late.

She didn't know if it was the alcohol or the situation, but Monica dropped her empty glass on the chair next to her and hid her face in her hands. The first sob to burst forth was powerful enough to shake her whole body, but the sound was worse: like an abandoned child wondering why she was all alone in the world yet again.

What was wrong with her? What made her so easy to abuse? What made any man, let alone the man she gave her heart to, decide to take her heart, her virtue, and her dreams for their future and crush them with his polished shoe? What made Jackson think he could hit her, spit on her, and force her to do things that went beyond the line of harmless sexual humiliation? She gave him several years of her life. In return, he gave her a prison and a broken heart.

Henry's arms wrapped around her, a much welcomed veil of protection from the world she was too exposed to. *I don't need this...* She didn't need these welling feelings overflowing in her body, telling her to cling to him, to feel the strength of his arms, his chest, and his shoulders enshrouding her. He was so tall that Monica easily nestled into his embrace, hoping that he would hold her there in their small world forever.

She wanted a lot of things. Like the pat on her back, the nose in her hair, and the kind words that said she was worth more than any man must have shown her. *I'm so weak.* As if he read her mind, Henry said, "You're one of the strongest women I've met. Who can come back from that and do as much as you have? I've seen men crumble from less."

No matter how much Monica wanted to tell him that it was an absurd thing to say, the words still sank into her brain, and she thought of the very few men in her life she ever saw cry. None of them had been her lovers. She wasn't even sure Jackson was capable of producing tears – besides tears of laughter at her expense. "Why am I such a mess?"

Henry tipped her chin up and gazed into her tear stained face. There should have been something comforting in the way he looked at her, but all Monica could think was that *this man had seen her cry.* That was her second most vulnerable.

The first was…

Her heart exploded into a burst of sparks when he kissed her, Monica's brain screaming no while the rest of her resisted reason and gave in to her strongest desires.

She hadn't kissed a man who wasn't Jackson in so long that she forgot men all did it differently. Henry, in particular, kissed with the entirely of his lips, not favoring one side or the other as he devoured the woman in his arms, each kiss stronger, more intoxicating than the last. Monica clung to him, her arms stretching to reach up around and bring him down closer to her, body slipping toward the sofa behind her with Henry following.

How liberating it was to give herself away, freely and without reserve. The heavy breaths hitting her skin were laced in an aphrodisiac that made Monica's legs spread around Henry's hips and her head fall back against the arm of the couch. Her chest heaved toward his mouth, which descended to her bodice, ripping apart the buttons of her dress and kissing both mounds of her breasts. Every time he thrust against her thighs, Monica whimpered, her hesitations unraveling the longer Henry Warren showered her with comfort.

Isn't this what she expected when she invited him into her room? A part of her certainly hoped that her flirtations would lead to this. To deny that she wanted Henry was a grievous mistake. Monica knew herself too well to know that she could fool her heart like that. *I won't call it love.* She wasn't looking for *love*... but she needed passion. She needed to know that there were men out there still willing to take her how they pleased, their bodies using hers while still thinking of nothing but the woman they held in their arms and pushed into with every famished movement. Monica begged for him to have her, to rip away the one thing separating them and let her know him. Carnal knowledge was the next best thing to enlightenment.

"Mr. Warren," she whispered, her skin bruising from the forceful way he kissed her throat and the shoulder that quickly emerged from her tearing sleeve. "Henry!"

He was too strong, too eager to deny any longer. Monica melted around him, her legs locked around his waist as he thrust against her. *He's hard already...* And unless Monica was mistaken, Henry Warren had a lot to offer. Now. Right now. Her hand pushed between them, determined to open his zipper and pull away her lingerie so he could have her as he liked. *I know men. I know what they like.* Lucky that she liked it too.

Monica wouldn't stand to wait another minute. "Take me, Henry," she whimpered again, her breaths ragged as he sucked her nipple through her bra, his tongue dipping into the padding in a futile effort to taste her intimately. "Ravage me."

She wanted it like she wanted to breathe the sweet air flooding her bedroom. For the first time in months, maybe *years* Monica looked forward to the fearless pleasures of sex. *Not just any sex.* The kind that made her scream into a man's ear that he was tearing her apart, and to not stop until she was incapable of feeling a damn thing anymore. Henry could take her like this, right on her couch, but she would rather he take her to bed and mount her there. And it had to be *now.* Quick. Even forceful. There was time to serve him better as a sub later. *Now* was about sating the desires fueling her like mad and making her fantasize about Henry Warren throwing her down on her bed and defiling her body – and not only with some hair pulling and dirty, disgusting words.

"Deep down you're a wild one, I see." Henry took her wrists and held them above her head, his demeanor primal as his stony blue eyes drank in the skin she showed him. Her skirt slipped down her leg, exposing the white of her thigh and the black satin underwear she wore that day. *They're wet already.* Now, damnit! He could have his fill of her in fewer than five minutes. Even at his biggest and roughest he could probably enter her with no hesitations. The more she thought about it, the more Monica wanted to claw his arms and scream at him to fuck her. "Like a sweet, pretty wolf."

Now he pulled her arms back down, pinning them to her sides as her back arched and she presented her chest to his mouth again. Henry did not indulge.

"I've trapped you, Queen of the Wolves. Here in your den." His voice, low and vibrant, sent shivers through Monica until she nearly wept in frustration. "Do you know how badly I want to shoot you in the heart?" His lips ravished the valley between her breasts, his tongue wetting her skin, caressing her nipple, and making her pelvis shudder against his hips. "Do you know how much I want to leave my mark in you?"

His words were so delightful that Monica could barely form any of her own. "Be a menace. Hunt me down and claim my body." She pushed her hips forward, rubbing against the hardness straining against his trousers. "I'm yours."

Monica almost got off on the situation alone. Her, the dangerous she-wolf, chased into her den in the lonely woods, her hunter too strong to resist. Truly, her only hope was that he would mount her well and good, a mate worthy of calling her alpha. Based on what she felt between her legs right now... *The odds are good.*

She thought Henry would fuck her there and then. His breath was harried against her breasts, his hardness still rubbing against her clothed, wet slit. Monica wanted to reach between them and show him what he had done to her, but her arms were still stuck to her sides. *Hold me like this and take me.* Being immobilized was one of her biggest turn-ons. Henry was doing a fantastic job speaking to her kinky mind.

"What are you waiting for?" she asked. "Or do you want me to struggle?" Like a wolf who would bite until the end.

"I want you." If that was so, then why wasn't he doing it? What did Monica have to say or do to get him to have her? "I want you so much that I know now is the wrong time."

He released her, sitting up on the couch and doing his best to ignore the response between his legs. Monica also sat up, covering her chest with her torn clothes and the hair that fell out of her bun. "What do you mean it's the wrong time?"

"I'm the first man after that after all that, aren't I?"

Monica didn't say anything.

"I don't want to be patronizing, but I wouldn't feel right doing that until you were sure it was what you wanted. And I mean *sure*. Not from the heat of the moment, but because your heart and mind are also ready, not just your body."

Monica didn't argue with him. A part of her knew that he was right. When he came to visit that day, she had no idea that this would actually happen. That it would feel so *good*. After her last relationship, she had vowed to eschew all future ones unless she was absolutely sure she would not be as hurt should something happen. For as much as she wanted Henry, Monica knew it wasn't enough.

"I won't come back here," he said, and for a moment a flutter of panic struck Monica's heart. "Not until it's the right time. If that time ever comes."

He kissed her, not with the ardor of earlier, but with a warmth that said *"No hard feelings."* Henry straightened out his clothing before seeing himself to Monica's door.

"This isn't farewell," he said, hand on the door. "Only goodbye for now." He left.

Monica had never felt so alone in her room before.

Chapter 7

Love Letters

When Monica received her first letter a few days later, she thought she was losing her mind. Nobody sent letters anymore. Certainly not to her.

But that was definitely what she received the morning a courier deposited a thick envelope in her hand before asking her to sign for a package containing better knives for the kitchen. "There's no return address on this," she said, signing the courier's device but not looking away from the letter. "I thought you couldn't accept those."

The courier merely tipped his hat and wished her a good day. As soon as the front doors to the Château closed, Sylvia said, "That means someone paid him to personally deliver that."

Monica could only think of one person who would do such a thing. She handed Sylvia the package, told her to take it to the chef in the kitchen, and darted upstairs to her room.

She never thought she would hear from Henry like that again. In the back of her mind she had pushed him aside as a momentary fling – the type of man who had wanted her one moment and then rejected her the next. When he never even bothered to call her, Monica assumed the infatuation was over.

Not so. The moment she tore open the envelope, a piece of paper fluttered to her desk. She snatched it up, eyes devouring every word.

***

"It's been three days since that small amount of time we spent together, and since then I've done nothing but think of you. My intention was to put some space between us so we could sort out how we really felt. In truth, we've only met a handful of times. I admit that I pushed things too quickly by sending you that gift. From the moment I laid eyes on you, Monica, I've thought of nothing but making love to you.

"Although we need space, I don't want to give it to you anymore. You're beautiful, yes, but you are also so much more. Since getting to know you better, I see a brilliant woman with a shrewd mind and a great sense for business. Not everyone could be in your position and do as well as you do. When you told me your harrowing tale of that other man, I felt my heart break on your behalf. There are foul men in this world. I like to think I am better than that. I also need to think about whether or not I can give you what you need.

"You're not a woman who can be won with flowers and jewels. I've known women like that. You're the type who must be won with deeds and reassurances. I can reassure you that I only have the best intentions. If I have ever wronged or offended you, or if I ever do so in the future, know that you are free to chastise me so that I may become a better man.

"Even so, my need for you burns. Your beauty caught me so off guard that it took me days to process your soft skin, sweet dimples, and hair enveloping your body. The other day I wanted nothing more than to make love to you, like an animal, like a man, everything in between and something that transcended both at the same time. You're a woman who deserves only the finest sexual pleasure. I want to deny you it until you feel as if you're dying. Then I want to give it to you until we both appreciate what this life has to offer us.

"It's not that simple, is it? The other day I came to your Château with every intention of seducing you into bed. Yet after you told me what you did, I knew that it couldn't happen. I won't tell you how you feel or how you're recovering. All I can do is prevent myself from becoming your next mistake. Now, before you protest, let me explain.

"Years ago I had a lover who was also heartbroken from a previous relationship. Not the same exact situation, but close enough that you reminded me of her. We were together for about a year. She wanted to use submission as a way to forgive herself for the pain she had been through at the hands of another man. One night I was too tough on her. Not only did I rip open her wounds again, but I scared her away from me, a man who had said he loved her.

"I don't know where she is now. I hope that she's happy, wherever she is. I hope she found a man that could give her what she wanted better than I could. I think about her often. Mostly because I wonder what I could have done differently to make her understand what I meant when I did the things I did to her. I was trying to help her heal too.

"So you see, I can't escalate a relationship between us. Not when it's like that. I don't want you until you're ready for me to take you. I want your heart completely open, your mind blind to the past, and your body prepared to accept what I have to offer. I won't deny it, Monica, but I often fantasize about what I want to do to you. I want to make you feel like it's only you and me in the world. Like we're alone in the universe, if only for a little while. I don't think I would disappoint you. I do think I might hurt you.

"I won't come around again until it's time. I hope that you are in good spirits and that your business is thriving. The next time I see you will be to either say my final farewells or to give you what you need. Either way, it will be your choice."

"Yours, Henry Warren."

***

"Mr. Warren, I hope that you know it took me no fewer than three hours to track down an address to send this to. As big of a man as you are, you are equally difficult to get a hold of. My persistence was not in vain, and now here I am responding to you when I should be downstairs making sure all is ready for a busy night.

"I admit, I was nearly torn in two again when you left me the other day. You don't understand the extent in which I *want* you. If you think you desire me, carnally or otherwise, then you still don't comprehend how much I want you to dominate me. I'm not a silly little girl looking for her daddy Dom. I want a man who will be my partner in the bedroom. You said so yourself that we are two halves of the same whole. What we both bring is equal in its relevance and passion. To an outsider we look, perhaps, barbaric. I do not doubt that it's those primal urges that make us so attracted to each other in the first place.

"I've been hurt, yes. Have there been times with you in which I thought of that man? Yes, and they frightened me. I won't mince my words – I am scared. I'm scared to not only love but to also be dominated. I'm not scared to be submissive. It's my nature to want to serve others, especially men. Do you know which wonderful ways I could serve you?

"I will bring you what you want, you need, and even put the spoon to your mouth so you don't have to move another muscle at the end of a long work day. I will put my hands on you, gently, massaging whatever you please as I begin to fantasize about the other things you will ask of me. Serving makes me so needy. The moment you force your hand, Mr. Warren, is the moment in which I belong wholly to you and am ready for you to use my will and body in any ways you please.

His Domination

"The other day here in my room I wanted you to not only dominate me, but to use my desires to fuel your own. Why didn't you ask me to take off your clothes, to take off *my* clothes? You could have asked me to do anything. I would have pressed my lips and tongue to your manhood the moment you asked for it. I would have bent over, climbed on top of you, even turned myself upside down for you. Just thinking about it now drives me insane, Mr. Warren. I need you. The fact that you are not coming through that door right now to use me is breaking my heart, not you doing it.

"Nevertheless, you are right. I should not rush into anything. *We* shouldn't rush into anything. Perhaps I am a delicate flower who hasn't taken root again yet. I wish I wasn't. I wish I wasn't scared to know exactly how you will use me and make me serve you. Trust. That's the word, isn't it? I barely know you. I have your word, but I long learned that a man's word may as well be dirt. My fantasies are only that. What do they mean when you're hurting me anyway?

"See? I assume that you will. I'm pathetic.

"Give me some time. In the meantime, I should like to hear from you again like this. Please write to me any time.

"Patiently waiting, Monica."

***

"Dearest Monica,

"You flatter me with your fantasies while also confirming what I suspected. Don't think I don't know how you would have behaved that day. I wanted it too. Tonight I came home from the office and imagined you giving me that massage before we bathed together. What man doesn't want to imagine a beautiful woman serving him in the tub? Don't mistake me for a man who gives nothing back. I will serve you too, in a way. Not just with my body, but with my mind. Or at least I hope you think I'm a good conversationalist. I want to know your opinions, your personality. Tell me what your favorite season is. Tell me what you think of recent stock prices, for God's sake. I know you keep track of them. Maybe you have a portfolio. How's it going for you? I love to talk business.

"I will give you my heart. It's frightening, isn't it? This heart exchanging business. It's been a while since I was last properly in love. I want to make that love with you.

"I also want to ravage you, as you asked. I want to know what you feel like beneath me, your body on the other end of mine as I reach deep into you and touch your soul. Do you moan? Do you cry out? Do you whimper? I want to know. I want to know how warm you feel inside and how you sound in my ear as you cling to me and dig your nails into my skin. There's nothing more exciting than getting to know a woman for the first time. There's nothing more rewarding than knowing that same woman over and over again.

"Don't take me for a man who only wants to use you, Monica. I'm not a casual love kind of man, especially at this point in my life. I want to build a life and sustain it. I'm a lifestyler, like you. An equal partnership that expresses itself in a different way. I may tie you up and tell you what to do, but I will also turn to you as my confidant. I want you to trust me like that too.

"Trust is a funny thing. To have a woman's trust is a bigger deal than most of my fellow men give it credit. But I want to earn it. I will prove myself to you until you know to trust me wholeheartedly. Even if it takes me years, I will do this.

"Is this a courtship? Are these letters our way of working up to that moment when we truly begin? You may not have let me be your patron, Monica, but I certainly hope that you let me be your intended. However you wish to interpret that.

"Please continue to take care. I am waiting.

"Yours, Henry.

"PS. I have included one of my private numbers. It is text and email only."

***

"My dearest Henry,

"You speak to my romantic sensibilities. Perhaps you're that much of a smooth talker. Your charisma certainly leaves nothing to desire. In fact, I would venture a guess that you don't usually have such difficulties getting a woman's attention. Not that you had difficulties getting mine. As you say so yourself, it is not as easy as we would like it to be for us to simply be together. This cat and mouse game we willingly play will be the death of me.

"Just yesterday I was thinking of you while we had our monthly patrons' dinner. I can't believe it's been a whole month since you came into my life. Mr. Witherspoon was here, but I did not dare ask about you. I assume that you have not told anyone about us. Although I hadn't mentioned it yet, I prefer things this way. I can't afford for people to speculate and say things about me. I already pushed boundaries being so open with my dinners with you.

"When I think that it's only been a month, I'm both surprised and accepting of it. You and I, Mr. Warren, are people who know exactly what they want and how to go about getting it. We're practical, aren't we? Waiting until the time is right. As frustrated as I was with you for leaving me that day, I understand why you did it. I will continue to improve myself until I can fully love you without hesitation.

"Should I use that word? Even though I am a romantic, I am also a sensible woman. 'Love' is something we can't know about until later. I loved too easily the last time I was in a relationship. It was that naiveté that led to me being taken advantage of.

"I've been doing some research on you, Mr. Warren. You're a hard man to track down on the internet. I like that you're not a public persona. They can be exhausting.

"This past week I decided to start doing some redecorating in my room. You might not recognize parts of it the next time you come by. The decorations are the same, and I have no desire to give up my recently acquired items... I've merely started adding in a few things here and there. It created a commotion when I had a single contractor in here giving me a quote on the work he could do. I haven't added any crosses, but there is potential for the hook in the ceiling above my bed. Eventually I want to convert some of my closet space into a... well, you'll see once my plan has come into fruition. I think you will like it, assuming I have pegged you as a certain Dom.

"Even though we cannot meet face to face right now, please know that I look forward to every one of your messages. Sometimes I convince myself that this relationship of a sort is completely in my head and that you don't even really exist. Perhaps I made you up after all. A man I created in my mind because you were cool and kind to me, when so many men weren't. I fill my heart with images of our life together, like any silly girl in young love would do, but at the end of the day I see your letters and know that this is real. This is true. One day, when I am ready, you will come to me and give me everything that I crave.

"Or at least I desperately hope so. When you're in my position, Mr. Warren, hope is all you have.

"Truly yours, Monica."

***

"Monica,

"As long as we're sharing, I will tell you that I too thought you might have been an illusion. Never before had I seen and spoken with a woman as elegant and intelligent as you. I am only more attracted to the fact that you wish to enter that sort of lifestyle with a man, let alone me. When I think about you, I also convince myself that I have it all in my head and heart. I'm supposed to be a composed man. I can barely keep myself together in my business meetings, because suddenly my thoughts turn to you, and then I am transported to a world where we share our thoughts and then make love. I've had lovers who entertained me at the dinner table but lacked in the bedroom. In turn, I've had lovers who were everything I wanted in bed, but bored me to tears outside of it. I believe you could be both good things and so much more.

"I don't mean to put pressure on you. It's how I honestly feel. The sense I get from you is unlike anything I have ever felt before. Rarely does a woman make me feel the rush of lust and the intrigue of a new friend at the same time. It's usually one or the other. It's funny, because I've never considered myself a man with a physical type. I've found all sorts of women physically beautiful. After knowing you as I do now, however, I can safely say that I think you are my type. Should I never see you again, I would want to find a woman who matches you. Not to replace you, but because I can't imagine finding any other woman attractive than one who looks like you.

"Is that a strange thing to say? I'm sure it came out the wrong way. I'm sorry, Monica, but when it comes to talking to you, I discover that I suddenly lose my vocabulary and write the arguments of a university freshman who has yet to learn what a thesis statement is. Did I ever tell you that I have an uncle who is a professor at Harvard?

"I, too, look forward to our correspondences. I feel like a kid waiting for the mail every day. Your words, although they do not tell me what I wish to hear, make my evening. I go to sleep thinking of them, and in the morning I am rested after only having good dreams."

"I hope your business is doing well, and I hope that Sam isn't giving you any trouble.

"Henry."

***

"I disgust myself with how much I think of you."

***

"I see you decided to email me. I miss your beautiful handwriting, but this feels delightfully direct."

***

"I'm serious, Henry. I've become an unnatural creature. You appear in my thoughts even when you have no business doing so. Tonight we had a full house, with a party in almost every room and my girls working themselves dead. I could hear one of them with her patron when I passed by her room. I don't know what he was doing to her, but I could only imagine. Fucking her, I suppose. Whatever it was, she genuinely enjoyed it. I know the difference between her patron placating moans and her real ones. The longer I idled there, listening like a pervert, the more I thought of you and my desire to have you. I almost feel inhuman."

***

"And if I were there, what would you have me do?"

***

"No, that's not how it works. You're the one who decides."

***

"What would I do to you? I'd begin by tying your wrists together, and then blindfold you until all you can rely on are your ears and the top of your skin. I'd disrobe you, moving my hands over your body, exploring every inch of your curves until I know you in ways I never imagined."

***

"And then?"

***

"And then I would bend you over my knee and test your limits for that kind of pain. You'd cry out, but I think you would like it, yes?"

***

"I do love a good spanking. Then what?"

***

"I wouldn't go easy on you, not even the first time. I want to deny myself as much as I want to deny you. I'll take you to the brink of release again and again, making you beg until I can't stand it anymore. When I finally unleash myself upon you..."

***

"For God's sake, what?"

***

"Use your imagination."

***

Monica didn't want to use her imagination anymore. She was tired of tossing and turning every night, losing sleep because all she could think about amounted to one of two men. She already dreamed of Jackson every night. Sometimes they were the rogue dreams of fancy, the kind that said, "Things could have worked out so much better," while others turned into absolute nightmares from the onset. The hateful things he said to her, the way he treated her in public, the way he shut her up in his guarded palace to ensure she had no agency. Love had trapped her with him. No amount of reasoning could have saved her, until he went out and brought another woman home.

Maybe I'm not ready. Monica sat at her desk, wishing she had a crystal ball to tell her what to do. This was why she didn't like having relationship balls in her court. Too much pressure. Too much anxiety for a submissive like her. She wanted Henry to set the rules and then follow through once the conditions were met. If only there were some magical words Monica could say to make him appear.

I'm desperate. A slut. An easy woman. She was sure that's what people would say about her. The first man to pay attention to her like that after Jackson… and she goes running into his arms? Shit, Henry was right. If she were him, she would have abandoned the situation as well, no matter how hard her cock got.

Except there was a fallacy to his way of thinking. If he waited for Monica to be completely over Jackson, then he would be waiting forever. There was no way she would ever be completely over a relationship like that. Wasn't that part of the reason she hid herself away in her brand new Château? So she could stew in her misery while watching other people around her enjoy themselves?

What did other women do? Did they force themselves to move on? Did they go up against men who told them that they weren't ready? Did she insist that they were, then live happily ever after? Monica wasn't even sure she believed in happily ever afters. She wanted to build a life with a good man, yes, but she also wasn't a naïve little girl anymore.

Henry might hurt her. He might break her heart and cast her out. At one time Jackson was a kind, attentive lover who seemed to love nothing more than pleasing his sub. Who was to say that all Doms weren't like that? Monica would like to see someone try.

She pressed her face against her hands and contained a sob as best as she could. She wanted to be much younger again, back when she first discovered the lifestyle and instantly jumped into all of the possibilities. Her first boyfriend had been as clueless as her when it came to domination and submission. At least those mistakes could be explained away with inexperience. What Jackson did to her later... there was no excuse for that.

Monica didn't want to make that mistake again. She owed it to herself to find a man who both understood and respected her. If such a man could be found.

Either stop hoping or give it one last chance. Monica wouldn't say she was jaded. Just cautious. In her lifestyle, she had to be cautious.

***

"To Mr. Henry Warren,

Cynthia Dane

"You are cordially invited to attend a party thrown by Madam Monica Graham at Le Château on the night of Friday the 27th. Parking and dinner will be provided.

"Formal wear is to be expected. Black tie not necessary.

"Failure to arrive may mean a severance from all future invitations. Please RSVP."

***

"I'm ready."

Chapter 8

To Serve And Be Dominated

Butterflies danced in Monica's stomach that Friday night when she descended the staircase to greet the first guest. Contrary to what her invitation to Henry said, it was simply another night in the Château. Two patrons were scheduled to come in for appointments, but otherwise the only business that night was two walk-in clients who happily walked away with Chelsea and Judith to their rooms.

Mr. Carlisle entered, although he was early and thus Sylvia was not ready for him yet. Not until Monica took his hat and coat for him did he speak besides the usual greetings.

"That is a lovely shawl, Madam," he said, gesturing to the light red shawl adorning Monica's otherwise bare shoulders. "The color suits you."

"Thank you." Monica bowed her head, but Mr. Carlisle's attentions were soon taken by Sylvia, who bounded down the grand staircase in her little black dress, pearls, and freshly curled hair. Her ecstatic greeting was probably half truth, but Mr. Carlisle didn't care. He paid for her time, and he was here to take what he paid for.

Monica waited in the front hall for Grace's patron Mr. Andrews to arrive. He brought his wife with him again. This time Mrs. Andrews, in her fur stole and emerald necklace, looked much more comfortable standing in a house of damning pleasure than the first night she came. *And how many times she came...* If she believed Grace, anyway. *I should start charging by the orgasm if we're getting more female clients.* Monica's girls were talented.

When it looked as if no other clients were going to suddenly show up, Monica put the doorman on standby, informing him that only one girl was open that night, and she had no idea if and when either Judith or Chelsea would be available again. Their drop-in clients might take the whole night for all Monica knew. Although knowing Judith, she would want to take as many as possible, even if she decided sex was involved. *Note to self: don't hire nymphomaniacs.* Of course, some clients paid extra to meet with a girl who recently had intercourse. Whatever opened their wallets. *Probably makes them feel cuckolded.* She briefly wondered if that was something the Andrews were into.

Monica went back to her room, passing both Chelsea and Judith's rooms. The first one was silent, but the second came with the sounds of a whip cracking and some poor fool living it up while a beautiful mistress informed him what a bad, laughable boy he was.

The dangerous part about waiting was the sitting around and second guessing her decisions. Mostly her clothing and hair choices. Monica donned a red satin dress, falling to her knees and hugging her svelte curves. There were no sleeves to contain her shoulders – mostly because she wanted to wear Henry's gift, laced in rubies.

She had few accessories to go with it. Simple shoes – that men rarely noticed – and gold earrings. Monica decided to forego other jewelry in favor of styling her hair in a large, curly bun that rested easily on the back of her head, one carefully released chestnut tendril falling along her neck and stroking her clavicle.

Usually Monica did not wear much makeup. Men always called her a natural beauty, whatever that meant. Yet she wanted her intended to see her in a new way – to blow his expectations into another universe the moment he laid his eyes on her. So Monica opened her makeup tray and considered her options. Smoky eyes, yes. A faint pink lipstick, definitely. Some rouge on the cheeks, of course. The only thing she was unsure about was the eyelashes. In the end, just when the doorman called up that someone had arrived, Monica curled her eyelashes until they made her look like a different woman.

The moment she stepped out of her door, her role in the Château changed. No longer was she Madam Monica, the matriarch of young women looking to make a lucrative career in BDSM. She was Monica, or whatever her Dom wanted to call her. *She-Wolf.* She stopped in front of the Cigar Lounge and cracked a small smile.

Everything went to according to plan. Henry stepped into the foyer, where a maid took his coat and presented him with a silver tray. On the tray was a piece of folded paper Monica wrote on that morning.

"The safe word is Blossom. Meet me upstairs for dinner."

Monica raced to the balcony where dinner was already halfway served. By the time she reached the railing overlooking the garden, she heard a familiar voice behind her.

"Good evening."

She turned, fingers clutching the railing as if she would fall over. *I'm on the verge.* Henry Warren wore a pristine suit and tie, his sandy hair combed to perfection and those blue eyes alight even in the setting darkness of twilight. A chill spread through Monica's skin. She clutched the ruby-studded shawl closer to her body. "Mr. Warren." She bowed her head.

"You look lovely." He continued to stand in the entryway even after Monica gestured to the nearest chair. "That color really does suit you. Complements your skin and hair."

Monica blushed, letting her fingers touch her cheek before looking away again. "Thank you. You are quite handsome yourself. Shall we dine?"

He pulled out her chair for her, and she began putting portions of salad and chicken on his plate. *Tonight I serve you.* It had been ages since she last served a man for her own pleasure. She served men every day in her job. Poured their drinks. Took their coats. Inflated their egos. Gave them girls to fool around with. Tonight? Monica finally had her turn. She doubted any of her girls felt as giddy as she did at the thought.

Monica did not sit until Henry had enough food on his plate and enough wine in his glass. The closer she got to him, the more she wanted to ask him, *"What do you want? How can I serve you tonight, Mr. Warren?"* She didn't say these things because she didn't want to risk him thinking this was a patron-mistress situation. After all, he had tried it already.

And yet she was disappointed when he began their dinner conversation by asking how her business was doing. "I still wish you would let me invest a little," he said, eyes lingering on the twinkling rubies in the shawl he gave her. "Name something you want to add to this place and I will give you the money for it."

Monica held his gaze. "You."

Henry dropped his utensils and sat back in his chair. What was he thinking? That Monica was already too clingy and that he had made a mistake? That he didn't want to talk about them at that moment, even though that was the whole point of this evening? *I am ready for you to be my Master.* Monica forced her visage to stay pleasant, or else she would frown.

"I'm afraid I'm not for sale, Monica."

She tried to eat, but her body was too distracted by the movements of his arm, his impeccable posture, and that strong jaw chewing tomatoes and tasting wine. *Ask me to do anything. Ask me to crawl beneath this table and suck you off.* Monica never told people that one of her biggest kinks was getting a man off at the dinner table. She was a master of sliding her hand between thighs or disappearing beneath tablecloths. The game was intensified if her lover could maintain his demeanor and even carry on a conversation on the phone or with guests.

It was too soon to start doing that with Henry. Yet she had a feeling he would like it.

"Isn't this wine delicious?" she asked, taking a sip before insisting on filling Henry's glass up more. "It comes from…"

"Monica." Henry's voice gave her another chill – or perhaps it was the moonlit breeze tickling her skin again. "Come sit next to me." He gestured to the empty spot between the table and the railing.

Happy to oblige, Monica shot out of her chair like an eager pup and dragged it forty-five degrees around the table. She didn't bring her dinner with her… too much in a hurry to sit down and let her knee brush against Henry's. "Yes, Mr. Warren?"

His knuckles brushed against her cheek, those piercing eyes digging through her own and toward her soul. Monica bit her lip to contain her excitement. Everything, from her chest to her thighs, responded with an alacrity of arousal she hadn't felt since the last time she was in love.

Don't think of him.

"I've thought about you constantly these past few weeks."

Monica let her hand roam over his knee, but did not venture farther. "And I you." His fingers pushed into her tight, fine hair, making it tug against her scalp and arouse her even more. Images of him bending her over the table and pulling her hair flashed before her eyes, and she knew her skin flushed to behold it. *Spank me while you're at it.* Monica was far past due to have a proper spanking.

"I had to have my man drive me here tonight because my thoughts were full of you, it was too dangerous to come alone. I sent him home. I hope that wasn't presumptuous of me."

"Not presumptuous at all. May I...?" Monica picked up his wineglass.

"You drink it."

She wasn't a sub to disobey. Some were. Girls like Sylvia desired to be brats even on the submissive end. They toyed with men by making them work harder to get them to obey. They both got off on it. Not Monica. Her greatest pleasure came from doing exactly as told. Such a goody two-shoes.

Still, would it be too much to ask him to take her right here, right now? Or at least to ask that Monica get acquainted with certain parts of his body? She was ready to bring him both emotional and sexual pleasure. She didn't need anything in return.

The wine was sweet on her tongue. But not as sweet as Henry Warren's lips on her neck.

He kissed her as she drank the last of his wine. The glass slipped through her hand and landed on the table, her other hand bunching up her skirt to channel her frustration. "Shall we begin now?" she asked, hopeful. Monica couldn't wait to throw off her public propriety and revert to her natural submission. She needed him to liberate her with his domination.

"Your perfume is exquisite," he said, words rolling directly into her ear. Henry's hand lingered on her breast. "I can barely contain myself. Do you know what I want to do to you right now?" Oh God, oh no, here came his hand sliding between her thighs and stroking the line of her slit. Monica whimpered, legs coming together and toes curling in her shoes. "Too many things to keep up with myself. I'm only one man. What can I do? I want to do everything with you."

It took every ounce of strength she had left to reply. "You are one man, but I am a woman who can take many things. Deny me my pleasure. Force it upon me over and over until I'm so sensitive that I beg you to stop, and then keep doing it anyway. Whether you last five minutes or five hours, Mr. Warren, know that it doesn't matter. Tomorrow is another day with more possibilities."

"I certainly hope that I last more than five minutes." He squeezed her thigh. "If I don't, I'm sure there will be no problem doing it again tonight. You're so beautiful, and being here with you wakes me up in ways I haven't felt in years."

"Please, Henry. I can't wait any longer. The moment I told you that I was ready for you to take me was the moment I could no longer live without knowing your touch."

"I'll give you more than my touch, Monica. I'll give you my words and my vigor. Every last bit of them. Do with them as you like."

"And do with me as you like. The moment we walk into my room, I belong to you. Command me. Punish me. Reward me."

He kissed her, shutting off her words, but not her passion. The scent and taste of wine lingered on their lips, but all Monica could taste was Henry's essence, and all she could smell was that powerful cologne. *I want it on my bed. I want to wake up every day this next week and smell him in my bed.* Even better if she smelled like his cologne by the end of the night.

"I might ruin you." Henry's voice was low, but frantic, echoing in her ear in between frenzied kisses. "I might not be able to hold myself back. I'll think of nothing but claiming you. Every part of you." He squeezed her breast and bit her ear. "I don't want to scare you."

"You cannot scare me tonight. You don't understand… I need this. I need a man like you to own me tonight. Again and again. I'll wait in between. Control and own me. I *need* it."

"Not as much as I need you, surely."

"I wouldn't count on that."

Dinner was called to an early end, which delighted Monica but also made her nervous. Organic escalations of a relationship were one thing. Last time had been organic. There was nothing to be nervous about in her bedroom, Henry's cock about two seconds away from thrusting into her. This was planned. Monica didn't know what he would do to her, but she did know that this was their initiation, and she wanted to die from anticipation.

They walked separately down the hall to her quarters. As she produced the key, however, she saw Henry stop in front of a closet-like door that said "PRIVATE, MDM. ONLY."

"That's a security room," Monica said, fumbling for her key. "It's…"

"Let's watch for a bit."

How did he know what it was? Monica approached the door and unlocked it with another key.

It was her personal surveillance room. In it, which was nothing more than a walk-in closet, were a dozen closed-circuit televisions letting her see every major room in the house. There was another security room that showed the public areas and the outdoors, manned by her security chief and his part-time deputies. This room, however, focused on the private areas, so Monica could make sure no awful business was going on in the girls' boudoirs.

They knew about the cameras. Some of them even got off on them, although Monica rarely came in to keep an eye on things.

"Do your clients know about this?" Henry said the moment Monica latched the door shut behind them. He sat in the only chair in front of the TVs and zoomed right in on the one featuring Grace's room.

"No, they don't. These aren't recorded to anything. Just a live feed to make sure nobody's actually getting hurt. Sometimes the girls don't know when to report something."

"I hope they don't report this, because it's damn fantastic."

He pointed to the TV, and Monica leaned in to see what he meant. *Should have guessed.* It was Grace with Mr. Andrews. And Mrs. Andrews.

Henry pulled Monica into his lap as they watched. *I'm not supposed to get off on this.* She was human, and it couldn't be helped. Grace was naked, bent over and chained to her wall while Mr. Andrews fucked her from behind, his hand coming down for a hard spank every few seconds. Even on that tiny camera Monica could see how red Grace's ass was.

"Please tell me there's sound."

"No," Monica said. She wished there was.

Mrs. Andrews slipped off Grace's bed and approached the fornicating couple, her hand rubbing her husband's bare chest before going to rub Grace's bare back. *I really need to charge them extra.*

"Sex isn't supposed to be expected, right?"

"No. It's made clear to every man. Tying up, whipping, humiliation, that sort of thing… legal things."

"That ain't legal."

"It is if they're not specifically paying for it."

"Do all those ladies fuck their patrons and clients?"

"The patrons? Yes. Not usually the clients. Unless they want to, but then they risk starting rumors that we're an actual brothel."

"Travesty." Henry's hand moved over Monica's mouth, silencing her. She slid farther along his lap and leaned against his chest. "Now be quiet. I want to watch."

So did Monica. Mr. Andrews was fit, albeit a bit older. He had good endurance too, apparently, since he had been going at Grace for a good three minutes now, and who knew how long before that. The spanking had stopped, but Grace continued to make faces that could only be from moaning in unexpected pleasure. *He found her G-spot, I guess.* No wonder Grace liked him so much.

He pulled out, still hard, and Mrs. Andrews unchained Grace from the wall. Her husband pulled her arm and brought his wife in for a kiss, their passionate embrace only foiled by the naked woman slumping over and grabbing Mrs. Andrews's ankle. The well-to-do woman sank to her knees and began sucking her husband. Grace disrobed Mrs. Andrews, even going so far as to rub her breasts and kiss her shoulders.

It came as no surprise when Mr. Andrews took his wife to bed, pushing her down, half-dressed and spreading her legs. After having been inside another woman only a minute ago, Mr. Andrews was now inside his wife, and Grace came to them both, biting the wife's nipples and rubbing her clit for her.

Something hard dug into the top of Monica's ass. Henry's breath was heavy in her ear, his hands groping her through her red dress.

She wanted to unzip him and ride him right there, letting her breasts slide against the table as they watched this threesome unfold, but Monica hadn't been told to do anything but stay quiet. She took those kinds of commands seriously, especially when they came from a man like Henry Warren, whose large bulge was even harder now.

Mr. Andrews pulled out of his wife and tossed Grace over the side of the bed. He finished inside of her.

I want Henry to do that. Monica shouldn't on their initiation. The code of conduct for the girls was to use a condom with all walk-in clients and for the first month with a patron. Monica should follow her own rules, but the temptation was too strong to know what her Mr. Warren felt like coming inside of her. Deep, deep inside of her.

She whimpered, grinding against his bulge as he continued to grope and kiss her. "Are you wet, Monica?" he asked, hand covering her mouth again. *I won't talk. You didn't tell me to.* "Because I'm so hard for you that I don't want to wait any longer. Tell me!"

He released her mouth as she gasped and slammed her hands on the table. "Yes, Mr. Warren," she said, reveling in his name like that. Henry liked it too, because his fingers dug into her flesh and threatened to push the short skirt of her dress up. "I'm ready."

All it would take was three movements. Move her lingerie, take out his cock, and thrust upward. At this angle he could even pull her hair as he liked. Even spank her! "I'm ready too." He released her. "Let's go."

It wasn't what she wanted, but she knew that's what she needed. Henry opened the door and led her out. Monica barely had time to lock the door before she had to unlock the one to her chambers, Henry taking a look down the empty hallway before wrapping his hand around the back of her neck and whispering something into her ear.

"I'll show you the night of your life."

Chapter 9

A Long Lost Release

"Don't move."

Monica stood in front of her bed, staring at the swirls in her comforter as Henry Warren came up behind her and put his hands on her hips. She didn't move, as told. Nerves were killing themselves inside her stomach, her chest, and her groin – all because Henry's voice growled every time that head of dark blond hair came closer to destroying Monica's sanity.

"I can't tell if I should call you a princess…" Henry kissed the nape of her neck, his tongue trailing down to her shoulder and then the space between side and arm. "Or a queen."

He undid her hair. Fine locks of chestnut landed on her shoulder and fell toward her breasts. The clip holding it together dropped. "Call me whatever you want, Mr. Warren."

"I like it when you say that." Henry's hands pushed beneath her breasts and lifted them up, making her cleavage even more ridiculous in that dress. Her zipper slowly came undone toward her rear. "Tonight you will call me Mr. Warren or sir. Do you understand?"

"Yes, sir."

"I mean it, Monica." His fingers were like daggers shooting into her flesh. "Don't disappoint me."

"I would never. Disappointing you would break my heart."

"Neither of us wants that. Now be silent and do as you're told. Do that, and I'll take care of your needs."

Monica shivered for the millionth time that night. Her skin was on fire, her stomach broiling, and her heart fluttering so quickly she thought every breath would be her last. The anticipation would make her come before anything Henry did to her. Yet she said nothing, as told. *I love being told not to talk.* The real challenge came when her Doms told her to be silent during her orgasms. She hoped Henry wouldn't do that tonight.

"Stay still." Although gentle, his voice was still rigid. "I want to explore you."

He sounded like an adventurer when he said that. The type of man who climbed mountains and tamed wild horses. *I'm neither.* She was a she-wolf queen inviting this stranger into her den for mating. A queen who usually had the reins, but tonight she was turning them over to this alpha male.

Henry poked his finger into the dip of her zipper, tickling the top of her rear. His teeth bit the shawl and pulled it off her back and arms. She saw it fly across the room and land on her dresser. The skirt of her dress pulled up over her rear, exposing her black lingerie.

Monica waited for him to tell her to bend over. Or to push his fingers inside of her because he wouldn't believe any testimony as to how wet she was. Yet he didn't do either. Instead he wrapped his arms around her midsection and pressed his hardness against her.

"Do you want it, my princess?" he asked, licking the tip of her ear. "You're not a virginal princess, are you?" When Monica didn't answer, he remembered his order and said, "You can answer that."

"No, Mr. Warren. I'm not a virgin."

"How many men have been inside you?"

"Inside me? Five."

The silence killed her.

"I'm sorry, sir, it's too many."

"No, not at all. It's a good amount of experience. I'm assuming you like it."

"Very much so, sir."

"And what do you like most, Princess?" Henry rubbed himself against her, reminding her that he had something to offer besides money and conversation. "The size? The entry? The ending?"

"I like all three, Mr. Warren."

He grasped her shoulders and pushed her down. Hair obscured her face as she looked toward her carpet, her lingerie straining against her slit. "Get down on your knees."

The sound of another zipper coming undone thrilled Monica as she dropped, shoes kicking off behind her and hands helping her to turn around toward her Dom. *My master.* She didn't want to say that out loud yet. That was too intimate.

Not as intimate as what she saw right in front of her face the moment she looked up again, however. Henry's erect and ready cock was out.

She didn't wait for her order. Monica could sometimes be a naughty princess who anticipated exactly what her Dom wanted. When a man told her to get on her knees and took out his cock, it only meant one thing.

Monica sighed, hand wrapping around the base of his cock as her lips pressed against the side. Henry stirred within her grasp, hardening more, his one moan encouraging Monica to keep going. Her other hand disappeared into his trousers and massaged his sack. Her tongue followed a single vein down his shaft before encountering dark hair that tickled and delighted her lips.

"Fuck." The first time hearing him say it like that, and it couldn't have come at a better moment. Monica wanted to know that she was undoing this man. He may be her Dom, but he was still a man, and to topple him in pleasure was one of her many skills as a talented submissive. "Suck my cock, Princess. I've been waiting for this moment for half an eternity now."

So had Monica, but she didn't mention that.

She went to work on him, not in the least disappointed by the size he gave her to adore. His girth was the most impressive. Monica could wrap her mouth around most men, but Henry gave her a little trouble at first, until she remembered to relax and let him meet her halfway. Even so, she anchored her hand around the bottom of his hard shaft, letting her fingers nestle in the soft hairs as the roof of her mouth and the back of her throat welcomed him into her. Nothing leading up to this moment had been as satisfying.

Deep breath after deep breath filled Monica as she pulled him into her mouth and used her tongue to stimulate him the most. She found that vein again and traced it, letting it lead her to the head of his cock and then back down to her hand. When he proved not interested in thrusting into her mouth, Monica relaxed her gag and let him slide farther down her throat. Her teeth lightly – *very* lightly – grazed him.

"Look at me."

She glanced up. Henry had undone his tie and lost his jacket on her bed. *Let me undress you.* Monica's free hand circled his waist and grabbed his ass, firm, and flesh unyielding. There was power in his hips. Monica almost closed her eyes again to imagine the cock in her mouth fucking a different pair of lips.

"Enough." Henry lost their staring contest and looked toward the ceiling. "For God's sake, Monica, enough."

She eased off him and sat on her legs. "Are you pleased?"

"I told you not to speak unless I give you permission. Did I give you permission?"

She shook her head.

"Then behave." Henry grabbed a chunk of her hair but did not pull it. It tugged on her scalp, but pleasantly so, his fingers burying into her head while he studied her form. "Turn around on your hands and knees. Keep your ass in the air."

Monica did as told, coming face to material with the carpet as her elbows supported her and her knees dug into the floor. *Fuck me, Henry.*

"Move your hair out of the way. I want to see your back."

It fell beside her, and the air was warm against her skin.

"Now stay still and don't make a sound. Be a good princess. It's not time to punish you."

She had no idea what he was doing, and she didn't care. He could light a cigar and have a drink while she stayed like that, and it would thrill her all the same. Of course, she hoped against hope that Henry would pull her onto his cock and end the frustration brewing between them for over a month.

Monica did not look up, so all she knew about what was going on came from the quiet groans in Henry's throat. He sounded so far away, yet close, and they shared an intimacy that told Monica few got to hear him so vulnerable. *He's no virginal prince.* She preferred it that way. Much preferred it that way. She wanted him to know what he was doing and how he should give it to her. *Hard. Fast. I don't care. Be slow and sensual, just do it!*

His groans turned into grunts. Monica focused on them, wanting to reach between her legs and stroke herself to the sounds of Henry Warren taking pleasure from *her.* Sometimes serving wasn't about doing anything at all. Sometimes it was about getting on one's knees and exposing one's bare back to a man towering over her.

"You're mine, Princess." It was the last thing he said before climaxing onto her skin.

Monica gasped into the carpet, the warmth of his seed hitting her skin most unexpectedly. She never anticipated him coming so soon. Then again, the man was so wound up for a night that was supposed to be long and purposeful that he probably needed the early release. Now Monica was left with *him* all over her. At first it hit her between the shoulders, then the small of her back, and then the base of her zipper where her ass poked out. *That's a lot…* Was he normally that generous, or was it *her?*

He didn't have to tell her what he meant by his words and action. *I'm his. I'm all his tonight.* The primal instinct for the alpha male to claim the she-wolf as his.. *I'm his.* It allowed him to take his time with her now. And in turn, Monica got to revel in the fact that Henry Warren wanted her enough.

"Get up."

Henry was no longer erect when Monica gingerly sat up and turned around, her Dom's spent seed sliding down her back and wrapping around her sides to her breasts. Some of it remained on the head of his cock, and it took every bit of restraint to not lean forward and lick it off for him. *I would. I love that.*

"Did you like that?"

"Yes, sir."

The thumb touching her chin was both gentle and demanding. *Give me more.* "Do you want to stop?"

"Absolutely not."

Monica walked away from him.

"Where are you going?"

She opened a drawer in one of her dressers. What she pulled out was none other than the silver and diamond collar.

Two minutes later she was strung up by silk rope to the hook hanging above her bed. The collar wrapped snugly around her throat, but did not choke her. The leash fell around her in a spiral, Henry Warren yanking it until she yelped in surprise.

"You're a foul princess now, aren't you?" He tugged again, Monica's head nodding backward as her hair became tangled in the metal links of the leash. "Tied up in bed with a man's seed dripping on you. Tell me how filthy you are."

"I'm filthy, sir. My skin has been corrupted."

"I wouldn't go that far," Henry mumbled. He knelt on the bed with one knee, the other foot supporting him on the floor. His buttons were open now. *I want to touch his bare chest.* Toned, firm... the man worked out. "You like being a filthy princess, don't you?"

"I wish to be defiled."

Something smacked her ass. It wasn't his hand, but the end of the leash. Monica couldn't move with her arms suspended above her, but her legs buckled, splitting apart and making her slit come closer to the bed. "Make as much noise as you want, Princess."

Gladly. Henry ripped her dress upward, smacking the hard, silver leash against her ass in quick succession. *Smack!* One. *Smack!* Two. *Smack!* Three. Monica shuddered every time, her teeth biting her bottom lip as she whimpered and then cried out in beautiful pain. She waited for a fourth one, but it never came.

"Do you want more?"

"Yes, Mr. Warren!"

"Too bad. You'll have to earn them now. Do you know how to earn another spanking?"

"No, sir, please tell me."

"Every time you show me your filthy side, I'll punish you with a spank. You don't get anything else until you've proven to me that you are the filthiest woman I know."

Henry was generous in the examples he let her show. When he pulled her dress off her, letting it pool around her, he commented on how hard her nipples were. *Smack!* Four.

Her knees shook whenever he came close to her breasts. *Smack!* Five.

His seed had spread across her back, wetting her underwear. *Smack!* Six.

She whimpered when he pinched her nipple. *Smack!* Seven.

"Please give me one more," he made Monica beg. "Only I want your hand."

Henry dropped the leash and spanked her with his hand. When it lingered on her ass, he finally realized how wet she was.

It prompted him to remove her underwear. Slowly at first, but even Henry could not deny how eager he was to see what she kept inside them. His frustration reached the point that he ripped them, and they fell away from her thighs and slit.

Smack! Nine. For being wet.

I can't stand it. Her arousal was so great that her wetness dripped from her center and trickled downed her thighs. The scent alone, mingling with the scent of Henry's seed on her skin, made her look to the ceiling and curse the rope keeping her immobile. Otherwise she would turn around and demand he take her right now.

"One more, Monica," he said. "Your ass is so red. And you have no idea how much I want to fuck you."

"I do, Mr. Warren," she replied out of turn. "Because I want you to just as badly."

She was naked, and he was almost naked. Henry removed his shirt, standing before Monica and showing her what she longed to touch. His cock was half-erect again. She wanted to touch that too.

Henry looked at her spread thighs and chuckled. "I guess so. I should be flattered, Princess, I doubt you get that ridiculously wet for any man."

"I've wanted you for so long that I can't help it. Please, Mr. Warren, use my body."

His smile disappeared. "I like the sound of that."

First he had to stroke himself back to a full erection. His large, wide hands massaged his cock in the way he liked, and while Monica enjoyed the show, she also took many notes for future reference. *Tug on his sack more. Rub my thumb at the bottom of his head. Stroke quickly upward but slowly downward.* A man knew best how he liked it. Monica's job as his submissive was to learn and employ it.

Now he crawled onto the bed, erect, his hands grabbing her as he kissed her mouth and lifted her hips into the air.

She came close – so close! – to having his tip touch her slit. Monica sobbed in frustration, her core aching for him to reach up to it and stroke the innermost parts of her. Henry wasn't kidding when he said he would deny her, however. He tapped his cock against her thigh, making her squirm, and making him wet all over as she released her arousal right onto his shaft. When they finally got around to it, Henry would slide in so effortlessly that Monica would cry.

"My princess," he muttered, kissing her once, then again. His fingers pinched both of her nipples, and his cock came dangerously close to her entrance. *Fuck me fuck me fuck me!* "You are quite a woman."

He leaned back on his arms, directing his cock at her slit and rubbing the head against her clit. Monica in turn rubbed against him, although her movements were stilted thanks to the ropes. Finally, after what felt like an eternity trapped in a prison of sexual frustration, Henry's cock pushed into her.

And didn't go any farther.

"Tell me how much you want it." Henry was on the verge of giving up and fucking her anyway, but his restraint was unreal, and Monica knew he took pleasure in making her suffer. "Tell me how much you need my cock."

""Yes, please." Monica wrestled against her binds, futilely trying to ride him. "Please, Mr. Warren, I beg you… fuck me!"

She was almost crying real tears by the time he untied her and let her fall to the bed. Before Monica could scramble into his lap and ride him until she came too hard and too long, Henry held her down and whipped the leash back into his hand.

The collar closed in around her throat. It wouldn't hurt her, but suddenly Monica was reminded of what they played at.

"I've done a many things to you tonight, Monica." He pulled on the leash and forced her head up, her legs already dangling around his hips while she continued to search for his cock. "Fucking you will mean that this is it. You're my sub. You're my servant. You want to be defiled? Then I'll use you as I use all my subs."

He saved one last thing for the moment he finally thrust into her.

"This means I own you forever now."

Monica cried out, his cock filling her as easily as she anticipated. Good thing, for his girth would have been too much to handle otherwise, especially the first time. *I'm going to die. He's going to kill me. I can't wait.* As satisfying as it was to have Henry Warren finally fill her up, nothing compared to the moment he sat up and yanked on her leash.

His defiled, tarnished, *ruined* princess had no choice but to grab the leash by her throat, bracing against it as her knees shoved up toward her head and Henry fucked her with the strength of a primal beast. Never before had Monica felt so small and cornered during sex. She realized she truly was Henry's plaything, a servant to be used and discarded when she became too sullied to be of any more use.

That's all she was.

That's all she needed to be.

His forcefulness was what she needed. Maybe not wanted, but needed. He ravaged her, his cock thrusting into her at alarming speed and never missing its mark inside; he pulled the leash every few seconds, snapping her head up and reminding her that she was a beast too; the sounds in his throat were more animalistic than hers, which were shrill, pitiable, and blissfully irrelevant. The more Henry Warren fucked her, the more Monica fell away from reality and entered that torrid world where she only existed to be a slave.

No worries. No debts. No terrible past full of heartbreak and guilt.

Monica squeezed the leash until her hands ached. Eventually she had to close her eyes and concentrate on Henry thrusting into her, one hand tightening around her hip while the other pulled on the leash and held her chest down at the same time. He was using her, his first orgasm allowing him to last a lot longer this time, although his breaths were quickening and his hips shaking in impending climax.

Monica lifted her hips at the right moment. Henry hit her where it counted, and she screamed in pleasure to the point it felt like fate.

Her orgasm turned her into a famished creature who slammed back against him, devouring him until he became the one who couldn't run away. When his fingers tightened on her breast, Henry let out a sadistic sound that was only matched by the sudden, quick bursts of warmth filling Monica deep inside.

He lingered inside her, although his breath labored in his chest and his body nearly collapsed on top of her. When he did embrace Monica, it was with kisses to her skin that were more loving than passionate.

The collar came away. At first it saddened Monica, for that collar represented more than a good time in the bedroom. It represented an intimacy that she couldn't have with just anyone. When her Dom took off her collar, it meant she couldn't escape into his world for another day.

Sometimes those days were so long.

"Monica." Henry caught his breath and used it to nuzzle her neck with a sigh as warm as the rest of him. "Or should I keep calling you my princess?"

"Call me whatever you want," she said, wrapping her aching arms around his broad shoulders. *He's so strong.* Deceptively so. In his suits he looked like an ordinary man. Not overweight, but for all a woman knew he might be less than attractive beneath those expensive clothes. *It wouldn't have mattered.* Feeling his muscles on top of her petite body made her feel like the most protected woman in the world. It helped that he spent more than a minute kissing her, his affections most welcomed as he slowly pulled away from her below. "I don't mind."

"Of course you mind." He slumped to the side, his hips and torso off her but his legs still curled with hers and his arm propped up next to her head. A tender touch came to Monica's cheek once again. "There is always something that makes you happier to hear than all others."

"I truly do not care… if it makes you happy to call me, then it makes me happy to hear."

"Spoken like a true sub."

"I aim to please."

Henry laughed, rubbing his eyes and fighting back a yawn. Monica pressed her hand against his chest and hid her smile in the crook of his arm.

"Were you pleased with me?"

"I should be asking you that."

You're too nice. She almost meant that. On one hand Monica was relieved to know that her new Dom was a good man at heart – or at least as far as she could tell. On the other, Monica much preferred a man who would keep the act up a bit longer after climax. Oh well. There was always time to work out the kinks of the kinks.

"I'm happier right now than I have been in…" She didn't want to scare him by saying years. "A long time."

"What would make you even happier?"

Many things. So many things that she was afraid to tell him. *I'm content now, but things can change.* Monica was willing to take a risk again, but she was aware that this may be the final time she took a chance on love.

"If you stayed the night, Mr. Warren, I would be the happiest woman you know."

He pushed against her, stroking her soft skin and kissing the bottom of her ear. "You can call me Henry."

"Yes, sir."

Henry smoothed back her hair and tasted the skin on the back of her neck. "Oh," he said, lifting his head, "maybe we should get you cleaned up first."

Was it too early in their relationship to tell him that was the wrong thing to say?

Chapter 10

Le Monstre

"Somebody's in a good mood."

Monica looked up from her grapefruit and newspaper. Sylvia pulled out an adjacent chair and plucked some fruit out of the nearby basket. She passed on the bread. *Trying to watch her figure, I'm sure.*

"I have no complaints at the moment. How could you tell?" Monica needed to work on her poker face, apparently.

"You've been smiling these past few days. You don't show it much, but when you do smile, we can tell."

"We?"

Sylvia stole a piece of the newspaper. "Of course. We've all noticed. You're acting like a teenage girl." She had yet to touch her banana. "Wouldn't happen to have anything to do with that man you've been inviting over, eh?"

Monica leaned back in her chair and held her newspaper up. "No idea what you're talking about." There was a headline about a plane crash in South America. For some reason, Monica didn't feel compelled to compare her situation to that of a hundred people dead. "I haven't been seeing any man."

"You can't hide it from us. Chelsea was the one who noticed, because apparently the guy is one of her patron's friends. And she was right... since that guy was last here, you've been like a different person. Subtly, of course." Yes, because God forbid Monica show grand expressions outside of the bedroom. *Or so some would say.*

"I still don't know what you're talking about."

She drank coffee, ate her grapefruit, and perused the business news, trying to guess what the clients would be talking about tonight. *Stock prices, as always. Some company buying out another. The best brand of brandy.* All Monica wanted to think about was her Henry.

He was away on business, supposedly only a phone call away but too busy to talk to her most of the time. Something about Austria or Switzerland. The time difference was too inconvenient for them both. Text messages and emails littered their phones, some of them sweet, and others scorching. *"Strip, lie down, and imagine me fucking you,"* was one message Monica received the night before. She did as told. *I'd rather he be here with me.* They had a date in another week, assuming work didn't come up, but another week was much too far away.

Cynthia Dane

Monica wanted to talk to him. She wanted to hear his voice, that tone that said he was thinking of her fondly and lasciviously. She wanted more than anything else to have him there with her, holding her, kissing her until it was time to take out the collar.

I'm falling in love. It was scary to think. At the same time, it was liberating to free herself from the shackles of her past.

Sylvia didn't press the issue. After breakfast, they went to their usual routines, Sylvia to going over her appointments for the evening and Monica to checking in on the kitchen and other staff who might need help that night. It was going to be a busy one.

"Mail!" someone in the front hall called as Monica approached the grand staircase. "What do you say, Madam?"

Since she was there, Monica approached the doorman and the maid signing for the mail. There were the usual packages, bills, and letters from patrons to girls, but also an unidentified letter for Monica.

The envelope was thin and light. Monica flipped it over, looking for a return address, but all she saw was her name and the Château's address.

After making sure the rest of the mail was taken care of, Monica stood in the middle of her vast estate and opened the letter she assumed was from Henry.

However, her smile faded within the first few words she read... written in a familiar, elegant handwriting she hadn't had to see for a good many months.

His Domination

"I know where you are. I know what you're doing. I know that man you're whoring yourself out to."

That's all it said. It was enough to shake Monica's mind where she stood.

"Ma'am?" called the doorman only a few yards away. "Is something the matter?"

Monica rushed to the door, pushing it open before her staff could do it for her. Out on the concrete stairs she found the mailman, still finishing up his paperwork before hopping back on his truck and going to the next estate.

"You!" She approached him, each step more forceful than the last. "Who gave you this letter to deliver?" It shook beneath the man's nose.

He looked at her as if she had lost her mind. "I have no idea where it originated from, ma'am. You get a lot of letters like that. I know where to deliver it. Excuse me." He closed his tablet and stalked off toward his truck. So much for that help.

Monica wasn't convinced. She looked around the front lot of the Château, into the trees of the surrounding woods, even into the neighboring valley in between mountains. Still not convinced, she ran back inside, up the stairs, and burst through the balcony doors to see who was in the garden.

Grace, reading a book. Judith, sunbathing in the middle of the labyrinth. The gardener trimming the hedges and trying not to get distracted by half-naked Judith.

It didn't matter that Monica didn't see *that man* anywhere. It didn't matter that the staff knew to turn him away should he even come within a mile of the Château.

It doesn't matter, so why am I so...?

The letter shook in her hand. Jackson Lyle's words had never cut her so deep.

She needed Henry. Now, and for as long as that other man breathed down her neck.

I don't want to be alone. Monica clasped her hand over her mouth and turned away before anyone in the garden could see her shaken. *And yet I never am alone.*

Jackson made sure of that.

Part 2

CAUGHT

A Confession

I'm a fake.

A fraud.

And above all else, I am a liar.

The things I've lied about... they're not things other men would think twice about. They lie all the time too. The amount of lies I've seen pile up in my business is nothing. For those men, it's easy to lie. I admit it's easy for me to lie too. Spin a few tales to get what I want. Do you know how men like us stay so damn rich? We lie. Constantly. Eparither by layering pleasantries upon you or outright lying about data we have. When you're born with a silver spoon in your mouth, it's second nature to lie.

We lie to keep clients. We lie to keep staff around. We lie to get laid. And we definitely lie to make ourselves look better than we actually are.

Suffice to say, there's a lot I've lied about.

His Domination

I haven't lied about my identity. My name is Henry Warren, son of Gerald and Isabella Warren. My father was a millionaire when I was born, and my name alone carries over a billion in my personal coffers. So, I'm rich. I'm filthy rich. I never lied about that – if anything, I downplay my worth to keep people off my tail. Not that it works.

You've never heard of me because I keep a low profile. I don't go to many social gatherings, and I don't make my business transactions public. There are some men who are always on Page 6 and making waves in *The Wall Street Journal*. That's not my style. Why would it be, when I would much rather watch the world unfold elsewhere?

Because you've never heard of me, you have no idea what I'm lying about. Neither does Monica, the woman I'm falling over backward to lie to.

I didn't mean to start lying to her. I only told her the simple lies I tell everyone when I first meet them. Like how I never heard of her, or knew what kind of woman she was.

Of course I've heard of Monica Graham. Who the hell hasn't, even if she doesn't come from a great background. Middle class, white suburban America. Average university. Even more average major. It's what she did right out of college that everyone knows her for: become the long-term girlfriend of Jackson Lyle, one of the most mercenary businessmen in the world. Now *there's* a guy everyone has heard of. A lot of people admire him too. Not surprising, since people are always trying to figure out how to make a billion more bucks.

So I lied when I told Monica I had never heard of her before. Hell, that I had never *met* her before. We had come across each other's paths several times over the past decade. Except I never saw her sans Jackson Lyle until a few weeks ago, when my friend and colleague Sam Witherspoon dragged me to her place of business.

Here's a secret – and it isn't a lie.

I've been madly in love with Monica Graham for years.

She's a gorgeous woman. A subtle beauty, who doesn't wear much makeup and doesn't do anything special with her hair. I like that in a woman. I'm always around women who are done up to the nines. It can be beautiful as well, but there's something special about a woman who blends into the crowd. I want to know more about those types of women. What's going on in their minds? What are they privy to see that others aren't? The first woman in a room that I notice is a woman like Monica. And I've noticed her many, many times.

Of course, Monica doesn't know that I've been in love with her for years. *Of course,* "love" has different kinds of meanings. The love I felt was more infatuation for a woman I could never have. Then something happened between her and Jackson Lyle, and Monica disappeared from my social spheres.

Until Sam Witherspoon dragged me to that blasted Château and I was face to face with Ms. Graham all over again.

She didn't remember me. I didn't expect her to, but she was as beautiful as ever. Perhaps even more so, because she was no longer in that man's shadow. She seemed more confident, surer of herself...

Sadder.

It wasn't until later that she told me what happened with her ex-Dom. Abuse. Sad fact of this lifestyle we choose to live sometimes... men in power, especially those born with it like Lyle, will use it as an excuse to hurt people, particularly women. I've seen it happen countless times. I was enraged to find out it happened with someone as kind and interesting as Monica.

Don't tell her this. I'm already in deep water because of the lies I've told her. I need to find out the best time to tell her for myself. She's already shown me more trust than she has any right giving a man in my station. Any man at all. I fully realize that I may be her last chance, so to speak. If I botch this, then that woman may never trust another Dom again.

It's a lot of pressure. Pressure I've put myself under because I foolishly believed I wouldn't become more besotted with her. Well, I have. The deeper I fall in love with Monica, the more I sense certain darkness on the horizon.

How deep can I go with her? Is she in love with me?

I wish those were the most daunting questions I have to answer. For, you see, there is one secret I'm still hiding from the both of you that would completely destroy everything I've built. There's no way for me to tell her about that.

So what do I do? Fall in love and hope it never comes up?

This happiness I've suddenly found myself in is a ticking time bomb. When – not if – it goes off, there will be more than one casualty.

Me.

Monica.

The one bit of happiness we've managed to carve between us.

I'll keep smiling for her, because she needs to believe she can put all her trust in me. I don't want to let that down. But I will.

The secret I'm hiding is too personal to survive.

Chapter 11

Appointments

"Can I talk to you for a minute?"

Monica looked up from her piles of papers strewn across her desk. "Now's not a good time," she said to Sylvia, the girl currently standing in the office doorway. "I've got the tax company coming in about thirty minutes and I barely have my shit together."

Sylvia took a step back but did not excuse herself. Monica continued to rummage through her desk, looking for a damned folder that supposedly held receipts from a certain cleaning outfit. *I really don't have time.* Monica had this meeting scheduled for nearly a month. If those tax people showed up and she didn't have her receipts for the past quarter put together, she would be feeling more pain than any of the subs taking up residence in her Château.

"I mean it."

Finally, Sylvia bowed her head. "All right. I'm sorry, ma'am, but I would really like to talk to you sometime soon. It's rather serious."

"Unless you're quitting or someone assaulted you, I *really* don't have time."

"Well…"

Monica glanced up again. *Well, what?* Did Sylvia have something to report? Or was she trying to take up Monica's precious time? Sometimes the girl could be flippant like that. Monica would humor her if she wasn't too busy, but… *I am definitely too busy right now.*

She shooed Sylvia away as the first of the tax people arrived downstairs. It also happened that Monica found the receipts she looked for. Somehow the folder managed to slip behind the file cabinet instead of being properly stored within it.

An hour of endless tax chatter commenced, shortly after she served her CPAs tea and cookies from the kitchen. Whatever these people thought of her business, they never let on. *As long as I make a lot of money, they don't care.* Monica consoled herself with the knowledge that other clients probably gave them a harder run for their money in the tax universe. Sure, Monica's Château skirted the edges of legalities here and there, but she was sure other clients were doing much more nefarious things. What was a BDSM dungeon between her and the IRS?

Nevertheless, there were always snags to hit, especially when it came to the large sums of money that passed in and out of this business. Monica had to be extra careful in order to not be audited. What a nightmare that would be!

By the time they left, she was more than ready for a bath. Or a massage. Except she didn't have time for either when a long night of entertaining clients and guests loomed in front of her. It was Friday, and more than one party was scheduled to show up that night – and that didn't count the patrons coming to see their girls. Monica had about two hours to eat dinner and get ready for her actual job by the time the last CPA bid adieu and saw herself out.

"I must say, you've been looking extra radiant recently, Madam," said Mr. Andrews, a common patron around those parts. It was the first time in a good while he didn't bring his wife with him. When Monica inquired about this, he explained, "She's in Vancouver visiting relatives. Afraid Grace has to deal with me all by herself tonight." He patted Grace's knee when he said this. The girl gave a wan smile and motioned in secret code to Monica that she was feeling tired that night anyway. *When will I started charging the Andrews double?* The rate things were going, Mrs. Andrews would become Grace's second patron. The couple apparently kept the spark alive in their marriage by sharing a kinky mistress.

"Thank you for the compliment, Mr. Andrews," Monica said shortly thereafter. She sat in the salon with him and Grace. Only a matter of time before someone else was announced for her to deal with. For now, her attentions could be solely given to one of the most generous patrons to enter the Château's halls. "I admit I've been feeling pretty good recently."

Grace nudged her patron. "It's because there's a man."

Monica sent her employee a look, but Grace chose to ignore it. Mr. Andrews, on the other hand, perked up and smiled at Monica. "A man? Wouldn't happen to know the guy, would I?"

I don't know, do you? Monica would have to chastise Grace later for sharing personal information like that, even to her patron. Nobody was supposed to know about Henry Warren, the kinky billionaire who came to the Château solely for Monica. *We've only been together once.* It was one of the hottest nights of Monica's life, but their relationship was fated to be strained from the beginning since her Mr. Warren had many places to be. They were supposed to have a date two weeks ago, but he had to cancel at the last minute in order to fly to Paris. And then Amsterdam. And then Beijing. *I hope he's not being facetious.* Monica knew how busy billionaires like Mr. Warren could be, but she needed more this early in a relationship. *Is it a relationship?*

"Miss Grace speaks of things she doesn't know," Monica assured Mr. Andrews. "I have had good fortune of my own recently, but we can attribute it to my business."

"What a business it is! I wish I could bring more money through those doors for you."

"In due time, Mr. Andrews." Better to gradually grow her business than have too much to deal with up front.

The doorman announced one of the parties scheduled for that night. Monica excused herself and tended to the business she was trying so hard to grow.

Another night, another dollar made. It wasn't until late – well past midnight – when Monica finally had a breath to herself and was able to retire to her quarters. Either the guests had gone home or were passed out drunk in spare rooms... *or* shacking up with a girl for the night. Not a single girl was alone, as far as Monica knew. Not a single one except for her, as she was reminded when she entered her quiet room and had no one to talk to.

Or make love to.

She pulled out her cell phone and looked for a message from Henry. Voicemail. Email. Text. Anything. He tried to send her something when he had the chance, but recently it was all Monica making a fool of herself and sending him text after text. She even went so far as to leave him a voicemail stating she was ready to serve him. On a personal level, it felt right to say that. But when she considered her position in that mansion, she was reminded that she was supposed to be the calm and collected one. Leaving frenzied voicemails would only scare Henry away.

Maybe he's no longer interested in me. Monica had initiated a pursuit on his end. Now that he had her once... perhaps he was no longer interested in having her again.

That wasn't why Monica was so on edge lately. Nor did it have anything to do with her taxes. Not really. She kept pristine records and always stayed within the law.

No, what made her antsy so much lately was…

She stared at the pile of letters stacked on her bureau. She couldn't help it when there were so many.

The first letter, received the day before, called her a "cheap whore who gives it to any rich man." The second, received a week ago, insinuated that Monica's body was so used up that she better not be charging too much. "There's this thing called shelf-life, my pet," it said in Jackson Lyle's disgustingly nice handwriting. "The longer you sit on the shelf, being tried out by various customers coming through the door, the less value you have. Are you so stretched out and beat up that nobody will buy you for full price now? That's unfortunate. You were really svelte when you were with me. You know, I'll take you back no matter what those other brutes say or do to you. When you get tired of playing house with whores and fooling around with inferior men, come back to me. We'll pretend none of that old junk happened."

Monica wanted to tear up those letters and shove them in her fireplace. Yet something prevented her from taking such agency. *You idiot.* She continued to sit on the edge of her bed and stare at those letters. *You know he's lying to you.* Of course he was. Jackson didn't love her. He wouldn't respect her. Monica never once entertained the thought of going back to that man.

No, what unsettled her was that he not only knew where she was, but that she had been with Henry.

At first Monica thought it was a fluke that she got that letter so soon after her first night with Henry. Then she got another one. A letter that said, "My birdies tell me that some sandy-haired buffoon is in your bed now. What did he do to you? Tell me in great detail, and I might forgive your treason toward me."

She hadn't told anyone. Certainly none of her girls. Not even Henry. Then again, she didn't want to worry him, and they hadn't seen each other since that one night.

Hence Monica's disbelief when her phone lit up with a call.

The disbelief was fleeting, for within a few minutes she expected the worst. *Jackson.* If he knew what was going on in her bedroom, then surely he knew her private phone number. He was a man with means. He could find it out if he paid the right people enough money.

Monica tentatively picked up the phone, fully expecting to see Jackson's phone number.

Instead, she saw Henry's.

Never before had Monica slammed on a button so hard. She pressed the phone to her ear and said, "I thought you would never call me again."

Warmth spread in her heart when she heard his chuckle on the other end of the line. "No need to be so dramatic, Princess." The bite in his voice was what Monica needed. "I've been away on business. I only got back in the country earlier today. Once I had some time, you were the first person I called... I hope it's not too late. Or that you're too busy. I know Friday is a dodgy time to try calling you."

"I'm done for the night." Monica turned away from the pile of letters. "I'm alone and have some time right now. I'm glad you called."

Henry took a while to respond. *What are you thinking? That I'm pathetic and needy?* Monica wanted to project the image of a "good sub." Or, a woman who could fill her role but without all the trappings. *And yet I feel this way.*

"I'm calling because I need to make good on that rain check I sent you when I had to cancel last time. What are you doing Monday? I made sure I have some time off this next week. I have to see you."

Monica held her hand to her chest. "I want to see you too." She imagined him sitting in some office somewhere... no, it was too late for that. Surely he would be sitting in his bedroom by now. What did it look like? What kind of bedroom did a man like Henry Warren have? *I want to find out.* Sooner rather than later.

"Then it's settled. I'll come pick you up on Monday."

"Pick me up?"

"Well, you don't think I'm going to insist you stay cooped up in that mansion of yours the whole time, right? I want to take you out for a couple of days. Nothing fancy. Just my place and maybe a couple of nice restaurants. I want to spoil you, Princess."

Leave the mansion... Monica rarely stepped off her property. Hell, she rarely ventured beyond the walls. The occasional chat in the front driveway, or maybe a stroll through the gardens when the mood struck her. She wasn't agoraphobic by any means, but she also wasn't the type to wander out on her own. *Am I naturally that way, or did* he *make me this way?*

"You can spoil me as soon as I've spoiled you."

"You spoil me talking on the phone." Monica could practically hear the grin on Henry's face. "Anyway, I can't be away for too long. Lots to keep running around here. I should be back by Thursday at the latest."

"Three whole days." Henry whistled into the phone. "What am I going to do with you for three whole days?"

"I'm sure you'll figure something out." Monica rose and went to her desk, picking up the top letter from Jackson. *Three days without worrying about him.* All Monica had to do instead was wonder if she should tell her new Dom about the old one harassing her. *I don't want to worry him.* She also didn't want to sound like someone who needed constant protection. Bad enough that as a sub she already gave off that "protect me" air. *I want to be protected.* If Henry could take her somewhere that Jackson could never find her... she would probably move there and serve Henry for the rest of her life.

He sighed into the phone, a delightful kind of sigh that made Monica shiver to imagine it blowing against her skin. "I'm sure I will figure something out. Monday. I'll tell you all about it on Monday, if you can wait that long."

Can I? Monica thought about playing that flirtatious game, but instead she said, "I look forward to seeing you, Mr. Warren."

"Call me Henry."

"No, no, Mr. Warren, I think in these circumstances it's better to..."

"Fine. You can call me whatever you want. Until I tell you otherwise."

There was that bite again. Monica bit her lower lip, slapped Jackson's letter onto her desk, and turned away. "I can't wait until you tell me otherwise."

"Goodnight."

Monica hung up. Not that she wanted to, but it was late, and there was a long weekend of work ahead of her. She made a mental checklist of everything she would have to finish before running away with Henry for half a week. *I wonder what he will do to me.* So nice to think about that instead of other, more malicious things.

Chapter 12

Stepping Out

Monica didn't think anything of packing one of her small suitcases Monday morning, when half her girls were hungover and the other half enjoyed the equivalent of their weekend by sunbathing in the garden or making their own escapes into the city. Nothing seemed amiss to her until more than one person showed up to watch as the most shut-in woman around prepared for an impromptu trip.

"Where are you going?" Chelsea asked, donned in a pink bathrobe and cucumber mask. "This isn't like you. What is it? An emergency?"

Monica finished wheeling out her overnight bag for one of the maids to take downstairs. "I didn't realize I needed an emergency to get out of here for a couple of days. Are you worried that I'll miss something?"

Chelsea shrugged. "You bend over backwards to make sure you never have to go into town. Excuse me if it's weird that you would go on a trip for more than one day."

"I'll be back by Thursday."

Grace sauntered down the hall. "Where are you going?" she asked, standing next to Chelsea. "Ah, you're going to see that guy, right?"

"What guy?" A cucumber fell off Chelsea's face. Nobody was in a hurry to pick it up. "Boss has a boyfriend? Since when? Fuck it, I'm always the last to know these things."

While Monica went back into her room, she heard Grace say, "What are you talking about? It's that guy your patron brought that one night."

"Who?"

"Seriously? Do you pay attention to anything going on around here?"

"Apparently not."

Monica popped back out before rumors could spread like wildfire in her Château. *These girls are terrible gossips.* Half of them didn't care for one another, but they would still gossip about their boss until the cows came home and then turned around to go back out to pasture again. "As lovely as it is for you to speculate on my love life... well..." Monica smoothed down her hair. "Yes, I am going out for a few days with a man. Why not tell you? You get to gallivant all over the countryside with whatever man asks you out."

Both girls rolled their eyes. "Because that's our jobs," Chelsea reminded her. "You going out with a guy all of a sudden is like… I dunno… Sylvia no longer playing dress up or Yvette taking on another client. It's weird. I don't like weird."

"So you don't like me going out with a guy?"

"Not if he's my patron's friend, apparently!"

Monica didn't have time for this. Henry was going to be there any minute, and at this rate Monica would be cornered by all her girls. "There's nothing to fret about," she said. "Mr. Warren…"

"Oh, right, that guy. I remember him sniffing around here off and on. Wow, Boss, you work fast."

"Excuse me."

"Not trying to imply anything. We all screw on the first date around here."

Monica stepped into her room, picking up her travel gloves and sunglasses before heading out and locking the bedroom door. "I'll pretend neither of you are up to no good." She put her keys away and pulled her gloves on. "Anyway, everything should be in order. You all know how to reach me if there's an emergency." She sent them a stern look. "*Only* for an emergency."

"Got it."

"Not a problem."

They remained standing by her door even after Monica made it halfway down the hallway. She turned, eyeing them from behind the sunglasses sliding down her face. "He's not my boyfriend." She sniffed. "Not yet, anyway."

"Go get 'em."

Monica left Chelsea and Grace to their no good. Perfect timing, too, for when she reached the top of the grand staircase she received word that someone was there to see her. "In a Rolls-Royce, ma'am," said the doorman. "Since you asked me to keep my eye out for one."

It took great pain to not let her excitement bubble over. *I'll save the giddiness for him.* He wanted a princess? He would damn well get one. "Thank you," she said, handing a small list of instructions to the doorman. "I should be returning Wednesday evening. Hopefully in time for any rush we receive. Keep an eye out for that Rolls-Royce during that time too."

"Will do, ma'am." He opened the door and tipped his hat to Monica as she stepped out with her suitcase in one hand. "Have a pleasant holiday."

The Rolls-Royce parked right in front of the fountain, the driver side door opening to reveal Henry Warren in a light brown summer suit, no tie, but his jacket buttoned down far enough to make Monica smile. His sunglasses were designer, and his hair more golden than ever in the late spring sunlight. His smile when he turned to her was a most welcomed sight.

"Oh, I think I will," Monica said to the doorman. "Thank you. I'll be going now."

Henry met her at the bottom of the front steps, taking her by the arm and escorting her to his car. *I want to kiss him.* Right there in front of God and Château. That would give the girls spying on them from the second floor windows something to gossip about over dinner.

Monica refrained. She would unleash what she offered later.

"Beautiful day for a joyride." Henry opened the passenger side door and motioned for Monica to enter. The door shut behind her. Yet the window was down, and Henry Warren folded his arms on top of the door and peered through the empty space. *I can smell his aftershave.* Memories of their one night together flooded Monica's head. She was not surprised when Henry picked up her suitcase and instantly frowned. "What did you pack in here?"

Monica smiled sweetly. "You'll find out later."

This time the grin she got was laced in nothing but naughtiness.

A minute later they were pulling out of the driveway, Henry's hands on the wheel and out the window as he let the fresh air weave in and out of his fingers. Monica followed his example, sticking out her arm and watching the shaded trees breeze by them. The cool air invigorated her senses until she thought her face would burst from the smile splitting it in two.

She had to yank her arm back into the car when they reached the main road and Henry gunned the gas. With a shriek louder than anything she had uttered in years, Monica held herself to the passenger seat and made sure her seatbelt was fastened.

The car was too loud for them to converse. For the duration of their afternoon drive, Monica took pleasure in the tingles wallowing in her skin, in the fresh air whipping through the car, and in the touches of Henry's fingers every time he reached over to caress her hand or arm. *Is this how my girls feel when they're being spoiled by patrons?* Monica wasn't as young as them, but she could imagine this kind of rush becoming addictive.

"So how's the carriage?" Henry shouted over the roar of his motor. "Is your great escape everything you ever wanted?"

Monica couldn't raise her voice as loud as his. Instead she laughed, showing him her mirth in the only way she knew how.

The Warren Estate wasn't just in another county, but it was in another state. Monica thought it would be too far for them to travel in one day, but Henry proved her wrong when he got them there in as few as four hours. One moment they were speeding on the highway, and then the next he whipped into a hidden driveway, taking them beneath towering oaks and along a small river that was as pristine as his eyes.

The house – well, mansion – was in the shape of a horseshoe, with the east and west wings jutting toward the front gardens while the main house sat in the back. The circular driveway meant Monica got a grand view of both towering wings as Henry pulled up to the front steps and flagged down the nearest man he could find. Monica was too distracted by the Baroque-inspired architecture that matched Henry's personality to the point she would believe he had this place built instead of inheriting it from his parents. Nevertheless, her handsome chaperone led her out of the car and up the steps into the grand foyer.

"This is the Premier House," he said, helping her remove her coat and gloves. Henry handed them to a butler who stood behind them. "Staff live here, as well every common area to be shared between household and guests. I live in the East Wing. My sister lives in the West. Perhaps you'll meet her later."

"I would like that."

He introduced her to the primary staff who came up to greet them, welcome Henry home, and take their coats and bags. Everyone was polite and discreet to a fault, as Monica had come to expect from the people who worked in such places. *Even in Jackson's homes.* Those people could be brutish, however. They had to be in order to put up with what went on in that household. *They knew what he was doing to me. They saw it all.* Jackson liked to… *No, no.* Monica couldn't put herself down that path. She was here to have a getaway with Henry, the new man in her life. She wanted to get to know him, to enjoy what he had to offer, and maybe escape into their world of pleasure they were beginning to build.

"Is this your parents' house?" Monica asked as she admired the gild work on the nearest banister. "I know they live in Montana now, but I'm guessing this is a family home."

"My parents technically own it, but my sister and I are the only family residents here." Henry put his hand on the small of her back, eliciting a smile. "My grandparents were the original owners of the house. Guess you could say it runs in our family."

He had a habit of doing that – dropping hints that he was expected to continue his family line. *Or maybe I'm reading too much into it.* Monica followed him up the stairs into the East Wing. A man had already taken her bags up there after Henry told him that she was to stay there for the next few days. *Which means these people know I'm sleeping with him.* She hoped he paid them well enough to stay out of his business.

"Does your sister have any children?" Monica had no idea why she asked that. *Yes I do.* When she was with Jackson, there was no idea that they would have children. *Perhaps in another life where he didn't turn out that way.* Monica was not opposed to the idea of being a mother one day, but she wasn't about to get tangled up with a man who would eventually leave her because she wasn't good enough to birth heirs.

Henry stopped in front of a door and looked at her over his shoulder. "No, she doesn't. Honestly, the idea seems so preposterous."

"Does she not want any?"

He opened the door. "You'll see what I mean if she decides to join us for dinner."

The master quarters of the East Wing were simple yet elegant in design. A receiving room boasted ample seating space and an entertainment center that spoke of intimate nights watching movies in front of the fireplace. Attached to the receiving room was a small kitchenette with a microwave, mini-fridge, and advanced hot plate that looked more sophisticated than the common oven.

Of course, that did not compare to the master en suite, with its jetted tub, high-tech shower, his-and-her vanities and enough storage space to hide Monica's wardrobe if she were the type of woman to shove it in the bathroom. Henry showed it to her out of propriety, since, "I'm sure you'll have to use it at some point."

While nice, Monica only really cared about the bedroom. Especially when Henry opened a pair of double doors and carried her luggage through, gesturing to the four-poster bed bedecked in a soft blue comforter and white Egyptian cotton sheets.

All told, the common man would not imagine that Henry Warren was a Dom. But Monica was not the common man. She felt the sturdiness of the posts, saw the hooks hanging from the headboard, and caught a whiff of romantic candles that mixed calming vanilla with exciting cinnamon. It was a smell she could get used to.

Since they arrived so late, Henry informed her that dinner would be ready in less than a half hour. He excused himself to tend to house matters, leaving his guest to change into a loose cotton dress that hugged her chest but merely flirted with her hips. She thought about letting her hair down, but chose to sit in front of Henry's vanity and coif it on top of her head into a tight bun. The finishing touch, which she completed the moment Henry stepped in to tell her dinner was served, was a string of pearls around the bun. They nestled nicely in her fine chestnut hair.

Dinner was indeed served by the time they reached the dining room in the Premier House. Henry pulled out a chair for Monica to sit in, to the right of the head. Naturally, Henry sat there, his posture perfect as he pulled a silk handkerchief into his lap and pulled roast off a platter. Monica lifted her hand to either serve him or herself, but Henry insisted on "spoiling" her. *When do I get to spoil you?*

Not anytime soon. A loud voice echoed in the dining room, feminine, yet full of bite.

"Henry!" A woman dressed in a Givenchy suit strutted into the room, her five-inch heels clacking on marble and her jewelry jingling on her wrists and neck. At first Monica thought the woman also had her dark blond hair pulled into a bun, but on second glance she realized it was a short, choppy pixie cut above the ears and the nape of the neck. The bold and dark makeup on the woman's slim face made her look like the type to waltz into an office and grab a man's balls. "Where have you *been* all day?"

"Monica Graham," Henry said, pushing back in his chair, "I'd like you to meet my sister, Evangeline Warren."

"Please. Eva." She pulled out the chair on Henry's other side and sat down, although she did not face dinner, nor did she act like she was going to eat any of it soon. "Evangeline is some other woman I don't know."

"I admit I don't know an Evangeline either." Henry put his utensils down and regarded his sister with a mixture of contempt and affection. "And I was out. I told you that I would have a guest this week. I had to go pick her up."

Finally, Eva looked at Monica, a smile cracking on her face. *That's not a happy smile.* Monica concentrated on her most political countenance, refusing to show Eva Warren that she was at all intimidated by her. *I'm not intimidated.* For one, Monica knew she was older than Henry's sister. Not that Eva was a "kid" by any stretch of the imagination. *She doesn't seem to like me*. Monica was usually good at determining whether someone wanted anything to do with her or not.

"Yes. Your guest." Eva stared straight at Monica, her heavy eye shadow making her look like a supermodel from a high-fashion magazine. One long, slender leg crossed over the other as Eva took out a large smart phone and looked something up. "There's your message from this morning. I must have forgotten to check them."

"Would you like to join us for dinner?" Henry pushed a glass toward his sister and offered to fill it with wine. "Surely you haven't had anything to eat yet this evening."

"Afraid I can't. I'm meeting someone later and wouldn't want to ruin my appetite."

"Who are you meeting?"

Eva pulled her fingers across her lips as if she were closing a zipper. "Last time I told you there was that whole fifth degree thing. Remember? Because I sure do."

"Ah, so it's a date."

"Now I regret telling you. At least you're on a date of your own." Eva flashed Monica another look. "What did you say your name was?"

"Monica." She said it before Henry had the chance. "I don't believe we've met before."

"No, but I've definitely heard of you." Eva accepted some wine and downed half of it in one gulp. "I guess my brother has… eclectic tastes."

"Eva…"

"Now, now, I didn't mean to be rude." Yet Eva would still not look her in the eye, as if Monica would give her a terrible affliction from a glance alone. "You have to understand. My brother has a habit of bringing in women I tend to recognize. Small circles, you know."

"I see."

"Isn't it about time you got ready for this date of yours? Don't you have some *homework* to do?"

Eva stood up without finishing her drink. "Don't do anything I wouldn't do, Henry." She patted her brother on the shoulder and sashayed out of the dining room. "Especially with that lovely lady!" Her voice echoed, loud and melodic.

It took a few moments before Henry or Monica could pick up a fork again. "Please pardon my sister. My parents let her get away with murder growing up. Truly the spoiled one."

Monica finished chewing before responding. "She seems lovely. I can see the resemblance between you two." Not just the hair, but the way they confidently carried themselves through the room as if everyone should be in awe of them. *I would say it's a Warren trait, but I've been around enough rich people by now to know it's every last one of them.* Sometimes they expressed it in different ways. "Don't worry about her, Henry. I sensed no malice in her words."

"That's good, because I doubt she intended them." Nevertheless, Henry looked back to where his sister walked. "A date, huh? I should see what kind of person it is…"

"She's a grown woman."

"You don't understand. I'm not worried about her. I'm worried about her date."

"Oh?"

Henry finished his sister's wine. "Let's say more than the hair runs in our family."

"I see." Monica contained her smile. If she didn't know any better, she would say that Henry and Eva were twins. "So, does her bed have hoops and chains on it too?"

"I don't want to know. It's bad enough I heard an ex of hers go on about how she works a flogger. Oh, and you know that BDSM club in the city?"

"Of course." Monica had been there a time or two. Most recently to hire a girl for her Château – Judith, to be exact.

"I ran into her there once. I don't think I had ever vacated a place as quickly as I vacated that one." Henry sighed. "From then on, we had to come up with a code word for it. 'I'm going on vacation tonight.' That way the other one knows not to go and we don't embarrass ourselves. Some things still stay sacred in this family."

Monica hid her smile behind her hand. "That sounds... well, I don't have any siblings, so I couldn't tell you how weird that is or not, but I'm sure it's disturbing from your perspective."

"You truly have no idea."

They finished dinner, eschewing dessert and instead deciding to head up to the East Wing. Henry insisted that there was a good movie they could watch. Monica, on the other hand, had a few ideas of her own – which she shared with

Henry the moment they entered his chambers and the twilight of the day cast shadows on the both of them.

"I don't want to watch a movie," Monica said, placing her hand on Henry's firm abdomen and playing with his belt buckle. "I want you to fuck me."

Chapter 13

Her Master's Chambers

Neither surprise nor boredom entered his eyes. Henry leaned one hand against the wall, cornering Monica by the door but not doing anything to incite her. "That's pretty forward."

"Please. You invited me to your estate and thought I wouldn't be thinking of this?"

"Quite the contrary, not a minute went by today in which I didn't imagine you on your knees in front of me." He lowered his head and touched her cheek with his nose, breath hot on her skin. "In fact, I spent so much time thinking of what I want to do with you, that I ended up confusing myself. So little time. So many games we could play."

Monica shivered. "Will you kiss me?"

Cynthia Dane

Henry wrapped his hand around half her neck, his thumb pushing against her tender flesh as his lips came for hers. *We haven't kissed since we last parted.* Now here he was, mouth touching hers, their kisses heavier with each passing second. Arousal burst within Monica, and while her bun pressed against the wall, she searched for Henry's jacket in an effort to bring him closer to her.

"My sweet Princess," Henry said, his grip tightening. "There are some things I can think of making you do now."

"Tell me." The thought of doing as he bid brought more arousal to Monica. *I'll please you. I'll make you proud.* And in return, she would also feel good for a while. "I want you to be my Master." Monica was on vacation, after all. Time to escape into a different world where she didn't have to worry about a damn thing in her life.

Henry, however, did not jump at the chance to make her serve him. "And what are you in such a hurry for?" He touched the top of her cleavage and watched his finger disappear between her breasts. "You just got here. You've barely had dinner. Are you so wound up that you can't keep off me?"

Monica gasped when his fingers found her nipple within her dress. "Please, Mr. Warren," she said with a careful tone. "It's only right to thank you for inviting me into your home."

He loomed over her, and for a fleeting moment Monica thought he would take her right there against the wall. *Do it.* She would either take the drawn out game of dominance and submission, or she would take the quick, needy sex he offered. *Let's get it out of our systems. Out of my system.* Didn't Henry know how much she fantasized about coming to see him? Monica was ready to feel his touch again. His *absolute* touch.

"You try my patience. I was going to wait until tonight to treat you to something, but now you come in here and attempt to seduce me. I'm a strong man, Monica, but even I have my limits. Tempt me too much and I may give you what you want. To my own ends, of course."

Whatever that meant, Monica wanted it.

"There must be something I can do for you." She touched his chest, fingers working the buttons of his silk shirt while her eyes darted to his belt buckle. "Tell me what to do. My knees, my back... do whatever you want to me."

"Maybe I don't want to do anything to you." Henry guided her hand to his cock, hardening within his trousers. "Maybe I want to make you do all the work."

That's fine too! "You're the master of this household. It's only right that I serve you." Monica pushed off the wall and against him. "Use me in any way you want. Even if it means using my actions."

Without a word Henry smoothed down her hair – his fingers played with the pearls before hovering around her ear. Her hand did not leave his cock. "If you're not careful, I will take full advantage of you."

The man knew how to speak to her. Monica clasped her hands on his shoulders and lifted herself up, kissing his chin and attempting to bring him down upon her.

In her desperation all she could think was how happy she was when Henry finally lured her to bed, his body sitting on the edge while he forbade her from joining him. "Kneel," he said, the bite of Mr. Warren clouding his voice. "Kneel and lower your dress."

She did as commanded, her knees sinking to the carpet in between his legs while her hands reached for her straps. One by one they fell down her arms, gathering at her elbows while the bust of her dress gave way to her breasts. Her braless breasts, since Monica knew what she was doing when she dressed earlier that day. *I brought one whole bra on this trip.* Just in case it was socially necessary.

It definitely wasn't right now.

"Where did you get these pearls?" Henry rubbed one of them, nuzzling it into Monica's hair. "They make you look so prim and proper. And yet here you are, kneeling before me with your tits out. Do you think that's proper, my princess?"

Monica shook her head. "No, Mr. Warren. It isn't proper."

"A good girl would keep that sort of thing hidden away. You must not be a very good one. Would you say you're a sullied girl?"

God willing. "I'm afraid so. I'm sorry if it displeases you."

"It doesn't matter. I don't like you because you're virginal. I like you because you know how to serve. Do you think I care that other men have seen you like this? Other women, perhaps? Never. You seem like an assured woman who knows what she wants. And you want me to punish you for your indiscretions, even the ones I don't know about… right?"

"Yes, Mr. Warren." Monica tried to mask the excitement in her throat.

"Turn around and bend down. I want to see your ass."

The carpet rubbed against Monica's knees as she did as he bid, her skirt falling along her back while she pushed her ass into the air and against Henry's cock. *Fuck me.* Being pushed into the floor as he did her from behind sounded... well, Monica couldn't think of it without wanting to pass out in her fantasies.

Not that she could pass out. The first spank she received made her torso shoot up, her voice cracking in the air as another smack hit her ass.

"How many times should I spank you today?" Henry kneaded her flesh, his strong fingers rolling her skin between them as Monica moaned into the carpet. "You tell me. I don't know what naughty things you've done since I last saw you."

I don't care, I just want more. Henry knew how to spank. He was hard enough to send a tender flash through her system, but considerate enough to not dish long-term pain. Monica liked the shock of the here and now. She wasn't interested in being bruised and sore the next day. "I've been terrible," she said meekly. Monica was careful to not sound childish. A woman with a lot of guilt was the ticket. "I've thought about you so many times."

His grip on her ass tightened. "Did you touch yourself?"

"Every time."

"Every time?" She got a spank for that. A harsh one that made her yelp. "Touch yourself now. Right here." Henry took her hand and pushed it between her legs. Monica touched her own thighs before meeting the cotton of her lingerie. "Just like that. Touch yourself until I can see how wet you are."

That wasn't difficult. Just hearing Henry talk about punishing her with more spanking was making Monica shudder in all the right ways. When she pressed against her lingerie, she already felt her arousal appearing, right in full view of Henry's eyes. Somehow that was hotter than him taking off her clothes.

"Ah!" Both hands came down on her ass at the same time.

"Do you like it when I call you filthy, Princess?" The gentle way he rubbed her red flesh lured Monica back into reality. "Do you like being punished because of how dirty you are?"

"Yes…"

"Yes, what?"

"Yes, sir."

"In that case you're unbelievable. I don't think I've ever come across a woman who takes so much pleasure in parading herself like this in front of me. Do you think it pleases me?"

Good Lord, Monica didn't care. Her fingers were burrowing beneath the fabric and relieving some of the tension he left inside her. "I hope so, Mr. Warren."

"It does in that it tells me I can use you as I wish. It's one thing for you to tell me that. It's another to see it for myself." Henry bent down, hands clasping on her shoulders before yanking her up and pulling her into a half-embrace. Monica clutched his shirt and fought to unbutton it. *He's so warm.* Anxious fingers felt his skin and the hard muscles beneath. Some of her hair came undone from her bun – Monica was almost too busy rubbing her arm against his erection to notice.

"Since you're purely a vessel for my pleasure, I'm sure you won't mind taking matters into your own hands, so to speak."

He strained against his trousers, the zipper already halfway down by the time Monica fumbled with it and drew his erection out of his clothes. *Now we're getting somewhere.* Her sore ass reminded her that more discipline could be coming if she played this scene right.

Henry's groan excited her, and all she did was kiss and stroke his cock from the side. Monica wrapped her hand around the head and lowered her tongue so she could have the chance to graze her teeth against his sack. That was apparently the right thing to do, for Henry braced himself against the bed and unleashed a groan so loud that Monica briefly worried that he would come just from that.

But Henry was a practiced Dom who could withhold his own pleasure while his princess, lover, sub, slave serviced his cock with her hand and mouth. Monica took her time, both in the hopes of pleasing him better and fending off her own rising needs now that she had a good distraction.

"You're a talented lady," Henry growled, his hand wrapped firmly around her bun. "Show me how talented you really are."

Monica situated herself squarely between his legs, her knees trapped against the carpet as her hand gripped his base and her lips parted over the head of his cock over and over, another inch entering her mouth with every attempt. His size was the only thing stopping her from taking it all at once – that and the fantasies filling her mind every time she tasted his musk and turned her mouth over to what her thighs craved for. *Do I make him come?* Monica wanted to feel him come inside her throat. Especially when he stroked her cheek and told her to look at him while she kept him hard and built his desire for her.

"Isn't that the image of a naughty princess?" Henry's voice wavered every time his cock slipped into the back of her throat. "If only your other suitors could see you like this. Don't give me that look. I know there must be other men out there who would kill to have you serve them."

Monica wanted to tell him that she didn't care about other men. *You're the only one I want to please.* Yet she didn't dare stop what she was doing without being told to. Anticipating his next order led to her nipples hardening against the end of the bed.

"Don't stop." Henry's nails dug into her skin. "Suck my cock until I make you swallow."

Now that it was official, Monica threw everything she knew into making him come as hard as possible. She pushed him into her throat, relaxing her gag and relegating her breathing through her nose; she grabbed his sack and squeezed it; she flicked her tongue against the underside of his cock and then over his tip when she eased his length out far enough. *Tell me more about what a slut I am.* Undo her bun and pull her hair. Demand she finger herself. Remove her mouth and bend over the bed so he could enter her from behind. *I really want that.* Monica wanted to know what his raw power felt like… push her into the bed and thrust his cock into her as if that was all that mattered.

Henry tensed beneath her before he released a long, loud groan that matched the pulsing of warmth and wetness down

Monica's throat. The taste of his seed was not surprisingly unique, but it did arouse her even more, inciting Monica to use her free hand between her legs and stroke herself.

Three waves of his orgasm ran down the back of her throat before Henry settled against the bed, released her shoulders, and began to soften in her mouth. Monica eased back. The moment she licked her tongue against his salty tip, a small stream of his seed dribbled from the corner of her mouth.

Henry tipped her chin up, but did not wipe it clean for her. "Even now you look so put together. I bet inside you're begging me to fuck you."

Monica's legs quivered at the thought of him hardening and taking control again. "Yes, sir," she said.

"Say it. Beg me to fuck you."

"Please fuck me, sir. Make me yours on both ends."

His finger teased her skin, and for a moment Monica thought he would at least flip her over onto the bed and eat her out until he was hard enough to penetrate her. *Yes, yes!* Monica could see it, her petite body completely enveloped by his, his cock splitting her open and thrusting into her until he came deep inside her. *I want his seed in my mouth and on my thighs.* Anywhere was fine. As long as she got it.

"Just like you've been fantasizing about what you want me to do to you for so long now," Henry began, tapping his thumb against her chin. "So have I planned out what I want to do to your body. Hold tight, my nymphet. I have a wonderful plan for giving you pleasure unlike you've ever felt before. I just hope you remember your safe word."

Chapter 14

Denied

The sun was barely up when Monica awoke the next morning. Birds chirped on the tree branch outside the window to Henry's spacious bedroom. Best of all, the chilly air wasn't so chilly beneath his plush comforter... and the firm arm holding Monica's body to Henry as he continued to doze in the crook of her neck.

Monica tried to go back to sleep, but was too frustrated. Not emotionally, but physically. After all that build up yesterday evening, Henry informed her that she would get no relief until Tuesday at the earliest. Monica was agreeable only because it was a part of her role. Inside, she was screaming to have him do her at any moment.

She didn't even care about the kink anymore. All right, so she cared. But not to the extent that she would demand it. *I was sent to bed so aroused I almost had a dream.* A dream in which Henry held her to him much like he did now, only with his cock thrusting into her from behind.

Monica would be more irate about it if she didn't know this was a part of their ongoing scene. Even last night, when they cuddled on the couch and watched a movie while sipping wine, Monica knew they were more in a scene than not. Henry was keeping his princess locked in a palatial tower so he could take his time with her. Why not, when he got an orgasm even if Monica did not? *He's denying me.* It seemed to be one of Henry's favorite games. Rile Monica up and then make her beg for it for twice as long. Well, there would be no begging right now. Not until he asked for it.

Then Monica would turn on the begging like her life depended on it.

Henry woke up not long after her. "Good morning," he mumbled, rubbing his hand on her arm and looking at the time. "Bad news, lovely. I have a couple of short meetings this morning. I hope you don't mind. You'll have me for the rest of the day afterward and then all day tomorrow."

"That's fine." What was she supposed to say? "I can wait for you here."

"I'll make sure you're taken care of." Henry got up and went to the bathroom while Monica stretched and admired the view outside. Not too much, since she was dressed in her underwear and hadn't brought a robe. When Henry emerged dressed in a casual suit, he plopped a box on the unmade bed. "Open it."

Monica hopped onto bed and brought the box toward her. Inside was a lacy purple negligee that looked like it would barely cover her. *It's lovely.* It wasn't red or black, but it was a healthy mix of the two. Monica hardly wore enough purple, when she thought about it.

"Put it on."

Henry was fastening his cufflinks and applying cologne. *I guess he wants me to model at seven in the morning.* Monica obliged, pulling the lingerie over her torso and letting the lace settle on her breasts and around her hips. It fit just right.

"Good to know I guessed your size correctly. Never know how that's going to turn out." Henry rounded the bed and drew her into a kiss. "You're beautiful. The perfect gown to wear to our ball today."

"Ball?"

"A ball for you and me. I'm so smitten with you that I plan to keep you entirely to myself today." He squeezed her, hand roaming toward her rear. "I'll make sure you're well taken care of, but you're to stay in here, all right? And keep this lovely thing on for when I get back."

Then will we make proper love? Monica remained still as he kissed and nipped her bottom lip. "I will."

"That's an order." His stern voice was authoritative enough to make Monica shiver. "I'm going to have breakfast downstairs with a colleague. I'll make sure some is sent up for you. Use the bedroom and bathroom as you please."

"And the den?" Monica asked, gesturing to the room they watched movies in last night.

Henry released her and stepped away. "I don't think so. I want you to stay in here and think about what you've done."

"What have I done?"

He stopped shy of the door. "Stolen my heart. You'll be disciplined for that indiscretion later."

Before Monica could bid him farewell again, he slipped into the main hallway. And locked the door behind him.

Locked?

Monica tested the door for herself. Even when she turned the lock on her side of the door, nothing happened. *He locked me in here!* Heart racing, Monica went to the bathroom door and found it opened with no resistance. The drawing room door, on the other hand, was as stubborn as the main door leading to the hallway.

Monica sank on the edge of the bed, a terrifying image entering her mind.

He tied me to the bed and locked me in our room for a whole day. Twenty-four hours. For twenty-four hours Monica was trapped like a prisoner in her own bedroom. What could have been a hot dalliance in power and control had left Monica strained, bruised from her binds, and on the verge of tears because she had never felt so *used.* And not in the good way.

Henry didn't know any of that. In his mind, this was business as usual with a sub.

Calm down, dumbass. Monica pulled her legs up on the bed, folding them until she was in a meditative position. After a few deep breaths she managed to settle her nerves and remind herself that *Henry was not Jackson.* He was playing games. They were in a scene. Monica wasn't confined to a bed for almost twenty-four hours, left to cry in her pillow while her arms hung painfully above her and her bladder screamed for relief. There was nothing fun or pleasurable in that. Maybe some subs got off on that, but the problem was...

By that point, Monica no longer trusted Jackson.

The kind of relationship Monica wanted with a Dom could not be achieved without a high level of trust. It wasn't possible. A sub who couldn't trust her Dom was one of the lowest things on Earth. Monica swore she would never go back to something like that.

Breakfast was delivered by a servant about twenty minutes later. That was Monica's chance to escape if she wanted to. *The fact I'm even thinking about it...* She once again had to regroup and remind herself that Henry was not Jackson. If anything, he was simply ignorant to the extent of the hell Monica had been through only a year ago.

So when the servant bowed to her and then stepped out again, Monica did not panic when she heard the door lock again. Nor did she feel ashamed that such a person saw her in a sexy piece of lingerie. Brand new lingerie, insinuating that it had recently been given to her. In a mussed bed, no less.

Monica was used to nonplussed help. Yet how many women had they seen in Master Henry's suite?

She ate her breakfast and left the tray sitting on the dresser. After a quick trip to the bathroom, Monica curled into bed, this time bringing Henry's pillow to her nose and inhaling as if she would never again have the chance to revel in his scent.

Such a moment was brought to an end after Monica dozed off and slept for who knew how long. When she awoke, it was to the sound of someone unlocking the bedroom door and helping himself in.

"You fell asleep?" Henry shut the door behind him. He glanced at the empty breakfast tray and clicked his tongue. "If I didn't know better, I'd think you're taking advantage of me."

I should tell him. Tell him about that horrible experience she had at the hands of her ex. On the flipside, Monica wanted to see how their scene played out. *I still want him after all.* Henry, standing straight in his business suit and a clean shave. Monica pined for him like she had pined for him during their time apart. "I'm not, sir. I was sleepy."

She pushed herself up and knelt on her legs upon the bed, hands in her lap while Henry stepped forward and looked her up and down. "Well, if you were sleeping, then you didn't think about what I told you to think about. How can you ask me to forgive your indiscretions if you didn't even bother?"

What should I say? On one hand, Monica did not want to displease him. On the other? Discipline was one of her favorite words. "How was your meeting, sir?"

"Don't change the subject." Henry took her wrist and brought her hand up to his cheek. His face was dangerously close to hers, as if he would plant his lips right on her – but he didn't. "I spent my whole meeting thinking of you. Thinking of your mouth on my cock yesterday. Did you like that?"

"Of course, Mr. Warren."

"I bet you wanted something a bit... more, though. Tell me, how badly did you want me to fuck you?"

"Badly."

Henry stepped back, although his eyes never left her form. Monica leaned back enough to push her chest up in his direction. *Come on my breasts for all I care.* She was beginning to starve for his attention. Just according to plan, probably.

"No, I don't think so." Henry backed away. "I don't think you really want me that badly."

"Of course I do!"

Henry opened one of the dresser drawers and pulled out a silk restraint. "You say that, but I have yet to see you really writhe in need."

"Tell me what to do. I'm yours to command, sir."

"I told you what I wanted you to do." Henry pushed her onto the bed, her head hitting his pillow while he pressed her wrist against the headboard and tied it there. He did not reach for the other one. "I want you to think about your indiscretions. You've been a terrible, wicked woman, Monica. Lie here and think about what you have done. I have another meeting to go to."

He's not... The man was. He was going to restrain her to the bed and then leave her locked up in this room until he felt like playing with her again. Monica yanked against the restraint, her arm pulling and her teeth chomping down on her lip.

"Are you all right?"

His Domination

It was that soft, kind voice of Henry's that Monica hadn't heard in a few hours. She opened her eyes and saw Henry looming over her, his hand on her abdomen and his eyes large enough to swallow her whole.

Monica stopped writhing – not that it was the writhing Henry sought anyway. "I'm… fine." She forgot the words she owed her Dom. "It's just…" Her history. Her fears. Her ex-boyfriend who tried something like this and never gave her a payoff.

Henry didn't untie her, but he sat on the bed and caressed her cheek with smooth fingers. "Do you trust me?"

He wasn't judgmental. He was, however, firm in the way he gripped her shoulder and eased her back into his pillow. *He still wants me to obey.* Monica's safe word flashed in front of her eyes. She could say it. If she said it, this would all be over. The scene would end, and Henry would either send her home to her Château or unlock that door to let her roam free. *And I would feel awful.* Monica knew that she would never forgive herself if she didn't see this scene through.

"I trust you, Henry," she said, hoping that he would bend down and kiss her.

He did. His lips, warm and soft, tended to her romantic needs, his hand wrapping around her breast while his tongue snaked into her mouth and down her throat. *He won't hurt me.* Monica had to believe it. She couldn't live the rest of her life assuming that every billionaire who tied her to his bedposts was going to leave her to her own misery.

"You'll be back soon, right?"

"I will be back. Before you're missed by the rest of the household." Before Monica could express her relief, he continued, "And sometime later we'll talk about why you're so nervous right now."

"I'm not nervous."

Pleasure suddenly jolted through her as he lowered one side of her negligee and squeezed her bare breast. "You shouldn't be. Once I think you're sufficiently ready… I'll give you exactly what you want."

He kissed her once more before sitting up, his hand wrapping around her thigh and prying her legs apart. "I won't tell you when I'll be back. When I do come back, you better be ready for me. I expect my girl to *always* be ready for me."

Monica blinked away the dust from her eyes. "Yes, sir." She had a free hand. She knew what to do. *All I care about is that he won't do what Jackson did.*

"I don't know what you're thinking about right now." Henry rubbed her bent knee before stepping toward the end of the bed. "But you don't have anything to fear from me. I care about your pleasure. I also care about your discipline. You understand that you have to be disciplined?"

"Yes, sir."

"Good. When I get back, I want to see you ready to be disciplined."

He left, the door latching behind him once again. Monica exhaled a heavy breath and looked at the ceiling, her arm still tied behind her head and her mind full of conflicting thoughts.

His Domination

Did she really trust Henry? In truth, she barely knew the man. They met a handful of times, had sex once, not counting the head the day before, and now were testing boundaries like they had been together for months. *How stupid I am.* Monica was too easy to trust. Too easy to get into relationships. What happened the last time she hopped into a relationship? *I got caught up in Jackson's world for almost ten years.* A naïve college graduate who wanted to explore the world of BDSM more. *I liked the taste I got with my first boyfriend.* When Jackson offered her more? On a scale she could have never imagined? Riches beyond human comprehension? Every trick in the book? How could Monica say no back then?

So why wasn't she saying no right now?

She lay there, for a few minutes, for a half hour, thinking about her lot in this relationship. This was what she thought she wanted. To serve. To submit. To be used once in a while. The idea of a man controlling half her life, taking charge and taking care of her, was all she cared about at the end of the day. She wanted him – whoever *him* was – to coddle her, to make love to her, to make her feel like the most wanted woman in the world. In return? *I'll make him feel like a king.* There were many simple pleasures in life. There were also many extravagant pleasures. Monica wanted a healthy dose of both, and making a well-to-do man feel like that was a good representation. *Just get through today.*

Sexual pleasure. Flashbacks. Monica shouldn't push her own boundaries and conflate the two, but here she was, tied up in Henry Warren's bed waiting for him to do God knew what.

Monica imagined him pushing her down again, using her body for his own whims, and whispering into her ear what a filthy woman she was. Even without him touching her, Monica's skin tingled at the thought of him spanking her, fingering her, and bringing her down onto his cock with promised relief. Sometimes she imagined him wearing that suit, his buttons undone but that material hugging his form with a hint of the forbidden fruit he carried for a sub like her. *"Behave, and I'll reward you."* Other times he was naked, his strong body steady as he pulled apart her legs and drove his cock into her. *"My princess."*

She certainly felt like one. A princess locked away in a king's tower, ready to be claimed by him. There was no queen in the castle yet, but if Monica pleased His Majesty, she may see a change in her fate yet.

Her hand hovered around her thigh. Without any idea of when Henry would return, Monica pressed her fingers against her slit and moaned into the pillow.

"What a beautiful sight for these sore eyes." Henry's voice wafted into Monica's ear ten minutes later. "Not every man gets to come into his bedroom and see a lovely woman touch herself in anticipation of him."

Monica said nothing, but she opened her eyes, gazing into Henry's as he stood above her.

"You look... quite ready." Henry's hand hooked beneath her knee and lifted her leg into the air. Monica gasped, her slit open and bare to the cool bedroom air. *I think I might be a bit wet.* And now with Henry touching her again? His pants straining against a slight bulge between his legs and mere inches away from Monica's face? *It's getting worse.* A shudder ripped through her as Henry tapped his fingers against her thigh. Her arousal burst from her, caressing her skin and dipping into her most forbidden regions. "Yet what are you ready for?"

Monica bit her lip. "For you, Mr. Warren."

She didn't ask for much. Just for him to climb onto the bed, unzip his pants, and give it to her. Was that too much? This long game was killing her. "You think you're ready, but have you thought about what a temptress you are? I think you're doing all of this to keep me from going to my final meeting today."

How many meetings did this man have? *Too many!* But he proved that he would come back. Keep coming back, again and again, if only to taunt her. "I'm sorry for tempting you, sir. I can't control it."

A blissful shot of pain shot through her body as he smacked the side of her ass. "Find a way to control it. I forbid you from coming until I tell you to. Understand?"

"Yes, sir."

"If you come before me today, I won't forgive it."

"Yes, sir."

"Good. Close your eyes. I have a present for you for being so patient."

The world went dark as Monica did as told. Henry rolled her hips over and gave her ass another light smack. She hissed, a tiny whimper escaping her lips. Henry must not have heard it, for he did not chastise her.

"Keep your eyes closed."

Something warm dripped onto her rear.

It took her a bit to recognize what it was. Wet, slick, and heading right for where she puckered most. *Is he...?* Monica wanted to open her eyes but did not dare. Not even when Henry opened and closed a drawer next to her head and pressed something hard against her ass.

"You know what this is?"

Before she could say anything, her body released more of her arousal, drenching the plug.

"Of course you do. It's a small one, don't worry. I haven't assumed anything." The tip of the plug pushed slowly into her, stretching her tender muscles and making her groan in both discomfort and ease. "You have such a lovely ass, Monica." His other hand rubbed it, those strokes opening her up a little wider as the plug slipped into her body. *I haven't done this in so long.* Her body almost resisted it. Yet between the lube and her own wetness, Monica would lose that battle if she chose to fight it. "One of these days I'll have to take it for myself. Not today. This is fine for now, right?"

A sigh escaped her. The free hand she was allowed rested on her stomach, her hips wiggling beneath Henry's touch. "Yes, sir."

"I'm glad. Now, I have a very important job for you, Monica." Henry stood and opened another drawer. Within moments he had another silk tie wrapping around her eyes to blindfold her, and yet another bind bringing her free wrist up to her confined one. If that wasn't maddening enough, Henry then pulled apart her legs, lingerie bunched around her waist, and hogtied her calves to her thighs at a stark angle.

Monica felt like she was ready to be served to her king.

"Your job is to lie like this for a bit longer. From now on you're not just my princess, but my doll. When I'm down there talking to someone, I'll be thinking of you up here, tied up like this and waiting for me to come take care of you. The best part will be knowing I can do whatever I want to you, because you'll be begging for me to put an end to your carnal misery."

She was already there. "Yes, sir." Monica contracted around the plug, and it sent a wave of undeniable desire through her, striking her right in the loins before shooting to her breasts and throat. An inaudible gasp wracked her.

"What if I told you that you're not to come while I'm gone? I'll know if you do. And if you do, I won't give you anything at all. You have to earn your reward. Now, I will ask you if you understand, and after that, you're not to say another word until I give you permission later. Do you understand all of this?"

"Yes, Mr. Warren."

That was it. The last thing she was allowed to say.

Monica took that seriously. Even after he left, she didn't say a word as she lay in Henry's bed, tied to herself and his furniture. It was uncomfortable, but only physically. She could think past the cramped muscles and the strained limits. After all, Henry was testing her as much as she was testing him. He wanted to know how far he could push her... and Monica wanted to know how he would react when she decided she had been pushed too far.

Not that she was anywhere near that. All she could think about was how much she couldn't wait for this to end – in the best ways.

There was one problem. No matter how disciplined Monica was, there were a few things she had no control over. Like how the plug inside her was pushed farther in thanks to the weight of her body on top of the bed. Every time she slightly moved to relieve pressure in her legs, other parts of her moved, and suddenly she was taking deep, steady breaths to contain an orgasm. Because one was threatening to claim her now.

Don't do it… don't do it… Henry had warned her that an orgasm would prevent her from getting what she wanted. And while she definitely wanted some punishment, she *didn't* want to be denied his intimate touch and the chance to share something so wonderful together. If he were a Dom of his word – and that's what Monica wanted more than anything else – he would make good on his promise of leaving her to stew in her own needs if she couldn't follow such a simple command.

Except he wanted to push her. He wanted to test her and see how well she could obey. Henry Warren knew that Monica was a seasoned sub. That meant she knew how to practice mind over matter in order to play the long game.

Mind over matter was not working super well right now. Monica stared at the back of her blindfold, sucking in her breath every time the plug threatened to make ripples of pleasures tear through her. With her luck, Henry would walk back in during the moment. Yet the result would more likely be him coming back in after one, two orgasms, and sighing at his new girlfriend's inability to follow the simplest of instructions.

Please come back soon. What was he even doing? Who was he talking to? Monica couldn't believe that Henry would schedule at-home meetings on a day they planned to spend together. Was it his intention to tie her up and draw things out like this? Did he know, from the moment he picked her up the day before, that he would do this to her?

Was he downstairs talking to a business associate while thinking of her? Was he practicing his own method of mind over matter? His cock straining to become hard, but his mind telling it to hold off a while longer? *I don't know anything about him.* Her previous partners... Monica knew how they would react. Maybe they were taking things too quickly.

Stop. No. Don't! She had to stop moving. No matter how cramped she got, she had to realize that moving around and shifting this or that part would end in her betraying Henry's orders. The more she became aware of the plug inside her, the more it hurt, stretching her enough to make sure she felt it.

It was harder to fight off pleasure. If Henry hadn't explicitly told her to not climax even once, then Monica would have given in to it. She was denied the day before, and now she was so wound up that tears of frustration began at the corners of her eyes. *I'm just one woman. This man is torturing me.* A long time since she was able to think that in such a positive way.

Just when she thought she wouldn't be able to fight her desires any longer, she heard the bedroom door click and admit what Monica was beginning to recognize as Henry's steps.

"There she is." His voice was heavy, commanding. "Just like I left her a while ago. How are you feeling?"

That was a trick question. Monica remembered that she wasn't supposed to say anything, and she didn't believe for a second that Henry forgot. He was testing her. Again.

"Your silence must mean you're holding out. I admit I'm rather disappointed." The bed turned downward as his weight sat upon the side. Soon, his firm hand was on her knee, curling around it and advancing toward her spread thighs. "I was looking forward to punishing you. Guess I'll have to up the stakes even more."

He stood, his steps carrying him to another part of the room Monica couldn't see. *Up the stakes?* What else could he do to her? Start using the flogger or whip? That was sure to make her come at this point... was that what he actually wanted? Should she give in and hope for the best?

She gasped when a cold clamp pinched her nipple. *Oh no.* Monica bit back the words threatening to stumble past her lips.

"You're tougher than I ever took you for." Henry clamped the other nipple, sending Monica into a stratosphere of bitter frustration. He knelt next to her and murmured into her ear, "Most women would have folded by now."

I'm not most women. Didn't he know that by now? Monica came from a past built almost entirely on submitting in the bedroom. This wasn't how she always did it, but Henry was kidding himself if he thought she didn't have lots of practice in holding back her own pleasure.

His Domination

"Excuse me, my sweet doll." Henry ran his hand across her stomach, dipping his finger into her navel and threatening to touch her mound below. "I've got one more thing to tend to before taking my pleasure with you. I won't be long. And neither will you be long for this carnal coil, I see." He tipped his finger against her chin. "Hold back a few more minutes. Remember... not a word until I tell you otherwise."

Monica didn't dare nod. She had the power to say her safe word if necessary, and that was enough.

The door opened and closed again. What in the *world* was he doing? Was this a part of his game with her? Not that Monica didn't like it. But obsessing over Henry's true motives gave her a distraction from the plug in her ass and the clamps on her nipples. Every time she gave herself the luxury of thinking about *those* she had to fight off an orgasm biting at her toes and squirming inside her stomach. Whenever she moved, she became wetter between the legs until she moaned from the effort it took to try to hold her climax in.

What a sight she must be. A small woman dressed in brand new lingerie and tied up like this in a rich man's bed. For all she knew, a door had been left open for the staff to glance in and see. *Wouldn't that be something...* Monica shuddered. She liked some sexual humiliation. Throw in some exhibitionism and she might have the time of her life. The only thing better than pleasing her Dom was letting the whole world watch her do it. In another life, Monica would make her fortune catching it all on tape.

I'm his doll. Her legs hurt and her arms cramped from being held together so long. *Dolls don't feel anything. They don't have any needs.* Monica pulled herself into the back of her mind, imagining what it would be like to actually be a doll. Not just any doll. A man's plaything – his vessel of pleasure. A life-sized doll that didn't come cheap. No… only the richest, most affluent man could buy a specimen like her. Henry had tied her up according to how he wanted to see her. Monica was his plaything, with careful attention paid to her erogenous zones… not necessarily to please her, but to give him something to admire the next time he walked through that door.

She had to think lifeless. She had to think quiet. She had to think *his.*

When she released the trappings pinning her to worldly pleasures, Monica was able to turn off the torture going on in her body. Henry would return soon enough. And when he did? She would be ready for him. Whatever he wanted, she would deliver. After all, she was a doll, and all she cared about was being played with.

Just as she achieved this kind of nirvana, the door quietly opened and closed a final time.

Henry did not immediately come to her. He took his time meandering around the room, having a drink of this and clinking that into a glass tray. Monica heard all these details. She even heard the heavy breaths coming out of his nose, and the unbuttoning of his shirt before it fell to the floor. What puzzled her the most, however, was the feeling of his knee resting on the bed followed by the welcomed sound of his zipper coming undone. Then nothing.

Nothing aside from some breaths and the occasional grunt slipping out of his throat.

Is he stroking himself to the sight of me? Monica wished she could see him with his hand wrapped around his hard cock and taunting her like he taunted her with the plug, the clamps, and the thighs forced apart. If the man were feeling ostensibly cruel, he would come on her mound and then make her wait for him to get hard again. Yet she never heard the hurried breaths of a man on the brink, nor did she feel something wet and warm hit her skin. All she could hear now was the beating of her own heart echoing in her head. *Breathe, idiot.* The clamps hurt. In a good way that was going to drive her mad.

Henry's hands groped both of her breasts. He loomed over her now, his threatening weight almost making good on a promise to crush her. Monica waited for a kiss, but one never came. Why would it? She was a doll, and a man like this would not kiss his doll.

Nevertheless, she almost spoke when he lifted her hips into the air, tied legs touching his biceps as he directed his hard cock toward her desperation.

Monica barely had time to collect what was left of her bearings before Henry Warren drove himself into her.

Relief claimed her. After who knew how long of sitting, waiting, and wishing to feel him like this again, Monica finally got her reward. Henry held himself inside her, letting her stretch and accommodate him before he began to gently roll his hips against her. Monica kept her lips sealed shut and her throat quiet. Well, the latter was easier said than done. Countless groan after groan bubbled in there, and every time Henry smoothly pulled out and pushed himself back into her she nearly wept.

He felt so good. Especially when he pushed her hips into the bed and drove into her, his cock stretching her wide but meeting no resistance. Not after a morning of touching herself, feeling the plug inside of her, and having those clamps constantly stimulate her nipples.

It was sensory overload. Henry held her hip with one hand and her shoulder with the other, keeping her still and steady as he thrust into her over and over, his breath becoming ragged and his motions more erratic. The man swelled within her, but kept his thrusts even – long, purposeful, and deep enough to drive Monica mad. Yet she still did not speak, and she managed to keep her louder moans within her, channeling them toward her loins, which were on the receiving end of Henry's pursuit for pleasure.

He didn't say a word to her, not that he had to. His hand slipped from her shoulder and to her breast, tugging on the clamp before smacking and grabbing her flesh. Monica lifted her hips involuntarily. Her Dom's cock filled her as much as it could.

She was quickly slipping. Thighs wet and stuffed to her core, Monica concentrated on the sensation of Henry thrusting in and out of her, his thrusts increasing in speed and intensity.

Monica could have held out longer if it weren't for the angle at which he entered her now. Between gravity and his own skill, Henry hit her where it counted, and a giant spark of pleasure tore her apart.

"Mmf!" She couldn't help it. Orgasm was breaking her, the one that had built up inside of her since the last time he pleased her like this. A wave of relief and pleasure washed over her warm skin and settled in her stomach, now held down by both of Henry's hands. The clamps clinked as her breasts bounced before his eager eyes; the plug in her ass seemed to grow in size as her muscles contracted around it; the gag in her mouth drowned in saliva and from the groans erupting from her chest. Most of all, she relished in that full and perfect feeling of her Dom continuing to fuck her at the same rhythm even after she began to hold onto him with the brute strength of her orgasm.

Not for long. An excited grunt hit Monica's ears, and the next thing she knew she was in the middle of her orgasm when Henry began his. He filled her with more than his cock. The sheer amount of heat expanding inside of her told Monica that Henry was more than satisfied with her performance. Even though they did not speak to or kiss one another, they shared an elation that only a well synced Dom and sub could have.

Henry slowed his movements before pulling out of her. Instantly his seed spilled out, running down her skin and covering the flared base of her plug. Henry removed it without a second thought – another relieving contraction sent some of his seed into her opened hole.

The clamps came off one after the other. Henry bent down and blew against her nipples before gently rolling across them with his tongue, keeping them hard but easing any swelling. This time Monica let a moan escape her. When her arms and legs were released from their binds, she carefully moved them, feeling the tension evaporate as Henry helped her change position so her joints would not be hurt.

Finally, the blindfold came off. Then the gag in her mouth.

She was halfway onto her stomach by now, legs closed but seed still easing out of her body. Henry massaged her side before curling up behind her and wrapping an arm around her midsection. The lips on her neck only made Monica sigh.

"By the way, you can speak now."

She didn't want to. She wanted to sleep. Not even when Henry began covering her sore spots in cream and tender touches did she open her mouth to say anything.

"Did you enjoy that?"

His leg was hooked beneath hers. Monica rolled back into his embrace, relishing in the easy way he loved on her. *Why does this man want me so much?* Was it because she was such a good sub? Or was there something else about her that he admired and wanted to have? Men were such a mystery to her sometimes. "I did." Her voice was hoarse from disuse.

"I thought about you until I couldn't stand it anymore. Knowing that you were up here waiting for me like this… all I could think about was taking you. And then to see the way your body begged for it when I got here… you're destroying me, Monica. You don't know how much power you have."

He kissed her ear and fingered her slit. Monica collapsed in exhaustion, her only request that he keep doing that and then take a nap with her. Henry would not commit to anything until Monica started to orgasm once more, his fingers inside of her and teasing her ass as well.

"My princess," he whispered into her ear before sucking the side of her breast. Monica was still coming, this second orgasm taking much longer to accomplish than the first. Her body shook in fatigue but would not give up the pleasure she felt. "There's still so much I want to do to you. I haven't seen your limits yet. I want to find them and shatter them."

He gave one final thrust of his fingers and made her quiver around them, her arousal drenching his skin in her inability to care anymore. *You're already pushing my limits, Henry.* His wet fingers rubbed the inside of her thighs as he mentioned how swollen and wet her nether lips were. *You don't know that you are, but it's happening.* Monica clung to him the moment he embraced her, a kiss the size of her uncertainty blossoming between them.

Chapter 15

The Dark Hour

"Of course I've been here before," Monica said later that night. "What, you think I was never aware of the most exclusive BDSM club in America?"

"I never said you weren't aware of it." Henry took her by the arm and led her through the front entrance of the club, a spacious, dark abode deep in the center of the local city. "I merely asked if you had been here before. There's a difference."

They approached the doorman, a fellow dressed in a designer suit but liable to bash someone's head in if they looked at him wrong. Monica flashed him a sweet smile while Henry pulled out his ID and shared his name. The doorman checked it on a member list and showed them through.

His Domination

"And I told you, I've been here before." Monica let Henry remove her coat and pass it on to the girl behind a counter. She wore a gold, glittery mask and a smile the size of the building.

"Hello, Mr. Warren," she said with a hint of flirtation in her voice. "And who is the lovely lady with you?" The girl handed him a claim check for the coats.

Henry put it in his wallet. "Don't tell me you don't know Monica Graham. She says she's been here before."

The girl stepped back from her window, her blond hair swishing in the dim light. "I've heard of you, ma'am. Forgive me. I didn't start working here until a few months ago."

They both returned her smile. Henry put a tight hand around Monica's shoulder and directed her toward the hallway leading to the main sitting area. Not that they would deign to sit so low in one of the country's most private members-only club.

Monica had been here. *The Dark Hour.* There were elite BDSM clubs all over the world, but this was the Western Hemisphere's #1 abode. Any man – or woman – who had the financial means and the love for the relationship between a Dom and sub came here. Just like they would visit Monica's Château up in the rural hills, they would make some time to check out The Dark Hour. Men in expensive suits and smoking cigars; women in flashy dresses and collars; both crawling on the floor and wielding whips. A center stage bathed in red and blue lights boasted the occasional show and demonstrations. Monica saw on the calendar of events that they recently had a shibari demonstration. *I should find out who did it and hire them to tutor my girls.* Always the business-minded woman.

Henry apparently had a membership important enough to give him a VIP table in the corner upstairs. Monica sat next to the railing and looked down at the stage, all while Henry flagged down a scantily clad server to order them drinks.

"What will you have?" he asked. "I'm getting a gin and tonic."

Monica batted her eyelashes at him. "Whatever you want to get me, Mr. Warren."

He looked at her for a few seconds, completely ignoring the server in favor of sharing a smirk with his girlfriend. "Get the lady a Manhattan. Put them both on my tab."

When the server left, he turned to Monica and wrapped his arm around the back of her chair. "Did I guess right? You seem like a woman who loves hard liquor and some fun."

"You haven't seen me with a good amount of hard liquor yet. I'm pretty giggly."

"Hang on. Let me get that girl. I'll load you up with Manhattans."

The drink was perfect. *Amazing that he knew I like vermouth.* A lucky guess, really. Monica liked most liquor, so that wasn't an issue. She even dared to ask to taste his gin and tonic mere seconds after enjoying the first sip of her Manhattan. Henry slid his glass toward her and stole her Manhattan. Unlike her, he did not enjoy both.

Their intent coming to The Dark Hour that night was not to merely taste expensive drinks. They could do that back at Henry's mansion. Instead, Henry had suggested the club in town for "the sheer thrill of it." Although they had spent most of the morning and early afternoon playing on their own, Henry thought they might like to unwind by watching others and being around like-minded people.

Monica knew his real motive. *He wants to show me off.* This was their first time being seen together in public, let alone sitting together so intimately. *I haven't been here since…* The last time she came to The Dark Hour was when Jackson had it in his mind to watch other people whip each other for a change. Back then, he always made such a show of arriving and spoiling others. *He liked to flaunt his wealth.* That was something often associated with men of new money, but Jackson, born with a silver spoon in his mouth, fell into those same traps… wanting to be loved for his money, respected… it always bothered Monica to a point, but she could overlook it. For the most part.

The first show that evening was a Domme and her male sub. *Just like being back at the Château.* In fact, the woman in leather stepping onto the stage with a young man on a leash looked a lot like the Judith whom Monica stole from this establishment back when she opened her Château. *"How would you like to make more money, set your own schedule, and have a fabulous place to live?"* The woman down there wasn't Judith, but if Monica was thinking about hiring more girls, this wasn't a bad place to poach from. *I wonder who that lady down there is.* First, Monica wanted to see how good she was.

So did Henry, as evident when he leaned over Monica to get a gander at the stage.

The Domme made her sub kneel on the floor, his arms tied behind his back and his head bowed. She told him to do something, and when he did not immediately obey, he received a gentle lash on the bare back.

"Oh boy." Henry leaned his elbow on the table. "There's a man with fortitude. I never cared for being whipped."

"You tried it?" That only surprised Monica because Doms almost never flipped the script. "You don't strike me as the type who wants to be a sub. Ever."

"You say that because I'm a man." Henry curled his fingers on her arm and spoke directly into her ear. "A long time ago I had it in my mind to try many tastes. At this point in my life I know what I like. Everyone reaches that point in different ways."

"Color me surprised that you would rather whip than be whipped, as you put it when we first met."

Henry bit her ear as the man moaned below. "That was a good day."

"Well look who finally showed his face around here after God knows how long." A curt voice interrupted their moment of affection, forcing Henry to back off his date and turn around. "Henry Warren, you ridiculous shit."

To the sounds of a whip cracking in the air, both Henry and Monica stared up at a man and his date. The man wasn't very tall, but he wore a slick suit and clean facial hair that suggested he came from as many means as Henry, if not more. His date, on the other hand, was a svelte blond woman wearing a see-through brown dress that did not hide a single thing, including her breasts and thighs that were both pale and pink even under those lights. She wore a diamond-studded choker around her throat. *A baby sub. Cute.* They always went with the demure – but expensive – collars.

"James Merange." Henry stood up and shook the man's hand before settling back into his seat. Without invitation, both man and woman slipped into the chairs on the other side of the table. "And this must be the lovely Gwen I've heard about."

The blond woman blushed. Flattery always worked, even if a girl had no problems walking around in a public place with her nipples showing through her outfit. "You flatter me, Mr. Warren."

Monica bristled. *Great. Jealousy already?* That didn't take long. When she lived with Jackson she didn't get jealous of other women deferring to him. But she didn't have a special name for that man. "Mr. Warren" was something Monica already associated with her new romance. She took a drink before anyone could see her face.

"Nonsense. James talks about you all the time." Once the other two were settled in and had ordered drinks, Henry turned to Monica. "Have you been introduced to Mr. Merange before?" The implication was not lost to Monica. *He wants to know if he's been to the Château.* What a sneaky man.

Monica reached across the table and shook the other man's hand. "I think we may have met a few years ago. At a fundraiser." That was always a safe answer in these circles.

The man down on the stage cried out in pain. Nobody at the table flinched. "Monica Graham, is it?" James sat back in his seat, arms crossed and eyes never leaving Monica's face. "Boy, I certainly know you. Who doesn't around these parts?"

Cynthia Dane

Gwen glanced at him. "Is that so?"

"Ms. Graham here runs that house of ill repute up in the hills, dear." James cleared his throat. "Not that I've ever been there, mind you." He then looked at Monica again. "No offense."

"None taken."

"Wait, the BDSM house?"

"I suppose you could call it that," Monica said.

"Oh, I know you! Didn't you used to date Jackson Lyle?"

The table fell silent. Monica maintained her poker face but had to look toward Henry before having the strength to answer. "Once upon a time, yes."

The pride Gwen boasted for being right quickly fell off her countenance. "Sorry…"

While James shifted uncomfortably, Monica smiled. "Nothing to be sorry about. I'm hardly doing poorly for myself."

"I'll say." James perked back up and pointed to Henry. "Didn't think I'd see you with such a classy lady in a place like this, Henry. Look at you! Becoming a regular Don Juan. Although it's kind of funny, isn't it?"

Henry was not smiling. "What's funny, James?"

The server returned with drinks for James and Gwen, as well as refills for the original couple at the table. Monica snatched her fresh Manhattan and nursed it while the two men had a battle of secrets across the table. *Business bullshit.* Back at the Château she would be taking notes. On a date with her

Dom? She was under no obligation to listen to a thing – unless Henry told her to, of course.

"Oh, you know." James patted Gwen's thigh. "Just some things I've heard on the grapevine."

"I'd ask what those are," Henry stirred his drink with the thin straw he was given. "but I don't think I want to know. Not tonight."

"Of course." The knowing smile on James's face did not inspire any confidence at the table. All Monica knew was that Henry did not look like he was enjoying himself any longer. Whatever went on in his brain right now had nothing to do with her, however. "So how did you two meet, exactly? I'd love to know."

"How does anyone meet Ms. Graham in this world?" Monica didn't like the undertone to Henry's voice. It was similar to the way he spoke to her in the bedroom, but tinged in anger. Was this the Henry who did business? "We met at her Château, of course."

"Of course."

"Of *course.*"

Tension covered the table. Monica glanced at Gwen, who averted her eyes and pretended to be enthralled with the show wrapping up on stage. *What do these two know?* Something that Monica didn't know? It made sense, when she considered the fact that she had only met Henry a few times. *A few times, and yet it feels like we've been together an eternity already.* There was something dangerous about that thought.

Things didn't change until another couple arrived. Then another. Men and women from the business world coming together on a Tuesday night, of all nights, simply to enjoy drinks and watch people be tied up and talked down to on a stage. Not that many people were watching the shows once they connected with others and made bawdy jokes over drinks. Eventually Monica had to get up from the table and join the new party at a bigger table in another corner. She recognized some of them from work and from her old life with Jackson. None of them were interested in her.

Because she knew their sexual secrets.

Because she knew who owed who money.

Because she heard them make judgments while at her place of business. Or through her girls who would feed her information so Monica could use it to her own advantage. *"Oh, Mr. So-And-So, you should really speak to Mr. What's-His-Name. I think you two would get along really well."* It was in Monica's best interest to have only good words leave her Château. If other rich denizens heard that good deals – and good times – were made in her home, then more of them would show up.

If they heard that someone was drunk enough to make a bad decision… somehow that would give her a bad reflection in the mirror.

Monica was content to sit next to Henry, his arm around her and nobody asking why. *They pity him.* None of the people at the large table would say so, but they probably thought Henry was being taken in by Jackson Lyle's leftovers. They certainly spent a good amount of time glimpsing at them and then pretending to brush something off their shoulders or be taken in by their empty glasses. *Unfortunately for them, I can look right through that.*

Part of it bothered Monica simply because she didn't need reminders that she was a pariah around these parts. No, people didn't hate her. They probably felt sorry for her, maybe even admired her for her business, but they all feared and pitied her because of her relation to Jackson. Lots of these people had to deal with him in their everyday dealings. If he heard on the "grapevine"… Monica didn't want to think about it. By now he knew that she was seeing Henry Warren. What he thought of that? A part of her didn't care, but another was afraid.

Afraid of what? She had no idea.

"Excuse me, Masters and Mistresses." A woman dressed in a black skintight suit stepped to the end of the table, where she distributed a couple of fliers advertising an upcoming event. "I would like to remind everyone that our annual auction is coming up in a few weeks. Thank you." She bowed and stepped back before turning to head to the next table.

James picked up the nearest flier and raised his eyebrows. "What do you think, my dear?" he asked Gwen, handing her the flier. "Should I auction you off to the highest bidder? Maybe I'll win and a woman will buy you for a night."

Gwen took the flier and folded it in half, lips pursed. "I'm not for sale, *my dear.* But we should come that night to watch."

The rest of the table laughed, including Henry, who glanced at another flier before sliding it to someone else to look at. Monica caught sight of it. *"Annual Submissive Auction."* She had heard of this. Every year The Dark Hour put on an event like this, in which a sub auctioned him or herself to the audience. The happier the audience was, the more money they gave the sub and their Dom. It was always one of the biggest nights of the year. *Unless I have a lot of appointments, we might as well close the Château that night and come ourselves.* Hm, maybe Monica should try to convince one of her girls to auction herself and then split the profits...

Another drink was placed before her, and that was the end of those thoughts.

If Monica thought that she was going to get to spend an intimate date with Henry, then she was sorely wrong. Most of the evening was spent entertaining these other people she barely knew and only had a passing interest in. Sometimes she gazed at the stage, hoping for something exciting to happen, but Tuesday nights were slow in that aspect, even when a million people showed up for fun.

Some people talked to her. Mostly those asking about her business out of politeness. A few asked about her relation to Henry. *What do I say?* Monica was practical and not about to say that he was her new Dom. Yet calling him her "boyfriend" felt juvenile, especially in their type of relationship. "We're dating," was all she said. Two people left it at that, while another glanced between her and Henry before looking away with a snort.

People could be so rude.

As the evening wound down, Monica imbibed more alcohol. She wasn't kidding when she said liquor made her giddy. While there wasn't much for her to talk about with these people, she wouldn't say she was *bored*. Especially when she lost most of her inhibitions and draped herself across Henry's shoulders, reveling in the way people looked at them – like they had room to talk. Most of them had men and women hanging all over them as well.

"You should wrap things up so we can get out of here," she said into his ear, her hand snaking around his thigh. "I wanna make out in the back of your car."

They had taken a Town Car there, driven by one of Henry's chauffeurs. Monica wasn't above rolling up the partition and giving her Dom whatever he wanted in the backseat. Making out, nipple play, a hand or blowjob… there were some crazy times bending over the seat while the driver turned up the music to save his own sanity.

"You weren't kidding when you said you got giddy." Henry rubbed his hand on top of her knee. "Give it another twenty minutes. We'll wrap things up here and do whatever you want in the car."

Twenty minutes was too long. The tingles of arousal were filling her with impatience. *I'll show him to make me wait again.* First drawing out her pleasure that morning, and now this? Forget that! Monica was full of booze and ready to party.

While Henry resumed his conversation with another man across the table, Monica used the cover of darkness to slip her hand between his legs and brush against his crotch.

Henry froze up, but did not interrupt his conversation. Monica smiled into the back of her other hand. Too easy.

His zipper came down with little resistance. Monica rubbed her fingers against the silk of his boxers and bit her bottom lip at the scandal of what she was doing.

Only while intoxicated would she think taking her Dom's cock into her hand beneath a table felt indecent. Like she was a teenager. A freshman in college getting freaky with her frat boyfriend at a social meant for the brainy elite. *Maybe that really happened.* Whether it did or not, it wasn't as good as now when she wrapped her hand around Henry's cock and drew it out of his pants.

It was as if she did nothing, if one went by the expression on his face. He was still laughing at one of James's jokes and reassuring Gwen that she was a beautiful woman who could model for any designer in the world, if that was her pursuit. The other people were either wrapped up in their own conversations or too far away to ever notice what went on beneath the table. *Always good to have a nice, public thrill.* Alcohol made that more fun for Monica.

She worked her hand up and down his shaft, her fingers rounding his head until he stiffened in her touch. The man had driven himself into her over and over only a few hours ago, and now he was getting hard again from this? Monica had to contain a grin of self-indulgence. Henry was thick in her grip, and the thought of him taking her like he did that morning made those tingles in her body flow like a strong river, the only dam in its way the public around them. Nevertheless, Monica wasted no time tightening her grip and moving her hand as quickly as she dared without calling attention to her actions.

Her hand was wet. When she glanced down she saw the gleam of precum on the tip of Henry's cock. And yet he sat there so coolly, talking about dividends and how they related to a tasteless joke about strippers. The only time he showed any emotion was when James made yet another quip and incited his tablemate to laugh.

Oh, he was good. If Monica was the queen of poker faces, then Henry Warren was the god. Perhaps there were other things he could teach her outside of the bedroom.

Not today, however.

Monica rubbed her palm against the head of his cock. *Let's take this as far as I can.* She would do it. She would make Henry come right there in front of everyone. What was going through his head right now? The sheer amount of power he held in front of these people? Who else could possibly have this kind of service from their sub? All the other subs at the table had both hands above the surface, holding drinks, stroking shoulders, and twiddling thumbs as they waited for something to happen. *Something's happening beneath this table.* If Monica were feeling *really* frisky she would lean in and blow into Henry's ear. That would make him come.

To her disappointment, Henry put his hand around her wrist and yanked her hand away as his cock stiffened to its hardest point yet. *Darn.* Monica retracted while Henry covertly buttoned up. She still had her wet hand, and she rubbed it against her bare thigh.

In the middle of a conversation, Henry cleared his throat and sat up straight in his seat. "Excuse me." He buttoned up his jacket, probably in order to cover up his erection when he went to stand. "Waitress seems to have forgotten our next round of drinks. Monica?" He looked at her.

She waited a few seconds before standing as well, her arm going around his as he escorted her away from the table – and nowhere near the main bar.

Henry knocked on a VIP room door, and when there was no response, he opened it and pulled Monica in after him.

"Cute," he said, pushing her against the nearest wall and barricading her with both arms. Monica shrank in front of him, keeping a grin to herself. "And what do you think you were doing back there, hm?"

His breath was delightfully hot against her cheek, and he was so close, so intruding that Monica felt herself become weak between the legs. "Call it a mild attempt at reading your mind. Are you telling me that you didn't want that… sir?"

"In front of all those people?"

"With all due respect, Mr. Warren, we're in a sex club."

"And I didn't ask you to do that."

"Didn't you like it?"

She gripped his jacket, attempting to pull him down to her level for a kiss. Instead, Henry grabbed both of her arms and held them above her head, pinning her wrists to the wall as his breath increased in intensity against her skin. "I should punish you for being so out of line."

Yes, you should. Monica pushed against the wall, her breasts straining against her dress again. "Please."

"Please, *what?*"

Monica ran her tongue against both lips. "Punish me, sir."

"I should make you get down on your knees and suck my cock. Finish the job you started out there."

"Yes, sir."

"No, don't call me sir." Henry's fingers tightened around her wrists. "Call me *Master.*"

"Yes, Master."

Such a satisfying word to say. Monica hadn't called a man her Master with such conviction since… Now Henry glared at her, his eyes hungry with desire. Desire to punish her, and desire to have her. Now this was the kind of thing Monica was hoping to have tonight.

"Let me suck your cock, Master."

"As charming as it is to hear you say that, I don't think so."

Monica bowed her head. What had she done to displease him? If she had learned anything from her years as a sub, it was that being denied things like that meant her Dom was angry with her. *Did I really go out of line when I did that to him?* Wouldn't he have brushed her off if he didn't want it? He knew the safe word. How hard was it to work the word *blossom* into conversation? She even wore a flower-patterned dress. *I'm so stupid.*

Henry must have caught the disappointed look on her face, for he said, "I want to hear you beg for it. Tell me how much you want me to fuck you right here."

Relief swept through Monica, and finally she felt that dam let up in her body, releasing a new wave of arousal. Now that she could fully express it, she did so, rotating her hips in his direction and lifting her chin toward his face. His eyes went straight to her chest.

"Fuck me, please."

"Do better."

Monica sucked in her breath. "Fuck me, Master."

"And why should I do that? What have you done to deserve that sort of reward?"

What haven't I done? "Everything you've wanted."

Henry kissed her, quickly, as if the man couldn't control himself. *Go ahead. Lose control.* What Monica would give to feel Henry completely go alpha on her! "You haven't given me *everything* I want yet, Monica."

"What do you want, Master? I'll give it to you right now." She tried to free her hands, but Henry was too strong.

"I want you," he began, staring deep into her eyes, "to beg for whatever I give you."

She could do that.

"Yes, yes, take me right here!" Monica felt like a loose woman on the verge of losing the last of her morals. Henry was on her, kissing whatever he came into contact with, his arms falling to touch her breasts and to lift her hips around his waist. Monica slid down the wall but kept her balance by wrapping her arms completely around him. When he discovered that she wore no underwear that night, she could only smile and say, "My Master didn't tell me to put *all* my clothes back on earlier."

"You sly vixen." Henry held her up with one hand and undid his zipper with the other. "Look at what you do to me. I'm supposed to be a collected man."

It didn't take long for his cock to pierce her where it mattered most. By then he had given in to his base desires, growling into Monica's ear and squeezing her flesh as he drove himself right into her. She cried out, nails digging into his suit. Sure, she had been aroused for a good twenty or so minutes, but her body hadn't been prepared for this kind of quick and rough sex. Pain seared through her as Henry forced himself deeper, his teeth in her shoulder and his determination winning out over how dry she still was. Not for long. The sheer rawness of his actions sent Monica to a different plane of existence in that dark abode.

This man wanted her so badly that he pulled her into this room to fuck her. Didn't matter if she was ready. When Monica threw down her gauntlet back at the table, she had signed herself up for whatever punishment he felt like dishing out.

Taking her with a side of pain felt pretty appropriate.

"Henry!" Monica clung to him, her head bumping against the wall as he thrust up into her. "Yes! Fuck me! Please!"

It hurt, but not for long. Given the intensity of the situation she quickly acclimated, her arousal flushing her skin in time to Henry's thrusts. The next time he completely pulled out and slammed into her again, he met almost no resistance.

Monica never forgot what he asked of her.

"Punish me, please!" Somewhere in the frenzy Henry found the ability to smack the side of her ass as he took her against the wall. Monica's legs dangled around his waist, one shoe falling off and clattering to the floor. The front of her dress was pulled apart, her breasts hanging out for Henry to indulge in whenever it pleased him – which was every single second he wasn't kissing her lips or leaving a bruise on her throat. This primal showcase of his affections had Monica riveted to the point she squeezed his torso and sang her pleasure into his ear.

"Shit!" Henry pinned her to the wall again, his cock buried deep within her and his cologne overpowering the last of her senses. This was it. This was what it felt like to be caught by the man who pursued her.

And claimed by him, which happened a mere moment after Monica began to climax, her voice echoing in the VIP room.

His grunts of release were better than any music playing in the main room of The Dark Hour. Monica squeezed her eyes shut so she could concentrate on the warmth filling her, connecting her to the man so enthralled with her that he couldn't wait until they got home.

"Thank hell," he muttered, staying still within her and catching his breath. Monica opened her eyes, leaning against him, kissing the underside of his chin as he tipped his head back. "You're something else."

Henry released her, and the first thing Monica noticed was that she missed the way he had held her against the wall. Now, watching him zip up and straighten out his clothes, Monica was aware of his seed spilling from her for the second time that day.

"Don't," he said, snatching her wrist as she began the walk to the bathroom. "That's your punishment until we leave."

Monica stared at the floor, her sense telling her to clean up. But when her Dom told her she was being punished, well…

Besides, she liked feeling him trickling down her skin, his claim on her spreading from her core to the world beyond. It made her feel like a glorious extension of him – just what she wanted that night.

"You go on ahead and rejoin the party." Henry cupped his hands on her cheek and gently kissed her lips. "I need to use the restroom. I'll catch up."

Monica kissed him again, this time harder, their tongues searching for one another as Henry embraced her again. *I want to smell like him.* Even though Monica had to detach and fix herself up in the nearest mirror before heading out into The Dark Hour, she still wanted to bring as much of her Dom as she could with her.

Life went on as if nothing had happened in the VIP room. People mingled in the club. A show began on the main stage. Waitresses wearing collars carried trays of drinks. And Monica Graham sauntered back to the large table in the back, alone but not without Henry's marks on her.

A chilling laugh came from the table.

She stopped. Her legs turned to mush. *No.*

She'd recognize that laugh anywhere. She had heard it in her dreams. Her nightmares.

Sure enough, as soon as she turned the corner and encountered the table, she saw that a newcomer had taken Henry's chair in their absence.

The conversation stopped. A blond man in a tan suit pulled a cigar out of his mouth and looked to his left.

Monica looked right back into the eyes of Jackson Lyle.

Chapter 16

Crossing Boundaries

Everyone was silent and uncomfortable. Save for the man gazing at Monica over his shoulder.

"Monica." He stood, and Monica took a step back. "Long time no see."

Yes. A long time, but not long enough. "Jackson."

Her resolve was weak. For a woman who had felt like she was in heaven, she now stood like a statue, hoping that the stiller she stood the less likely Jackson would pay attention to her. Things didn't work like that. Jackson approached, keeping a respectful distance but holding back what he really wanted to do and say. *Hit me, probably.* Monica refused to shudder in his presence.

"How are you doing?" He stuck the cigar back in his mouth like a pompous ass. To think that Monica once found his behavior attractive. *What did I know? I was younger and dumber.* "I've been hearing interesting stories about you. If I didn't think it would make you uppity, I'd come visit that lovely business you started up with Cole's money."

Monica inhaled deeply. "I'm fine." She didn't ask how he was doing.

Now he approached, closer, his aftershave taking Monica back to those dark days in which she was a prisoner in his mansion. "What brings you here? Never thought I'd run into you in one of my... favorite places."

He's trying to get to you. Monica finally had to look away to keep from giving in to the chills she felt. "I go where I please."

Jackson tilted his head. "With whomever you please, it seems like."

Monica turned. Henry stood two feet behind her, his brows furrowed and his jaw set. "Jackson Lyle."

The man in question took a long drag of his cigar before blowing a longer trail of smoke into the air. "Who are you again? Harry Wilson?"

"Henry Warren."

They didn't shake hands, thank God. "Oh, right. I've heard of you. Well." He winked. Monica wanted to vomit. "I must be going. Merely stopped by to say hello to some friends." His wave to the table was a bit too enthusiastic. "Hope to see you around, Monica. Always good to see a familiar face."

He slowly passed by them, staring at Monica through the corners of his eyes. She stood, stoic, wishing Henry would do something, anything. *What can he do?* Besides stand protectively near her as that man went by.

"Warren."

Henry's hand went to the small of Monica's back. "Don't satisfy him," he muttered into her ear.

The moment Jackson disappeared around a corner, it was as if a fog lifted. People went back to chatting and the music became louder. Monica pushed herself from Henry's extending embrace and cleared her throat. "Can we go?"

"Of course."

They said curt goodbyes to everyone at the table before going to the coat check and collecting their deposited belongings. On their way toward the door, however, Monica released Henry's hand and made a detour toward the bathroom. "Sorry. I need to."

He said nothing aside from, "I'll see you by the door." Monica left her coat with him and slipped into the ladies' room, which was blissfully empty at that moment.

She had to clean up. As erotic as it had been a few minutes ago, seeing Jackson made her feel... dirty. It was an irrational thought. Jackson had nothing to do with Henry. Henry had nothing to do with Jackson. *I should feel comforted.* Yet the last thing Monica wanted right now was something sexual left on her. *That man makes me hate sex.*

Not only did she clean herself up from head to toe, but she stood in front of the sink, staring at the makeup on her face and the way her hair curled across her skin. This was the face Jackson saw. The face he used to see every day. What had changed since their last meeting over a year ago?

Monica had changed her hairstyle. She also wore bolder makeup when bothered. Otherwise? She looked exactly the same. No new wrinkles. No scars – aside from the ones residing inside her. With a sigh, Monica splashed some water on her face and sucked in some strength from the air. She would need it to walk out of that place with her head held high.

In front of all those people who knew what Jackson had done to her.

It was never public knowledge. As far as she knew, Jackson had only told people that they broke up, and that was that. Yet people talked. And she and Jackson had been together for about a decade. That kind of intense relationship couldn't be swept beneath the rug. *People talked.* Monica heard them all the time in her Château. *"Did you hear that he was beating her? No, not in the fun way. The bad way." "I always knew there was something off with that guy. Have to be if you're going to bust balls like he does in the boardroom."*

Monica turned off the sink and used a paper towel to dab her face dry. After throwing the towel away she went back into The Dark Hour, where Henry patiently waited by the entrance.

She made it all the way to his car before breaking down. Henry opened the door for her and she crawled in, muttering a greeting to the driver while Henry got in on the other side. The partition went up the moment he told the driver to take them home. Henry kept to his side, but his eyes lingered on Monica as she grasped the door handle and stared at the back of the seat in front of her.

The first sob to claim her was like listening to an iceberg crack.

Monica covered her face with her hands and leaned forward, elbows digging into her legs as her scalp came dangerously close to scraping against the leather seat before her. *I'll never be rid of him.* As long as Jackson lived – as long as *Monica* lived – he would be lurking in the shadows, reminding her of the hell he put her through. The more Monica thought of that toxic smile and that bone-breaking laugh, the more she howled into her hands.

And the more she thought of that prison she was taken back to earlier that day.

Something pressed against her back. When she sat up, she saw Henry caressing her, his other hand gesturing for her to come to him. Monica flung herself into his embrace, her tears wetting his shirt and the jacket on top of it. This wasn't like the affection she received after lovemaking earlier that day. This was the comfort she craved after going for so long without it.

"It's all right." Henry held her close, his protective arms encircling her and giving Monica a tight squeeze. "I'm here."

That only made Monica cry harder. As the car lurched through the streets and made its way toward the highway, Monica held herself to him as if he would abandon her if she let up. "I'm so tired of thinking about him."

"When else have you thought about him? Today?"

She didn't want to say it. Yet when Henry stroked her hair, his comforting touch sending a ripple of relief through her, Monica sat up and told him what had happened to her earlier that day.

"I wish you had told me," Henry said, both hands still gripping her arms. "I wouldn't have done that if I had known."

"You didn't need to know. It's my problem. There's nothing wrong on your end."

"Still, I need to know these things. I can't go pushing boundaries I don't even know exist."

Monica sat up, wiping her cheeks. "You're not. You're not that man."

The solemn look she received didn't inspire her. "You don't know that, do you Monica?"

She pursed her lips. "I…" Something choked in her throat. "I have to believe that."

"And I have to keep proving that to you. Come here."

When they embraced again, Monica couldn't tell if she was holding him the tightest or if it was him holding her. It didn't matter. Her soul was weary, but her heart was opening with love.

Chapter 17

What She Needs

It was the sweetest day of the year thus far. The sun was warm, but not scalding to those choosing to sit in it; the breeze brought with it a nice chill, but was not too strong to blow about the lunch Monica laid out.

She was dining on the main balcony with two of her friends. Well, if a man like Ethan Cole could be called her friend. *Ex-boyfriend. Business partner. Confidant.* When Monica made her great escape from Jackson's prison, it was Ethan who was there for her. The same man who once shared her with his former best friend before he decided the ménage life wasn't for him. *Too bad.* In truth, Monica and Ethan made better friends than lovers. There was a lot of mutual respect, but without the drama Jackson infused everywhere he went there was little romantic passion. Just as well. Monica had her life, and Ethan had his.

Part of that life was also dining with them that early afternoon at the Château.

"This place is a lot bigger than I expected." Jasmine, Ethan's girlfriend of over a year said as she looked around. Even though she came from a lower middle-class background, she hid it well with her boyfriend's money adorning her body – in the form of a black and white dress and a wide-brimmed sunhat that covered most of her silky dark hair. Yet when she picked up a regular spoon to eat her soup, Monica saw the tell-tale sign of a woman new to the world of billionaires and their desires. *Took me two years to figure that out.* She hoped she wasn't being obvious when she picked up the large soup spoon.

"For the amount we paid, it better be big," Ethan looked at Monica across the table.

She picked up her iced tea before answering. "It's adequate for the job. Still a few rooms leftover if I decide to hire more personnel."

Ethan jerked his thumb to the woman sitting at the end of the small four-person table. "She needs a job. She's unemployed now."

"Ethan!"

"What?"

Jasmine stuck her tongue out and Ethan pretended to be offended. *Another one that was almost destroyed by Jackson.* She wouldn't bring it up today, but Jasmine was the poor soul Jackson kidnapped and intended on "breaking in," her consent be damned. Only because of Monica's fortitude were they able to make their escape. Oh, and Ethan providing the getaway car, of course.

Monica didn't get to see them often enough. They lived farther away, although Ethan made a concerted effort to keep in touch on a weekly basis – and not just because he was Monica's #1 investor. He put up most of the start-up costs and gave Monica the money necessary to buy the Château. She had made sure it was a good investment for them both.

She wished she could see what few true friends she had a bit more often.

"Oh, excuse me." Yvette appeared in the doorway, wearing her tanning bikini and a straw hat on her head. In her hand was a tablet, although Monica had no idea how she read it in this sunlight. "Thought the balcony was empty."

Both Jasmine and Monica caught Ethan staring at Yvette's backside as she walked away.

"Hate to break it to you, but she refuses all clients who aren't her patron," Monica said, blowing on her soup before eating it. "You'll have to find someone else to play with tonight."

Jasmine blushed, but Ethan smiled. "Afraid we have to leave before three. Unfortunately, since I know how much Jasmine has been looking forward to coming here."

They both looked at the woman in question. She shifted in her seat, grabbing her drink and pretending to be so thirsty that she couldn't answer. *She would like Grace.* And Grace would probably like her!

"Sweetheart," Ethan said, pulling out his wallet and handing his girlfriend a slip of paper. "Do me a favor and go give this to the driver. I forgot earlier."

Jasmine scoffed. "Can't it wait?"

He cleared his throat. "No. Afraid not."

She turned her head between the two of them. "I see. I'll be back." After putting on a plastic smile, Jasmine stood up, pushed in her chair, and disappeared into the Château, leaving Monica alone with Ethan.

"Subtle."

Ethan sat back in his seat, crossing his legs while balancing his wineglass on his bent knee. The look he gave Monica made her feel like she was about to get the fifth degree from her older brother.

"Guess what I heard from a birdie named James Merange."

Ethan drank his wine but did not take his eyes off Monica. She, in turn, shrugged as if to say, *"I have no idea. What in the world is James Merange saying?"*

"Says he saw you at The Dark Hour acting really cozy with a date. *Really* cozy. Oh, what was his name..." Ethan looked right into the sun, his eyes narrowing as he sucked on the inside of his cheek. "Henry Warren."

Monica's façade faded with another shrug. "I was there."

"Come off it, Monica. You're seeing that Henry Warren fellow, huh?"

This time she looked him in the eye. "And what if I am?"

"I'd say good for you. Was a bit worried."

"About what?"

Ethan put his glass down and rested both hands on his chair. "That you wouldn't date."

How nice of you to be concerned for my love life. She knew what he meant, however. Even Monica wasn't sure if she would ever give a man a real chance again. That was before Henry... convinced her. "He's a remarkable man. What do you know about him?"

They laughed abruptly. *That's how this world works.* One man brought up another, and the best course of action was to ask, *"So what do you know?"* In Monica's case it was in her best interest to find out more about Henry before she fell deeper in love... if that's what it was.

"I don't know much. Just his name and some of his holdings. The only person I know less about in that family is his father. He retired long before my time."

"His parents live on a ranch in Montana."

"That's so... provincial."

They laughed again. Those were some of the words they both heard when they were thrust into the world of rich people however many years ago.

"He has a sister too," Monica continued after her laughter died down. "Evangeline. I only met her once, but she's..."

"Ah, yes. Evangeline Warren. Now *her* I know." Ethan leaned against the table, hand cupping his face and eyes sparkling as if they were sharing middle school gossip. "I haven't dealt with her directly, mind you, but she comes into the office sometimes. Spends an inordinate amount of time hitting on my receptionist."

Monica drew her lips into her mouth. "Everyone hits on your receptionist. *You* used to hit on your receptionist." That pretty young redhead couldn't catch a break. If Monica were single, alpha, and gay, she would totally hit on that woman every time she went into that office. *Those sound like three words to describe Eva, though.* Monica didn't want to feel too smug about guessing Henry's sister's sexuality based purely on her appearance and mannerisms, but when a woman knew, she knew.

"So what we've deduced about this suitor of yours is that his parents ran away to Montana and that his sister spends half her day trying to pick up chicks. It would be scandalous if everyone in this circle didn't already have a million skeletons in their closet."

Monica poured herself another glass of tea. "He's a bit more than a suitor right now."

Ethan straightened his back. "That so? Was under the impression you're merely dating."

"Like I said. It's a bit more than that." Ice clinked against Monica's glass as she drank.

Seconds passed. Ethan studied the look on Monica's face, and she pretended that she didn't notice him staring. Instead she focused on the sun shining on her skin and reflecting off the crystal they drank from. *More things Ethan helped pay for.*

When Ethan spoke, the frivolity of the previous moments evaporated with the tweets of birds. "Does he treat you well?"

Monica met his gaze across the table. *He really is my older brother now.* That meant she could roll her eyes and pretend there were no grounds for him to say that at all. Now, if he were looking at her like a *friend*, then maybe she would take it a bit more seriously. *I guess he's both.* Now she had to answer.

"He treats me…" She suffered to find a word to say. "Like a princess."

Her balled fist gently tapped the arm of her chair. A princess. That's what he called her. The beautiful, gleaming girl Henry Warren doted on. The girl in the tower. The girl constantly harassed by a dragon.

A princess.

It was as if Ethan picked up on this. "There's nothing wrong with being a princess, as long as he's a worthy prince."

"And what about you? Are you a prince?"

"I believe the technical term is 'pauper douchebag.' I come from the slums, unlike your Mr. Warren."

"Not this New Money vs. Old Money bullshit."

"I'm stating the facts. Men like me don't become princes. You're born one."

Monica picked up the small bottle of wine and poured her ex-boyfriend another glass. "Then what are you?"

"A damn good imposter."

Ethan turned down another glass of wine. Apparently someone was driving later.

"I don't think Henry is posing."

"Does he love you?"

"It's too early for that!" Flustered, Monica folded her napkin on her empty salad plate with a huff. "We've only been seeing each other for… well, not long at all."

"Uh huh. And that's why you're acting like this."

Monica slumped in her seat. "It's too fast, isn't it?"

"I can't tell you that."

"It's true. I met Jackson and two months later I was practically moving in with him." Back then Monica could blame her stupidity on naïveté. Not this time. She was old enough to know better... or so she believed. "I can't help it, though. When I find a man who I think can give me what I need... I go for it."

"There's nothing wrong with that." Ethan finished his drink and turned in his seat. "You're talking to a man who used to pick women off the street to work for and sleep with him."

"Worked out for you."

"It may work out for you too. Live a little."

Monica wished she could. She wished she could run into Henry's arms and trust him with all her heart. Give herself over to him, completely and wholly. It sure felt like they did that sometimes. Then there were times like Wednesday, when Henry took the whole day off and spent the day with her in bed. No kink. No spanking. No orders and no "sirs." Just two people curled up in bed until they felt like eating in front of the TV and then taking a shower. *He washed my hair for me.* Pros of having a boyfriend that much taller than her. For as much as Monica enjoyed serving her Dom, she also enjoyed being spoiled with affection.

"I saw Jackson at The Dark Hour."

Ethan sighed. "I had heard that as well."

Word travels too fast. Especially with men named James involved. "I spent the rest of the night crying." Monica pulled out her phone, hoping to see a text from Henry. Nothing. "Will I ever get over that man?"

"No."

Monica looked up at him.

"Ten years is a long time for a man to get to you. You loved him, Monica. Nobody has ever debated that."

"Just whether or not he loved me."

"Some men are monsters. Some men are saints. All men are complicated."

Where's Henry on that spectrum? "Sometimes it feels too good to be true. That this man happened to find me and decided to dominate me while being the sweetest man in the universe. I feel like I'm falling into a trap again. A trap I can't stop myself from walking into because I'm a sad piece of shit."

"Sounds like you need to be upfront with him about that. If he's as generous as it sounds like he is… he'll understand."

"Will he? You just said that men are complicated."

"Boy howdy are we complicated. One minute we're throwing tantrums because we can't get anyone to sleep with us, and the next we're throwing tantrums because we fell in love with one person and now they're saying we have some ulterior motive. What gives?"

"You're right. I need to tell him how I really feel. I need to figure out what it is I want."

"No. You need to figure out what you *need.*"

The balcony door opened. "This place is a maze," Jasmine said, shuffling back to her seat. "On the way back here some girl taught me how to tie about five knots."

At least the conversation went back to something she could handle. Too much talk about Henry, Jackson, and God knew who else would send Monica over the edge. When she had friends over, she wanted to talk about frivolous things. Especially when she didn't get to see them often.

I'll figure out what I need later. Monica already knew what she needed.

She needed to know that she wasn't making a grievous mistake – again.

Chapter 18

Leaving The Nest

The confines of her chambers usually brought Monica comfort, but that Monday evening she could only think of her loneliness. Not the true kind of loneliness that would leave a man crippled on the floor, but the kind of loneliness that made her wish she could blow Henry's phone up with messages even more than she already had.

He had yet to respond. Of course, it was Monday, and the man was probably working. All Monica knew was that Henry had an office in the city. One office. Unusual for a man of his means and various enterprises. He had shown her a picture of it the last day they were together. It was... exactly what Monica expected after hearing the man had one office.

His Domination

Papers everywhere. Coffee stains on the desk. A permanent impression on one of the chairs from where his secretary sits and takes notes. His sixty-eight-year-old male secretary.

So Henry didn't keep an impeccable office. Neither did Monica most days. She looked at the stacks of papers on her desk and smiled. At least hers was an organized chaos.

The curlers in her hair pulled against her scalp. Not big curlers, but tiny ones, meant to make her hair spiral down like springs. She hadn't curled her hair in so long that she wanted to test it out before styling it for her date with Henry that weekend.

Yes, weekend, because she wanted to see him that badly. So badly that she would leave her Château to the mercy of Judith, who cleared her appointments that weekend in order to fill in for Monica. *I need a reliable back up anyway.* Really, it had been foolish to not think about that. What if she got sick? Had to fly to her family's? Decided to take a real vacation? Henry was a convenient excuse to start training someone to fill in for her on the busy nights. Everyone liked Judith. *She'll be fine.*

To take her mind off any regret she already had, Monica pulled one of her monogrammed papers toward her and took a ballpoint pen out of a drawer.

Before she saw Henry that weekend, there was one thing she had to make very, very clear. And Monica was not used to expressing herself and her needs out loud.

"Dearest Henry," she began, her steady hand moving across the paper. *"I've very much enjoyed our time together…"*

Monica stopped writing. This was going to be harder than she anticipated.

The phone rang.

She jumped, her hand slamming down onto her phone anyway. "Hello?" she greeted, dropping her pen. The phone pressed against her curlers. "This is Monica Graham."

"You really should set a ringtone for me. I hear that's a thing you can do these days."

Monica smiled at the sound of Henry's voice. "Funny you should call right now. I was just writing you a letter."

"As much as I love your beautiful handwriting, I much prefer listening to your lovely voice. Hence why I called."

"Are you busy?"

"I should be asking you that. I'm calling, so I must not be *too* busy."

"I'm not busy. Slow day."

"Yes, Monday. You don't know how much I would have rather driven down to pick you up again instead of talking shop with a bunch of stuffy nobodies. One of my companies is buying out Grand Wires. You know, that dying electronics store."

"I may have heard of it."

"Apparently we need more retail stores to sell smart phones and tablets in. Maybe I'll get you one. Have it set up so the camera is always going and I can peek at you whenever I want."

"Coming from anyone else that would be creepy."

"Pretty sure it's creepy coming from me as well." Henry drank something on the other line. Bourbon? Water? Whatever it was, Monica wished she could pour him another glass. "How is my princess doing in her palace? No dragons, are there?"

Funny he should say that. Monica frowned. "No. No dragons." At least Jackson had yet to send her another threatening letter. "There is something I need to talk to you about."

A pause lingered on the line. "What is it?" Henry's voice was soft for a hard working man at 4pm on a Monday.

"It's about... well, us."

Her conversation with Ethan the day before still bounced around her mind. *"He needs to know what you need from him, Monica. Contrary to popular belief, we men don't like to play mind readers. Just be upfront."*

Henry didn't sound perturbed. "Tell me."

Monica inhaled a deep breath, her resolve better suited for pen and paper than a phone conversation. "After what happened Tuesday night... you know, at The Dark Hour..."

"Uh huh."

"Well, I've been thinking. A lot. Because I'm always thinking about him." Somehow it ashamed her to admit it.

"I understand."

"No you don't."

The silence permeating their line was almost deafening. *Is he angry?* Men didn't like being told they didn't understand something. Monica had a feeling that Henry couldn't even begin to comprehend what Jackson had done to her over the years... it didn't matter how much he tried. There were some things he couldn't...

Cynthia Dane

"I'm sorry," Monica said, both elbows leaning against her desk. "What I meant was…"

"That you're a guarded woman who has been through some… times."

"You could say that."

Henry sighed into his phone, and Monica heard the creak of his chair as he sat at his presumably messy desk. "I hope that I haven't done anything to lose your trust."

"Of course not. You've been an absolute gentleman."

"Minus the part where I spank your ass raw and fuck you against public walls."

Monica smiled. "Who said a gentleman doesn't do that?"

"Nobody. But I'm not deluded into thinking I'll make all your problems go away. What do they call it in those books and movies? The 'healing cock'?"

Neither of them laughed. "You could help me. Maybe not get over him, but move on. Learn to love all those things again. Trust somebody."

Don't put too much pressure on him. Ethan had warned about that as well. "What things, Monica?"

The way he said it… purred her name right into the receiver… sent shivers of ecstatic hope through every neuron in Monica's body. Her own phone shook in her hand, rattling against a curler. "You know what things."

"I'm sure our imaginations are veering in different directions. I can't read your mind. Look out your window and see your prince bumbling on a thin string of rope, and that's me. Either throw me a thicker rope or start heaving me in with your own brute strength. Go on. Either method works for me."

Monica wanted to laugh at the image. "Not here on the phone. Besides, you've already made me waste some of this paper. I'll write you a list of the things I want to do with you."

"Christmas isn't for another few months yet. Santa Claus can only do so much right now."

"I don't want Santa Claus." Monica cleared her throat. "I want you, Henry."

Him, his body, his kindness, his dry wit, and the rough and easy way he made love to her. Even before he spoke again, Monica was already writing something down on her paper to mail to him the next day.

"You want more than me. You want what I do to you, Monica."

"Yes. I want your domination." Her mouth was dry. "Because I'm a sub, Henry. I want to serve you. And I want to know that I can trust you with my life and world."

"Of course. Well, get that list to me. And I look forward to seeing you on Friday."

He said it so easily. So casually. It was moments like those that made Monica wonder if he was that self-assured or not taking her seriously.

"I look forward to it too. I…" The words caught in her throat. "I'm quite fond of you."

"And I'm quite fond of you."

They hung up.

Monica stared at the paper in front of her. Just as she picked up her pen again, there was a knock at the door.

"I'm so sorry, ma'am." It was Sylvia, helping herself into Monica's chambers and office without being invited. *Well, then.* "I really need to talk to you."

Monica flipped her paper over and sat back. "Sure. Have a seat." Poor Sylvia had been begging for an audience for a while now, but their schedules had yet to sync up. The girl looked like she was about to burst if she didn't get out whatever was eating her up inside.

"Sorry, again."

"Anyway?"

Even with the curlers stuck in her hair, and her silk bathrobe covering not much of anything, Monica attempted to look like the boss she was meant to be. Not that she wanted to look *intimidating...* but Sylvia was a girl who responded best to a firmer hand. Or mouth, in Monica's case.

"It's about Mr. Carlisle, ma'am."

"What about him? Did he do something unsavory?" This was it. The day Monica dreaded. The day a patron got himself kicked out.

Yet Sylvia was doing her damndest to contain a smile from blooming on her rosy cheeks. "Mr. Carlisle has asked me to marry him."

If Monica were still holding her pen, she would have dropped it. "Excuse me?"

"Two weeks ago. He took me out on a date and, well, asked me to marry him!" Sylvia slapped her hand down on the table, revealing a monster rock on her finger. How long had she been hiding *that?* And how had Sylvia contained that piece of news from the other girls? "Isn't it amazing? I guess dreams do come true sometimes."

"Yes." Monica forced a smile. "Congratulations. I will have to have a talk to Mr. Carlisle about these turn of events."

Meanwhile, the smile on Sylvia's face disappeared. "I thought it would be okay... look, ma'am, we won't be getting married for at least a few months so you can find a replacement... and it's not like I'm going to stop working..."

"No, no." Monica drummed her fingers against her desk. "I'm happy for you. I simply need to work out the details between you and him." Another forced smile. "Again, congratulations. I'm sure you'll be very happy together."

Giggling, Sylvia hopped out of her seat and waved at Monica before going back to the halls of the Château. Monica remained sitting at her desk, the paper still turned over and her brain exploding with memories of the day Jackson asked her to move in with him. Never to marry him.

Chapter 19

Leaving The Nest

The last time Monica was monetarily spoiled like this she bought a Château and stocked it with BDSM-loving women ready to make that money back.

"How about this one, Miss?" A docile woman in her early 20s knelt in front of Monica's dais and showed her a purple gown covered in sparkling sequins. Made by anyone else and it would look like a tacky prom dress. Styled by M. Francisco, the latest and hottest designer from Italy? It was a gorgeous piece meant for charity dinners or a wild night on the town.

Monica fingered the material and decided it was too scratchy for her skin. "Thank you, though. It's a lovely color. Do you have something like that, but in silk or satin? Cotton voile?"

"Certainly." The girl got up and hustled to the back of the dress shop, where she stopped to confer with a woman older than her on where she might find such garments.

So far Monica only had one purchase, and this was after trying on gowns for about an hour. Her choice of the moment was a deep red Queen Anne dress that cutoff at the knees and had a hem of black Chantilly lace. Bonus: she already had the perfect pair of red and black heels to go with it, as well as the gold jewelry to accent it.

Standing a few feet away was Henry, having decided to stay close but stay out of Monica's way as she found new and exciting ways to spend his money. At first Monica vehemently turned down the opportunity to go shopping with Henry's credit card. Yet the moment they entered the city he brought it up again, insisting that they stop at a boutique or two.

"Why?" Monica had asked, content to pass through the city and go straight to his mansion. "I have plenty of dresses and shoes. My closet is practically overflowing with cocktail and cotton dresses. They're all I wear, Henry. If you ever see me in pants, check my temperature."

"You may have a lot of dresses," he said, pulling out his wallet and thumbing through his myriad of golden credit cards, "but none of them came from me."

Monica liked the red dress because it went with the shawl Henry gave her on their first supposed date. Oh, and because she looked great in a nice red dress. But she couldn't live with only red. And if she only bought red, Henry would give her a hard time about that as well.

"My dear," Henry said, leaning against the wall and flipping through slides on his smart phone. "Come here."

Monica, standing alone on her dais while the girls of the shop looked for things in her petite size, turned to him with bemusement on her face. "Everything all right?"

"They will be the faster you get over here."

With her shoes already off, Monica hopped off the dais and went to him, her eyes darting around the room in case someone was watching. Unless Henry wanted to show her something on his phone screen, who knew what he would ask of her.

"Am I taking too long?"

"I don't care how long you take." He put his phone in his front jacket pocket. "Just as long as we make our dinner reservations at seven. Until then, who cares?"

"As long as you're not bored."

"Around you?" He leaned down and pressed his head against the top of hers. "How could I possibly be bored? Now..." His hand appeared between them, palm up, fingers wiggling in expectation. "Give me your underwear."

"What?"

Henry's voice, as deep as it was expecting, rumbled into Monica's ear. "I told you to give me your underwear. Or are you a bad girl who isn't wearing any?"

A smile tugged at her lips. "I'm wearing a dress. Of course I'm wearing them."

"Excellent. Give them to me."

"Why?"

She looked at him with the expectation that he would tell her exactly what she wanted to hear.

"Because I told you to. Or should I punish you later?"

"No, sir." Monica looked around the room, making sure that none of the staff were back yet. She pressed herself against the dark corner of the gallery and reached beneath her skirt. "You realize that I have to try on dresses here, right?"

"Yup."

Well, that was one way for a man to enjoy himself while his girlfriend shopped with his credit card.

Monica waited for him to shield her before she slipped out of her silk panties and shoved them into his waiting hand. With a smirk the size of the sun on his smug face, Henry stuffed the silk into the same pocket he held his smart phone in. He crossed his arms across his chest and pretended to find the crown molding of the boutique fascinating as one of the shop girls came back with a white dress tossed across her arm.

Even though she wore a slip through her taking off and putting on, Monica was still acutely aware of the lack of clothing between her legs. While she pulled off her current dress and put on the white one, she thought of Henry standing at the entrance, holding her underwear in his pocket as if he owned them. *Today he does.* Ah, now it all made sense.

The way he asked for them.

How insistent he was on buying her clothes that day.

Now, how he gazed at her as she twirled in a white chiffon gown that looked like it could be a wedding dress at a golf club. *What a way to get married.* Monica stopped and laughed, the girl looking at her as if she were loony while Henry held in a laugh of his own.

He does own me. He was dressing her up like the princess he was going to kidnap and have his way with. This meant that while Monica *should* find something she enjoyed wearing, this was more about Henry's tastes than hers. *Find something that knocks his socks off.* She turned down the white gown because it was too frou-frou for her seductive style. *I need to make him hard the moment he gets a look at me.*

"Bring me something black," she told the girl. Before she departed to the back room, Monica took her by the wrist and brought her in close. "Something sexy."

The girl took a look at Henry and then back to Monica again. She nodded, her feet whisking her to that back room again with the white dress in tow. Monica didn't want to look like a fairy princess. She wanted to bedeck herself in a gown fitting a sultry one.

She stood in nothing but her half-slip and bra, her delicate curls resting on her bare skin and falling before her face. At first she didn't mind avoiding the mirror, but then she caught a glimpse of it, and inside the reflection was Henry gazing at her in the hungriest way imaginable.

Chills shook her body. Suddenly Monica was *very* aware of her breasts pushed up in her lacy pink bra, the one she put on that day to entice him when he would undoubtedly start undressing her that evening. She never counted on being taken to a boutique and put on display in front of him. *Nobody batted an eyelash when she stayed behind as I started changing clothes.* Perhaps the staff people here automatically assumed they were a couple. Did they look and act like one? Henry certainly put his protective hands on her more than once.

Ah, Monica had forgotten how exciting it could be... this paraded around business.

Men liked to show off their money. They liked showing off their business conquests. And they definitely liked showing off their women. Especially those alpha Doms with nothing better to do than take over other companies and then carry their subs around.

It sounded so animalistic. So primal. So what Monica needed – and wrote in her missive to Henry two days ago.

She saw him take it out now. A single piece of paper he kept in a different pocket. With pen in hand, he crossed something on the list off. Monica didn't know what it could possibly be.

"Here, Miss!" The girl returned, carrying two different black dresses. She held them up in front of Monica. One was a svelte mermaid that would more than adequately hug her curves. Monica looked it over for a while, fingertips feeling the soft fabric and debating whether or not the restrictive movement would be worth it.

Then her eyes went to the other dress.

A short, flared skirt supported a high-neck and strapless bodice that, when Monica looked closer, sported a keyhole on the chest. She plucked that dress from the girl's arm and held it to her body. "I'll try this one on."

Sure enough, it was perfect.

What set it apart from a regular brunch dress was the keyhole that rested right at the top of Monica's cleavage. Combined with her curls, she had the air of a woman ready for a fancy dinner. Like the one Henry was going to take her to shortly after this.

"Looks like a winner to me." He was behind her, peering over her shoulder but not touching her. "You should get it. And wear it out of here."

That was her cue that they were done shopping.

She did as subtly ordered. The clothes she wore into the store were boxed up with the red dress, and the helper snipped off the tags once Henry's credit card went through. Monica excused herself to the powder room to freshen up her makeup and ensure that it matched her new dress. Once the mascara was gingerly applied and a fresh coat of blush put on, she pulled back her curls into a loose bun that rained upon her shoulders.

When she stepped back into the boutique, the bags were already in Henry's car – and he was staring at her, eyes dancing between her face and the dress on her body.

Restlessness didn't settle in until they stepped outside, Monica without her coat or shawl. For a spring day it was rather cold, the temperature snapping against her arms as she waited for Henry's driver to open her door. The moment Henry put his hand on her back a cold breeze blew by, reminding Monica that an important piece of clothing was currently in her Dom's front jacket pocket. *Holy...* Her eyes widened, and Henry had to push her toward the car to get her to sit.

Dinner reservations had been made with privacy in mind. That's what Monica discovered when they arrived and the host took them into a small back room with low lighting and candles burning brightly in the center of a two-person table. Champagne was readily available, but Henry ordered a vintage wine the moment they were seated.

"Very good," their waiter, a man dressed better than most office workers said. "Would you like to order dinner or at least appetizers, Monsieur?"

French food, huh? Monica smiled over her water glass. She deferred her order to Henry who decided she would like the chef's choice. "No appetizers. The wine will tie us over until the main course."

"And should the meals be served at the same time, monsieur?"

"Absolutely."

"The lady's meal will take about forty-five minutes to prepare."

"That's fine. We'll be extra hungry." Henry winked at the waiter. The man in a tuxedo was off, and the door to their private paradise clicked shut.

Both wineglasses remained empty. Henry sat expectantly across from Monica, candlelight licking his skin and making his eyes glow in the same hunger she saw in the boutique.

Monica crossed her legs. It was the only way to keep her naked thighs from going crazy.

"You know," she began, reaching for the wine bottle and opening it without a second thought. A steady stream poured into Henry's glass. "I love it when a man knows how to order for me."

Now it wasn't just candlelight licking his lips. It was a smile, too. "I know."

Steady. Low. Monica had entered a scene and barely realized it. "Should I pour myself a glass too, sir?"

"Of course. And I expect a different word out of you, Monica."

She steeled herself in her chair. "Of course. Master."

This was it. This was what Monica had been waiting for. *What I wrote in my letter.* Her need to serve *and* submit at the same time. Henry was good at getting her to submit easily enough. But she wanted more. She wanted to serve – to have him become her whole world for a while.

She poured herself some wine and held it up for a toast. Henry matched her. "To new adventures," he said. Their glasses clinked together and he drank, his eyes still boring right into hers.

Bitterness washed down Monica's throat. She did not flinch. "Are you pleased with my dress?" She tugged on the keyhole, revealing more skin for Henry to devour in the candlelight.

Be honest. Monica didn't want platitudes. She wanted compliments, but only if she had earned them. The dress? Henry chose that. Her hair and makeup? That was all her. While Monica liked the way she looked that night, she would be happier knowing that Henry also thought she was gorgeous. From the way he pulled his bottom lip into his mouth and licked it… perhaps she was on the right track.

"I think you tempt me on purpose."

Well, of course. Monica couldn't say that. Her stomach also growled, but Henry had made a point of making sure they weren't disturbed for a long while. *What's his plan?* He wasn't…

Was he?

Monica really, really wished she had her underwear on right now. Especially when this dress was brand new and she was waking up to certain ideas.

"It's not my intention to tempt you, Master."

Henry drank more wine. "Yes it is. You've been tempting me since we first met. Do you know how hard I have to work to keep myself steady around you?" He leaned forward, his dark blond hair almost brown in the low light. "Women like you get off on grabbing a man's cock in public."

Did this count as public? "I'm sorry, sir."

"No you're not. Look at the way you're wearing this dress. You want me to stare at your breasts all night." The last of the wine disappeared past his tongue. Monica picked up the bottle and offered him more. He readily accepted.

"What can I do to please you?"

Henry glanced into his pocket. His phone? Her underwear? *The list.* The damned list of things Monica said she wanted from the Dom who promised to help heal her. *Anything off that list right now would be…* She sucked in her breath, which made her chest more prominent.

As expected, his eyes lingered on her keyhole. "Contain yourself. We're in public."

Tingles forced Monica to cross her legs in the other direction. She looked at the fine tablecloth, mind racing with what Henry could be playing at. Deep down, she knew. *Humiliation.* The thought shouldn't have made her nipples harden in her dress, and yet... "I'm trying, Master."

The best part? She didn't have to be demure. She didn't have to sweeten her voice. She was still the same Monica she had always been. For her, this wasn't acting.

"Try harder, for God's sake." Henry held his wineglass but didn't drink. "If you don't tone it down, I may be forced to deal with you."

Neither of them said anything for a few moments.

"Shit." Henry stood, his chair shooting out behind him and the wineglass nearly spilling on the white tablecloth. "Why do you have to be so bewitching? You're turning me into a sick man, Monica."

She cast her eyes down. "I'm sorry, Master," she whispered.

"Sorry isn't good enough. You clearly don't know your place." Slowly, Henry rounded the table, standing only a few inches from his sub. His hand gently patted her head and fingered her curls. "You need to learn that you can't tempt me twenty-four hours a day. I'm a man with a schedule. I need to be... collected... for the other people around me. Whenever I'm with you..." His hand slipped down her chest, clutching her breast and rolling her nipple through both dress and bra. Monica whimpered. "I want to lose my fucking mind."

Two fingers pushed into the keyhole, wetting themselves in the sweat of her cleavage. Monica regulated her breathing but could not stop the fluttering of her eyelashes as she sat perfectly still.

"I have to constantly ask myself if I'm going to deny my need for you." Henry pulled his hand out and placed it on top of Monica's untouched water glass. "Or am I going to indulge in you? You know what I want to do, of course."

Ice swirled in the glass. Monica watched him pick a sizable cube and pull it out in one motion. "I want the same thing, Master."

"Of course you do."

Cold. Bitter, biting cold stung Monica's cheek as the ice cube began melting against her skin. Her lips parted, some of the water dripping into the maw of her mouth. When Henry drew the ice cube back toward her ear? The lights blurred before her.

"You can't contain yourself."

The ice awakened every part of Monica. Her hips tightened in her dress. Her legs parted. Her hands created hard fists on the table. The only thing keeping her in place was the fact Henry had yet to ask her to do anything.

"No, Master." Her voice was already ragged. The ice cube, now smaller, made its way down her neck and onto the dress. "I'm so sorry. I can't contain myself."

"All you want is sex."

"I want to serve you, Master." The ice cube teased the edge of the keyhole before disappearing into her cleavage.

The ice in her glass rattled again. "You can serve me by knowing when is and when is not an appropriate time to arouse me." Another ice cube disappeared down her cleavage. The melting sensation against her skin made her cold breasts jerk beneath his touch. "Remember when I took your panties earlier?"

Monica nodded.

"There's a reason for that. Stand up and bend over the table."

Oh my God, he was going to do it!

Monica obeyed, head down and curls playing with the ice water spilling from her breasts. Good thing they hadn't been served dinner yet. It gave her an empty space on the table to bend over, legs spread across her chair.

She thought he would thrust into her. Instead, Henry picked up another ice cube.

"Lift your skirt."

The moment Monica presented her ass to him, she received a hard, *hard* spank.

"Ah!" The surprise echoed in the private room. Another spank, and her fingers clutched the edge of the table.

"Do you apologize for tempting me at an inappropriate time?"

"Yes, Master!"

"Do you know your place?"

"Yes!"

He spanked her again, her hips snapping.

Something cold touched her raw skin.

"Oh…" Monica both wished for and against someone coming through that door right now. "Henry…"

The cold numbed her to the pain she received. Slowly, *slowly*, the ice cube traveled down her ass, the water left behind both soothing and a nuisance. It made her legs shake, her arms bend against the table, and the already melted ice in her cleavage spill water onto the table.

"What did you say?"

"I mean…" The cold was on her slit now, pushing toward her opening. "Master."

"I like the way you say that word. Or I would if it didn't make me want to fuck you. Don't you remember what I said?"

"I'm so sorry, Master." Monica tried not to pull away from the cold swirling around her opening, but she couldn't help herself. Henry pushed her torso down with his other hand. "Please go easy on me."

"No, Monica. I want you to beg for the exact opposite. If you're so insistent on seducing me, then I'll make you work extra hard for it."

The ice cube felt like it was tearing her apart as the cold invaded her body and ventured toward her deepest recesses.

Her pitiful whimpers must have placated Henry, for he picked up the last ice cube from her glass and rubbed it against her skin.

"Does it burn?" he asked softly, the large ice cube hovering outside her entrance. "Does the ice hurt?"

"No, Master." It hurt, but in the good way. Her neurons were alive with perpetual pleasure, a feeling unlike anything she had experienced in so long. *I'm going mad.* Keeping perfectly still as the ice spread its chill throughout her body? Not easy! And as that chill turned into her body's natural warmth, she was reminded how wholly human – how wholly woman – she was. Small droplets of water dripped onto her thigh.

Before she knew it, a quick, snapping spank hit her ass.

"How about that? Does that hurt?"

Another spank.

Another.

Three spanks in a row, and Monica was about to come undone. The pain of his touch and the pain of the ice made her wiggle in his grasp. "No, Master!" She gasped the reply, for the biggest ice cube was now melting and threatening to pop out of her body.

After a tiring shudder, it dropped to the floor anyway.

Henry clicked his tongue when he bent down to pick it up. "I knew it. You can't control anything right now. Looks like I have some training to do." The ice cube, warm and tasting of her arousal, pressed against her mouth. "Open."

She took the ice cube into her mouth and pressed her tongue upon it.

"Don't swallow it."

She wasn't going to.

"Sit in the chair."

Monica obeyed, careful to keep the smaller ice cube within her as she eased back into her seat and pressed her hands against hard wood. Her skin was on fire. Freezing. Freezing with fire. She didn't know if she wanted Henry to fuck her or stay like that until the end of dinner.

Good thing she had a Dom to make the decisions for her.

"Over here." Henry yanked on her curls, pulling her head toward his hips.

Sucking his cock at the dinner table with ice in her mouth was easier said than done.

"Oh, fuck." Henry clutched all of the curls he could, pushing her mouth onto him. "That is some serious ice."

Monica nearly gagged upon him entering her mouth, but she persevered. Her tongue pushed the ice against him, rubbing it along his shaft as she grabbed him by the base. He coached her, telling her to take it easy, to go slow before he came too soon, and to remember to breathe. Monica didn't need help with any of that, but she enjoyed the sound of his soothing voice.

Yet the worst part was what happened between her thighs. Her new black dress was wet, and she didn't know if it was from the melting ice inside of her or her own arousal.

She didn't care.

"That's it." The ice was small enough to ride on Monica's tongue up and down his hard shaft. "Good girl."

That simple comment filled her with so much joy that she almost forgot where she was.

"Stop."

Monica halted her movements, easing her mouth off him. She looked up into his stern visage and pressed her face against his waiting palm. *Is it my turn, Master?*

"Up."

She didn't need to be told twice.

"Remember your safe word?"

"Yes."

The next few moments were nothing but a shocking blur. Henry grabbed her by the shoulders and whipped her around, shoving her chest onto the table and lifting her skirt back up over her ass. Her thighs were so wet he had no problem entering her on the first try.

She squealed into the tablecloth, his girth invading her, his hands squeezing her hips, and his strength bringing her back onto his cock before shoving her forward again.

Henry grabbed her curls and yanked.

"How's this, huh?" The pain on her scalp was only rivaled by the pain between her legs. When Henry pulled out, Monica's thighs were wetter than ever, and not just from the melted ice. "Is this what you wanted all along?"

She could only whimper again.

His next forward stroke came with a determined grunt.

There was nothing sophisticated about the way he fucked her. From beginning to end he was crude, taking her like an animal that could no longer control himself. *Because of me.* How dare she? Taunting him like that!

Every thrust hurt, but brought with it more pleasure than the last. Henry yanked on her scalp one minute and pushed her down onto the table the next, his body overshadowing her as he lifted a leg to get better access. "Tell me how much you like it," he growled.

He had both hands on her shoulders now, holding her arms to her sides as he steadily thrust into her, deeper, deeper, *harder.* Monica's lips twisted as she fought to speak. "Thank you, Master!" she cried. "Please give me more!"

An orgasm traveled through her. Moans fell from her lips. She clamped down onto Henry's cock and encouraged him to give her what she really wanted.

Proof that she really was irresistible.

He lost himself within her. Henry pushed down on her so hard that she grimaced, but didn't think twice about accepting his gift into her. *This never gets old.* Every time Henry came inside her she was reminded that he had chosen *her.* Marked *her.* Out of all the women he could easily have, there was something about Monica Graham that made him unable to control himself.

And she reaped the benefits.

"Yes, Master…" she murmured against the wrinkled tablecloth. "Thank you."

He pulled out, hand still steady on her. "That should tie me over for now." Somehow he managed to regain his steadiness as he zipped himself up and straightened out his jacket and tie. Monica stood up, her Dom's seed rushing down her thighs and gathering behind her knee. The more she moved, the more came out. The melted ice did not help. Or was it helping? *Both.*

"No." A firm hand pushed her shoulder so she was forced to sit in her seat, seed still wet on her skin. "Now we eat dinner."

Henry returned to his seat and poured himself another glass of wine. Not even two minutes later the waiter arrived, announcing that their meals had been given priority and that their food would be ready any moment.

Monica stared at her plate of food, no energy within her to eat. Henry ate as usual, wine washing down his meal as he talked about his parents' latest messages from Montana and some idle thing that happened in his office the day before.

Finally, he said, "Eat up. You need your energy for later."

Monica looked up. "Later?"

"Of course." Henry gave her that hungry look again. He pulled out the list and crossed another item off. "We've got a lot to accomplish tonight."

Monica kicked back her glass of wine and ate. Her ass was sore, her chest was wet, and her thighs were so worn out already that she could barely press them together – but had to, if she wanted her new dress to remain unstained before they got back to his place later. Even though she ached on the outside, she ached even more within.

Tonight.

He was going to do even more to her.

Tonight!

Chapter 20

Cut, Take, Free

"Let's see what you brought with you tonight." Henry crossed in front of the bed and flipped open the top of Monica's overnight suitcase. "Oh. I see."

Monica watched him from his bed. She sat on her legs, arms pulled behind her... and with a silk black rope tied all around her torso. Her body ached in more than the pleasures of discomfort. With the rope pressing into her skin and her arms forced behind, she felt like a sweet specimen on display for her master perusing her belongings. Her underwear poked out from his side pocket.

"I packed with you in mind."

She wasn't under any orders to stay silent. Nevertheless, Monica was mindful of her manners when in her Master's quarters. So when Henry lifted the silver and diamond collar from her suitcase, she said nothing, and only flashed him a sheepish smile.

"I have good tastes, don't I?" Henry held it up to the light, the chain falling against his arm and tapping against his hip. "Did I ever tell you that I had this custom made?"

"No, Master."

Henry stepped away from her suitcase with the collar still in his hand. It swayed in the muted light of his room, diamonds twinkling and the end of the leash scraping the carpet. "I did." He stopped in front of the bed. "When I thought of the perfect gift for you, this was what popped into my mind. I had it rushed so I could give it to you as soon as possible. Cost me a pretty penny." He opened the collar and glanced at Monica. "Money well spent."

Go ahead. Put it on. It made her think of the first time they made love in her room at the Château. When Henry strung her up with the collar on... "Thank you."

Yet the collar hovered a few inches away, secure in Henry's hands. "I bought this when I thought I would be your patron, not your actual boyfriend. It was something like a bit of fun. Now that I think about it, I overstepped some lines buying you a leash and collar, didn't I?"

Monica didn't say anything. The ropes dug into her arms.

"Have you ever been collared before? Officially."

She lifted her eyes and looked into his. Blue. Calm. There was serenity in those eyes that Monica rarely saw in men. Even though her brain took her back to that one day Jackson wrapped a marital collar around Monica's neck, she didn't feel scared or pained. Not if she could look into Henry's eyes.

"Yes."

The collar lowered. "Jackson."

"Yes."

Henry sighed. "How long ago?"

Why was he asking this now? "I'm not sure exactly. We had a collaring ceremony when I broke up with…"

"Broke up? With whom?"

There was surprise in his voice. "I used to be in a ménage with him and Ethan Cole. A long time ago."

"I see."

"Does it anger you?"

"Of course not. I never considered it."

"I guess that was about four, maybe five years ago."

"Was it a nice ceremony?"

Monica had to look away again. "Yes." Candles. Wine. A red dress. Ethan had been there as both of their witness. *He gave us his blessing.* He was Jackson's best friend. Of course he had. "I was very happy."

"Was."

Neither of them commented on what that meant.

For the first time that night, Monica spoke completely out of turn. "Have you ever had a collaring ceremony?"

Henry's eyes widened, and yet he didn't look at all surprised that she asked that. "Yes. Also a long time ago."

"With that girl you scared away?"

A brief cloud of sadness overtook his countenance. "Yes."

"What kind of collar was it?"

Henry reached down and traced a line around her throat. It made her shiver. *Touch me more.* If only. "Black. Thin. She was a very understated woman. Liked leather, so I got her a leather collar with flecks of emeralds. She took it with her when she left. I don't know what she did with it. What do subs do with their old collars?"

Well, if they were going to chat, Monica was going to go ahead and fall off her legs. She sprawled them to the side, her arms still bound but her toes wiggling in relief. "I can't speak for all subs… but I know a lot of them leave them behind, or take them with them, or keep them. Sometimes they sell them if they're valuable. It's highly personal. What do women do with their wedding rings from old marriages?"

"I wouldn't know about that either." Henry fingered the outline of the silver and diamond collar before tossing it onto the floor. "Doesn't feel right to use that right now. Maybe sometime again in the future, Princess." He put a hand on her head, smoothing down her curls and caressing her cheek. Monica leaned into his touch. "Are you happy with me?"

With her cheek still pressed against his palm, Monica looked up at him with as much reassurance as she could muster. "Very much so."

"I've done my best to please you. As you know, it's not just subs who want to serve and make another person happy." His strokes lessened. "A good Dom takes his sub's happiness into account above all else. I want you to trust me, Monica. Do you trust me?"

"Yes."

"You barely know me. You've had a rocky past. I don't believe you trust me wholeheartedly quite yet. And that's okay." He kissed her forehead, "I will earn more of your trust. Sit up."

Monica pushed herself back onto her legs, her heart beating furiously in her chest at the thought of what her Dom might do to her. *He's already done so much tonight.* Her ass was still sore from the spankings she received on the restaurant table. And her thighs... the way Henry fucked her... Monica wasn't sure she could take more that night, and yet hearing Henry speak made her crave his intimate touch once again.

He went to a drawer on the other side of the room. The man was still in his suit, but minus the jacket. This was the most casual Monica had ever seen him dressed. His creased trousers were wrinkled in all the right places, and his long-sleeved shirt clung to his body in a way that made her shudder in anticipation. Just his shirt tucked into his belt alone was enough to make her want him. If she could, Monica would have clutched that belt and undone the buckle with her tongue. *Next time.*

Henry pulled something long and gleaming from a drawer. "I need you to sit very still."

When he turned, there was a skinny knife in his hand. Monica involuntarily shot back on her legs.

"Now, now. I'm not going to cut you." He stood in front of her, the knife at his side. "I need you to trust me. I don't want to hurt you. I want to take you to new places. No blood. No skin. Do you trust me?"

Monica nodded. "Yes, Master."

"Good. Now what did I tell you to do?"

"To sit still."

"Can you do that for me?"

"Yes, Master."

The edge of the blade lightly touched the top of Monica's shoulder. She sucked in her breath but did not move. *He won't hurt me.* Thank God Jackson had never done knife play with her. She could only imagine what state of mind she would have been in right now had that been true.

The blade descended to the keyhole in her dress. Monica released her breath as the tip pierced the fabric.

"I really liked this dress on you," Henry mused. "Remind me to get you another one later."

Before Monica could inhale again, the knife cut into her dress and sliced away the fabric covering her breasts.

Henry did it so lightly that she barely felt it. The blade never touched her skin, as he promised, but that was partly in thanks to her perfect posture and stillness. Yet feeling the fabric pull away from her almost felt like having the edge of the blade drawn across her skin.

"My beautiful princess." One hand wrapped around the back of her neck while the other held the knife steady against her dress. "It feels like unwrapping you after the ball. You already served me so well in the restaurant. I keep thinking of how I should repay you after such just punishment." The knife teased her bra, but he didn't cut it. *Because he didn't buy it for me.*

Anything he bought her was fair game. He could always buy her another.

"I will love anything you do, Master."

"That's not true." The knife was back in her dress, slicing it down the center until meeting the top of her navel. "It's not possible for you to like *everything*. Besides, half the fun is discovering what you do like. Did you like the ice earlier? I think you did."

"Yes, sir." It still gave her chills.

"Good. Now, this list you gave me…" The top of the knife pressed against her skin but did not penetrate it. "There are quite a few filthy things on here. I'm not in the mood for a lot of them tonight. Some of them… I'll do my best."

Monica shuddered inside, but held still against the knife.

Henry tossed it onto the floor, far away from the bed and where they would make love. He kissed her, that hand still around her neck, but now the other groping her breasts and freeing them from the front of her bra. His fingers pinched her nipples one at a time, making her groan into his mouth.

The pinching stopped and was replaced with his lips, Henry's tongue tracing large circles around her nipple. Whenever he pulled away to take a breath, Monica's nipple was harder and more pronounced than before.

"You were such a good girl in the restaurant." Henry ran his tongue along her chest, pushing up to her throat and then her chin. His hot breaths burned her ear as he climbed onto the bed and held her close to him, her bound arms struggling to embrace him back. "You did exactly as I told you to do. You always suck my cock without question. You're such a sweet, attentive sub, and you will be rewarded."

Those words were like music dancing in her ears. Even when Henry pulled away and began undoing the ropes around her bodice, Monica remained in a state of adoration, her eyes rolling back and her sighs gentler than the air around them. The ropes dropped to the bed. Henry disappeared around the side and opened his drawer of goodies. Monica was left to stretch her arms and flex her fingers. Who knew how much longer she would have this freedom.

Not much longer.

A small pulley hung from the ceiling. Behind Monica, Henry stood on his bed and looped a stronger rope through it. Monica could lean her head back and rest it against his thighs, but when she tried this, Henry pushed her forward and grabbed both of her arms.

Within seconds she was taken back to their first night together, when her arms were raised above her head and tied to a simple rope. Henry wasn't content with that. He had to pull harder, forcing Monica to get up on her shaky, cramped legs and stand on the bed. Her bare toes wiggled against the soft comforter.

Henry secured her before pushing his hands beneath her skirt and feeling her hips. "Did you enjoy our time in the restaurant?" he murmured into her ear.

"Yes, sir."

"What did you enjoy?"

"What you gave me."

"And what did I give you?"

Monica wasn't shy about these things. For years she was used to talking frankly about sex and her desires – and her Dom's desires. "You gave me you."

"I did. It's easy for men to do that." His hands tightened around her thighs, coming dangerously close to her center. "Women, I find, have a harder time giving themselves like that."

His fingers brushed against her slit. Monica steeled herself, hissing through her teeth.

"You're still wet."

"Not as wet as I was back there."

"I can fix that."

He kissed her neck. Monica rolled away from it, letting Henry explore the white of her throat while his hands felt her intimately, reawakening her body to the idea of lovemaking and all that it entailed. The bed had some give beneath their standing weight, but Monica was the one secured to the ceiling. It was Henry who had to check his balance.

"I want you." His urgent voice lit a fire beneath Monica's skin. When he tore apart the front of her dress with his bare hands, she gasped, her will crumbling.

Alphas were always such thrills. They could be kind and considerate one moment, and ripping apart a girl's damned dress the next. Monica loved both sides equally. Especially if one naturally followed the other.

With her bodice and sleeves ripped, Henry was able to drop the dress to Monica's feet and tell her to step out of it. Once the pile of defiled black fabric was sent to the floor, he unhooked her bra and unsnapped the straps. That soon followed the dress, and Monica was presented to her Dom completely naked.

"As pretty as you are in your ball gowns, Princess, I much prefer you like this." Henry wrapped his arms around her, placing another kiss on her neck and then her shoulder. Feeling his soft clothing against her skin lulled Monica back into comfort. "Let's see what we can do about that." He pointed to her feet, struggling to maintain her balance on the bed.

Henry hopped down and opened a closet by the bed. Monica couldn't see in it from where she stood, but from the way her Dom paid careful attention to what was inside… she could only assume good things were stored in there.

"Spread your legs."

Easy. Monica had to do so in order to maintain balance. Yet she wasn't surprised – but definitely excited – when Henry latched one end of a spreader bar to her right ankle.

Apparently she wasn't spread enough for his liking, even though the bar was adjustable. Henry eased her legs open farther, taking care to make sure they weren't *too* far apart when he latched the left ankle. Strung up, spread, and naked, Monica had never felt so delightfully vulnerable in front of Henry.

Except this wasn't her reward. That came from a sharp, painful hit to her ass.

She yelped, her legs buckling but unable to close. The hit came again, this time harder, and the skin on her ass felt like it was about to cry from the impact.

"Oh my God!" she cried, as the pain morphed into pleasure throughout her body. She anticipated another smack but didn't get one. Instead she saw the end of a black leather crop round her stomach and caress her breast.

"Perfect." Henry was beside her, massaging her injured flesh with a kind hand. "Your body and its responses to what I do to it are perfect. You really are a natural at this, my dear."

Monica managed to crack a smile through the pain. "Did you ever doubt it?"

The crop tapped her breast. "Knowing and seeing it for yourself are two different things. There's nothing that sates me more than seeing a woman who enjoys this sort of thing."

"I assure you that I do."

"I know." Henry nibbled her ear, just the way she liked. "You're the total package. Beautiful, intelligent, savvy… and a lover of painful pleasure." The crop caressed her nipple, threatening to smack it at any moment. "No wonder I'm falling so hard for you."

If Monica weren't trapped in her position, she would melt into the bed, carried away by the sweet words her Dom offered. Most of her was more than happy to hear them. Happy to take them in and turn them into the fodder she needed to feel that holy emotion of love. But another small part of her was afraid. It was easy for men to say that they loved someone. They were so free and yet fickle at the same time. What did they have to lose? Nothing. A man like Henry Warren had nothing to lose. He could say he loved Monica and suffer no repercussions if he changed his mind later.

These thoughts almost dwelled in Monica's head – and then the crop slapped her breast.

It stung for one blinding hot white second, and then the pleasure settled in, spreading from her nipple to the rest of her chest. "Again," she begged, as the crop circled her stomach and patted the top of her mound. ""Please, Henry."

Not sir. Not Master. Monica wanted all those sides of him, but it was Henry she desired the most in that moment. The caring and understanding man who knew how to hit her with a crop.

"Whatever you want, Monica."

A shriek of pleasure took them both by surprise when he smacked her breast once more. Streaks of red appeared on her flesh.

Time slowed, then quickened, then slowed again as Henry circled her body and picked specific places to hit with the crop. Sometimes he struck the soft skin of her ass and breasts. Other times he gave a lighter smack to her stomach, the small of her back, and the top of her shoulders. When he hit the inside of her spread thighs, Monica moaned, her body on fire and ready to douse the flames on her own.

"Can you feel it?" Henry embraced her from behind, his hard cock pressing into her sore ass. "Doing this to you... seeing you respond like this... I want to fuck you until neither of us can breathe anymore."

His hand rubbed the brunt of her mound, her slit, and the tender flesh in between. One thick finger rubbed her clit, sending waves upon waves of pleasure through her. Pure pleasure. No pain. After mediating all of her pain with pleasure, Monica didn't know how to handle just one of those things any longer.

"You may be my sub, Monica." Henry's voice was becoming more ragged the longer this played out. *How long until you can't help yourself?* Like in the restaurant... when his cock ravaged her, the rest of his body thrusting it into her for the pure need of it. Nothing got Monica off more than knowing her Dom wanted her so badly that he turned into a mad man. "But my desire to serve *you* right now outweighs everything else."

"Henry..."

His wet finger lingered on her lips as he sank to his knees and kissed her tender skin. *He's never done this before...* Monica was used to Doms who only doled out that level of pleasure once in a blue moon. Jackson definitely did not taste her often. The only lover who regularly gave her that kind of pleasure was Ethan, but he had always been the most conventional of all her lovers.

Henry's tongue slid along her slit, caressed her clit, and massaged her folds until she was squirming in her binds. When the pleasure abated long enough for her to think again, the first thing Monica thought was *I can't believe he's letting me watch.*

Dark blond hair scraped her thighs as Henry kissed her nether lips. Occasionally his deep blues looked up and met hers, but it wasn't the look of a submissive that Monica was used to seeing from someone in this position. It was that intense, claiming gaze of a man leaving yet another mark on his woman.

Henry Warren wasn't lowering himself beneath Monica. He was reasserting his role in her life – a harbinger of pleasure who wouldn't let her go until he was good and ready.

And he was clearly a man who had plenty of experience in this realm of love, for the way his tongue, his lips, and his breath all came together to pleasure her was like someone who wanted to please. So while he was her Dom and purely in control, Henry still had that romance inside of him. *"Relax and enjoy, Princess."*

Monica closed her eyes and eased into it. Within seconds she was moaning into the open air, her eyes trembling but unable to close. Not with the spreader keeping her thighs far apart and granting Henry all the access he wanted to her innermost places.

He brought her to the brink of orgasm and then pulled away, teasing her thighs with his tongue and the tips of his teeth. Monica shuddered again, her arousal to the point that even she could detect its scent in the air. Henry growled against her, pushed himself up, and touched her with his fingertips.

"Relax," he whispered, one hand stroking her below while the other spread across her back. "Give yourself to me."

Monica knew what he meant. "On your bed?"

"It's fine."

His touch drove her forward again, yanking on the rope above her head and straining against the spreader. With her slit opened to him, Henry had no problem sliding his fingers into her and tempting the inner recesses of her body. *A man with long and thick fingers is either an angel or a demon.* An angel would take her to orgasm – a demon teased her until she cried in frustration.

Henry was a demon.

"No, don't stop," Monica begged whenever Henry pulled his fingers out, wetter than before. Her legs were wet for a second time that night, and it had nothing to do with him or ice. It had everything to do with what her body was capable of. "Please, Henry…"

"What was that?" His fingers hovered near her entrance.

"I'm sorry. Master… please…"

"Not until you give me what I want, Monica."

The only way for that to happen was to completely surrender, allowing Henry to do whatever he wanted, stopping when he wanted, and trusting that he would give her the ultimate pleasure when he was damn well ready. Monica bit her lip and felt him enter her again, this time with a third finger pushing its way in while his thumb rubbed against her clit. The rest of his body surrounded her, the silk and cotton of his clothes comforting Monica as she collapsed into his embrace and let out breathy cries of impending orgasm.

He stopped.

The sound coming from Monica's throat was pure frustration. There was orgasm denial, and then there was this. She was so pent up that she was about to burst right on his hand – especially when he pulled his shirt open and pressed their skin together, his belt coming undone and his zipper dropping. His stiff cock brushed against her back.

And his fingers reappeared inside her.

"Come if you want," Henry said, both of his hands working her until she was likely to scream his name. "Just give me what I want in exchange."

Between his touch, his words, and the heat of the situation, Monica began to orgasm. Yet before it hit her like a meteorite crashing into her body from the heavens, she gave Henry exactly what he wanted: enough wetness to slide his cock into her even at that angle, and enough wetness to mark the comforter beneath her.

"That's it, lovely," he said with a gruff tone. His fingers shook within her, filling her deep and sending her eyes to the back of her head. "All over my bed. Give yourself to me."

It seemed like a fair trade. Him in the restaurant, and her in the bedroom.

Of course, Monica would prefer to have him yet again.

When her orgasm dispersed within her, she opened her eyes to see Henry unlocking the spreader and freeing her legs. He waited until the spreader was off the bed before untying the rope and catching her in his arms.

Henry laid her down, her head touching the nearest pillow. He continued to loom over her, his clothing coming off as Monica prepared to take him one last time.

"Are you ready for me?" He eased her legs open again and hovered between them. Although he did not thrust into her, Henry lowered his lips and kissed her cheek lightly. More kisses meandered down her throat and then back up the other side. "Don't tell me I wore you out already."

Monica wrapped her arms around his shoulders and brought him closer, their lips melding together until she had to answer again. "Never," she mumbled against his mouth. "I always want you again."

"Good." With that, Henry entered her, his lips taking over hers once more.

Although she was not tied up, bound, or otherwise immobilized, Monica still felt the crushing weight of his body on top of her. Muscles moved beneath her grasp as Henry thrust into her, his groans of pleasure echoing between Monica's ear and the pillow. There was no pain, aside from the ache in her thighs. All Monica was aware of in those moments was her body, Henry's, and the bed they made love on.

I feel so liberated. He held her down, and yet it was for a union of their hearts and minds, not just their bodies. Truly, it was impossible for them to achieve this sensation on their own. Monica needed him as much as he needed her. And the way he kissed her, as if he were so famished that she was the only vessel for replenishing his spirit? *I can barely stand it.*

His thrusts became more powerful the more he overtook her. His shadow dominated Monica's world, her nose buried in his scent and her legs locked around his hips. Henry fit so easily into her now. The more they made love, the easier it became for Monica to take him into her body and not have to think about the consequences of giving her heart to a man like him.

"Henry," she whimpered, her nails scratching a trail down his shoulder blades. "I'm…"

Her words were cut off by a moan echoing in the enclave between their bodies. Henry grunted against her – his cock held firm inside her, and nothing, not even the end of the world, could have stopped him from pinning her to his bed and filling her with his seed for the final time that night.

For once he was louder than her. Monica bit back her cries and listened to him release his urges into her, at first eager, and then so determined that the bed creaked and their wet skin created a familiar sound that lulled Monica right into another orgasm.

"Yes!" she cried, her fingers clawing at his back and her next shout trapped in her throat. Long, steady strokes slammed into her as Henry lost his mind and his ability to withhold orgasm. Monica anticipated and welcomed the warmth filling her body until Henry had to stop and slowly pull from her.

They collapsed into each other's arms, their harried breaths only interrupted by a kiss here and a sigh there. As Henry dozed against her neck, his legs and arms entwined with hers, Monica had to admit that she never felt safer. It had nothing to do with the mansion, or the money, or the privacy in such a large home. It had everything to do with the way Henry held her, as if she were the most precious being in the universe. *I'm not a princess. I'm a queen.* Queen of the wolves, and this was the mate helping her protect her life.

Chapter 21

The Princess And The Dragon

"A girl could get used to living like this." Monica rolled over in bed, extending her arm so she touched Henry's wrist.

He got up from where he sat, his clothes mostly on but his tie still dangling around his neck. "Used to living like what?" Henry stood up straight, folding his tie this way, that, and then looping it downward. *Naked or dressed like that, I'll eat him alive.* His navy blue trousers made Monica want to fling back the bed covers and remind him that she was naked.

And sore, but the sweet way Henry took care of her after their long night was almost as good as the sex itself. His tender touches, his kisses to her aching flesh, and the way he massaged her tiny bruises took her to a place of peace that she had yet to experience in such a long time.

"Used to living like a queen."

"Not a princess?"

"I believe you were calling me a queen of wolves before a princess. Which is it?"

He bent down and kissed her cheek. Aftershave already on, he smelled like the million dollars he carried in his pocket at any moment. *I don't really care about the money, but I care about the money.* Money was security. Money meant a certain lifestyle could be maintained. Money meant Henry could do what he did while Monica lay naked in his bed all morning.

"Depends on the day. You're either about to bite someone or beg to be rescued. I follow the patterns."

Monica sighed. "Don't leave me."

"I'll be back by lunch. Until then, there's biscuits and tea in the other room. If you get hungry or need anything else, you're free to call the butler. He'll take care of you."

"Not as good as *you* do."

Henry adjusted his cuffs. "Thank God. I'd have to fire him then." His wink sent ripples of heat through Monica's body. "He shouldn't be going through my stuff like that."

Monica sat up, keeping the comforter around her body – not that she was shy about showing Henry what he had seen many times by now. "Am I your stuff?"

"No. I was thinking of the crops and whips and whatever the hell else I've got hiding around here."

He shrugged into his jacket and gave Monica one more kiss. "I've got video calls to make in my office a few doors down. When I get done, we'll go have lunch in the back gardens. You'll like them."

Biting her lip, Monica rolled onto her stomach and huddled beneath the comforter. "Or I could stay right here."

"Whatever you want, lovely."

Henry patted her through the comforter before departing his quarters. The door closed gently behind him and locked – on the outside. Monica could easily unlock it. They weren't playing any games today. Not yet, anyway.

Monica remained in bed for another fifteen minutes, enjoying the comfort and the sweet sunshine coming through the bedroom window. Even though Henry's bed probably wasn't any better than hers in the Château, it somehow seemed better. Probably because it was his. And smelled like him.

Eventually she had to get up, especially when she remembered there was tea waiting in the other room. Monica pushed herself out of bed and searched for her red silk robe in her overnight bag. Once it was on she fluffed out her hair – now devoid of her curls – and went looking for the goodies.

The tea was Earl Grey, and the biscuits were, well, *English*. Monica poured herself a cup and took a biscuit to the nearest couch. She debated turning on the TV, but instead picked up her cell phone and read a message from Judith saying that everything went smoothly the prior night without her.

She called the first person to come to mind.

"If you're calling me at ten on a Saturday morning, then something must be up." Ethan sounded like he was halfway through his first cup of coffee. "So, what's up?"

Monica brushed biscuit crumbs off her lap. "The best day of my life."

"Congratulations. Dare I ask why?"

"Because…" Monica blushed, even though nobody was there to see her embarrassment. "I think I'm in love."

The silence on the other end made her wonder if Ethan was about to chastise her. "With that Warren fellow?"

"Henry Warren, yes."

"I see."

"Ethan."

"I'm happy for you."

"You sure you aren't jealous?"

"Why would I be jealous? Besides, I'd be a hypocrite if I told you not to go around falling in love all willy-nilly."

"Indeed. Yet I feel like there's a but coming on."

"No buts. Just that… I did some digging on your boyfriend."

"Of course you did."

Whatever Ethan was eating, it probably wasn't as good as these English biscuits. "Don't know what you want me to say. He is beyond *boring*. No wonder I couldn't remember him. Man sequesters himself in offices and signs off on buyouts and sells. Bunch of money simmering in the stock market and property investments."

"You sound disappointed."

"You know me, Monica. I like people who are go-getters and start innovative businesses. Seems your Mr. Warren saves all his innovations for the bedroom, not the boardroom."

"I'm not complaining."

"Again, I'm happy for you." The line crackled. Where was he going? "His whole family is boring, minus some events his father was involved in a long time ago. Oh, and I have it on good authority that Ms. Evangeline Warren has left a string of broken hearts and thighs in her wake. I suggest you don't go falling for her Sapphic charms."

"If your gay receptionist can't fall for them, then I think I'm safe." Eva wasn't her type anyway.

"Regardless, I *am* happy for you. You deserve all the happiness and spankings in the world, my dear."

"Don't get me riled up again. Don't think my current boyfriend would appreciate my ex doing that."

"If he has a problem with me, he can come find me in the boardroom."

"Ah, the pissing contests of the elite."

"Better than drawing blood."

Monica almost told him about the knife from the night before, but thought better of it. Instead she said, "Like how you and Jackson used to fight about nothing all the time?"

"Don't go bringing him up. You need to stop thinking about him."

She frowned for the first time in many hours. "It's not that easy. Even with Henry, I am always thinking about *him*."

"You'll find that it goes away after a while."

"How would you know?"

Ethan sighed. "Because it has to be true."

They hung up a minute later, Monica promising to do her best to stop thinking of Jackson. Besides, she was in Henry's manor. Nothing could touch her here.

She rose from the couch and took her tea to the window overlooking the front courtyard of the mansion. Across the way was the West Wing, where Eva lived – and currently stood on a balcony looking at the same courtyard as Monica.

Their eyes never met. Whatever Eva was looking at was more interesting than looking into the windows of her brother's quarters.

Monica sipped her tea as Eva disappeared into the house.

And as a nondescript car pulled in from the driveway.

The driver remained inside until Eva showed up in the grand entrance. She stood, perched like a disapproving mother watching her teen's walk of shame after a late night of partying. Between the hair, the body-hugging suit, and the stark makeup on her face, she even intimidated Monica.

Nobody intimidated Monica as much as the man stepping out of the parked car.

She dropped her empty teacup onto the carpet.

Her heart stopped in her chest.

Jackson Lyle closed the door, his hat slicing through the air as he approached the front steps to Warren Manor. Eva remained in place, nose turned up in the air.

Monica couldn't hear what they said in greeting to one another. She didn't want to know.

She held herself to the edge of the window, wishing to be seeing things. But Monica knew every angle of Jackson Lyle.

She knew the way he stood, the way he carried himself when he thought he impressed somebody. That was him. Jackson, in his pastel suit and hands in his back pocket.

Eva said something and turned back into the house. Jackson took one step forward before glancing up toward the East Wing.

Monica ducked behind a curtain, but she was too late.

He saw her. The smile spreading across his face like a plague confirmed it.

When he entered the house, Monica did the first thing she thought of. Namely making sure the doors were locked and that nobody would come for her, least of all someone like Jackson.

There was no time to contemplate why he was there. Why *there*. Why the *Warrens*.

Did Henry know about this?

Monica collapsed onto the floor and debated between trust and flight.

Did she trust Henry? Should she run for her life? For her sanity?

All she could do was cry and wish she never got out of that bed.

Cynthia Dane

Part 3

HEALED

Cynthia Dane

Notice Of Payment Due

To Whom It May Concern,

This is a reminder that payment of $200,000, which includes the agreed upon interest rate of 10.78%, is due on the 10th of this month. Failure to make the payment by the end of business day will accrue a late fee of $10,000 per day late.

We thank you for your continued cooperation and wish you well.

Sincerely,

The Offices of Bernard, Grant, and Sullivan
Representing the estate and holdings of Mr. Jackson Lyle

Chapter 22

Goodnight, Innocence

"Today we toast to the engagement of this young and happy couple." Monica raised a glass of champagne in the Receiving Room of the Château, the other guests at the intimate party raising theirs as well. Polite cheers and good wishes echoed in the room, with everyone's attentions turning to Sylvia and her patron – now fiancé – Mr. Carlisle.

Two months ago Sylvia told her employer that Mr. Carlisle had asked her to marry him. With it came the promise that she wouldn't be quitting work anytime soon. Until three weeks ago when Monica was informed that Sylvia would, in fact, be moving in with her new fiancé soon. Like tomorrow soon.

Now I'm down one girl with no time to replace her. Monica would not tell someone as rich and influential as Mr. Carlisle that he could not have his girl, especially when said girl worked as a switch in the BDSM pleasure industry. One thing for her to whip other men while she waited to move in... but what if a man wanted to whip *her?* Not acceptable.

Monica was all smiles, however, as she worked alongside Mr. Carlisle's personal assistant to arrange the move, from the day a crew showed up to carry out Sylvia's personal belongings to this very party wishing them the best life possible.

It was the closest thing to a wedding the Château would ever hold.

"I promise to take good care of her." Mr. Carlisle, with his arm around Sylvia's midsection, kissed her forehead and drank half a glass of champagne. She giggled, looking every other girl right in the eye with the knowledge that she was the first in the house's history to move up in the world. Yvette ignored her; Judith shrugged and drank; Grace was distracted by both her patrons, the Mr. and Mrs. Andrews. Only Chelsea gave the young flapper what she was looking for – a sad demeanor that quickly turned to a smile when her patron Mr. Witherspoon patted her on the shoulder to ask for more champagne.

"Good to see real energy around here, Madam," he said to Monica, once Chelsea made herself scarce. "Although I thought maybe my friend would be here tonight to keep us company."

If only he knew what that sounded like. Monica had to hide her grin behind her glass. "I'm afraid that he couldn't make it tonight."

"Of course. Toronto called."

His Domination

Monica sucked on the inside of her cheek in lieu of making a disapproving face. Her dearest Henry was up in Toronto trying to convince the board of a pet supply chain to sell their company to him. His entire career of buying and selling businesses for a better profit made him a considerable amount of money, but the appeal of it went right over Monica's head. She preferred concentrating on one lifestyle that came with a degree of predictability. She usually knew what to expect at the Château. She knew how to please men looking for a Domme or a sub for the evening. She was a natural hostess with a head for her own numbers.

Monica also didn't have to travel around for business. More than once Henry canceled plans on her because he had to go to Dubai, Sydney, San Francisco… he promised to take her to one of these places one day, but Monica wasn't as interested in that. She was a homebody. Besides, if she were accompanying her Dom on an international trip, then she expected to spend it with *him*. Not sitting in a hotel room waiting for him to get back from his business responsibilities.

No, it was much better to stay in her Château and make sure it ran on a day-to-day basis. If Henry's plans changed… well, they hadn't lately.

Not that Monica was in a huge hurry to see him.

Ever since she woke up that day to see Jackson Lyle waltzing up to the front door, Monica had a bad feeling in the pit of her stomach, and it wasn't the stench of her ex-Dom stinking up the place. She didn't come face to face with him that day two months ago. Nor did any of the Warrens mention his visit. If Henry knew of it, then he never let on to Monica.

There were two possible reasons for that.

First, Jackson's visit had nothing to do with Henry and he was protecting her, assuming she never found out about it. The other? Shit, it meant that Henry had no idea at all. Evangeline was the one who welcomed Jackson at the front door. What was she up to? Did she dislike Monica? Their few interactions didn't lead her to believe anything.

All right, so there's a third option. The one that said Henry not only knew about it, but...

No, Monica didn't want to think about it.

That they were in cahoots together.

That she was being strung along on some gross joke the whole time.

When she thought about it – including now, at Sylvia's going away party – her throat closed up and she could barely breathe. Nobody wanted to think about that, least of all Monica.

So when Sam Witherspoon brought up their mutual friend Henry Warren, Monica could only smile, nod that she knew he was in Toronto, and hope that he would change the subject

"I'm still surprised that you two became such a quick item," Mr. Witherspoon continued, much to Monica's annoyance.

"What do you mean by that?"

The man shrugged. "I see it now, but when I introduced you two I hardly thought that there would be such an attraction. In fact, when I heard about it from a third party and not directly from him, I figured it must be a *baseless* rumor. I see that I was wrong now. But, forgive me, Madam, but I didn't think you were interested in a relationship. I know Henry wasn't."

"Is that so?" This was her first time hearing such a thing.

"His last relationship soured him on dating for a while. Granted, it was years ago, but Henry's always been a deep romantic. When he's not in a relationship? Phew. Loses himself in work. Barely pays attention to what's even going on with the rest of his family. Did you know his father...? Ah, never mind, Madam."

Monica was curious, but wasn't in the mood to speak more on the subject. "Excuse me, Mr. Witherspoon, but I'm afraid that I have some duties to attend to."

He released her from his words, but they remained with her as she went about the small party making sure everyone was refreshed and happy. The only girl without an appointment or client that night was Judith, who sat by herself in the corner. She wasn't being idle, however. She kept in touch with the kitchen on Monica's behalf to ensure the refreshments kept coming.

I made a good choice in picking her as my second-in-command. Monica no longer worried about leaving the Château in her hands. Even when Monica was there, Judith often oversaw some of the day to day operations. One of the cooks referred to as "The Other Madam."

These days Monica spent more time thinking about her future. What if she moved on from the Château? She couldn't leave the girls hanging with no job and no one to take care of them. The more Monica considered these things, the more she thought about talking to Judith about more serious matters than, "Do you have any appointments tonight? By the way, I'll be out next weekend."

"Congratulations once again on your happy union," she said to Sylvia and Mr. Carlisle. She gave them both fresh glasses of champagne. After tonight, Sylvia no longer lived or worked at the Château. Her room was empty, save for the furniture, and her role had gone from potential serving woman to honored guest.

"Thank you so much for everything you've done!" Sylvia slammed into Monica, knocking her off her feet but keeping her locked tight in a firm embrace. "This happiness wouldn't be possible without you."

"You're quite welcome." Monica managed to foist her off and back into Mr. Carlisle's care. *She's yours to deal with now.* Monica had no hard feelings, but there was an empty room no longer making money in her Château... now if it were *Yvette* leaving...

All parties come to an end, even if someone like Sylvia attempted to keep things going with more drinks and more pleas for people to stay. *There will be plenty of time for you to go to parties like this in the future.* On her wedding day she had many things to look forward to: like being the center of attention as Page 6's luckiest woman in the world. Just think! An eligible bachelor like Mr. Carlisle picking a woman like *her* of her all people. It was the stuff dreams were made of. Even if girls came in there never thinking they would marry a patron, the idea that they could was a tempting one indeed.

Final jokes of "I'm making an honest woman out of her," and "Sure, you think she's fun now, but wait until she becomes your wife!" made the rounds as the happy couple received their final farewells in the front hallway. Once Mr. Carlisle and his blushing fiancée Sylvia stepped toward his car, Monica took her leave and began delegating cleanup tasks to the staff.

"Didn't even have time to read the paper this morning." She picked up a copy in the dining room as she ate an after-party snack of fruit and buttered bread. Her head ached from everything going on. Or maybe it was the uncertainty plaguing her ever since she saw Jackson at the Warren estate.

"Anything good in the paper?" Judith sat next to Monica.

"I didn't see any disasters."

"I don't know what you're talking about." Monica turned the paper over and pretended she wasn't interested in the obituaries. *It's not morbid, I swear.*

Judith didn't say anything as they passed the bowl of fruit back and forth. She didn't say anything, at least, until a smile cracked on her face. "Going to be weird without that pup around here anymore. Who will wear the pearls now?"

Monica sighed. "I don't want to think about it. I'm going to have to replace her soon, and I'm already swamped as it is." She glanced at Judith. "Maybe I should poach at The Dark Hour again. Seemed to work for me last time."

"I still have some contacts there. I could ask around to see if anyone is interested in working here."

"Would you? That would help out a lot."

"Sure." Judith pulled her bag closer and removed a small folder from its depths. It slapped onto the table between her and Monica. "Why don't you get started with these?"

Laughter, as forced as it was, shot from Monica's throat.

"You've got too much time on your hands. I need to put you to work more often."

"Yes, you do." Judith patted the folder. "Let's start by making me choose who I think is the best candidate in here. Some real whippers and floor-crawlers in here."

That night Monica learned to let go of more of her work. What she couldn't let go of, however, was the anxiety in her chest.

Chapter 23

Unpaid Debts

Nothing should make Monica happier than seeing her phone light up every time Henry called. However, these days it was more like that sinking sense of dread.

"Good evening," she said, attempting to summon those good feelings from before. Yet every time she heard Henry's voice, she now thought of Jackson. That was not an association she needed.

"How is my beautiful princess doing?" Henry sounded tired, although he did his best to mask it in the depths of his voice. "Keeping her fort happy, I'm assuming."

"Don't I always?"

He jumped right into the topic at hand. "I have great news.

I'm finally back in town for a while. You'll be pleased to know that we got the company in Toronto."

"Congratulations." Business mergers were always a big deal, although Monica barely understood what went into them. Schmoozing. Promises. A shitton of money. Henry could do all of those with ease. *How much of his own money does he put in?* Not enough to feel it.

"So you know what that means, of course."

"Of course. You want to see me."

"Well, don't you want to see me?"

He almost sounded unsure, as if he had misinterpreted Monica this entire time. *He's thinking of that other woman he lost.* The one Sam Witherspoon said nearly broke his heart. Monica could almost relate.

"Naturally, I want to see you. I wish you were here right now." Monica was in her chambers, sprawled out across her bed and staring at the dark ceiling. Not an uncommon place to find her after a busy night. *I wish he were here...* Lying with her. Stroking her forehead. Whispering into her ear that she could have whatever she wanted. *I want the truth.*

The way her chest constricted at that thought told her that she wouldn't be able to move on until she knew for sure what game Henry played at.

Before Henry flirted with her, Monica said, "There's something we need to talk about."

She hoped her voice was stern enough that Henry did not mistake her mood. From the way he cleared his throat, she had a feeling he had no idea what this was about. "What is it? Have I offended you… again?"

What did he mean by *again?* Was he still hung up on the faux pas he made sending her that collar and leash a long time ago? "No, but there's something I need to ask you. In person."

"I'll come there, then. This sounds rather serious."

"Don't come now. Give me a couple of days to put my thoughts together."

"What have I done?"

Men! How typical. "You haven't done anything. I only want to clarify something."

"All right."

They made a date for that upcoming Wednesday, but Monica didn't consider it a date. Not with such a weight pushing down on her shoulders. Until Henry clarified why Jackson Lyle was at his house – assuming he knew about it – then Monica wouldn't be able to touch Henry Warren again.

The thought chilled her. Only a few weeks into a new relationship, and this was already happening? She didn't know if she could handle having her heart broken again so quickly.

On Wednesday, Monica awoke with a clear frame of mind. This was not a date. This was not romance. Even if Henry made her so happy with his words that she could barely speak, she still would not let him come into her innermost chambers. Namely, her bedroom.

Monica had to be like this. Life with Jackson taught her that she had to set hard boundaries and honor them. Not just get other people to honor them, but to honor them herself. *If I can't honor my own boundaries, then how can I expect others to?*

So even though she dressed up for Henry, it was not in a way to entice him. She left her lingerie, silk robes, and come-hither dresses in her closet. Instead she pulled out the nice outfits she wore for her CPAs and the occasional visit from the police. While the deep crimson dress accentuated her hips and bust, it was conservative, coming up to her neck and meeting both her wrists. It wrapped around her knees and did not draw attention to the black flats she wore on her feet. She wore no makeup. Nor did she wear any jewelry outside of a simple gold chain and a pair of studs in her ears.

Her hair was washed and brushed, but not curled. It fell past her ears and brushed her shoulders, but was not anything more special than she would wear on a trip to the grocery store. By all accounts, she was the most nondescript she had been.

Likewise, the staff was told to not treat Henry as anything more than a special guest. Not "the boss's boyfriend" special, but "someone who is supposed to be here" special. She was awaiting him, but not in a way that demanded her immediate attention. *I have to believe it's like when we first met.* When Henry was nothing more than a fantasy. Monica knew how much his touch could hurt – and please her. She knew what it was like to be safely wrapped in his arms and gaze into his blue eyes. The man was Kryptonite to her heart. The more Monica realized she loved him, the more important it became that she put up the barriers – until she got some answers.

She watched him get out of his Rolls-Royce and approach the Château. The first time they had seen each other in a while. All Monica could feel was dread.

How sad that their relationship reached this point. She was so ready to love and be loved again. Now all she could hope for was Henry giving her a good explanation. Yet she couldn't believe such a thing was possible. Not if Jackson Lyle was involved.

"The madam will see you in her office," the doorman said. A maid took Henry's coat and showed him up the grand staircase. Monica disappeared into her office, where she nervously looked over some papers until Henry arrived.

"Monica," he greeted, although it was more a plea. "I…"

"Have a seat." She motioned to the chair in front of her desk. The same chair he sat in when he declared they were two sides of the same coin. *Don't think I can't remember.* Oh, she remembered. She remembered how her body tingled and her heart raced to feel the mark of a Dom on her, let alone one she was so attracted to. *Henry, I…* she could play that game too.

Henry took his seat, tentatively, his body lowering into the leather while his concerned eyes never left Monica's face. He did not speak. If the man had a tail, it would be tucked between his legs.

"Thank you for taking the time to drive all the way out here and meet me." Monica took off her glasses and pushed her paperwork aside. "As I said on the phone, there is something we have to discuss."

"What in the world is going *on?*" Henry clutched the arms of the chair as if they held the answers they both sought. "Monica, this isn't like you. When I called you the other night, I could've sworn you would be all over me like I was you. Instead you do this? I feel like I'm in the headmaster's office. Clearly, I have done something. I'm not even sure what to expect. That you're pregnant? I feel like if it were that… this would be a very different scenario."

Monica had to refrain from laughing. No, if she were pregnant, she would be throwing herself into his arms and sobbing like a woman who didn't know whether to be happy or scared. *I feel like that anyway.*

"Please forgive me, Henry," she said.

"Oh, God. You're breaking up with me."

Again, she had to spare herself from laughing. No, she wasn't breaking up with him… yet. *Although if I have to, I will.* She made a promise to herself long ago.

"There's something I have to ask you, Henry." Monica folded her hands on the desk, as if she were about to ask a girl if she were stealing. "I don't want to ask you this, but I have to."

"All right…"

The tension between them was unlike anything before. It wasn't sexual. It was barely professional. All Monica could think about was how much she wanted to throw herself at Henry and reassure him that she still cared, that she still wanted to fall in love with him over and over again. *How often does a girl get to feel that way?* Not often enough.

"When I was at your home a couple of months ago," she began, wondering if she should be more specific since she had been to Henry's home a couple more times since, "you left me alone to do a video call in your office. Do you remember that?"

Henry searched his brain for the reference, then nodded. "I don't know what that has anything to do with…"

"No, let me finish." Monica leaned forward, her elbows scraping against the desk. "When I looked out the window while you were gone, I saw your sister…"

"My sister what?" The look flashing on Henry's face suggested that he expected anything other than what Monica said next.

"Jackson… came to your home, and she invited him in."

There. It was out. The look on Henry's face was one of both shock and disbelief.

"Jackson Lyle came to my house… and Evangeline invited him in…"

"Not only invited him in. He looked quite comfortable there." Monica cleared her throat. "You can imagine how I felt about *that*."

Henry shifted in his seat. Monica did not like how he did not immediately refute anything. Yet his shock was still palpable… was it because she knew? Or that he was genuinely surprised at his presence?

"Please explain, Mr. Warren."

She gave him her best serious look, the one she unleashed on people who wasted her time. Too many people were aware of this look. *I never wanted Henry to know it.*

"I can, in fact, explain." He was serious too. Hands folded in lap. Jaw set. Demeanor almost princely. That was the kind of look Monica could fall for... in the bedroom. In this environment? She only wanted answers. "I'm not sure you'll like the answer, however."

"Fucking hell, Henry!" Monica stood, hands slapping upon her desk. Henry did not flinch. "Tell me what the hell is going on! I do *not* like being left out of the loop when shit like this happens. What are you hiding from me? It's true, isn't it? That you and Jackson are in on some joke together!"

"Monica!" He stood too, his stature overwhelming hers even with the desk between them. *What I would give to succumb to him right now.* To feel his arms wrapped protectively around her... "Don't you dare accuse me of something like that. What kind of man do you take me for?"

"I don't know, Henry. What kind of man *are* you?"

He sank back into the chair, almost defeated. "A man in debt."

"What?"

They reached an impasse, in which Henry slid down in the chair and rubbed his face... the truth was out, whatever the truth was. Monica could only look on in trepidation. Her heart neither fluttered nor stalled. Whatever was happening... she wasn't sure she was prepared for it.

"My father." Henry snorted into the back of his hand before shaking his head. "It's my father who is in debt, actually. Not me. Many years ago... God, you'll hardly believe this, but my father owes Jackson Lyle a half a billion dollars."

His Domination

The room was silent. Monica sucked in her breath and tried to remember such a deal being made during her tenure as Jackson's sub. *He lends people money, that's for sure.* It was one of the ways he made his billions. When he wasn't investing, he was loaning. Exurbanite sums. Outrageous interest rates. Jackson was the money-grubbing Scrooge who put on a smile every time he got someone to sign the dotted line.

She didn't remember any Gerald Warren coming through the door. It must have been before Monica's time. Since so many people owed Jackson money, she never bothered to keep track of them.

"I don't believe it. How?" The Warrens were filthy rich. Why would they need money?

"It's complicated. Isn't it always?" Finally, Henry sat up, but he lacked the confidence from the time he walked into the room. "I'd say it was about... fifteen years ago? Maybe thirteen. Either way, my father pissed away most of his wealth with some seriously bad investments. Technology."

"I see." Lots of rich investors lost serious money during the Dot Com bust. Jackson made a ton of it.

"I had already started making my fortunes, so it didn't affect me. However, my father was stubborn and insisted on keeping up the same lifestyle as before. So he borrowed money. Like an idiot. I told you. They're always boring stories in my family."

"That's *hardly* boring to me!"

"I'm sorry, Monica. I should have told you."

"You damn well should have."

"But I didn't want to…"

"Didn't want to what? Scare me off? Fuck that, Henry, I thought you were pranking me!"

"Pranking you?"

"Oh God, forget I said that."

"Look, Monica." He put his hand on the desk, toward her, but did not move to take her hand or limb. "I'm sorry. I hardly ever see that man. I don't know what my sister is doing with him. Maybe she's speaking on my father's behalf. I know they're *not* in a relationship."

"I'm confused, not stupid, Henry."

"He should have not been there while you were. Ever. The conflict of interest right now is… a bit much."

"I'll say. You remember what happened at The Dark Hour."

"Not only that, but I know what he's done to you. I don't like that man any more than you do. I don't respect him, not even in a business sense. He's legal, but shady. I'm not cutthroat like he is. I can afford to take my time with dealings. He's like a kid in high school, fucking with people's money and feelings."

"That sounds about right."

"I'm so sorry I made you feel unsafe at any time, Monica. I don't mean to keep things from you. How was I supposed to tell you? I hoped that it would never matter. I'm not a keeper of my father's wealth and debts. All I expect to get from him when he dies is some property, like the house and maybe the ranch in Montana. Oh, you know, that's why he's out west.

Jackson doesn't bother him out there. Only the lawyers. Ha, my father thinks if he 'retires' out west then he never has to face his responsibilities."

"I still wish you had told me. You don't – you *can't* – understand how that man has affected my life. If your father owes him a ton of money, then I need to know... and your sister needs to know that if I'm there, he can't be there either."

"So you intend to go back there?"

"Now that I know you're not being cruel to me, I may just yet. Not right now. This whole thing has dredged up a ton of bad feelings, and I intend on wading through them before I commit to you again."

"Ah, Monica, I'm so sorry."

"Besides..." She opened her drawer, fingers touching the top of a dangerous letter. "There's something I haven't told you either."

"Oh?"

Time came to a slow as Monica pulled out the latest letter from Jackson. She received it a week ago, after a lull in which she received nothing. Blissfully. *Now they're back.*

The letter landed in front of Henry. He snatched it off the desk, and Monica turned away. She wouldn't look at his face while he read the filthy words sent to her by a terrible man they both despised.

She could remember what it said.

My dear pet,

It seems so long since I saw your gorgeous face in that man's window. I was surprised to see it there that day. I didn't think you would be there... not that day. And yet there you were, your angelic complexion looking upon me as it once did not so long ago. Do you remember? You used to look at me as if I were your god. I miss those glorious days. I've long come to realize how much I needed you as my priestess tending to my altar.

Isn't it about time you came home? You've been having quite the sabbatical. Over a year since we last made love. Ah, do you remember it? That final night we were together? I never saw a woman covered in so many beautiful welts. Every time you cried out in pain, begging me to stop, I thought we reached a new level of paradise.

Then you left me, you ungrateful bitch.

I thought you had run off to be with Ethan Cole and his frigid whore. Not so. You struck off on your own, my pet! I could be content with that. Love you from afar, knowing that you were in your tower, secluded from other men's eyes. And then Henry Warren, that arrogant son of a bitch... not only did you let him touch you, but I bet you've fucked him quite a bit. My soiled pet. Who else would want you but me and that man? Nobody. You are worthless to everyone but me.

Come back. Let's put this behind us.

The letter crumpled in Henry's hand and found its new home in the wastebasket.

"How long has he been sending you this shit?"

Monica had never heard that edge in Henry's voice before. It wasn't erotic. It was genuine anger, the kind that broadcasted that everyone should get the hell out of the way. Was this a voice he used often? *I wonder what he's like at work.* She had always imagined charming Henry getting his way. Perhaps it was something else.

"A few weeks now. They started after we saw each other."

"He's trying to get to you, Monica. Don't believe any of it."

"I don't."

Henry shook his head. "You're still bothered by it."

"How could I not be? The man is a monster and won't leave me alone."

"I would suggest a restraining order, but…"

"You know that's impossible." If she couldn't even get him for his abuses, then the idea of a restraining order was laughable. "Really, Henry, I'm not afraid of him. He's purely mental at this point. I don't worry about him trying to touch or kidnap me. What he did is too public, even if no one will punish him for it. No.. I'm more worried about this business of your father and him. Is it possible for you to…" She couldn't believe she was about to ask it.

"It's too much money for me to pay off on my own," Henry said softly. "I've been trying for years. I pay some extra here and there in an effort to get my father ahead, but Jackson Lyle is shifty with the interest rates. Even with my sister's help, it's still too little. We've discussed it plenty over the years."

"I'm sure you have."

Henry stood, hands in his pockets and body turning from Monica. "This is not a pleasant predicament for any of us. Just… let me extend my sincerest apologies for having kept this from you. I should have been upfront from the beginning."

"Yes, you should have."

"Now I know why you've been so standoffish lately. I don't blame you."

"You're not angry?"

"No. Nor am I under any disillusion that I'm welcomed into your bed tonight."

"Maybe some other time."

Before Henry stepped out of her office, he turned and said, "I'm not that man. I want to make you happy, not hurt you."

A lump went down Monica's throat. *Don't break in front of him.* Now was not the time. "Thank you, Henry. I know that. I just need some time."

Time. She always needed time. Like how she needed Henry's touch to reignite her spark for life once more.

Now was not the time.

Chapter 24

The Princess Submits

The time finally came a week later, after Monica had more time to sort out her feelings.

Gerald Warren owed Jackson Lyle half a billion dollars. This happened long before Monica even met Jackson. *Long* before she met Henry. But Henry had known when they met that such a relationship existed. He continued to hold that information from her even after he learned the extent of Jackson's cruelties. Every time Monica reached this conclusion, she shook her head and had to distract herself with work.

Work was always the greatest distraction. It was the perfect mix of her ideals and an escape from reality. She could live vicariously through her girls, who were a fun fusion of bratty women looking for punishment, harsh mistresses with firm hands and firmer words, and sweet subs who reminded Monica of herself. *Wanting to please through submitting and serving. Wanting to receive pleasure from the hands of their Doms.*

The difference was that, even though the girls certainly had their preferences for which roles they played, they could do all three depending on the client of the night. Judith liked to dominate, but would purr like a submissive kitten for the right price. Chelsea wanted to pout and push her Dom to the edge until he shut her up and bound her hands behind her back. Grace wanted to kneel at the feet of anyone who came through the door, but was as likely to stick a heel in a patron's back if that's what he asked for. And Yvette... what did she like anyway? That girl was still a mystery.

Plus, Sylvia still needed replacing. Monica had gone through the stack of candidates from The Dark Hour that Judith provided, but nobody stuck out as of yet. She needed a versatile girl who could fill all three roles. Someone at least intriguing to look at, if not beautiful. Someone with experience in the lifestyle but no real desire to pursue it for herself. Sylvia was going out into the world to be Mr. Carlisle's full-time sub, probably. Monica was only a tad jealous.

Except why was she jealous? She had Henry, didn't she?

Of course. Every time she thought about him pulling her into his arms and taking her for his pleasure, she died. Died in her heart, in her mind, and in the pit of her stomach. *I want him so badly.* The few tastes she had were not enough. His gentle side, his firm side... when was the last time she met a man who understood both of her needs so well? Her need to submit and to be treated as a human being at the same time?

Men were usually only capable of doing one or the other. One was too painful. The other was too boring.

Being single was better than boring.

Henry wasn't boring. He was... problematic.

What else hadn't he told her? Monica wondered this as she watched Grace be led out of the Receiving Room with a leash around her neck. Mrs. Andrews was way, way too comfortable in her new role as Mistress. Monica would laugh, but...

"Whatever is bothering you, let it go."

Monica looked up from her leather chair. Judith took a seat in the one next to her. They were now the only ones in the room, meaning they could converse freely. "I don't know what you're talking about."

"You think I got as far as I have without being able to read people? You make it damn difficult, but I can tell when you're thinking poorly about something. What happened? Your boyfriend hasn't been around lately. What did he do?"

Monica snorted. Was it that obvious? "He betrayed my trust a little bit. I'm still trying to decide how quickly I want to forgive him."

"Men will always find ways to betray your trust. Usually by withholding something from you, right?"

"I suppose." Monica already had a bleak outlook of the world. She didn't need more reasons to distrust every man who showed interest in her. "He thought he was protecting me from something. Nothing of his own fault. Family matters."

"Then what's the problem?"

"I guess I only wonder what else he's hiding."

"Have you talked to him?"

"Yes."

"And?"

Monica was not prepared for this fifth degree. "He understands why I am not happy."

"What will it take to make you happy again?"

That was a good question. *To submit to him, without fear of betrayal.* A woman could only put her heart into a man's hands so many times before she had to run because he crushed it. "I needed some space."

"The poor man is probably being tortured."

"Hm, you think so?"

"His balls are so blue he's on the verge of popping a nut at a business meeting right now. I mean, I'm guessing."

Finally, Monica laughed, the image filling her head with the naughtiest thoughts.

Judith had to go get ready for an appointment, leaving Monica to her thoughts and admonitions to herself. *I want him. So why aren't I with him?* Perhaps the time had finally come.

Henry returned on Tuesday, a day he had to completely rearrange to fit Monica's whims. From gauging the desperation in his voice, however, he would have moved his appointments to the moon if Monica asked.

Although he didn't know it, Monica had no intention of asking him anything that night.

His Domination

Tonight is the night he sees my true self. She closed the curtains in her room and lit candles everywhere – on the dresser, on the end tables, on the shelves lining her walls. She poured wine. One glass, for him... although she sneaked one to calm her nerves. Suddenly she was back to their first night together, when anticipation nearly sent her to her grave.

Monica was hardly dressed to go downstairs, but dinner had been set for Henry to join – alone. A maid came to her chambers to inform her that Mr. Warren was currently dining with Judith to keep him company. *Judith?* Monica hadn't condoned that. Nor did she really hate the thought.

Knowing Judith, she didn't mean anything wicked. She was more likely sousing Henry Warren out in an attempt to get a feel for what kind of man he was. Well, she could do that. And Monica would get back to her plans for the night.

Henry was in her Château. He had no idea what awaited him, but he was downstairs, eating and drinking what Monica had arranged to be served. Meanwhile, she was turning her bedroom into a domain of pleasure, and the last thing to fix up was herself.

Her hair had tender curls caressing her skin. Her body was devoid of undergarments, only covered with a red negligee and a rose-red sheer satin robe that flowed behind her as she walked. She kept her feet bare, but her toenails painted to match her outfit. She wore no jewelry besides the studs already in her ears.

While she waited, she started a small fire in the fireplace she did not often use. Especially at this time of year. Yet it fit the

Cynthia Dane

mood of the room, and all Monica cared about was creating the perfect mood for when Henry finally walked through those doors.

He sent her a text message. *"This is nice and all, but where are you? This girl won't shut up, as sweet as she seems."*

Monica stared at the message until she thought of something appropriate to reply with. *"I am waiting for you, Mr. Warren."*

She turned her phone off after that, an excited smile splitting her face in two. No, no. She needed to get her emotions under control. Wouldn't do her well to face Henry with the giddiness on the verge of making her explode.

The maid returned fifteen minutes later to announce that Henry was finished with dinner and making his way upstairs – Judith in tow. Monica could hear their voices down the hallway. "Be sure she shows him in. Then escort Miss Judith elsewhere. Mr. Warren and I are not to be disturbed for the remainder of the night."

"Yes, ma'am." The maid bowed her head and showed herself out. Within moments, Judith's voice rang through the chambers.

"Do take care, Mr. Warren," she said sweetly. "I believe your lady waits."

"Pleasure talking to you... what was it, again?"

"Judith. Don't mind remembering me. I'm nobody here."

She didn't say it with malice, but with a tinge of playfulness that told Monica she knew what she was about. *Playing matchmaker, are we?* That was usually Monica's job. Hearing her girl say that made her realize that Judith wasn't really a *girl* after all. If anyone were to leave the Château and go her own way, it would be...

Henry knocked on the door to Monica's bedroom.

She took a deep breath. Not because she was afraid, but because she needed to change the space her head occupied.

On the surface, this looked like it was all about Henry. In reality? It was as much about her as well.

Monica opened the door, head pointed to the floor and her knees begging to touch the carpet beneath her feet. "Pleased to see you," she said softly.

"Monica..."

She glanced up. Regardless of how Henry felt before, he was now surely surprised to see his frail princess nearly prostrating herself in front of him.

"Please, come in." She backed away from the door. "Everything is ready for you, Master."

Henry's eyebrows traveled halfway up his forehead. *Was he expecting a different night?* Intimate chatter? Cuddling and snuggling or whatever? Sure, Monica liked those things, but tonight she wanted to rekindle their romance with *exactly* what she had to offer.

No more promises. No more "let me serve you tonight, Princess, and you can do it next time." This was next time. If Monica was going to declare how much she trusted Henry, she would do so in her own way. In a way that so few men ever got to see.

Henry seemed to sense these same thoughts. Although he took a step back in the entryway, he did not protest what Monica did or said. Instead he cleared his throat and stood up straight. "Thank you."

She led him to a chair by the fireplace, which crackled with ambiance but didn't burn too hot. Henry sat down, and instantly Monica's hands brought him the glass of wine before going to his shoulders.

"Tell me about your day, Master."

Henry took a sip of the wine before he allowed himself to relax in the chair and beneath Monica's touch. *Never told him that I'm a certified masseuse.* It had been her idea in the early days of her relationship with Jackson... to better serve him, of course. Those were in the Halcyon days in which he was a model Dom. Kind, but firm. Understanding, but demanding. *Whatever happened?* No, she wouldn't think about him right now. "Well, today has been fine. I took today off to come see you."

"Your recent trip to Miami?"

"Hot. It's hot in Miami."

Monica pushed her hands down his chest and covertly undid one of the buttons to his shirt. *I want to touch you, Henry.* Immersing herself in his aftershave wasn't enough. Monica wanted to kiss his throat, to massage his aching muscles, and to bring him the greatest form of relaxation a man could enjoy. Her lips curled in her mouth in anticipation.

"Surely there's more going on. You're tense. If today was so fine, then you're carrying worries from another day."

"How astute." As he drank more wine, Henry gradually opened up about his recent business endeavors. Boring, to be sure, but the emotions he felt were anything but. Frustration. Anger. Indifference. A man at Henry's level ran through all those emotions on a daily basis – and he had to be quiet about them. *That's what I was afraid of.* Men like Henry tended to push all their negative emotions deep down. They had to, in order to be as successful as they were. That's why Monica understood how important it was to calm him down, even if he didn't feel that way right now.

"How unfortunate, sir," she whispered into his ear. "Well, you can relax tonight. Forget everything as I take care of you."

"I *had* forgotten everything until you brought it up again…"

"I'm sorry, Master. I worry about you. That's all." As Henry tensed beneath her touch, she added, "I want you to feel comfortable enough to tell me what's on your mind."

"Well, there is something I want to tell you… but not right now."

"Oh?"

"It's nothing terrible. Let's enjoy the moment now."

"Am I making you happy, Master?"

"Very much so."

Those sorts of words brought felicity to Monica's heart. "I'm glad."

He caught her hand on its next trek down his chest. "I'd be happier if you sat in my lap."

"Whatever you desire." The thought made Monica smile.

His arms wrapped tightly around her as she walked before the chair and sank gently into Henry's lap. Her legs drew up over his, and her torso, barely clad as it was, leaned into his while her nose nuzzled the top of his head.

"I'm sorry for any ill feelings I have caused you," he said, arm pushing up her robe and touching the skin of her outer thigh. "Understand that I did what I thought best... I talked to my sister. She understands that man isn't allowed..."

"What man?"

Henry pinched his lips shut. "No man in particular, Princess."

"I like it when you call me that," Monica said, her demeanor demure but her heart crashing into her ribcage. "You make me feel special." Better than what Jackson used to call her. She was nobody's pet anymore. She liked the feeling of being exalted whenever Henry spoke to her, even if she were the one serving him. "Now I want to make you feel special."

She kissed him, the only overt act of dominance she would take that night. Not that Henry seemed to mind. From the moment their lips touched, happily rejoining after so much time apart, Henry gripped her flesh and nearly bruised her from how hard he wanted her.

"You always make me feel special," he murmured on her lips between kisses. "It's me who will always fight to make you feel as good as you make me feel."

Monica pushed farther into his embrace, enthralled with the way he held her, brought her closer, and nudged her with his erection below. *How long has he thought of me?* Monica wasn't vain, but she was pleased to know he had such a quick reaction to their reunion. She picked open two buttons and pricked his skin there.

"Is there anything else I can get for you, Master?" she asked, her hand wrapping around his neck as she leaned into him. "Your wish is mine to grant." She once said that to Jackson, and he laughed at her, saying she sounded like a horny genie. *Stop thinking about him.*

Henry did not move. "Sometimes the best subs are those who don't need to be told what to do."

Monica understood. She slipped off his lap, her fingers lingering on his skin as she placed one foot after the other onto her floor. The ties to her robe *happened* to catch on her nail, untying before Henry's eyes and revealing the lingerie beneath. It was a good night to be wearing a pushup bra.

She took his wineglass to her wet bar by the window. The sleeves of her robe fell down her arms, allowing Henry to gaze at the white of her skin as she poured him not wine, but bourbon, the kind of masculine drink she liked to have on hand for moments like these. *I'm a woman who gets off on fetching slippers and the newspaper.* There were words for women like her. "Bitch" came to mind, but she didn't like that word. She was still a human being.

One who poured a mean glass of bourbon and looked hot doing it.

She knelt beside Henry's chair and offered him the bourbon. He took it, smiling, his visage gentle and kind but his lips twisting with a bite. When his other hand began stroking

Monica's hair, she pushed into it, cheek rubbing against his palm as her eyes closed in beatitude.

The room was quiet. The fire cackled. Ice clinked in Henry's glass. Monica heard her own breath in her ears. Or perhaps that was her heart thumping wildly in anticipation. As much as she lived for this kind of life, she was still aroused enough to wonder how it would end.

"Would it be so bad?" she asked, her voice a sweet whisper. "To spend the rest of my life doing this?"

Henry regarded her with a concerned look. "You are really deep into the life."

"I don't think I am." Monica turned, her back leaning against the chair as her hand touched the back of his calf. "People tell me I am, but what can I say? It makes me happy. I like to know that *he's* pleased. I like knowing that he can come home to a sanctuary. There's nothing wrong with wanting to be a part of it."

"Don't you want to do anything else?"

She thought about it. She liked her business, most of the time. There was art in matching patron and girl. Joy in watching them share their moments. Love in hoping it could last forever. "I'm not saying that I want to do nothing but hide in a room for the rest of my life where I'm treated as a sex doll." Monica looked up at him. "Maybe only half the week."

"And your Château here?"

"I don't know."

His fingers felt like Heaven's touch on her scalp. "You deserve happiness, Monica. What you want hurts no one else."

She looked up at him. "What if I want you?"

It was the closest she had come to saying she loved him. *My chest is on fire.* Flames burst from her heart, licking at her bones and caressing her sinew. The heat extended to Henry, who placed a gentle kiss on the top of her head before leaning back in the chair again. The glass of bourbon was empty, placed on a table within arm's reach.

"You need only ask."

Something stopped Monica from asking. Something warning her that horrible things could happen again. That she had jumped into a relationship too quickly last time. She and Henry were already skirting the edges of madness. *I want to ask.* She wanted Henry to take her home and protect her for the rest of her life. To make love to her.

To dominate her.

"Please," she begged, clutching his legs, hands bunched at his hips. "At the end of the day, I'm a woman of simple pleasures. I only need small indulgences."

"You know what?" Henry's fingers curled her hair. "So am I. A man of simple pleasures."

Monica pushed herself between his legs, undoing his belt and feeling as if her body were about to collapse upon itself. "Let me spend this night serving you, Mr. Warren."

"Please. Henry."

"Henry…" It was the sweetest thing to call him. Master made her feel like she was in her place. Mr. Warren brought the intrigue and forbidden. Henry? That was the intimacy she craved. The touch to her heart she wanted to recapture again and again.

His soothing words continued to flow into her ear as she took him out of his trousers and eased her hand around him. Henry picked up his empty glass and searched for one last drop as his beautiful princess flicked her tongue against his half-erect shaft.

He never asked her to do this. He never suggested it was something he expected every time they met up. Yet it was quickly becoming one of Monica's happiest moments. Something so simple like running her tongue along his skin and feeling him tense up beneath her touch. *He responds so well to it.* Of course, all men did… but Henry would shudder, as if his whole body, as well as his mind and heart, embraced the intimacy Monica offered him.

For even cupping her hand on the head of his erection and turning her head so she licked the top of him was intimate. She understood the feeling of her hot breath on him like this. She knew what it meant to tease and stroke and suck. Learning what he liked best and how he responded to everything was a gift in itself.

I want to feel him lose himself like this. Her mouth opened over his tip, tongue licking the wetness emerging there. Henry groaned, the ice in his glass clinking back and forth as he absentmindedly shook it. It wasn't until Monica took half his length into his mouth that he said a word, and that was, "Astounding."

Yes, she certainly felt it.

Her grip on the base of his shaft was tight, her nails brushing against his sack as she lowered her mouth farther, farther, her throat opening to take him. *I can barely breathe.* Monica didn't care. She knew Henry would not hurt her. He would relax and enjoy what she offered, but he would not drive himself into her tonight.

Yet she squeezed, hummed, and concentrated on keeping him hard inside her mouth until he either told her to stop or finished inside her throat.

I'll do this for you every night. Every night when he came home, Monica would pour him a drink to enjoy while she brought him to this level of pleasure. She would constantly explore new ways to make him shiver. She would rely on the standbys most nights, but every so often, before he got too comfortable, Monica would throw in something new and delightful. All she wanted – all she *cared* about – was making her Master happy. There was no shame in getting on her knees. No horror in tasting him like this. *Dear God, I love him.* What an awkward time to realize it.

Or was it?

"Stop."

Monica slowly eased off him, keeping her gag relaxed as he emerged from her throat, hard and glistening. "I am willing, Master." She turned her lips inward. "Henry…"

"Call me whatever makes you happiest."

"Right now, I want you to be my Master."

"Then I will be. Sit back and let me look at you. Don't touch me."

Monica pushed back onto her folded legs, her visage expectant as she waited for her next order. What would he ask of her?

"Take off that robe."

She did as he commanded, removing the sheer satin from her skin and sitting before him in nothing but her pushup bra and lace panties. Henry took the robe and laid it on the back of his chair, the bright red satin touching his face.

"Sit up straight."

Her spine had never been so erect. Monica kept her chin up, looking into Henry's eyes, which widened from the suspense.

"You're beautiful. The most beautiful woman I have ever seen."

He can't mean that. Monica would not refute his opinion, however. "Thank you ,Master."

"How many men can say they have such a beautiful woman to serve them?" He held the glass to her. "Bring me another."

Monica responded with alacrity, her cramped legs feeling like nothing as she jumped up, took the glass, and returned to the wet bar. In poured more bourbon before she quickly went back to Henry and handed the glass to him.

"Kneel, my sweet."

She was back on her knees, shoulders straight while her Dom took a drink of bourbon and studied her form. It was the look of both a man in love... and a man plotting his next move.

"Are you here to serve me?"

Did he doubt her? "Yes, Master. Command me."

"Finish me off with your hands only."

Monica was about to lunge forward when a thought occurred to her. "Where…?"

"Use your imagination." Henry smiled into his drink. "Make it good and I'll reward you."

Music to her eager ears. Monica spared him a thankful glance before taking his shaft into her hand.

Surprisingly, this was almost more intimate than her kisses from before. She felt more vulnerable. Monica couldn't close her eyes and bury her face in his lap. She couldn't randomly decide when to look up and bat her eyelashes at him. No, in this position, with her body in front of him and her head held high, Monica's only option was to stroke him while they looked into one another's eyes.

They didn't say a word. Why bother, when everything they needed to say was expressed in Monica's clear eyes and the twitches in Henry's mouth? *I give him this, he gives me that.* The quicker and longer her strokes became, the more Henry leaned forward, his lips coming for hers as he kissed her with the invigorated passion of a man about to lose the last of his senses.

He stiffened. Wetness lined the top of Monica's hand. Her lips relaxed against Henry's as she incited him to do the work on that end. Yet his kisses were more sporadic. He wouldn't last much longer – not with his breath sharp in his nostrils and his hand encircling her throat, tight.

"Do you want it? Do you?" His voice was like a wave crashing into Monica's consciousness. "Take what you want. Anywhere you want."

Monica didn't have much choice. For when the last of Henry's words hit the air, he groaned, hard and rough, the first of his orgasm hitting Monica's breasts and covering her chest in his seed.

She did not relent. Just as Henry's grip around her throat tightened, he burst again, Monica's skin now covered in a heat she could barely anticipate.

Although she expected Henry to fall back in the chair and relax, he remained forward, both hands in her hair in an effort to keep it from getting sullied. "Did you like that?"

"Yes, Master." How could she not like the feeling of him dripping down her skin and running down her lingerie? "I.."

"You like it when I claim you, don't you?"

Monica blushed. "Yes. I like the idea of you owning me."

"It's hot, isn't it?" His thumb rubbed her lip.

She couldn't answer. Not without blushing more and possibly embarrassing herself... or was that even possible in front of Henry anymore?

"You don't have to be ashamed in front of me."

Monica lifted her eyes toward him. "Very much so."

His hand left her hair and caressed her chin. "Why don't you go clean up? I'll give you a sweet reward when you get back."

A kiss to her forehead sent her to the bathroom, where she did as bade. *This is almost too much.* Monica wanted Henry to claim her over and over. Inside her body, outside… he was right when he figured that she wanted it. Most "normal" women Monica knew thought the idea of being regularly marked by their men as disgusting. Not Monica. Nothing made her happier than knowing her Dom was pleased with her. Him doing that was one of the ways he could express that.

If Henry desired to come on her every time they had sex, Monica would rarely say no. As long as he could give her other things as well.

He stood in the middle of the bedroom facing the door Monica stepped out of, his pants still unbuckled but his face no longer flushed from climax. Still, he hung flaccid. *I'm almost disappointed.* Almost. Because Monica knew Henry was a man who could be ready again soon enough. If anything, this pattern of him coming before the main event meant Monica got it for a longer period of time. *How considerate.* She cracked a smile.

"Do you still wish to serve me, Monica?"

Cold tingles pricked her skin. Was the window open? No, even if it was, the fire would prevent her from feeling cold. "Of course."

"Then come take care of me."

She went to him, his arms embracing her as he kissed her lips with enough passion to knock her over. Monica did not fold. Nor did she sigh against his mouth when he pulled the cup of her bra down and brushed his thumb against her nipple. This wasn't about her. This was about him and – well, okay, so it was about her too. *What I get out of it being about him.*

The sub took care of her Dom, beginning with removing his jacket from his frame and folding it over the back of his chair. Henry's fingers combed through her hair until she turned around and unbuttoned the rest of his shirt.

"Thank you," he said, brushing his fingertips against her shoulder.

The shirt fell from his body, revealing the hard, unassuming muscles he kept beneath. Monica always marveled at how toned his body was. Henry was not the kind of man to advertise how fit he was. Some Doms liked to wear clothes that accentuated their muscles. Others found clever ways to show off their strength. Yet Henry was so subtle in the way he showed off his possessions that it felt like exploring a new world with him. He was almost... humble.

I still can't believe this is happening. Monica pressed her hand against his chest and batted her eyelashes in the hope that it would earn her a kiss.

It brought her a whisper in her ear.

"Let's go to bed."

They went, as soon as Monica pulled his trousers down and waited for him to step out of them. She folded all of his clothes together and left them neatly piled on his chair. The empty glass of alcohol went to the wet bar to be washed later. By the time she was finished, Henry was in her bed, leaning against the headboard while the silk sheets covered him from the waist down.

He extended his hand and motioned for her to come to him. Monica obeyed.

His Domination

Henry brought her into bed with him, enticing her to lie on her side while he loomed over her, elbow pointed into pillow. "Stroke me, my love," he said, pulling her hand to his cock. "Gently."

Monica's touch lingered on his length, her breath catching in her chest as he gazed upon her with an intensity that nearly made her melt. Yet their level of comfort at this point meant she felt no embarrassment doing as he asked, which began with simple strokes to his skin, and then wrapping her hand around the base of his shaft and giving it an easy pull.

As she slowly made him erect again, Henry kissed her throat, nibbled her ear, and licked the tops of her breasts as they pushed up from her bra. Once his tongue slipped between skin and lace, Monica gasped, her grip on him tightening until he groaned and grabbed her wrist.

"You're killing me," he mumbled. "I don't know if it's because you're good at what you do or because you're naturally so…"

Monica dared to speak. "So what?"

"Perfect."

"I'm not perfect."

"To me you are."

He kissed her again, his body overtaking hers until they were locked in that blissful world of lovemaking.

Monica had long missed sex being a way for her to escape from reality. Toward the end with Jackson, it became a place of fear. Love, and fear. With Henry, all she felt was relief. The way he grunted into her ear, moved between her hips, and kissed the inside of her mouth made her feel like the most protected woman in the world. It didn't matter that it hurt a little when he entered her. She didn't care that her foot twisted into the covers. All that mattered was the safe, yet passionate sensation of this man reclaiming her after so long apart.

I can't believe I distrusted him. A man out to hurt her wouldn't make love to her like this. She would feel used, repellant. Not like a sweet creature making love to her Master. When Monica thought of it that way, she couldn't help but moan into his shoulder and bite the flesh there. Henry groaned, his hips surging between hers as his cock reached deep within her, his thrusts long, hard, purposeful. *I can't believe I fell in love again so easily.*

Tears fell down her cheeks as Henry made love to her, his face buried in the crook of her neck as he left another mark of his love on her skin. He was all around her, within her, shielding her from the evils of the world and the people who would want to hurt her.

"Henry..." she said, her hips digging into her bed. "I love you."

At first she didn't think he heard her. Then his nose touched hers, those clear blue eyes staring into the back of hers. "I love you too." He thrust harder, as if to prove how much he loved her.

He didn't ask why she was crying, but he did kiss away the tears, their hands clasping together on her pillow as her arms were drawn above her head. *Don't leave me tonight...* Henry tightened within her. Monica was so wet by this point that it didn't matter what angle he tried or how fast his movements became. By the time he began to climax within her, Monica was already crying out in ecstasy, the tears flowing freely as she covered Henry in her love for him.

"Don't cry, my love." Henry stilled within her, his nose drawing circles across her cheek and jaw. "I won't let anyone hurt you anymore."

"I'm not crying... not like that." Monica kissed his face, where stubble grew and tickled her lips. "They're tears of happiness, I promise."

"If I had tears right now, they would be of happiness as well."

Monica wiped one from her eye and placed it on his temple. "There. Now we can be happy together."

"I am always happy with you, Princess."

They embraced, Henry still inside her as they slowly moved together and kissed with the knowledge that they loved each other. *Henry, my love...* The words felt so impossible. For the first time in so long, Monica loved without fear. She desired without remorse. Her heart was so full of happiness that there was no room for the pains of her past.

"Be mine, forever." Henry's voice brought her back to the bed. "I can't imagine spending my life with anyone but you."

Monica's nails pressed into his shoulders, his back, any skin and sinew she could find within his powerful body. "Yes," she wept, holding in the last bit of sanity remaining deep in her heart. "Yes!"

She didn't know what she said yes to. It didn't matter.

Chapter 25

White

Monica had never planned a collaring ceremony before. Not even the one she had with Jackson.

He planned everything. Part of the reason Monica was attracted to him for so long was that he took all the hard thinking out of life for her. He told her what to wear, where to go, and what to do on any given day. A collaring ceremony? That was like a party, and Jackson planned all his parties. Henry seemed like the kind of guy to delegate it to a professional planner and sign the checks with a shrug.

He wasn't quite as laissez-faire with the upcoming ceremony, but he made it clear he would like anything she planned. They would hold it at his house soon enough. Until then, Monica was knee-deep in planning the ceremony… and hiring a new girl for her Château.

"What are your predilections?" she asked the girl sitting before her desk. She had long black hair, draping on her shoulders and resting atop her large breasts which strained against her small T-shirt. *The types that come from that club…* Monica couldn't hold it against the girls. Sylvia showed up to her interview wearing overalls. "While we need women who can do a bit of everything, it's important to know what you're best at, so to speak."

A serpent-shaped smile crossed her face. "Every Friday night at The Dark Hour I put on a show with a guy named Scottie. If he's not crying uncle by the end of the night, I'm not happy – and neither is the audience. Does that answer your question?"

Monica cleared her throat. "Indeed. Would you be willing to move in here full time?"

"Sure. Place looks nice enough."

They shook hands at the end of the interview and Monica had a maid escort the young lady out. *Don't think we need another Domme.* Right now Judith was the biggest Domme of them all, and the others could do it well enough. Yet most of the clients coming to the Château were interested in submissive types. Just the day before Monica received a call asking if she had enough subs for a party. A part of her wished she could say yes just so she could peek in on what they did. Usually those sorts of parties ended with the subs on the floor, their leashes tight in a

Dom's hands and the spankings making their asses so pink that they couldn't sit for days.

Monica had to finish her coffee before she could think straight again.

With the last of her interviews done for the day, she went back to her ceremony planning. *I don't know, should there be music?* That sounded hokey. It was already strange that they were expected to write some vows for one another. What would Henry say about her? *Only good things, I hope.*

The fact she had to hope that...

"Ma'am?" A maid knocked on her door. "There's a package here for you."

"Sit it on the table over there."

"I think you better take a look at it first. It's not your ordinary package."

What now? Monica got up, the maid stepping out of the way so her boss could pass through the doorway. There, propped up against the wall, was a boutique box wrapped in silver paper and topped with a pure white bow.

It was the sort of box that could only hold one thing: clothes.

The maid saw herself out as Monica brought the box into her chambers. She shut herself in her room, locking the door behind her and admiring the beautiful package on her bed.

The first thing she felt was fear. *What if it's from Jackson?* Then she felt hope. *What if it's from Henry?* There was no note to tell her right away who it was from.

She would have to chance opening it to see.

Ribbons gave way to the lid of the box, which popped up without any effort on Monica's behalf. Inside was white, fine tissue wrapped neatly around a piece of... cloth? Silk? Monica gingerly pulled the tissue back to see white silk and lace, luxurious to the touch.

She whistled as she held lingerie in the air.

It was a white corset stitched in lace and tiny, sparse beads that dotted the bodice and ran down the sides. Lace trim bloomed beautifully from the bottom. If Monica wore it, her thighs would look like they were ready for Easter service... minus the fact that this was very sinful.

The corset attached to a white garter. A tag attached stated Monica's height, Sure enough the garters went with a pair of sheer stockings that were long enough to reach her knees when she held them to her body.

A piece of paper fluttered to the floor.

"A beautiful ball gown for a beautiful Princess," it said. Monica held her fingers to her lips. *"For the next time we meet."*

The next time was their ceremony. This was what her Dom wanted her to wear when he collared her once and for all.

Monica wrapped her hand around her throat. She hadn't worn a collar fulltime since Jackson. *Henry asked me what subs do with theirs when the relationship ends.* She looked to her dresser, where a slim black box rested in the top drawer.

She went there now, opening the drawer and staring into an abyss of silk, cotton, and satin underwear. Monica pushed two piles out of the way and pulled out the black box hiding at the bottom of her lingerie pile.

The collar she wore for Jackson twinkled in the light.

Her heart grew heavy. So did the collar, suddenly weighing five more pounds than it had a second ago. Yet Monica did not cry, weep, or sob. *There are better things ahead.*

She couldn't get rid of the collar. As much as she detested Jackson and everything he did to her, it was still… it happened. It existed. Monica ran away from the situation, but she would not run away from the memories. As long as she had this collar, she would remember. A bad man. A bad relationship.

It could never happen again.

Henry wouldn't like it, but he would understand. Although the circumstances of his old relationship were different, he probably kept a keepsake or two of his former sub who had to leave. In fact, Monica was grateful that Henry had memories like that too. He would be able to relate to her. Any other man may become jealous, but not Henry.

He's mine, now. Monica put the collar away and shoved the box to the bottom of her underwear drawer. *And I'm his. That's all that matters.*

She went back to the garment on her bed. White. Pure. Beautiful. It would look bridal if it weren't so sexual. Nevertheless, Monica would find her best accessories to go with it. Diamond earrings. Silver glitter for her hair. A diamond tennis bracelet Ethan gave her in celebration of the Château's opening. *Should I wear a ring?* Henry hadn't mentioned a ring,

Something else caught her eye in the box. After she pushed away more tissue, she came across a cut white blazer that matched the tone of the lingerie but would give her some formality for their ceremony. It made Monica smile.

Her phone rang.

"Are you looking through my window, Mr. Warren?" she asked the man on the other end of the line. "How did you know I opened your present?"

"I'm damn good, that's how." Laughter told Monica that it was pure coincidence that he called. "I just finished work for the day. Thought I would call and see how my lovely is doing."

"Your lovely is done with work as well." Monica put the items neatly away in the box and replaced the lid. A tuft of tissue stuck out, forcing her to redo the whole thing while her phone balanced between ear and shoulder. "Interviewed some girls today."

"Any good candidates?"

"I completely forget. Your present has jumbled my brain."

"Good. I want to keep you on your toes. Does it fit?"

"I haven't tried it on yet."

"I guessed your size again. It came from the same boutique as the purple negligee, so I'm guessing the sizes…"

"Henry." Monica chuckled into the phone. "I don't want to talk about shopping right now, believe it or not."

"You're right. There are way more exciting things to talk about. Like what's happening this weekend."

"Is there something I should know?"

Henry was silent for a few seconds. "Everything that you haven't planned is a surprise. You're always spoiling me. I'm going to spoil you that night."

"I think you're confused on who is always spoiling whom."

"Oh, no, our entire relationship may be founded on us trying to out spoil the other. Whatever will we do? It almost sounds like we'll be happy."

This time Monica laughed, and she was grateful to have the chance to. "I have to wonder about the white, though. You do know I'm hardly pure or virginal, right? Quite the opposite."

"If we were getting married, that would be one thing. You'll see why I sent you white. Besides the fact it will look beautiful on you."

"I already know what I'll wear with it."

"Don't wear a necklace. One of my surprises... I can't wait for you to see the day-collar I picked out for you. I'm fully confident that you would have picked it out as well."

"I look forward to seeing it." She was glad Henry suggested buying her a collar to wear in her daily life. The bulky silver and diamond one was great for certain occasions, but barely practical for going out to lunch or doing her work. "You have immaculate tastes. That's the real reason we get along so well."

"Is that it? Good to know. I'll mix it into my vows. Just you wait."

"The vows you're writing in French?"

"Okay, *that* was a joke."

"Aw. I would have loved that."

"I'll throw some in for you."

"Henry..." Monica sat on the edge of her bed. "Thank you. For everything."

"Don't thank me yet, Princess. I've still got a few more things up my sleeve."

It was that kind of talk that made Monica impatient. In this case, impatient for anything and everything Henry Warren wanted to give his favorite woman in the world.

Chapter 26

To Have And To Collar

Monica sat in a dressing room, far in the back of the East Wing in Warren Manor. The corset clung to her figure, accentuating her breasts and how bare her chest and neck were. She peered into a mirror, outlining her eyes with sleek black eyeliner that made her look sultrier than she actually was. *If I don't knock him off his feet when I walk out there, I've failed.* She wasn't too worried.

Her shoulders shivered from the cool air blowing in from the air conditioner. The white blazer hung on the back of her chair, but she didn't want to put it on until the time came to leave the room.

Just as she put in the first earring, someone knocked on the door.

At first it startled her. Who was coming to call? Henry wouldn't dare. Was it a butler with a missive? Something she forgot? Then the knock came again, harder. She wasn't exactly sure how she knew, but Monica was confident that Ethan Cole stood on the other side.

Sure enough, he peeped in, asking if she was decent. *As decent as I can be in this getup.* Even if Monica were shy, she didn't have anything Ethan hadn't seen before. She took heart in that when Ethan closed the door behind him and approached, hands resting on Monica's chair.

"You are gorgeous." He was dressed in one of his finest Italian suits, a kerchief poking from his front pocket and silver cufflinks adorning his wrists. The scent of his cologne took Monica back to the days of being with him and Jackson at the same time. At least his scent didn't give her *bad* memories. "That man doesn't know how lucky he is."

Monica smiled into the mirror, her other earring dangling from her ear and brushing against her shoulder. "Oh, I think he has a good idea." She looked up at his reflection. "To what do I owe this pleasure, Mr. Cole?"

His hand brushed against her skin, lingering in her curled hair and pulling some form of debris from its tendrils. It was not the touch of a lover, or a man making an advance. It was, however, affectionate, and Monica felt the most relaxed she had experienced in a long time.

"I wanted to see the lovely bride before I gave her away."

She rolled her eyes. "I'm not a bride. And nobody gives me away."

Ethan was there as her witness. She could have invited a woman, like Judith, but Monica instantly thought of Ethan the moment Henry suggested that they bring one witness each to the ceremony. Ethan had seen her at her lowest. He had helped rescue her from the abuses she endured. He even cut ties with his best friend – *ended their business partnership* – in the aftermath. For her. Because he cared about her.

Ethan understood her heart and mind better than any woman Monica currently knew. If anyone was going to speak for her at her collaring ceremony, it was him. *A part of me is still in love with him, I guess.* Monica never felt for him the passionate, heartbreaking love she once felt for Jackson and now Henry. She and Ethan knew how to please each other in the bedroom, but they were nothing more than friends outside of it.

"You may not be a bride," Ethan said, picking up the diamond tennis bracelet laid out on the vanity and taking Monica by the hand, "but you look like a beautiful one."

He wrapped the bracelet around her wrist and latched it together. After turning it so it faced the right way up, Monica said, "You're too kind. You're quite handsome yourself."

"I wanted to look good for your big day. I haven't been to a collaring ceremony since…"

Monica pursed her lips. "Since my last one."

"I didn't mean to bring it up."

"It's fine, Ethan." She stood, fixing her hair in the mirror and motioning for Ethan to help her with the blazer. "Nothing can bring me down today."

His Domination

The smooth sleeves of the blazer brushed against her arms as her shoulders were quickly covered. Ethan helped her pull her hair back and rub out the creases in the jacket. *I almost look formal.* Minus the fact she wore no pants. She did, however, purchase a pair of pure white heels for the occasion.

"He seems like a good man," Ethan said. "That's what you deserve most of all."

"A good man who knows how to spank me."

"I'll take your word on that one."

They smiled at each other in the mirror. Ethan patted her shoulder and turned away, hands going into his pockets.

"His father owes Jackson half a billion dollars."

Ethan turned enough to show that he was listening. "He told you this?"

"Yes. I saw Jackson here. I needed an explanation."

"Damn. The man has a lot of loan payments coming in, but I never heard about Gerald Warren being one of them."

"I hear it's very hush-hush. You can't tell anyone, I guess."

"You're okay with that?"

"Ever hear that you shouldn't blame the son for the sins of his father? It's like that. He's been honest and open with me about it. I don't care. I... Jackson did terrible things. He's stalked me since then. He wants to make me uncomfortable... what if I don't let him?"

"There's nothing wrong with reacting the way you have. Nobody should go through..." "I know that." Monica wouldn't feel bad for the times she felt like a victim. Like a runaway. Like someone who was so stupid to fall into a trap like Jackson's. *For ten years!* Even if the first several were fine, the last ones ruined the good ones. "But I can't shut down every time our paths cross. I can't give him a reaction when he mails me out of the blue. I need to face him and know that I can. Don't get me wrong. I'm not committing to Henry to prove a point about Jackson. Except let's be real, Ethan. No matter what I do or where I go in this insular world of ours, I will see him. And it will scare me."

"If you believe that he'll take care of you during those times, then I'll support you."

"Thank you." Satisfied with how she looked in the mirror, Monica stepped away from the vanity and motioned for Ethan to accompany her out of the room. "Let's see how long it takes me to cry."

They hooked their arms together, Ethan escorting her down the main hallway of the East Wing and to the grand staircase connecting to the Premier House. At the bottom of the stairs stood Evangeline, her slick look rivaling Ethan's as she pointed where to go. *Using his sister as his witness. What a strange family.* Monica hadn't even met the parents yet.

The servants were cleared out for the evening. The only people Monica saw between the East Wing and an open, marble-laden room overlooking the gardens were Evangeline and Ethan. It suited her fine. She liked being paraded around, but not necessarily in front of staff.

Evangeline disappeared into the marble room. Monica stopped near the entryway, Ethan stopping one step ahead of her and turning to see if she was all right.

"Second thoughts?" he asked softly, his fingers locking between hers.

"No." Monica squeezed his hand back. "I merely want to savor this moment."

No woman got married intending to divorce – not the ones in love. It was the same for a sub entering a permanent union with her Dom. *No sub enters a collaring ceremony expecting to break up later.* This was their marriage. For some, this held greater meaning than marriage. Maybe she and Henry would officially wed one day. With their families present, with everyone in the rich, wide world coming to celebrate their love. Monica didn't care about that. She cared about *this.* The rush she felt thinking of her Dom putting that collar around her neck... for now... forever... *I never want this moment to end.* God willing, it wouldn't.

Ethan helped her move again, but it was Monica who took the first step across the threshold.

Everything was as she and Henry planned it. Tea candles burned in an alcove, emitting a potent but lovely rose fragrance as well as a soft, warm light that cast Henry's shadow far on the wall behind him.

He stood in front of the alcove, dressed in a light gray suit that evoked the same bride-groom imagery but without being so obvious. Besides, white really wasn't his color. Monica smiled to see a red rose poking from his pocket and a soft silk shirt buttoned beneath his jacket. His sandy hair was combed down, and his shoes shined to perfection.

He held out his hand to Monica as she approached.

A few silent moments passed, in which Monica shared a look with Ethan. He nodded to Henry, unwrapping his arm from Monica's and giving her a gentle push. *You barely know this man.* Ethan never mentioned having a chat with Henry. Had they formally met before this day?

Did it matter?

Monica took Henry's hand. She left Ethan's protection and entered a new man's universe.

"You are…" Henry's eyes traveled across her body, taking in the glitter in her hair, the eyeliner winged toward her bangs, the light brush of blush pinking her cheeks, and the ensemble he had chosen for her to wear that day. The sparkling earrings caught his eyes more than once. "Radiant."

Eva cleared her throat and tried to pass it off as a cough. Ethan glanced at her.

"Thank you." Monica took a step back, putting a little distance between them so she could enjoy the moment more. "Have I told you lately that you're not so bad yourself?"

Another cough. Apparently someone had somewhere to be.

"I think it's best we got started. Eva?"

She probably thought he would never ask. Regardless of her real thoughts, Eva pulled a small slip of paper from her front pocket, unfolded it, and read the contents. "Does the man who gives away this woman promise that she is faithful, subservient when necessary, and deserving?"

Ethan was not slow to answer. "I do." He had a slip of paper of his own. "Does the woman who vouches for this man swear that he is a reasonable, kind, and diligent Master?"

"I do."

"Furthermore," and everyone in attendance turned to look at Ethan as he went off-script, "do you vouch that this man has never and will never betray or otherwise harm his beloved?"

A disturbing silence briefly erupted between the four of them. This time Eva's throat clearing was honest. "I... do?"

Down, Ethan. Big brother types. What was Monica to do with them?

Besides, it wasn't like she didn't have those sentiments covered already.

"Henry," she began, holding both of his hands in hers, "these past few months have been everything I ever wanted and more. Thank you for pursuing me so diligently. I daresay you caught me."

She ignored the silence in the room. She only had eyes for Henry's smile anyway.

"Before I met you, I didn't think I would ever be free to love again. To trust someone with my heart and body. You keep saying that you want to earn my trust over and over. I admire that. Because you're right. I will need that. You don't know this, but there were many times I expected you to prove my doubts right... and then you didn't. Every time that happened, I became more convinced that perhaps it was time to start trusting again. Thank you."

Something happened to Henry's expression. When before he had the plain, but happy expression of a man who had things going his way, he now had a poignant hue and brows turning down. *Has he never considered this?* Henry glanced at the two witnesses, including his sister and Monica's ex-Dom. *He hasn't.* Men could be so simple sometimes.

"That said, Mr. Henry Warren, I vow to be a faithful and obedient sub who will do her best to make your life easier and more pleasant. I am overjoyed at the thought of serving you for a long, long time. My only hope is that I can be the sub that you deserve."

"I don't know what to say." His hands were slippery in Monica's. "Except that I'm happy you feel this way."

When the silence became too much to bear, Henry realized that it was his turn to say something.

"I'm not sure how to follow that." Yet his grip on her hands was full of resolve, and Monica did not doubt that he would make her tear up. "I even had some notes I wrote last night. Alas, you've once again knocked me off my feet, Monica."

"Try it anyway, my love."

"Well, I was going to say some simple things about being your Dom, but… ah, to hell with it. I love you, Monica. I have from the moment I first laid eyes on you. I was intrigued by you from the first conversation. Your wit and intelligence is unlike any other woman's. Not to say other women don't have that, but yours invigorates me, and while you will be my sub, you will also be my equal partner. As your Dom, I promise to keep you in line, but I will never stifle your spirit or silence your opinions. I want to see and hear it all from you. We can be partners in many ways."

He picked a box up from the makeshift altar beside them and opened it to reveal a slender, black collar dotted in tiny diamonds. *How considerate.* It would go with any outfit. It was sophisticated enough to wear to work and formal functions, but also casual enough to wear around the house or entertaining friends. Monica did not miss the "In Care Of Henry Warren" etched inside the leather. *In Care Of.* Not property of. Not owned by. *In Care Of.* Henry was her caretaker, not just her Master.

The first tear threatened to sprout from her eye.

"I am honored to present you with this collar," Henry waited until Monica pulled her hair to the side before wrapping the leather collar snugly around her throat. "To know that you chose me as your Dom is an honor I'll cherish forever."

It sounded so sappy! Monica held in both a laugh and a sob of love. If it were her and Henry, she may have cried, but she didn't want to do that in front of Eva and Ethan. "Thank you, Master," she whispered, the collar latching behind her neck.

It was done.

The last matter of formality was the signing of the contract that stipulated their roles as Dom and sub. For a whole week they emailed it back and forth to each other when they had spare moments, changing wording here and adding things there. It wasn't anything they weren't already doing, but Monica insisted that they sign even a one-page contract for now. She added her signature after Henry's, and then both witnesses added their initials.

Before Monica could step away from the piece of paper, Henry pulled her into his arms and kissed her.

She had never kissed him in front of others like this before. Eva turned around with a groan, and Ethan respectfully averted his eyes while fighting back a smile. *I don't care.* Henry could start making love to her right now, and she wouldn't care. Having him kiss her so forcefully after they just committed to each other only made Monica more fervent in her desire to be with him.

They had dinner, the four of them, in the main dining hall. Aged wine and a five-course French meal were served. Monica sat beside Henry, who sat at the head of the table, and Ethan sat on the other side of her. Eva looked at her from across the table. While she showed Monica no malice, something clearly made her uncomfortable.

Was it because Henry was her brother and this pushed too far into his sex life? Or did it have to do with...

Him?

Monica had to brush it off. This was her day, as Ethan reminded her during dessert when they toasted to the happy couple and exchanged gifts. Eva gave them first edition texts chronicling one Victorian couple's foray into the lifestyle. Ethan gave them matching, monogrammed keys that were to go in their wallets. *As a reminder that someone else holds the key to their heart and body.* Monica was quick to place the key initialed "HW" in her coin purse, followed by an appreciative kiss to Ethan's cheek.

Ethan left shortly after dessert, but not before shaking Henry's hand and muttering something into his ear. Whatever he said, Henry did not flinch, so it must've not been *too* threatening. *"Break her heart and I'll do to you what I did to Jackson."*

Eva patted her brother's shoulder and nodded to Monica. "I've got a date to get ready for .After that sappy show I need to get the sugar out of my system."

"Just wait, dear sister, it'll be your turn to collar a special someone soon enough."

"I don't think so."

Henry waited until she retreated into the West Wing before replying. "That's what the young always say."

Monica wrapped her arm around his. "You're not *that* much older than her."

"We can say the same thing about our age difference." Not that there was much of one at the end of the day. "Anyway, shall we retire?"

She couldn't help the smile on her face. "I am ready to submit, Master."

"Oh," Henry said, directing her to the staircase. "You will."

Chapter 27

His

The collar was quick to come off Monica's throat. Henry placed it back in its box and gingerly left it on top of his sub's purse, currently stored in his room. *Their* room. Henry made it clear that Monica always had a place to call home here. Although she had no plans to formally move from the Château for now, she had no problem calling this her room as well.

The logistics of that could be figured out later. For now, she was at her Dom's whims on their collaring night.

"Hate to take it off you so soon, my love." A purr laced his voice. Monica stood in the middle of their room, wondering if she should follow him into the adjacent room overlooking the gardens or not. "We have something better for when it's you and me."

She followed him.

If she thought they would consummate their union as Dom and sub in the bedroom, she was mistaken.

There was a viewing room stocked with the usual: closets, alcohol, and extra storage space for clothing and jewelry that spilled from the bedroom. Monica was in here once to enjoy the gardens while she ate breakfast, but since that short stay the bench by the window had been pulled out to the middle of the space. Sheer curtains gave them privacy from any prying eyes outside, but still allowed plenty of early summer light in.

"Sit."

His commands were soft, but Monica still obeyed as if they were firm. *A command is a command.* It was her will to obey.

So she sat on the plush white bench and watched as her Dom carried in the silver and diamond collar that had been his first patron gift.

He's not my patron. He's my lifelong Dom. The thought still made her want to weep.

"This is so beautiful on you." Henry latched the collar around her throat, careful to keep her hair from getting caught in it. The leash dangled at her side. *I hope he spanks me again with it.* Monica had to bite her lip in order to keep her thoughts to herself. Her ass hadn't been spanked raw since that night Henry punished her most severely.

"Wearing this takes me back to when I first realized I wanted you." Monica's voice was so demure that she worried Henry couldn't hear her. Yet he caressed her shoulder, his fingers pushing beneath the blazer to help her shed it with ease.

"I know. Trust me, I do." Henry hung the jacket up on a nearby coat rack. Monica shivered, her exposed arms and shoulders having yet to pick up any heat coming through the window. Henry also took off his jacket and hung it up next to Monica's. "There are still things I want from you."

His hands were on her shoulders as he stood behind her. He began massaging her, releasing any tension she kept within her muscles.

And then his hands traveled down her chest, cupping her breasts through the bridal-white corset.

"Tonight I am taking every piece of you, Monica." His voice ravaged her ear, one hiss after another sending spirals of madness down her spine. *Oh my...* Henry squeezed harder, eliciting a whimper from her throat as her breasts begged for forgiveness in his grip. "You are mine. Do you understand? I will mark you in ways you never imagined. When I'm finished, there will be no doubt in this world that you belong to me. Your body is to be marked."

Monica's teeth made her bottom lip bleed. "I understand," she whispered.

"You understand what?"

"That I am yours, Master."

"You understand, but you have yet to experience what that truly means. I am going to take *all* of you. In return, I will push myself to limits even I have yet to pursue. I've been practicing all week for you."

Monica had no idea what he meant, but she looked forward to finding out.

"You remarked on my choice of such a bright white for you." Henry released her, stepping toward one of the drawers on the side of the room. He opened the top one and pulled something out. Body paint, it looked like. Red, black, deep royal purple. "The symbolism was not lost on you. White for purity. You are not a virgin, my dearest, but you are still pure in this relationship. I am changing that tonight." The paints opened, joined with a brush as big as Monica's thumb. "I will be rough with your body. I will push your limits. Use your safe word, if necessary, but I hope you won't. I intend on making it as pleasurable as possible."

"That would only be right on a night like this."

She trembled when he touched her again, his strong hands gently pushing her onto the white leather of the bench. The silver leash thumped against the carpet. "From now on," Henry began, "you may speak, but only softly. You can scream later."

Scream? What was he planning to do, exactly?

Henry yanked on the leash, prostrating Monica onto the bench. "You don't have to do a thing, Princess. You're to be doted on. Tonight, you serve me by completely and utterly submitting. All I ask is that you open not just your body to me, but also your heart and soul. Can you do that?"

Monica didn't answer immediately.

"I would never intentionally hurt you, Monica."

"I know." She kept her words soft, as he bade. "I am strong, Henry. There isn't much you can do to me that will scare me away. I know you have your own worries."

Cynthia Dane

He stopped pulling something else out of the drawer. "I know that if you are sincerely disturbed by something I do, you will tell me."

"You are not my old Dom, and I am not your old sub. We are the best for each other."

He closed the drawer. "You're wise, as always. Any man who asks you to keep quiet for too long is a fool."

"I am glad that you appreciate my thoughts."

Something jangled behind her. Henry cleared his throat. "I bought you another present, Princess." He revealed a pair of silver handcuffs glistening in the setting sunlight. "I'll be careful with your bracelet."

He took her hands and pulled them beneath the bench. The handcuffs cinched together, leaving Monica to stare up at the ceiling, on her back and mentally readying for what her Dom wanted to do to her – whatever it was.

All she knew was that she was to serve through submitting. Whatever Henry wanted, she would give. Her body. Her heart.

Her soul.

Henry eased her legs open. The bench was low enough that even a petite woman like her could touch the floor with her heels. Now her legs parted.

"Take a deep breath and relax. I want you ready for me."

Monica closed her eyes and breathed until she couldn't fill her lungs more. She felt Henry kneel between her legs and bring his head forward.

His tongue drew up the slit of her corset, flicking against fabric and teasing her skin beneath. Monica hissed, her arousal coming to life as her Dom showed her this level of unprecedented affection once again.

Although he did not touch her flesh with his tongue, he was still tender and efficient. Their first intimate touch as collared Dom and sub was as sweet as Monica could have hoped for. Henry would make sure she was ready for anything he gave her. *I'll take anything he gives me.* Monica would not say her safe word unless absolutely necessary. If Henry promised to push himself, then she would as well.

Together they would reach new heights.

"Henry…" The back of her eyelids turned gold as she relaxed into his erotic touch. They fluttered open briefly, giving her enough time to see his head of dark blond move between her legs. "I mean… Master…"

He stopped long enough to say, "Tonight, you can call me whatever feels best to you."

"Henry."

He resumed, drawing one long stroke after another along the fabric he picked out for her. Monica closed her eyes again and enjoyed the moment – until her arousal became too much and met him in the middle.

"That was quick," Henry said. "You didn't waste time showing me this side of you."

The air turned warm as Henry stood and went to the paints sitting out on the dresser. He picked up the brush and dipped the tip into the purple paint.

"Hold still."

Monica listened, watching him round her again and kneel between her legs. The brush dotted her slit. Her first mark.

She quickly caught on to the game.

"Tell me, Princess, do you yearn for me?"

Although he didn't request it, Monica kept her legs spread open, high heels digging into the carpet beneath the bench she displayed herself on. "Yes, Mr. Warren. I would very much like for you to make love to me now." She knew he wouldn't.

"I bet you would like that."

He sat on the open space between her legs and untied the strings on the bust of her corset. Monica batted her eyelashes and inhaled deeply as her Dom undressed her breasts, his fingers rolling across her nipples and making her whimper. When his head lowered and tongue flicked against one nipple, she released a whine only rivaled by his groan.

"The heat between your legs right now is incredible," he muttered, fingers pinching both her nipples. "I'm hard, Monica. Do you know what that means?"

"That it's time for you to claim the first part of me, sir."

"You are correct." Henry tightened the corset beneath her breasts, making them so prominent that they were all Monica could see aside from his head of hair. Yet she could feel his breath on her skin, and hear his voice as it groaned against the outfit he chose for her. "I think we're both ready."

He straddled her hips, the short height of the bench no match for his height. Monica held her breath for what she knew was coming, but Henry surprised her by bending down and kissing her on the lips.

As they kissed, Monica daring to show him just as much desire, his erection strained against his pants and rubbed against her abdomen. *I want anything you're offering me, Mr. Warren.* The more he ground against her, the more Monica moaned against his lips and pulled against the handcuffs in the hopes she could wrap her arms around him.

Instead, Henry sat up and lowered the zipper of his creasing pants.

"Did I forget to say that I want to hear your voice tonight?" Henry pinched her nipples again, eliciting more than a hiss from his sub. "I want to hear you beg for everything."

Oh, she could do that. There was little Henry could do to turn her off. *I want whatever you give me, Master.* "Please."

The tip of his exposed cock pushed between her breasts, but did not commit to anything more than taunting her. "Please what, Monica? You know I like what you have to say."

Her whimpers turned into moans. "Please fuck me there."

His clock slid between her breasts, pointing toward her throat and holding steady as Henry caught his breath. "Fuck you until what?"

"Until you come, sir."

"Why?"

Monica looked between the scene happening near her face and the swirling arousal in Henry's eyes. "Because I want you to claim me there."

"Since you asked so sweetly…"

Monica dropped her head to soft leather, her hair spilling over the edge in a cascade of silver-spotted black. Her Dom held her down by the shoulders, his cock moving with ease along her chest. *Should I beg for it?* Monica wasn't opposed to most things, especially in this frame of mind, but she never thought much of men full-on fucking her cleavage.

Yet somehow Henry made it exceptionally erotic. Perhaps it was the way his strength pressed upon her. Perhaps it was because Monica was immobilized. Perhaps... whatever it was, she opened her eyes and looked into Henry's. She did not miss when her nipples began to harden, even without his pinching. She wanted this. She would let him know.

"Don't stop," she whispered, the strength of his thrusts increasing until her breasts began to move and provide resistance against his cock. *He's doing it right if I'm turned on by my own breasts.* And turned on by the way his cock surged between him, his hips cutting through the air with purpose. "Please, Henry, I want this."

He didn't speak, although her words made him grunt louder, his cock hard and stiff between her breasts. Now her whole chest moved against the bench, the handcuffs clattering against the bottom and her heels easing up and down against the carpet. The bottom of the corset pulled against her slit, rubbing her clit beneath.

"Oh, fuck." She rarely swore so early during sex. Henry had a power over her that no man had before. "I'm ready..."
She had no idea that those were the magic words. For the moment her whimper disappeared into the warm air, Henry released his climax, covering the top of her chest, her throat, and the bottom of her chin with his seed.

It was on the top of her breasts too, evident when Henry stepped off his sub and disappeared behind her. Monica gazed at the swath of white covering her skin in slick warmth. Her nipples glistened. Her white corset was marked as well.

"Thank you, Master," she said, breathless.

A small towel patted her skin dry. Although most of it was gone, Monica could still feel some of the wetness on her skin, and it definitely remained on the corset.

"Hold still."

The brush covered in black body paint hit her breasts. One stroke down into her cleavage, and then another up, encompassing her tender nipple and making her moan without warning.

Within seconds, her breasts, chest, and top of the white corset were painted black.

When Henry Warren said he was going to mark her...

He wasn't kidding.

It was one thing to feel his seed on her skin. It was quite another to see how she had been soiled by her Dom.

The paint had time to dry on her skin and clothes, wondering what Henry would do next. A mystery that was answered when he reached beneath the bench and unlocked the handcuffs.

And yanked on her leash, forcing her up and turning her over so she faced him and his still half-erect cock.

She didn't have to be commanded. In fact, Henry said nothing as he placed the palms of Monica's hands on the leather bench and handcuffed them again. Her knees likewise dug into the leather, the stiletto heels of her shoes pointed into the air behind her and her hair covering her face. Henry pulled the latter out of the way and caressed her cheek.

"Do you want it?" he asked softly, his fingers tightening into her scalp. "I won't give it to you until you ask for it." Monica looked at his half-erect cock and then up into his face.

"Yes. I want it."

"Then take it."

His hands remained in her hair, gathering it in his fists until it spilled from his grip in a riot of dark and bright. Monica didn't care about the acute pain tugging at her head. She was more concerned with catching the tip of his cock between her lips and pushing the rest of his shaft deep into her mouth.

The head was salty, but good to taste. Monica loved tasting her Dom's seed on his cock – and she could safely say she rarely got to give head so shortly after a man orgasmed. Between the seed covering her tongue and him pulling her hair, Monica was quickly falling into heaven, wherever that was.

Here. It's right here. Her Dom's cock in her mouth, hardening, pushing into her throat while he went from slow, easy thrusts to the kind that nearly choked her.

Breathe. Breathe! It was so sudden, the way he powered into her, filling her mouth with his girth and taking her throat by surprise. Monica had about one second to relax her gag and accept him, the man she let collar her as his sub.

"That's it. I know you want it." He spoke on her behalf, since she could not. "Take my whole cock, lovely."

It drove her crazy being unable to touch him with her bound hands. She wanted to grab him, stroke him, even nibble other parts of his groin in the hopes of bringing him more pleasure. Except it also drove her crazy – in the best way – having him slide in and out of her throat without issue. Monica whimpered, her eyes appealing to him for what they both knew she wanted.

Henry pulled her hair harder. His grunt filled the room again, and to Monica's surprise, the first shot of his second climax hit the back of her throat and filled her mouth with that taste she appreciated.

More deep breaths. More of him inside of her mouth. Monica waited for him to start pulling out of her before looking down again. Her lips were wet, the corners of her mouth unable to hold in what he had given her.

"Easy." A fresh towel dabbed her mouth. Monica threw her trust into Henry and let him help her clean up what now covered the lower half of her face.

But like how he hadn't completely wiped clean her breasts, he also left some on her lips and chin, the rest of her waking up so quickly to arousal that the heat between her legs intensified, and her thighs begged for him to take them.

"I'm not done with you yet." Henry released her hair and helped her sit up straight on the bench. He was not gentle in the way he tugged on her leash. "Come." His free hand picked up the body paints. "I need the bed to take the rest of you. This is too low."

Monica said farewell to the view of the setting sun and followed her Dom into the bedroom. Rose petals were scattered across the bedding. *He really went out of his way.* Monica felt even more romantic when her Dom pushed her onto the bed, pulling her legs over the side before opening them and holding them up to her chest. Henry pulled the brush from the red paint and drew a line across her bottom lip.

"Two down." The paints dropped to the floor. "Now my real test begins. Encourage me to get hard again, Princess."

After two rounds of marking her with his seed, Henry was probably near spent. Yet he did not show any signs of fatigue, aside from his cock, which was more flaccid than last time. *He wants to go again? So soon?* Was that his test? To come multiple times?

Considering it was her thighs spread and presented to him now, Monica had at least one damn good reason to get Henry hard again.

"Please, Henry," she begged. her handcuffed hands holding fast to her bare, dirty chest. "I need you to fuck me properly. I won't really be yours until you claim the innermost me."

"Is that so?" Henry stroked his soft cock with one hand and the slit of her corset at the same time. Monica shivered, hoping that he would be stiff again soon. "How will I claim you like that?"

Monica didn't hesitate. "By coming inside me, Master."

"You'd like that, wouldn't you? I think you might be a particular woman. Asking me to fuck and come inside you like it's nothing." Henry's cock rested against Monica's groin, tormenting her – especially now that it was hard again. "Do you want me to go fast or slow?"

"Fast, please."

"I don't know." Fingers as thick as her opening pulled aside the meager piece of cloth covering her slit. Henry smiled at the amount of arousal Monica spared him. *I can feel it running down to my...* Everything was ready for them down there. All she needed was *him*. "Can you stay soft-voiced if I fuck you fast? Usually you're loud, and I don't want to hear that right now."

"I can be quiet." Monica held in a sigh as Henry rubbed his cock against her wetness. *I want to cover you in it.* Every time the head of his cock stroked her clit, more arousal emerged, spilling from her and leaving her skin too wet to bear. Henry sucked in his breath. Yes. He wanted her, still.

Thank God he was getting harder the longer he threatened to completely take her on their collaring night. "You must be quiet. No yelling, shouting, or crying out too loudly." Henry unlocked the handcuffs again, guiding her free hands to hold up her legs from beneath the knees. With the crotch of her corset pulled aside, she looked so ridiculous that she was turned on all over again.

"Fuck me, Master. Please."

The tip, although still trying to harden in Henry's grip, pushed slightly into her. "You want me to fuck you here and come inside you?"

"Yes, Master." Monica's own grip tightened beneath her knees, spreading them apart as wide as possible while keeping any eye on what went on down there. "It's my favorite thing."

"I know." He was harder. Sweat formed on his forehead, and his shirt was unbuttoned now, but Henry was nearly ready to take her once more. Monica held in a whimper of anticipation. "Now keep those legs good and far apart."

Monica didn't have time to think about that. She was too busy holding back a cry as Henry drove his cock into her.

He kept his promise in that it would be fast. Henry spared no moment before giving Monica exactly what she wanted. *I think I'm dying.* Her Dom thrust into her, hard, powerful, and promising to make good on another mark in her body. Monica moaned so loudly that Henry clamped his hand over her mouth – before he grabbed the leash and pulled it up.

"Ah!" Monica jerked up, hands still hooked beneath her knees and her Dom's cock impaled within her. "Henry! Don't…" she had to catch her bearings. "Don't stop…"

"Why not?" His thrusts slowed, but his cock still moved within her. Monica whined as his girth swelled, filling her depths. "Are you close? Do you want to come?"

A rib shaking moan meant Monica could only nod. *Please, please, I want to!* Her core had burst into a frenzy of arousal and the reverberating need for relief. Henry was inside her. All she needed now was an orgasm strong enough to make him come inside her. *I won't come alone.* She wanted to feel his seed fill her while she climaxed and hopefully transcended to another world.

The collar tightened around her neck as the leash jerked in Henry's hand. "Beg for it."

"Please spoil me, Master." Her nails dug into her thighs. "Please let me come with you."

"Now's the time to start being loud, Princess. I want this whole house to know how impure my collared sub is. How impure *I* made her."

"Yes, Master!"

Henry released the leash and allowed Monica's head to hit her pillow again. His hands went to her paint and seed covered breasts instead, forking his fingers around her nipples while he began thrusting below again.

"Thank you!" she cried, as her wetness displayed how easy it was for Henry to fuck her now. No resistance. No doubts that her body craved for this intense affection. "Oh, thank you..."

He reached so deep within her that Monica worried he would split her in two. After all, she was a petite woman, and her body sometimes felt barely big enough to take on a man like Henry. *I can't get any fuller.* Henry may be on his third round of sex already, but his virility was still strong enough to consume Monica and make her pray that this never ended. *I love it. I love it all.* The salt on her lips. The stains on her breasts. Henry wanted everything she had, and she would willingly give them over. Even better if she could prove to the world that she had been good enough for his gifts.

Monica was on the edge. Henry was going to let her come, and he made sure it would be worthwhile as he stood up straight, hands balanced on her bent knees while he fucked her welcoming body.

"I'm…" The words couldn't come out. Orgasm was hitting Monica hard, tingling in her toes before erupting through the rest of her. She tightened around Henry's cock. *Please come with me.* She wanted to feel that heat within her as she soared through pleasure and took solace in knowing that she fully belonged to this wonderful man

She exploded.

"I'm coming, Master!" He slammed into her with sheer brute strength, his powerful hips bruising her thighs. She didn't care. This was it. This was the height of pleasure with a man like Henry. The only thing missing was…

Henry groaned, relieved and exhausted.

His gift arrived now, catching Monica as she began her descent from nirvana. *Oh God, it feels so good.* Each thrust brought with it a new wave of heat that made Monica want to do nothing else with the rest of her life but experience this exact moment.

One, two, three… four quick thrusts marked her so deeply she could feel his seed already absorbing into her body.

"No, don't, please…" He was pulling out, the opening where his cock once was now releasing a steady stream of Henry's thick seed. It ran down her ass, across her skin, and onto the bed. Even more poured from her every time her muscles contracted. "Henry, stay like that."

Somehow, she doubted he would clean this up.

Sure enough, Henry had her ease her legs down, but kept them apart so the two of them could enjoy his handiwork. Monica was covered in his seed. Nothing compared to that, not even the black paint appearing on her inner thighs as Henry painted that beautiful white fabric.

"You're so fucking hot." He bent down and licked her nipple. "I wanted to draw that out, but I couldn't the moment I was inside of you. I had no choice but to give it to you hard."

"Thank you." A shudder relieved Monica of more virility. "But, sir…"

"What is it?"

"May I have one more?" She wanted Henry's cock to magically become hard again for one last round. Just like that. Or maybe from behind. Monica's corset had been profaned, thanks to Henry, so everything was extra now.

After a few moments Henry finally spoke. "You may have one more… but you'll have to please me indefinitely to make me hard a final time."

Slowly she rolled onto her side, her muscles aching but her heart on fire. Henry could do anything he wanted to her now.

Tonight, tomorrow, forever… whatever he wanted, whenever he wanted it. Those thoughts surged in her as she felt her used body. *I'm soiled all over.* Between the paint and the marks of her Master's seed, anyone looking at her right now would know how impure she was.

Granted, she was impure when she first met Henry Warren, but this was his way of telling the world how *he* had made sure Monica Graham was delightfully unclean.

Henry cupped his hand around her ass and squeezed her flesh.

"Look at you," he whispered into her ear. How was he not passed out by now? Few men could last as long as he had.

Three orgasms? In a row? *I wouldn't be able to do it.* Monica had one so far. Given to her by her Dom, who had already taken his pleasure from her more times than most men could even dream about.

Monica felt like the luckiest woman in the world.

"Look at you," Henry said again. His fingers dipped lightly between her wet folds and stroked her swollen clit. She wrenched away from him, shivering. "You belong to me, Monica. You know that, right?"

"Yes, sir."

His fingers, covered in the delectable mixture of her own arousal and his, pushed into her mouth. Sweet, salty.

He kissed her neck, his legs wrapping between hers, and his cock digging into the small of her back. It was far from hard now, but Henry's desire for her had not abated.

"You're all mine from now on. No other man can have you as long as you wear my collar." His teeth were on her ear. His tongue explored its depths. "And you'll wear it always."

"Of course." It was a part of her now. A sub without a collar was like a man without air.

"Then will you give every part of yourself to me, Monica?" Henry's hands squeezed her breasts, still stained and marred.

"Will you let me have and take whatever I want?" He pinched her nipples, hard, making her scream in the pillow.

"Will you let me take you that place I've yet to see you go?" He rubbed her thighs and ran his finger up the brunt of her ass. Then Monica knew. She knew what he wanted from her, and what deep, dark, and blissful place he was going to take her.

Chapter 28

Subspace

"Yes!" Monica's knees jerked forward, her shoulders pulling on her arms, which in turn pulled against her hands cuffed to the headboard. "Please, again!"

Henry's hand landed on her ass, hard, making her skin scream and her flesh cry for mercy. Except Monica didn't *want* mercy. She wanted her Dom to push her as far as she could go. She wanted to see the hot, white streaks of light behind her eyelids. She wanted to feel Henry's love for her manifest in the way he brought her pleasurable pain.

She wanted him to *own* her.

Every time he spanked her, the muscles in that area contracted, and the next thing Monica knew her thighs were so wet – with her wetness and his seed – that she felt the fringes of heaven in her grasp. And every time Henry smacked her ass, teased her thighs, and grabbed her hips? Yes, that was bliss. A bliss that Monica never wanted to let go.

"Have I told you how much I love you?" Henry yanked on the leash, bringing Monica's head up. Her hair fell to her side, and Henry was there, pulling that too. "Because I do. I love you unlike any other woman I've ever loved before."

Even more than the sub who broke you heart?

"Do you love me?"

She had been told that this was the time to be loud. "Yes, Henry." His caress against her cheek felt as good as the smacks on her ass. "I love you."

"I'm glad." Now his touch was gentle on her bottom flesh. Even when the cool metal of the silver leash stroked her there, she didn't think anything of it. "Tell me how much you love me now."

No words formulated. Not when the leash spanked her, just like that first night they were together months ago.

When the pain subsided, Monica muttered, "I love you."

She wasn't lying, but she was tired. Her body was on the verge of being spent, even though another orgasm built up in the pit of her stomach and threatened to break free if Henry kept up the spanking. He knew how to make her come from that alone. *I can't yet.* She knew she was being saved for one last thing. She first had to wait for Henry to be ready.

A man trying to get hard for a fourth time in the span of two hours faced his own challenges. If spanking Monica's ass bright pink helped him get there, then she had no qualms!

"I love you, too, Princess." Henry stood beside the bed, undressing the last of his clothing before dumping them unceremoniously on the ground. "That's why I want you the way I do. Because you and I are two sides of that same coin. Yin, yang... all that. We need balance, and we give that to one another."

Naked, Henry crawled onto the bed with her, his cock half-erect. He stroked it while he spoke to her. "Can I tell you a secret? I've never met a sub like you before. You know exactly what you want and aren't ashamed of it. You've wanted all of this, haven't you?"

"Yes." She sounded pitiful, but felt anything but. "This is exactly what I want."

"Good. I need to hear that once in a while. I need you to hear that you can say no anytime. I'll punish you for a lot of things, but not for that."

"Henry..." Monica broke out of her submissive headspace and turned her head to him. "I'm not afraid of you. If you do something I don't like, I'll *tell* you. I know my safe word. I'll use it, if I feel I must."

"I know. I like that I don't have to worry about accidentally pushing you too far." He bent down low enough to kiss her lips, his touch as gentle as the air.

"I want it." Monica trembled against his lips. "I want you to take me. Take all of me to that place. I want you to. Only two men have seen me in that place before. I want you to be the third. And last."

"I understand."

"Henry?"

He stopped on the edge of the bed. "Yes?"

"Thank you." Tears threatened to well in her eyes. Tears of happiness – and a little from the pain she still felt spreading through her body. "For everything."

"No, my sweet Princess." His touch ran down her spine, ending at her hips which he pulled up, forcing Monica to her knees. "I should be the one thanking you."

Henry had a different way of thanking the women he loved. Monica already knew this, but it manifested now, when he pulled himself onto the bed and settled behind her.

Monica did not expect him to drive himself into her so hard and so quickly.

Indeed, she had not expected him to take her *there* at all. A place he had already marked that day... not that she was complaining.

Monica shoved her face into the pillow and muffled her moans once more. Henry told her to be loud and grateful, but she couldn't bring herself to do it right this second. She was too enthralled by the way he so easily thrust into her.

She knew it would be short lived. Shortly after he started, he stopped. When he pulled out, he said, "Close your eyes and hold this position. I'll be right back."

Monica did as told... but now her legs shook in anticipation.

Sure enough, something wet and cold landed on the top of her ass only a minute later.

His Domination

And something flared and hard filled her center, causing her to gasp into the pillow.

"Hold it." Henry waited until Monica had the vibrator securely inside her before releasing it from his hand. *Ten years of kegel exercises are about to mean something.* Henry didn't have to tell her to keep it in or suffer the consequences. She knew *that*.

Whatever he did in those two minutes between commanding her and walking away, Monica had no idea. She didn't want to know – not because the truth would possibly scare her, but because she wanted to keep it a surprise.

Well, few things were more surprising than suddenly feeling one's Dom spread apart their ass and finger it with warm lube.

"You all right, my love?" Henry asked, his finger deep inside her. "I can stop."

Monica jerked on her restraints. "Yes. I mean…" Pain, pleasure shot up her spine and through her skin. "I'm fine."

"You tell me if you want me to stop."

She tried to withhold a laugh, but it came through anyway, her hot breath smacking back into her face as it ricocheted off the pillow. "You continue to underestimate me, Mr. Warren."

"Then do you want me to take you here as well?"

What in the world was he *waiting* for? Her birthday? Christmas? "I want you to take me everywhere, Master."

Her kegels struggled to keep the vibrator inside of her, but Monica persisted, her muscles there tightening in strength while her ass gradually opened to take the head of Henry's cock.

She was glad that Henry long gave her permission to be loud now. How else could she respond but by moaning so loudly that her chest shook? Henry was slow and gentle, but it was still intense. Monica hadn't taken it like that in a long time. It was one thing to have regular sex after a long time. This kind? Both her mind and body had to readjust to what it thought it knew about her physiology.

"That's it." Henry's breath was ragged, but he managed to find the words to coax Monica to take more of him. "Are you enjoying this?"

Monica released some kind of sound into the pillow, but it certainly wasn't in English.

"Don't be shy." Henry pulled her hair, forcing her head up and her moans into the open air. "Go ahead and tell me how much you love it."

It took a while for her brain to connect with her voice, especially with the sensation of the vibrator between her legs and Henry's cock thrusting into her ass. The moment she heard his groans erupt from his throat, loud and powerful, Monica found herself agreeing.

"Oh my God!" She tried to collapse onto the pillow, but Henry still held her hair and pulled with half his strength. "I can't…"

"You can't what?" The hand holding her hip dropped before smacking her hard against the ass. Monica shrieked, eyes slamming shut as the white light began to take over her vision. "You can't believe what a beautiful submissive you are right now? Because I can hardly believe it either."

Beautiful? Maybe. Submissive? Definitely. Monica rarely got to feel this taken, this controlled, and this much at the whims of a man. To have the amount of trust she had in Henry right now on top of that? Delirious.

"Please…" Her breath heaved in her chest, her whole body on the verge of falling over the edge of something wonderful. "Please claim my ass, Master."

"Do you want that?" He pulled her hair, harder. "Because I fucking will… and then every part of you will be mine."

Yes, yes… She wanted every part of her body to belong to him. A woman could give her heart, but it was a man who took her body. *The problem is finding a man you can trust with that…* The closer Henry took her to her favorite place, the more Monica began to believe that she could love and trust freely once more.

"I want it!" The white light was claiming her, a surge of endorphins opening her mind and elevating her consciousness to a safe, warm place that was only rivaled by… by…

Pure, unadulterated love.

Henry pulled her hair the hardest yet, raising Monica's chest and forcing her to look at the ceiling. His throat made a sound she had yet to hear him utter. Something raw, something powerful, and something that claimed every part of her body.

Just as his warmth flooded her a final time, Monica succumbed to the shadows dragging her away from the light. The light went out. Darkness claimed her.

She awoke sometime later, her body free to move but too tired to do so. She lay on her side, facing the wall. *How…?*

A tender hand touched skin, Henry's warm breath pushing into her ear. "Welcome back," he whispered, his limbs wrapping around her protectively. He was still naked, unlike her. "I missed you while you were gone."

Monica leaned into his embrace, overcome by the musk of his body and the breadth of his palms as they cupped her breasts and squeezed her arm. "How long was I out?'

"Only about fifteen minutes or so."

"Did you…?"

He spread her rear with his hand, and immediately Monica felt his warm seed spill from her. "What do you think, Princess?'

Monica closed her eyes, wanting sleep to claim her. *Don't be foolish.* She felt good, but she was coming down from her subspace high. Logic and reason were about to start winning.

"I think I'm worn the hell out."

"I'll say. Me too."

"You did it… what? Four times?"

"Somewhere around there."

"You're inhuman."

"Only around you."

Monica pulled against her collar, her breath slightly cut off at that angle. Henry unlocked it for her and let it fall to the floor, the silver and diamonds flashing in the bedroom light. "I feel so dirty. Not complaining, of course."

"You are delightfully filthy right now. Would it be uncouth of me to say that I'm really admiring it? I wish you could see the extent of it."

"You should be proud. No man has ever done this to me before."

Henry said nothing, but she knew she lifted his ego with those words.

"Come, love, we need to get you cleaned up."

Monica resisted his attempt to get her to sit up. *I don't want to.* She wanted to continue lying there, in his arms, feeling the heat of their bodies and basking in the glow of what he did to her. To give that up meant going back to reality. A reality that was full of terrible, bitter people and a world outside of them.

"Monica."

Henry stood beside her, his hands taking her again, but this time in an attempt to lead her to the bathroom. Monica continued to resist, the euphoria of subspace still too wonderful to leave. Tears rolled down her cheek. Tears she could not control.

He stopped trying. "I don't want my Princess getting sick."

Monica buried her face in the pillow. *Why won't he cuddle with me?* She wanted Henry to consume her again. To keep consuming her until there was no hope of returning to the real world. She wanted to be a part of him until her dying day.

It was the only way to keep the euphoria – and feeling euphoric meant certain people couldn't hurt her anymore. So when Henry scooped his arms beneath her and picked her up, she felt both comforted and irate. Her Henry held her, but he was taking her away from the pleasures of their bed, and to another room where he would cleanse her.

"Don't fight me, Princess," he said softly. Monica floated through the air, the room spinning until she had to close her eyes to keep from getting sick. "I'll protect you. We'll take a long bath together. This week is all ours."

Monica rested her head against his shoulder and felt herself carried into the bathroom, where steam from a bath already waited for them. She was propped up against the tub, Henry delicately removing her corset as she came in and out of subspace.

"Trust me, Monica." He stroked her knee, her cheek, and her hand, giving her a new charge of endorphins that made her smile again. "Do you trust me to take care of you?"

She nodded.

Monica didn't remember any of the rest of the night. She was too retreated into the back of her mind, where all she had to worry about was when she could go to bed and be wrapped in Henry's arms again.

Chapter 29

Plans In Paradise

They spent the next few days on a beautiful private island somewhere near Jamaica but not close enough to see other life. Of course, there were plenty of people on the island. Wait staff. Transportation experts, with their seaplanes and boats. Suppliers with boxes of fresh fruit and salted meats. The island was not inhabited year-round except for the occasional groundskeeper maintaining the place, but while Henry and Monica were there, it was a veritable bustling village from dock to vacation house.

The beach was for themselves. A hammock hung on a deck overlooking the bright blue sea, and although Monica spent a good amount of time in it alone, Henry often joined her in between phone calls back to the States. Monica had turned off her phone, but Henry didn't have such liberties, even on his collaring honeymoon.

On the day before they were due to return home, Monica spent some time reading the newspaper in the hammock, the quiet splashing of the waves keeping her head level as she read about tragedies around the world. Here in paradise, they didn't seem possible.

"Five shot and killed in Miami hit and run." How terrible.

"You shouldn't read sad things on a day like today." Henry, dressed in a light cotton shirt and khaki pants, stood beside the hammock, his sunglasses tight on his head and his hands on his hips. "There's plenty of time for that later."

Monica lowered the paper but did not answer her Dom.

"Scoot over."

He snatched the paper from her hand as she pushed herself to the side of the hammock, the net swinging toward the wooden patio floor just before Henry pushed it back down and claimed a spot for himself.

Monica rolled into his hold, head and hand on his chest as she gazed at the clouds roaming across the horizon. Henry's hand didn't wait to stroke her hair.

"I hope you've been happy these past few days."

"I have been." A few days of relaxing on private beaches eating fantastic food and making love after dusk? What woman could say she hated *that?* "I don't want to go back."

Going back not only meant returning to the Château, but the real world it inhabited. Not to mention being away from Henry for who knew how long. Monica wasn't ready to completely move in with him yet, or at least not until she figured out what to do with her business. *I don't want to give it up.* She still wanted to be the primary owner even if she groomed someone like Judith to take over as Madam. Her breakup with Jackson taught her to always have her own source of income.

"I know you don't. I'll miss you." Henry kissed her cheek before resting his head on top of hers.

She would have been content to spend the remainder of the afternoon there, swinging slowly in the hammock as they looked at the world passing them by. *Best way to live a life.*

"I have a confession to make. One I've been holding in for a long time."

Monica sucked in her breath. "Don't break my heart, Henry. We're on a private island. No one will hear you scream."

"Duly noted." Whether that was his dry wit speaking or his honest opinion… "I don't know how you'll take this, but… I already knew who you were before we met that night."

"Knew me as in recognized my name? Or knew me by sight?" She knew the first was true, if Gerald Warren owed Jackson a ton of money. No one knew Jackson without knowing who she was as well.

"Knew you by sight. Monica, we had met a few times before… not that I ever expected you to remember me."

"How had we met before?"

"Functions, The Dark Hour, parties… wherever Jackson Lyle brought you and I happened to be there as well."

"I see."

"I've loved you for a long time, Monica."

She lifted her head, studying the gaze behind his bright blue eyes. "That's bold to say."

"I always thought you were beautiful. Any man can think that, yes, but there was something else about you, even when you were in that man's shadow. You were quiet and demure, but commanded respect when people spoke to you. It's hard to find submissive women who still have spines in this world."

"Is that what your previous sub was like? You never told me about her."

Henry sighed. "She was too new to this lifestyle, I think. She only had one Dom before me, and he was new to Topping. So they didn't go as deep as I usually take my subs... as you know now."

Blissfully so.

"I always regret pushing her away from me like that. I should have seen it earlier. I learned a lot from that experience. I swore I wouldn't take on another sub until I thought we were truly a good fit and I had a better grasp on aftercare."

"I've yet to want for either."

"That's what I mean. I held longing in my heart the moment I heard what happened between you and Jackson Lyle. I admired you, first and foremost. Nobody likes that guy, unless they're licking his boots."

"You mean like I literally used to do?"

"No offense, my love."

"None taken."

"That's when I allowed myself to want you. Before, you belonged to some other man. It was verboten for another Dom to want you. But when I heard you left him, I was overcome with the desire to know you."

Monica waited for him to continue.

"When Sam invited me as his guest to the Château, I jumped at the chance. He knew I was a Dom, but I only cared about seeing and introducing myself to you."

"I hope I was everything you expected."

"And then some. You have no idea how much I loved you that night... even when I was hungover the next day."

"That explains your following actions. This whole time I thought you were simply persistent. Not... in love with me. Not like that. Yet."

"I was a slobbering mess in absolute love with you. Fuck it, I still am."

"That's sweet, Henry." She wished she could say the same about him back then. *I didn't know who he was... but he had loved me from afar for so long?* Had admired her intelligence and business tenacity? That turned so many men off, even Doms. Jackson used to belittle her business suggestions.

Jackson.

"He'll never be out of my life, Henry." She sat up, his hand rubbing her back. "Jackson, I mean. I don't want anything to do with him. I'll never go back to him, but he'll always find ways to torment me. It's in his nature. Your relation through your father to him does not help."

"I'm sorry. I wish there was something I could do."

"Paying off your father's debt would help. He would have no claim to bother us."

"I wish I could. As I told you, my fortune is all tied up in assets and investments. I don't actually have access to most of it at this time. Not enough to pay that man off and not end up in the poor house."

"I understand." Monica didn't have enough to help. Half a billion dollars was hardly anything to men like Jackson and Henry, but it was true. Those numbers were tied up in all sorts of things. These men rarely had stacks of money lying around. "But something needs to be done. I won't live the rest of my life afraid of him."

"I refuse to ask that of you. I can ban him from my property, but I can't ban him from other places we go to."

"Hence why something needs to be done."

She was not so subtly suggesting that Henry show her how alpha he could be in public. She knew how wonderful he was in the bedroom, in other private places, but not in the open world. She wasn't going to say, "Do something about him, or we're through," but something... had to be done.

Jackson would never respect boundaries. He only understood other men.

Henry seemed to understand. "He won't listen to me if I went to talk to him. He would laugh me out of his office, and that would only make things worse for you. It would have to be more... you know..."

Oh, Monica knew.

"So we, ironically, need money and a way to keep him away once and for all."

"Hmm."

"What if we could kill two birds with one stone?"

"That would be ideal."

As the ocean continued to rumble behind them, as the hammock continued to sway, and as their hearts continued to beat together, Monica had a good idea of what they needed to do. From the way Henry looked at her, they were on the same diabolical page.

Chapter 30

Least Expected

On the Thursday night following Monica's return to her Château, she was thankful that things were busy enough to take her mind off the fact that she would not see Henry for at least another week.

They were not overrun with clients, but Judith's patron stopped by, and a small group of merrymaking men having a four-day bachelor party decided the Château was their starting point. Chelsea and Grace were hired to entertain them for the evening, plying them with drinks and pretending to lose at video games. The last Monica checked, Grace was running around with her top off, and Chelsea had disappeared into her room with one of the guests who promised her an extra thousand if she whipped him for an hour.

I need to replace Sylvia. Back to work, indeed. If another client showed up that night, the only girl available would be Yvette. *Haha. Hahaha.*

Monica could not squirrel herself away in her office on a busy night. So she sat in the Receiving Room, covertly flipping through the other applications she received from girls while on her collaring honeymoon. Yvette came and went from the room, her clothing simple and her face barely clad in makeup. Although she never took on clients outside of her patron, she still made an effort to represent the Château decently in front of other guests. *Still, would a nicer dress kill her?* If she wasn't going to work, she could at least go outside or to her room. It didn't seem like the type of night where Yvette would offset her inability to entertain guests by helping out with the party managing.

"Madam, a guest has pulled up."

The maid disappeared from the doorway before Monica could give her any orders. *Great.*

She hated these situations. Rarely did she run out of available girls, but this was such a weird night already that she was kicking herself even harder. *I need. To replace. Sylvia.* No more falling into her pits of lovesickness. No more running off to get fucked in every orifice. Well, not until she took care of her other responsibilities first. *By this time next week, I will have my fifth girl again.*

Until then, she would have to come up with some way to make this man happy. *Damnit, Yvette.*

Men were impatient. They didn't like being turned down in a house of pleasure. Especially when their only crime was having imperfect timing.

She went to the foyer and waited.

And waited.

Some commotion erupted outside. Nothing bad, but there was certainly some confusion, some misheard words, and a flippant comment that brought the doorman inside with a look of "we've got a live one" on his face.

Monica steeled herself. *He wouldn't dare.*

Oh, yes he would.

Yet it wasn't Jackson who walked through the door. She doubted security would let him get that far anyway. Instead, she soon found out that the reason her staff was so confused was because the guest gracing the foyer was one of the least likely to arrive, let alone... alone.

"Monica! I didn't expect you to greet me yourself." Eva Warren, dressed in a navy blue Givenchy suit and wearing enough makeup to scare off a kick line, handed her coat to a maid and spared the madam another look. "Nice choker."

Without thinking, Monica's fingers went to the collar around her throat. The black one studded with diamonds. For a sub like her, it was basically a wedding ring. "Thank you." Monica shook the strange thoughts from her head. "Can I help... what are you doing here?"

"I don't know. What *am* I doing here?" Eva was so like her brother and yet completely different. They both could play long, coy games that must be how the Warrens made all their money in generations past. Yet Eva was very open when she was playing a game. Henry liked to horde it inside him, only letting people in on his dirty secret when it was time to spring the surprise on them.

So, Eva knew damn well what she was doing here… but she wasn't telling Monica a damn thing until the time was right.

Well, Monica would not let anyone, least of all someone in Henry's family, say she was not a competent hostess. After Eva secured her coat and large purse in the guarded closet, Monica led her to the Receiving Room, where she offered her Dom's sister a drink. Eva took a whisky highball, because of course she was the type of woman to drink one of the manliest drinks available.

Monica wasn't disparaging her. She tried to figure her out.

"I must say I am surprised to see you here." They were alone in the room, the door closed while Monica sorted out this situation. "I never thought I would…"

"Come on, we're practically family now." Eva crossed her legs and leaned back in a leather chair, her demeanor screaming *"I own places like this."* Under normal circumstances, Monica would find this scene exciting, or at least a puzzle to solve, but given their relationship it was nothing short of confusing. "Be candid. I'm used to it."

Monica didn't even know what she would *say* that would classify as candid. "Why are you here, Eva?"

"Hmph. You know, I was always curious about this place, but a girl like me never knows how she'll be accepted or treated. I'm a bitch, not because I'm a Domme, but because I have to put up with the bullshit people around us hurl at me. It's not easy… being like me."

"Of course." There were few lesbians in their world. Even fewer were so out about it. For all Monica knew, she got grief from her parents – she doubted Henry cared. Never mind anyone she wanted to work with in an ultra-conservative world. Well, conservative until they wanted someone to whack 'em with a flogger. Monica had seen it all. "You are the first solo woman to come through here."

"Oh? There have been other women?"

Only Mrs. Andrews, but Monica wasn't going to give that information up freely.

"Do you know Kathryn Alison?"

"Not personally. I've certainly heard of her." Kathryn Alison was one of the richest women in the country. Monica also had it on good authority that she took on male subs. Ms. Alison was not shy around The Dark Hour.

"I was hoping she may have come here before. She's a good friend of mine."

"I'm afraid I haven't seen her around."

"Damn." Eva drank some of her highball before setting it on a coaster and sitting up straight. "I actually have other reasons for being here. It's about my brother."

Monica perked up. "Has something happened?"

"Goodness, no. As far as I know he's in Madrid scaring the pants off a business we own there. Someone has *not* been performing well, and…" Eva grinned. "They're getting the Warren treatment."

Is that so? Monica was still interested in seeing how Henry worked outside of the bedroom. He must be effective at his job if he could manage so many subsidiaries and buy out even more. In those worlds, the only types of people others responded to were outgoing alpha types. While Henry was certainly alpha, he wasn't very...

"My brother is a subtle man." Eva cut into Monica's thoughts like a knife through cake. "A subtle man who always gets his way. For God's sake, how long did he chase after you?"

Monica didn't answer.

"Yes, yes, sorry. Keep in mind this is my *brother* we're talking about. I enjoy talking about him like this as much as you do. There's something I need to make clear to you, however. It's about... well, he told me that you knew about Jackson sniffing around our place."

Monica squared her shoulders. "He explained it to me. I understand that your father owes him money."

"Bit of a blunder, ain't it?"

Laughter bubbled in Monica's throat, but this was no laughing matter.

"Look, the two of us can't control our idiot father. Likewise, he can't control us. Henry and I have been doing a lot of talking about how to free our family's name from someone like Lyle's. Especially now that you're in the picture."

"I apologize for the inconvenience."

"Don't give me your submissive shit, dear. You don't have to impress me."

Lips curling inward, Monica decided to ignore that. *Fancy her calling me "dear."* Monica was an easy what, seven years older than Eva? Doms. Dommes. They were all the same when they got patronizing.

"What I'm trying to say is…" Eva leaned forward, her elbows resting on her knees as her bright blue eyes sparkled in mischief like Henry's. "He told me of this concoction of yours. Quite the… well, that is one way to get Jackson Lyle out of your life. Short of hiring a hit man."

"I doubt you came out all this way to talk about that."

"Not really. Not the event itself." Eva was interrupted by the door opening. Yvette sauntered in, her bored face bringing Monica down even more. *Would you work, already?* Clean the dining room. Make sure the guests in the other room had enough to drink. Walk around in something sexy. Yvette didn't have to take on a client in order to be useful around there. Sure, her patron was paying to take her out later that weekend, but…

"Get Miss Warren another drink, would you please?"

Yvette shot her a look over Eva's head. "Of course, ma'am." Sarcasm dripped from her lips like honey. Was someone having her monthly visit, or was she being a brat? *I can never tell with her.* Girls like Grace were open about how irritable they got while PMSing. Other girls like Judith could be like that all the time. Yvette continued to be an enigma to the Château.

"You must be one of her ladies." Eva flashed Yvette a smile. "You're very beautiful."

Yvette turned, her eyes widening the moment she saw Eva. "Uh... yes. Ma'am."

"Please. Call me Eva." She waited to receive a refilled highball before continuing. "My brother didn't tell me that such beautiful women work here. I mean, I expected it, but..."

The Warren game was afoot. Eva was one silver and diamond encrusted collar away from trying to one-up her brother.

And Yvette was blubbering like a teen meeting her idol in the most conspicuous place.

"That'll be all for now, Yvette. Thank you."

Reluctantly, the girl withdrew from the Receiving Room, her eyes locked on the back of Eva's head – and Eva could only spare Monica a knowing smile, as if to say, *"I know I'm good."*

I'll be damned.

"Anyway, as I was saying..." Bolstered by her oh so innocent flirtations, Eva draped herself across the couch, her metallic earrings sparkling in sync with the glitter on her eyes. "If you and my brother decide to go through with this, there's one thing you need to know. And yes, I partly came out all this way to tell you this in person."

"I appreciate it. What is it?"

"You think you've seen every facet of my brother, but you haven't. You haven't seen him when he's angry. He doesn't get angry often. Our mother says he's like a rock at the bottom of a river. He's constantly being beaten up, but he just stands there, waiting for the moment to cut someone's foot open. He was never the type of guy, even when he was a kid, to go up and slap somebody across the face."

Monica thought of Ethan, who punched Jackson in the face just for her. No, Henry was not like Ethan in that regard at all.

"He's... subtler than that. You know those snakes that wait in the grass? That's Henry. He'll wait for you to pass by, on high alert. If you pass him, he'll leave you alone. If you step on him? Hope you're carrying an antidote. I once pissed my brother off a few years ago, and now I'm careful to not do it again. Not like that."

"Are you warning me?"

"No. He adores you. I doubt you could do anything to bring that out in your direction." Eva laughed. "No, the person he's angry as fuck about right now is Jackson Lyle. Every time his name gets brought up in our house, Henry goes on a tear unlike I've ever seen before."

"I should like to see it."

"He keeps it far away from you. He's always concerned with worrying you or triggering you or whatever. Nope, I'm the dumbass who keeps bringing him up. Ha!"

Monica didn't know what to say.

"Look, what I'm trying to tell you is that Henry is waiting to completely destroy Jackson. He's pissed about what he's done to our father, and he's madder than hell about what he's done to you. His own father and his almost-might-as-well-be-wife? I don't know how he hasn't completely burst yet."

"Please get to the point."

Eva sat back as if Monica had bitten her. "My *point*, dear sister, is that this plan of yours may make Henry completely explode in ways you've never seen before. You think you know every side of him, but you don't. He can get scary when he's ferociously protecting someone. Except he won't resort to violence. The things he does… well, you'll see, I guess."

"I…"

"He's a subtle alpha. You know he's an alpha male. I know he is. Most of the world at large doesn't. If your plan works? The whole fucking world will know. Especially Jackson."

Monica cleared her throat. "That's the only language Jackson understands."

"Good." Eva stood, her half-empty glass left on the table. "I just want you to know what you're getting into. For your own sake, and Henry's."

The door to the Receiving Room opened. As Monica was about to show Eva out of the Château – for what the hell else would she *do there* that night – the only unattached woman in the whole damned building stepped in front of Eva.

"Can I get you anything, ma'am?"

Monica didn't know whether to gasp in disbelief or go pay someone over a bet she just lost. Eva, on the other hand, merely smiled at Yvette and said, "Your madam told me that there were no available girls tonight."

I said no such thing.

"The madam is wrong. I am available."

"Yvette." Monica fought to retain her propriety in the midst of these unforeseen events.

- 403 -

"Excuse me." Eva turned to her sister-in-lifestyle, suppressing the most satisfied grin. "Is she for real?"

"I have no idea. She always gives me trouble." There was a wink in that statement.

"How much trouble?"

Yvette took a step back.

"Too much. I'm thinking of replacing her if she can't hold her own around here. Don't expect her to give you a discount. She needs to be making me more money."

"So you're saying she's been a very bad girl."

"You could certainly say that."

Yvette's cheeks were as white as the platinum hair on Eva's head. "A girl who has been so bad that I couldn't possibly get the family discount around here. My word. She sounds like a fun troublemaker."

Wink, wink. Nudge, nudge.

"Do something about her, would you?"

Later that night, the whole house was as confused as Monica when they heard Yvette screaming for pleasurable mercy in her room. Monica finally allowed herself to laugh.

Chapter 31

Happy Never After

"Just to confirm," the polite voice on the other end of the line said, "you would like to offer yourself for the submissive auction next Saturday."

The ticking of the grandfather clock in Monica's office almost overpowered the woman Monica spoke to from The Dark Hour. *I thought I was clear enough already.* "That is my intention. Why? Have you had many other takers?"

"Naturally others have signed up for consideration."

Naturally. Every year dozens of subs and their Doms signed up to auction off their skills to the rich masses. Only one would be chosen. The one who served to make the most money for the establishment and give the greatest time. *That would be me, thank you.*

"You know me, and you know my Dom. We may be a recent couple, but we're both highly experienced in this world."

"Of course."

"Then there's my own history. That alone should get some seats in your audience."

The woman considered this. "I shall pass such information along, Ms. Graham."

"Be sure that you do. Mr. Warren and I are oh so looking forward to making you all *lots* of money." An inexperienced sub from the year before made nearly twenty million dollars. *That was her cut, not counting what went to the club for the privilege.* When the rich got together to throw money at a sub entertaining them, any amount was possible.

Or so Monica desperately hoped.

Usually a couple hundred people showed up to those shows. One of the biggest turnouts of the year for the club... billionaires from all around the country, let alone the world showed up to throw money at a woman they would never have for themselves. If someone who barely knew what she was doing could make that much...

It was their only hope.

Monica laid on more platitudes about the establishment and what was in it for them. Such as massive discounts at the Château for all the owners and managers. It was the least she could do for continuing to pilfer some of their best Dommes. *My olive branch.* When she hung up, all he could do was sit back in her chair and hope for the best.

She tried not to think about performing in front of so many people. She had done things publically before, but always at intimate parties where she knew everyone and what they liked.

The Dark Hour wouldn't let things get crazy between her and the audience, but their screening would only go so far.

Her cell phone buzzed with a message. Judith.

"You need to get down to the foyer." Before Monica could expect the worst, such as the police or Jackson, she received another message. *"It's Sylvia."*

***

The taxi idled in the driveway as Sylvia, dressed in a little black dress but devoid of her usual decorations, stepped out with a suitcase in hand. She closed the car door behind her and faced the Château, a smile so far away from her face that she looked like the unhappiest woman in the world.

Because she is.

The driver pulled out more luggage from the trunk. Without a moment of consideration, Monica told two maids to bring them in. "To her old room," she said, standing in the entrance.

Judith stood off to the side. Chelsea leaned over the balcony overlooking the driveway. Grace tried to hide behind a pillar, but everyone could see her. Yvette roused herself from sunbathing in order to see this spectacle.

That didn't account for every staff person gawking at the return of the one of the Château's daughters.

Nobody said a word as Sylvia ascended the front steps, her hand clutching her suitcase handle so hard that her skin turned red. Her lip trembled, but she kept her pride and did not cry. There was no engagement ring on her hand.

"Welcome home," Monica said, as soon as Sylvia was close enough to hear her.

She looked away. "I didn't know where else to go."

"Who said you had to go anywhere else?"

People respectfully cleared out as Monica led Sylvia back to her old room, which was still furnished in her style.

Sylvia sat on the edge of the bed, suitcase dropping to the floor. Behind her, Monica heard enough whispers to fill her ears for years. "Cheating bastard." "Had a mistress in every major city." "Promised to marry like three other women." "Does he think we're actual concubines or some shit?"

Tears fell down Sylvia's face now. She was so young, so naïve.

So in love, like they all had been at some point.

"He called me a whore," she mumbled through her tears. "When I confronted him about the other women, he called me a *whore*."

Monica did not move to touch her. That's not what Sylvia needed right now. "I'm sorry. You can stay here as long as you need to."

When she exited the room, she saw a maid eavesdropping around the corner of the hall. "Tell the doorman and all security personnel that Mr. Carlisle is no longer welcomed on these premises." The day Monica feared had come. That was the nature of the business.

Chapter 32

The Wolf Queen Returns

"Are you nervous?"

Monica turned from the window overlooking The Dark Hour's open room. The stage was empty, yet half the tables in the main gallery and up in the more private balconies were filling with people. Men in their finest suits. Women in risqué dresses that twinkled and showed off their bodies in enticing ways. Men in leather, gags in their mouths. Women with tight collars around their throats, some crawling on all fours while they waited for treats from their Masters.

On a normal night, Monica would find the spectacle absolutely delightful.

Tonight is not a normal night.

She wore her lavender silk robe, naked beneath. Her hair was freshly washed and styled by a competent professional. Body glitter covered her skin in case people couldn't find her in the darkness. Her leather collar pressed against her throat. The only thing easing her nerves was Henry's hand on her shoulder.

"I am nervous. Not for the reasons you think."

"NoI don't think you're nervous about getting on that stage and entertaining the masses." Henry smiled at her. "Not *you.*"

A shiver rippled through her. Oh, she was nervous. She looked at the darkened faces of billionaires, millionaires, their guests and lovers, coming from all over the world for this prestigious event that Monica was invited to participate in. Yet half the seats were empty, and the show started in a half hour.

"What if there aren't enough people?"

Henry shook his head. "You know how this works. People who came from far away want to make sure they get good seats, so they come early. The locals straggle in. Then there are the people in-between coming here right after business dinners or after waiting five hours for their dates to get ready. If an inexperienced talent could pack the place last year, what do you think someone like you will do?"

That was the rub. The Dark Hour hadn't explicitly named Monica as the main attraction that night. They usually didn't name the sub out of respect and to build intrigue. Instead the fliers and emails said, "The Experienced Madam, Coming To Us From Her Château On The Hill." It sounded like a grand re-debut. As if Monica had gone into retirement, never to be heard from again until this night.

Still, that wasn't what made her the most nervous.

"Don't think about that man." Henry stroked her cheek. "It won't do you any good."

"We're doing this *because* of that man."

"No, we're not."

She looked at him, her Henry, the man she let into her heart. "We're not?"

"We're doing this for us." Henry cupped both hands around her cheeks, "To make our future easier, and to test the last of our limits." His hands went from her face to her shoulders. "If you go out there thinking this is about that man, then you'll falter. Don't think about any man but me. That's what the people want to see anyway."

"You're not worried about your reputation?"

Henry laughed at that. "My reputation? You're kidding, right? If anything, this will bring me more business than ever. People who have never heard of me will know who I am. People who have heard of me will see how strong I am. And people who know me will respect me more. It's different for men, Monica."

"I know. Trust me, I do." Men who tossed their cocks and women about always got more respect than the woman baring herself to the world. Well, unless they were Monica Graham, experienced submissive extraordinaire.

"If our plan works, that man will be out of your life."

"Don't put conditions on it, Henry. My mind is already running in all the different ways this can go wrong."

"And don't think like that." He pulled her into his embrace, which instantly settled the nerves fraying within Monica. *Can I stay here forever?* His scent, his heat, his love... could a woman ask for more? *Safety.* Usually, Henry's arms were safe. Tonight, she wasn't so sure...

"I'll be fine once we start..."

"Do you remember everything we went over?"

"Of course." Monica stepped out of his hold and looked out the window again. People were settling into their seats. Bets were placed over this and that. Servers made the rounds with drinks and buttons that would let them make donations throughout the night. Monica's goal was to make them press it as many times as possible.

No pressure.

"You'll do great, Princess."

She shed the robe. A few feet away were the clothes she and Henry decided were best for that night. "Tonight I'm nobody's princess." Silk and lace filled her fingers as she looked at her naked body in the mirror, defiant. "Not even yours, Henry. I'm the queen of the wolves, and you'll do well to remember that."

Grinning, he stepped toward the door. "As you wish, Madam."

Indeed, the Experienced Madam was about to make her grand re-debut.

***

The chatter in the room was deafening. Businessmen who hadn't seen each other in years were suddenly old pals again. Women commiserated over spoiled kids, rich husbands, and the latest trend of candle wax going around the area. Workers struggled to hear the guests' requests over the rabble. The orderly rabble, of course.

Almost every chair was filled. The raised seats and tables around the center stage held not only the richest people in the region, but in the world – they could afford those premium seats. Monica wasn't embarrassed to see Ethan and Jasmine sitting toward the front, the latter's crimson and ruby collar glistening every time she slightly turned her head. If anything, it comforted Monica knowing her friends were there. It gave her someone to focus on.

James and Gwen were there, slipping money to other people as they placed bets. About what? If it were really Monica? If she would come too soon? *If Jackson will show up?*

She didn't see that man. She had looked.

Yet there were other familiar faces. The Château was closed for the night, since this would be prime advertisement. Thus, every girl, including Sylvia with her toned down style, sat together off to the side. Mr. Carlisle was a respectable distance from any scene he might cause with the pissed off girls on Sylvia's side.

Mr. and Mrs. Andrews tittered at a private table up in the balconies. Sam Witherspoon and a group of buddies took over another table, downing drink after drink in preparation for the show. Monica saw the illustrious Kathryn Alison, perhaps the richest woman in her own right, sitting with Eva at a table that was clearly reserved for women only. *Eva will leave.* Her job was to drum up interest, but there was no way she would stick around to see her big brother do what he was about to do. *Thank God.*

Bankers. Politicians. *Dictators.* If there were a rich man or woman with any interest in BDSM, they were here that night. Monica's worries that there wouldn't be enough interest were put to rest once she saw staff running around worriedly, forcing more space for people to sit and still see the stage. VIP rooms were stuffed. Bartenders worked overtime to keep the drinks flowing on schedule. The coat check overflowed.

They were all here to see Monica. They knew who she was, after all.

If she were the type to have stage fright, that would have done her in. But she never had stage fright in her life. Not even when she was giving controversial speech topics in front of her entire high school did she falter. Besides, this may be her biggest audience yet, but it wasn't her first time performing in front of a crowd. Let alone a discerning one.

In fact, one could say that Monica was a bit of an exhibitionist anyway. If there were no pressures to make a ton of money... if she could simply enjoy the moment... well, she would be very much looking forward to this.

The rabble died when a speaker came on. Monica couldn't hear him. She was too busy feeling the heavy silver collar wrap around her neck., feeling her wrists bind behind her, and feeling the leash pull against her body. The room opened up. People parted to get out of her way.

She was in front. Walking slowly, but leading her Dom through the crowd, head held high and shoulders back. She may be the submissive one, but the spotlight was on her tonight.

Some subs would still want to be led out by their Doms. That was fine, but Monica was a wolf queen. Nobody led her anywhere.

This apparently worked, for the announcer quipped that the first donations had already started rolling in. People were eager to spend their money on her. She only needed to earn it.

That was dangerous.

These people would want to see her limits, her boundaries completely violated for their own amusement.

They wanted to hear her choke on her safe word.

They wanted to watch Henry ruin her.

So be it. She knew this already. Henry knew it already. They went over, time and again, what the real limits were, and what would be for show. They weren't stupid, This wasn't their bedroom.

This was their freedom.

Monica stood on the stage while the announcer finished up his spiel, reminding the audience of the rules and how to keep spending money. *They'll remember.* Monica stood upright, her binds chafing a little, the collar catching everyone's attention.

All they could see her wearing, aside from her smooth skin and wavy hair, was a tailored black jacket hugging her arms and chest. It was buttoned in front, although the discerning eye could see peeks of white beneath. Whatever they thought of her outfit, nobody remarked.

No, this wasn't the type of audience to scream their demands at her. That happened at lesser establishments. These refined people wanted her to read their minds.

She had spent years learning to gauge a person's desires with one look. She enforced those talents at her Château every weekend. Now was the time to truly see how good she was.

The announcer left. They could start anytime.

There was a script in place, but Monica fully expected Henry to go off script here and there. She didn't expect it right away. Like when he yanked on her collar and nearly brought her to her knees from the force.

She gasped. The room remained silent.

Hundreds of eyes were on her. Henry rubbed her skin as if he could wipe them away, but within seconds he recognized that his precious princess was too tough to give in to his delicate touch.

When she stood, her leash still coiled around Henry's hand, she saw that half of the audience was intrigued. The other half considered her too defiant.

That changed when Henry snaked his hand down her bodice, slipping beneath her jacket and caressing her breast. Monica couldn't help but shiver against his touch, her teeth biting her bottom lip as her eyes fluttered shut.

The relationship between a Dom and sub was something most people in that room could understand. Of course, such a relationship differed between people, but at its heart, they all knew what it meant to be a sub who wanted to serve or a Dom who wanted to pleasure. Tonight, Henry and Monica were an extension of every desire manifesting between the men and women in the audience. They represented pain, pleasure, love, desire… they were current relationships, both new and old. They were old relationships of the past, gone but not forgotten. When Henry wrapped his tongue around Monica's ear, sending waves of need through her chest, the women in the audience swooned. When he pressed his hand against her abdomen, threatening to touch her between the legs in front of so many people, the men smiled and willed him to continue.

Everything they could want or need was there on stage. A table full of toys and other equipment. Rings hanging from the ceiling. Silk, leather, and metal binds and spreaders. Everyone in the audience had a preference. Their job was to appeal to as many of those as possible.

And remain authentic? *Bring it on.*

As much as Monica tried to remain focused, she was quickly succumbing to what Henry did to her. That was good… and a danger. She had to remain levelheaded if she was going to put on the best performance, but it would mean nothing if she couldn't lose herself to what her Dom did to her. Right now Henry was appealing to that possessive nature so many Doms had. He reached beneath her jacket and pulled her breasts free from the corset she wore. The jacket opened enough to show every man and woman what Monica Graham kept beneath her clothes.

"See what I have? See what I get to play with? Isn't my sub a beautiful woman? I bet you'd like to play with her. Do you want to fuck her? You don't get to. Only I do."

Monica could feel those words in the first pinch Henry gave her nipple.

The most pitiful moan in the world escaped her lips. People shifted in their seats. Half of them were enthralled already.

Monica could hear their demands now. *"Take off her clothes." "Bend her over." "Fuck her 'til she screams."* The most amazing thing? Monica responded to these hypotheticals as if they were nothing more than her personal fantasies. She wanted that.

Right here, in front of an audience.

She had to perform, but she also had to serve, to submit to her Dom as she always had. Since she was his servant, Henry could do whatever he wanted to her. Like slowly reveal more and more of her body to everyone staring at them.

They saw not only her breasts, but her thighs, her stomach, the white flesh of her ass, and even the fine hairs growing from her most intimate place. *He's humiliating me.* Not directly, since Henry knew this wouldn't bother her – they had cleared that up in the week leading up to this. The audience didn't know that. For all they knew, Monica was trembling inside as her Dom offered her up as some sexual creature to be admired and used by the masses. *That* was the thrill she now felt as Henry practically stripped her in front of these hungry beasts consuming her vicariously through her Dom.

Then she was untied, then retied again, this time with her arms hanging above her head as she was attached to the nearest ring hanging from the ceiling.

"Don't make a sound," he hissed in her ear as he bent her forward, her ass in the air in the moments before he spanked it.

His Domination

The pain was embarrassing – and exquisite. Monica was at her most vulnerable. Everyone knew she wanted the punishment her Dom doled out, but they still sat on the edges of their seats to hear her let out that squeal of arousal.

Monica wouldn't do it. She would swallow the sounds, because she was not green behind the ears.

New, untried submissives would squeal on the first spank. People would laugh. The Dom would scold her and punish her until she learned to no longer make those sounds until given permission. Monica was the opposite. She was expected to obey without fight. The joy she offered was being pushed until finally an experienced sub like her finally, *finally* cracked. Because they always did.

There were no rewards for her. Not like in the bedroom. The reward was for the audience.

Another spank hit her ass. Monica's lips parted, her eyes fluttering open as the pain quickly turned to pleasure. She made no sound. The only sound she couldn't control was the smack on her ass as Henry used his whole hand to turn her skin pink.

He left her side, rolling up the sleeves on his shirt as he observed the tools displayed on the table nearby. Monica regrouped in her head. It was only going to get worse.

Or did that mean it was going to get better?

A paddle. It was a damned paddle with *holes* in it. The first hit was merciless, making half the women in the audience jump out of their seats when Monica's flesh screamed in her stead. The world turned a hot white for a split second. Shudders upon shudders of blissful pain claimed her, warming her stomach and hardening her nipples for everyone to see. A quiet chatter of glee permeated the audience.

Henry struck her again on the other cheek. Her skin burned, but Monica did not falter.

However, if Henry didn't start holding up his end of their bargain, she might die from a lack of careful attention.

The edge of the paddle touched her collared neck and slowly drew down her spine. It tickled, so much so that Monica licked her lips and anticipated a strike to her ass again.

It didn't come. Instead, Henry lifted the paddle and addressed the audience.

"I've had the tremendous opportunity to spoil and punish this delectable beauty for these past few months. I highly doubt I'm the only man – or woman – who has dreamed about it."

The voices rose in intensity.

"It takes a lot to make a woman like this crack." He struck her, the paddle shrieking through the air before hitting her ass. Monica jerked against the binds, but did not say a thing. *This is getting harder...* Her skin pulsed in pain. Her need for a tender touch strengthened. "I'm sure most of you would love to see that happen."

Nobody said anything. They didn't have to. Their hungry eyes, as Monica looked into half of them, said everything. *"Spank her until she cries." "Make her come from that paddle." "Untie her and make her serve you."*

"Have you had enough?" Henry pulled her hair, forcing her head up. "Are you willing to serve me now?"

His Domination

The bite in his voice filled Monica with a need she would instantly act upon if they were alone. For now, she had to hold a little back. "I am yours," she said meekly. Half the audience couldn't hear her, but they still knew what she said. "Please, Master. Give me your bidding."

He released her from his hand, but not the binds. Not yet. First, Henry spanked her one last time, hitting her with the paddle so hard that Monica's knees buckled and a tiny whimper fell from her lips. Just enough to send a flurry of donations in their direction.

The binds came undone. Monica sank to her knees and propped herself up with her hands, hair creating a veil of darkness around her face.

"Look at me."

She did, but first she had to look at the audience. So many unfamiliar faces... so many ones she recognized. Her eyes met Ethan's behind a table. He kept his lips taut, but his eyes urged her to press on. Beside him, his girlfriend Jasmine gaped as if she were at the circus.

Henry brought her face near his hips, his long fingers pushing hard into her cheeks. "Go to the table and bring me what I'll punish you with next."

She pulled herself with her hands, for even if she wished to stand, her ass was in so much pain that her knees would buckle in an instance. Besides, it pleased her more to crawl toward the table, slowly, her bare skin squeaking against the stage floor.

There was a wide variety of tools on the table, all neatly laid out for her to easily recognize. Monica looked past the hole where the paddle had been and instead looked at its compatriots. A flogger. A whip. A cat. Monica pulled herself up until she was level with the table, the edge brushing against her nipples and making her gasp unexpectedly.

Her hand latched around the first thing it could grasp.

When she turned around to crawl back, she found Henry sitting in a chair, his nonplussed demeanor blocking out the audience as he waited for Monica to return. She did so, wincing every time she moved her hips too much and her raw ass cried in pain. *I can do this...* In private, she may ask for a small break. Then again, Henry wouldn't have struck her that hard in private.

As soon as she was by his side, Monica placed her next tool of punishment into his lap. "Here, Master," she said. "Is this sufficient?"

Henry fingered the long handle in his reach. "Present yourself."

Monica propped herself against Henry's legs, aware that more than one person in the audience mumbled about what he held in his hand. *"Is she insane?" "She really is a slut for pain."* Yet if Monica didn't push herself in front of these people, they would never make enough money to free the both of them.

There wasn't enough energy to pull herself across Henry's lap. With a grumble that she was more trouble than she was worth, he hoisted her across his lap, her ass pointed up and her chest pointed toward the ground.

His half-erect cock pushed through his trousers and into her abdomen. *Good.* If Henry was getting hard, then half the men in the audience were probably ready to ask their women to start stroking them beneath tables. That meant more donations for them.

Henry pulled her hair, searching for the clunky silver leash beneath her curls. "Do you want me to do it?" He tugged on the clothes covering her ass, baring more of her pink flesh for the feasting eyes around them. "Do you want me to spank you until you cry?"

She fought her attraction to the way he said those words. *If we were alone, I'd cry for you right now.* Especially if it meant feeling his erection harden against her stomach. "Yes, Master."

The cane she handed him hit her ass with the force of five men. She could not hold in her yelp of satisfied pain.

"Nobody heard you." The cane tapped against her tender flesh, inoffensive, but present. "Say it louder. Beg for it."

"Please!" Monica used every ounce of strength she had to project her meek voice into the void before her. She wanted it to echo like the sound of the cane hitting her ass. "Please give it to me, Master!"

Her prayers were answered when Henry smacked her. The snap of the cane was delicious even to Monica's ears.

However, she was slipping. The adrenaline pumping through her – that fight or flight sensation that so many subs experienced – not only made her squirm involuntarily, but began to shut down her brain's ability to process pain. She was slipping into that blissful subspace already.

Damn her Dom, who knew exactly what she liked and wanted.

"Please…" Her feeble words disappeared into the mess of hair surrounding her face. "One more."

"Please what?"

"Please, Master!"

Hot, white sparks exploded before her eyes as Henry hit her one last time. Monica's mouth was left gaping open, Henry's fingers shoving themselves inside before anyone in the audience got any *ideas*. He was definitely hard against her stomach now.

This was the moment at-home Monica would be most excited to experience. Her ass may be raw, but Henry would push her to the floor, holding her head down against the carpet as he drove his cock into her from behind. They enjoyed such a scene on their collaring honeymoon, with the French doors wide open and the ocean crashing against the beach only half a mile away.

There was no beach or sunshine now. No cool breeze kissing her skin. And Henry was definitely not going to spend himself inside her anytime soon.

He did, however, push her off his lap and onto the floor.

She landed most unceremoniously, her body crumpling in a messed heap, yet no worse for wear. Henry pulled her up as he stood, leading her back to the hook and silk binds hanging from the ceiling.

Before Monica could open her eyes and stare into the audience, Henry bent her head forward and clasped his hand over her eyes.

What is he doing? Henry was going off script. A blindfold took her face, preventing her from seeing how the audience reacted to the performance. *What?* They had decided to forego a blindfold so Monica could gauge how well they were doing. This completely defeated that purpose.

Trust him, Monica. Trust your Dom.

So she stood, docile, her skin on fire as Henry finished tightening the blindfold around her head and began ripping off her jacket.

She wished she knew how the audience reacted to that. For beneath the jacket she wore her collaring corset, still painted, and still stained from the night Henry took her everywhere he could. Were people shifting in their seats, full of ideas and desire? Did they blanche at what it meant? Did they even understand? Surely, some did.

What Monica would give to know.

She disobeyed her Dom when he told her to keep quiet and then proceeded to rip her cherished corset. Pitiful sounds crossed her lips. *I already knew it was ruined, but…* She had been surprised that Henry kept it after their collaring night. Now she knew why.

Her breasts spilled from her ripped bodice. Her thighs poured out of her torn seams. Even though everyone had seen her naked parts before, they now saw her at her most vulnerable. Spanked, humiliated, and now denied one of her most precious senses.

Low whistles echoed from the audience. Chatter filled the air. *Concerned* chatter. Did they think Henry was pushing her too far? Even when Monica's ankles were forced apart and a spreader bar shackled to them, she didn't fear what Henry had planned for her. This was part of the script, at least. Even the tap of the cane against her inner thighs – gentle yet ominous – was something she anticipated.

Yes, even the cold, hard clamps pinching her nipples were not surprising.

Monica sucked her breath through her teeth, refusing to make another sound until her Dom allowed her to. She was not some newbie. She may have been spanked and struck raw, but she was not the type of woman to cry out every time she felt an ounce of pain. She had been through hell before.

This was nothing.

With her arms raised above her head and her legs spread below, she had no choice but to accept the end of the cane wetting itself on her exposed nether lips. She wanted to moan. She wanted to tell the audience how good it felt to have that corporal toy now give her direct pleasure.

"Let them know how much you like it," Henry whispered into her ear – the rounded tip of the cane pushed into her wet folds.

A long, relieved moan filled the room as Monica was forced to take as much as she could. Although the cane couldn't have been more than an inch in diameter, she felt full. The other end of the cane fell from Henry's hand and smacked against Monica's calf. Her kegels would have to do the job again.

"If you drop that, you will not be allowed to come," Henry said, loud enough for the audience to hear.

On one hand, the audience would want to watch her falter. They wanted to watch her come a lot more than that.

Her nipples pulled against her breasts. Henry grasped her hair and pulled her head to the side, kissing her throat as his hand rounded her abdomen and slipped between her thighs. Her clit throbbed at the attention he suddenly paid it. When his hand cupped one of her breasts and his cock pushed against her worn ass, Monica nearly choked.

"Likewise," he bellowed into her ear. "If you come too soon, that'll be the end for you. Show these people what a good sub you are. No matter how much I push you, you won't come. And I'll reward you greatly if you fend off that demon scratching at your loins."

Henry was the demon here. As always.

Monica had to call upon all of her training from over the years. If she thought fending off orgasm was hard enough that first time she was in Henry's manor, then she was about to lose herself now.

The clamps tugged her nipples until ripple after ripple of pleasure filled her breasts. Her ass throbbed from the painful divinity Henry bestowed upon it only minutes before. The cane thrust into her, caressing her G-spot while Henry rubbed his fingers along her clit. Most of all, his erect cock pushed against her back, reminding her of the power he held here, in the bedroom, in her life...

...Against everyone judging her right now.

No, that was the most damning thing: the amount of people – including the women who worked for her, her friends, and the few remaining people who respected her – watching as she endured this pleasure and struggled to be a good sub. After all, Henry had partially trained her, although at the time Monica saw it as nothing more than lovemaking.

Whether people watched or not, Monica had to rely on herself. Henry was not going to hold back. That defeated the purpose of pushing her limits. *"Don't go easy on me. People will know if you do."* That's what Monica told him the day before.

Henry's onslaught ended. Monica let out a moan of relief, the cane disappearing from her body and dropping against the floor with a shocking sound.

The spreader bar unclasped.

The binds released her hands.

Monica dropped to her knees, Henry's hand on her head as he pulled her back against his hips. *He's decided to do it.* Monica didn't care what he did to her while they were there. However, *he* cared about what she did to *him.*

A part of Monica was relieved. How else could they show how submissive she was if she didn't obey one of their most precious displays? She was available to him, always. That meant giving him one of the simplest pleasures a man could ask for.

Everyone in that audience would love to see the madam of Le Château suck a man's cock.

Why not? They had seen her spanked and struck. They saw her with nipple clamps dangling from her chest – that were still there. They saw her get fucked by a foreign object. They saw her corset covered with her Master's seed and marked where he had claimed her.

His Domination

Nothing was sacred in front of these people.

Blindfold still on, Monica focused on the intimacy at hand instead of how this looked to others. Besides, nobody in the audience was uncomfortable with this thought. If anything, they had been anticipating it. Even the women, who probably often performed such intimate acts on their partners. That was the key. *Intimacy.*

These people wanted to see her be dominated. They also wanted to see them be intimate.

They were an extension of everyone's relationships, both good and bad. Every Dom imagined her as their sub, and every sub imagined being as good as her. What were her girls thinking? That they still had a lot to learn? That they never knew this side of her truly lurked within? She wasn't worried about being lowered in their opinion. She was far from that.

But she wasn't so far from Henry, who made it clear that he wanted her to *serve him now.*

Even so, a bit of apprehension crept into Monica's stomach. She had to push it away in favor of succumbing to her desire to serve.

For the first time all night, Monica used her hands to do more than crawl on the floor and hand her Dom something to strike her with. She pulled down his zipper and drew out his cock for everyone who was paying attention to see.

It wasn't unusual for a sub to want to keep this kind of adoration a secret. Not because they were ashamed, but because knowing the details of a Dom's cock was something for her to treasure. Sure, the audience couldn't see the precum already touching her tongue, nor could they inhale his natural scent, but every businessman worth his shit on the planet had a good idea of how big Henry Warren was in his pants. *That will get him business.*

The funny part? It actually would. Henry was not lacking, and the way he stood, stiff and arms crossed, showed that he didn't care if a single man in that room looked at his cock and compared it to his own. Why would it? He had a beautiful woman all to himself. Monica was the star of the show tonight, and her lavished attention was *all* for Henry. He was the envy of every man in the room.

Monica was given one minute to do as she pleased before Henry took over. She gently stroked him, remembering how he came on her breasts the day she was collared. She wrapped her tongue around his tip, tasting his musk and the seed that managed to emerge even though Henry was also practicing his own form of self-control. She relaxed her gag and swallowed his cock as far as she could, her breath puncturing her lungs as she inhaled deeply through her nose.

Henry took a handful of her hair and dug his nails into her scalp. Even though Monica knew what was coming, she still squealed in surprise when he shoved himself down her throat. He pulled her hair. He called her a slew of words that turned on the audience. He never let slip that he too was on the verge of climaxing at any moment. Monica could feel it, as his cock slammed into the back of her throat and almost made her choke. Henry was playing the professional Dom just as she was playing the professional sub. Just like she wasn't allowed to come earlier, he wasn't allowed to come now.

People loved watching others deny themselves pleasure. They loved it even more when that pleasure was finally granted.

Monica hadn't come. She would be rewarded.

Henry pushed her off his cock, a gasp of air tumbling down her throat and filling her lungs as she fell backward onto her hands. Her reprieve was short, for Henry yanked her off the ground and returned her to the hook a final time.

Monica bent over at the waist, dangling while her Dom took their leash into his hands.

The leash he had custom made just for her shortly after they met.

No, Henry had known her long before that. *Wanted her* long before that. Now he was going to take her in front of all these people – the woman he coveted for so long.

Monica allowed one short moan to burst from her lips when he entered her.

His domineering hand hit her tender ass, making her quiver on his cock as it thrust into her. His other hand lifted her right leg, spreading her thighs and allowing him to take her as deeply as possible.

Monica forgot what was happening. Why they were there. That so many people watched them ravenously, their hands on donation buttons as they watched a Dom claim his sub for their enjoyment. All Monica cared about now was the feeling of euphoria gripping her heart. Henry was inside her. His body filled hers, and they were becoming one, as it was always meant to be.

He spanked her again. The pain subsided and turned to nothing but blackened pleasure. Her eyes rolled into the back of her head.

Her bliss was short lived. Before Monica could succumb to the beauties of subspace and become wholly Henry's, the force of his thrusts loosened her blindfold and sent it halfway down her face.

Perhaps it was a cruel, cosmic joke. Perhaps it was her mind playing tricks on her as she entered a state of delusion. Either way, Monica never expected to see the one thing that would crush her heart.

There, sitting in one of the best seats of the house, was Jackson Lyle, the mirth on his face only rivaled by the joy once flooding Monica's heart.

Chapter 33

The Princess And The Dragon II

The room was quiet. Probably because Monica's ears closed themselves to the world out of pure shock. *Jackson!* Were her eyes lying to her? Was her ex, the man responsible for her woes, really sitting in the audience watching her with her new Dom? The Dom currently thrusting into her while Jackson continued to watch with that sick smile on his face?

Monica's fears had come true. Ever since she made the decision to do this show, she fretted that Jackson would show up and make her life hell. Yet she hadn't seen him in the beginning... wait, was this why Henry blindfolded her? Did he see Jackson sit down? Was he sparing Monica the trauma of seeing that man when they were in their most intimate moments?

Was that why Henry went off-script?

Reality came crashing back down. Monica averted her gaze, staring at the floor while Henry yanked her leash and pulled her hair. The blindfold had fallen far enough to cover her mouth, but not to muffle it. *I can't do this...* They were toward the end of their show, and yet Monica could only think of fear, regret, and so much guilt that she was caught in this compromising position. A church choir could have sat down in the seats and she would have relished it. Her ex-Dom? It was all over.

You're doing this because *of him.* Because the Warrens owed Jackson a ton of money that nobody could afford to pay back even if they pooled together their available money. Because Jackson wouldn't leave her the fuck alone.

Because he had stolen ten years of her life and wanted to make sure she never enjoyed emotional freedom again.

Even now, with another man inside of her – another man who had collared her – Monica could only think of what Jackson had done to her. *Hurt me. Hit me. Defiled me.* She didn't feel in love right now. Jackson's presence had managed to overshadow everything she felt before.

Apparently, Henry could feel her sudden apprehension. Under the guise of yanking her up and biting her ear to the titillation of the audience, Henry pulled her close to his mouth and whispered, "I love you."

I love you. I need you. I'll protect you. The dragon roosted only a few yards away, and yet Monica was in the hold of another man who wouldn't let someone like Jackson Lyle touch her ever again.

His Domination

Monica opened her eyes. Faces blurred. Voices mingled as people openly betted on who would come first.

The only one not leaning in to whisper to someone else was Jackson, who tapped his fingers against his knee as if this were all done for his own amusement.

He probably truly thought that. All of this had been an elaborate scene playing out in their usual relationship. The breakup. The moving out. The letters. And now this.

No.

No!

Monica couldn't let this go on. She didn't want to live the rest of her life afraid of Jackson's next move, wondering if he would find a way to bother her in her new life. That wasn't any way to live. Especially now that she had a new Dom wanting to build a life with her. Henry loved her. *Truly* loved her like a Dom was supposed to. Monica wasn't a toy to him. He was his partner, his equal on the other end of the Dom/sub spectrum. She felt safer with him in their short time together than she ever had in ten years with Jackson.

When Henry pulled her hair so hard that she let out a gasp of pain, Monica looked Jackson straight in the eye and dared him to do something.

It wasn't easy. She was at her most exposed, not just in front of the audience, but in front of Jackson as well. This was when he would hurt her.

She dared him to hurt her now.

Those eyes. That set demeanor. The look of a man on the verge of lashing out. Monica skated upon the thinnest ice in the world. While the man she loved readied himself for climax, Monica stared down the man she hated.

More than one person in the audience glanced to where she looked. Cheeks paled, reddened, and twitched. They knew. They all knew, whether they had ever done something about it or not.

Jackson lost his smile.

I'm not yours anymore. I never was. Monica opened herself to the pleasure her real Dom gave her, feeling his cock fill her, delight her with every quick stroke. His fingers traveled from her thigh to her clit, wetting themselves in her arousal as shiver upon shiver of need overcame her. Still she did not look away from Jackson's visage. She wouldn't until it was all over and he never bothered her again.

Although she felt pleasure, her face twisted into anger. The spirit of the wolf erupted from her, teeth baring, claws slicing through the air, her most primal instincts begging her to finish her rutting and tear out Jackson's throat in the audience. If she were Yin and Henry Yang, then he gave her too much now.

Her Dom was quickly losing himself, no matter how much he tried to hold back. The audience would love to see him make Monica come from his cock alone. They wanted to see her succumb to him like that. They wanted her climax to make that composed Dom come undone, the true sign of their mutual pleasure.

Monica wanted to prove that Henry was the only man who could do that to her.

His Domination

As she shot a thousand daggers into Jackson's eyes, she came, her body filling with rolling waves of pleasure that nearly knocked her off her one foot and sent her sprawling to the ground – assuming there were no binds holding her up.

Since her concentration floated elsewhere, her orgasm not only surprised her, but dragged her to another plane of existence that only Henry Warren could give her. She was *high*. Her mind escaped the dark club, laughing in the faces of everyone who wanted to see her be denied pleasure and then forced to take it. She felt more powerful than she ever had since the day she realized she wanted to serve and submit.

She was so high that Jackson couldn't touch her if he wanted.

A cry of relief burst from her body, her core holding on to Henry, refusing to let him go. He kept her grounded, as a Dom should, but he could not keep her from releasing the scream she had kept pent up inside her for ten years.

"Thank you, Master!" she exclaimed. The clamps on her nipples tightened. His touch on her clit quickened. His thrusts gave way to stillness, letting her ride out her orgasm on his cock while the world came crashing down around her. "I love you, Mr. Warren!"

The hand holding her thigh tightened before his release. In front of half the world's elite, Henry Warren spent himself inside her, his warmth filling her. Claimed, Monica let herself fall from the brief glimpse of subspace she had, her mind returning to her body.

Fatigue washed over her, but she could not fall from it as she wished. She still had to stare at Jackson, his lips taut, his ego bruised. For as much as he didn't mind watching "his" woman get fucked by another Dom, he was not charmed by the aftermath.

Henry released her. Monica's right foot touched the ground, her true Master's seed running down her thighs as gravity attempted to claim her. The binds gave in to the pressure she put on them and let her sink to her knees. Henry put his booted foot on her rear, as if to kick her over.

Instead, he pulled on the end of her leash, forcing Monica to her hands as one clamp came undone and clattered to the floor.

"Do you belong to me?"

His voice was both in her ear and a million miles away. Monica looked up, locking her eyes with Jackson's for what may be the final time in her life.

"Yes, Mr. Warren," she gasped. "I belong to you."

"You're pretty happy about that, aren't you?"

A diabolical smile crossed her subdued face. "You have no fucking idea."

Monica wasn't a knight. She couldn't cut off the dragon's head on her own. She could only distract him with her wiles and beauty, as any classic princess could. Even if the dragon tried to keep her locked in his prison, Monica still had the means to make him lower his guard. So while Henry ripped her corset off her body, stripping her completely bare in front of the audience, Monica sent every ounce of emotion she had right into Jackson's face.

Henry left her on the stage, still bound and spent on the floor. She lost her strength and collapsed onto her side, although her eyes never left Jackson's. Even while her Master's seed covered her skin for everyone to see, those same people were too busy focusing on Henry Warren – who made a grand ascent into the audience carrying Monica's soiled corset.

He stopped in front of Jackson's seat and dropped the corset into his lap, like a knight dropping a sword on the dragon's neck.

Never before had Monica heard such a large group of people fall utterly, reverently silent. She wanted to laugh, but she was so tired that the only sound she could make was a peep of retribution.

Chapter 34

His Healing Hands

The height of summer was not so bad that year. Every time Monica thought it a tad too hot, a cool breeze would start up and tickle her skin until she relented. Today, especially, it was refreshing.

Of course, it helped that she rode in Henry's Rolls-Royce, a blue Drophead Coupe that tore down the countryside highway.

The sun warmed her skin, but the breeze kept her cool, especially with her hair tied down to her shoulders and her sunglasses keeping the debris out of her face. Beside her, Henry drove with one hand on the wheel and the other hanging over the edge of the driver side door.

It felt like another paradisiacal weekend in their life. Not that it was a *bad* thing. Monica had no problem spending her days at Henry's house, in town with him, on a beach in the

Caribbean, or even in her own Château where he sometimes came to spend the night, even if it was out of his way.

Their current arrangement wasn't ideal, but it would do. Monica wanted to keep the Château going until she was confident enough to leave it entirely in Judith's hands. Otherwise, she prepared to move in permanently with Henry, the Warren Manor about to acquire one new resident. The East Wing sorely needed a woman's touch, anyway.

My future is mine. She was glad to spend it with Henry, however.

They turned down a familiar road leading up into the mountains. Here summer felt more like spring, the air chillier, the plants blooming green instead of brown. Yet Monica shivered, and it wasn't from the cold.

Henry gave her a sympathetic look before focusing his attentions on the road. It curved here, and he couldn't be too cautious.

It didn't take long for them to reach a gate manned by more than one security guard. Both men dressed in padded black took a good look at the well-to-do people in the Drophead Coupe before glancing at each other.

"I believe we are expected," Henry said. If he were at all intimidated by these men, he did not let on.

I'm intimidated. These weren't like the security guards on the perimeter of Warren Manor or keeping out the weirdos at the Château. Those men were genial to anyone not causing trouble. *These* men looked like they were waiting for trouble to shake up their day. Monica did not miss those types.

One guard was about to check Henry's ID when the other smacked him on the shoulder and pointed to Monica. "You're too new to remember her. Let 'em in."

The electronic gate slid open without a sound. Henry forced a smile at the guards before gently stepping on the gas and taking them to the private road leading up to a compound in the mountains.

Nothing had changed in the year and a half since Monica was last up this road. The same trees grew. The same outposts manned with armed guards stood tall in the shrubbery. Once upon a time, young and naïve Monica thought it was normal for a rich man to be this paranoid about security. Now she knew it was nothing but power – and not the fun kind. Henry didn't need this kind of security. Neither had Ethan, and he was more public in his persona than Henry. Since breaking up with Jackson, Monica had come to regard this kind of security as a sign that the man in charge had something to hide or was too paranoid to function – or both.

Once upon a time, Monica had felt trapped on this mountain. If she tried to leave, someone would drag her back. The fact she escaped when she did was a miracle.

Ten minutes later they passed the final gate leading to the front driveway of Jackson Lyle's luxurious mansion. The place Monica once called home. *Prison.* She frowned, body stiffening as Henry shifted in his seat and parked only a few yards from the main entrance.

Monica had promised herself that she would never pass through those doors. She was about to go back on her word.

Henry lightly touched her shoulder. "You ready? You can wait here if you want."

The sun glared off the windshield and into Monica's eyes. She shielded them, even though she wore a pair of thick sunglasses. "No. I need to do this."

Henry nodded. "Let's go, then."

He got out of the car, rounded the front bumper, and opened Monica's door for her. She was quick to take his hand, searching for his strength as one foot was placed in front of the other. *I can do this.* Breath steadied in her throat. Monica was sure to keep her chin up. The last time she was here, she ran away with fear striking her heart. Now she was returning on her own terms.

Not to be Jackson's girlfriend.

The doorman took one look at her and squared his shoulders. They recognized each other, but shared no greetings. If anything, the man was probably paid to keep his mouth shut around Monica. Lots of the staff had been like that. Jackson didn't like her getting too cozy with people. Jealousy? Maybe. Power-tripping? Definitely.

Jackson stood in front of the grand staircase, his lawyer beside him – and Henry's lawyer on the other side of him. *He came an hour ago to smooth things over for us.* Monica felt no qualms stepping right up to him with Henry behind.

The tension in that grand hall was thick enough to choke on. Nevertheless, Monica Graham kept her posture straight and her intentions clear. She was *not* here to make nice with

Jackson. Quite the opposite. She was here to make sure he never bothered her again.

Jackson opened his mouth as if to address Monica, but Henry stepped forward, and right away that stupid coward in a tacky tan suit backed down. Ever since the show at The Dark Hour, people had been laughing behind Jackson's back while flustering at the thought of Henry Warren flaunting his masculinity like that. Those people hadn't done shit when Jackson's abuses came to light a year and a half ago, but now they were more than happy to make jokes at his expense and declare Henry the much better man to admire and do business with. *I barely understand how men work.* Not on that level, anyway. A bunch of teenagers, really. Although right now it worked in Monica's favor.

"Let's get this over with," Jackson said with that false bravado of his. *I can't believe it used to turn me on.* Now Monica wanted to laugh at him like the others did. "I've got appointments."

Both lawyers cleared their throats. Before Jackson could throw a fit in his own home, Henry withdrew his checkbook and tore out the first check he encountered. "To whom do I make this out to?" He pretended to write something, though the check was filled out even before they left home.

"You know damn well, Warren."

"Oh, of course." Henry held the check up for both lawyers to inspect. "$416,578,430.98. The full amount, including the interest owed. I'm sure your lawyer is satisfied?"

The wiry old man took the tiny piece of paper and double checked the numbers he had written on a clipboard. Jackson tapped his foot against the floor, refusing to look Henry in the eye. *What a weak weasel.* He only knew how to throw his weight around when he had a woman to take advantage of. Right now, *no* woman in their circles would want anything to do with him. One day he might con another woman into being his girlfriend. That was another battle for Monica to fight another day.

"This is the correct, agreed upon amount." The lawyer handed Jackson the check. "Should I consider the debt paid in full and release Gerald Warren?"

Jackson didn't take his angry eyes off Henry's face. Not like he would do anything in front of the lawyers. But he would make sure Henry and Monica knew how much *disdain* he now held for them. They were no longer amusement. They were the people who had put some final nails in his business – let alone pleasure – coffin. First Ethan Cole, and now the "little cow and her impotent bull," as he called them in his final letter. *Not so impotent, now is he?* Monica got a regular demonstration of that.

"Sure. Paid in full. Now get these people off my property."

He said that, and yet the look lingering on Monica was anything but damning. Jackson was taking his last fill of her. *I suppose I should be intimidated.* She wasn't. If anything, she felt sorry for Jackson. All that money and nobody to share it with. It was his own fault, but still...

"Farewell," Monica said. She extended her hand to him.

Everyone, including Henry, took a step back. *So sue me. I'm a bit emboldened.* How could she not be when this was her new fate? After their show, the first thing Monica discovered was that she had broken the record for most donations. When she saw the number, she nearly fainted.

As soon as they were paid by the club, she, Henry, Eva, and even Ethan pooled together their available funds until there was more than enough to pay off Gerald Warren's debt to Jackson Lyle. Monica's first interaction with Henry's father came in the form of a phone call to Montana announcing that the debt was being paid off – and to never, *ever* do something as stupid as that again. The senior Warrens were content to remain out west while their children cleaned up their mess.

Jackson turned away from Monica without deigning to touch her.

"Come." Henry put a gentle arm around her and turned her toward the door. "It's a long drive back."

The sun felt warmer when they stepped outside. The doors closed firmly, security guards standing before them, trying to look powerful and almost failing. Monica didn't care. She was content to take Henry's hand and walk down the steps to his car.

They were both free. Between the debt being paid off and Jackson's lack of interest in her, Monica had never felt so confident about her future.

"Thank you for all you've done for my family," Henry said in front of his car.

Monica turned to him, dumbstruck. "What are you talking about?"

His hand still in hers, he brushed the curly hair from her face and teased her ear with his fingertips. "Who knows how long my family's name would have been beholden to that man. If it wasn't for *you,* my dear, the future would've been quite complicated."

"Don't do that. I should be the one thanking you."

"All I've done is love you."

"That's what you think." Monica turned from his touch and placed her hand on the hood of his car. "You've done so much more… you've helped me heal."

Henry said nothing as he opened the car door for her and made sure she was comfortably in the passenger seat. He closed the door and went to the driver's side, the sun warming the leather seats to the point Monica shifted and pulled her hat over the top of her head.

"I take that back," she said the moment Henry was in his seat and fiddling for his keys. "I haven't healed."

He looked at her, keys dangling from his hand but not nearing the ignition.

Monica explained. "I'll always be moving on from that man. There's no fighting that. For the rest of my life, he will be a part of me. He'll be souring my heart, just a little, but I think the longer I'm with you, the smaller that piece of my heart will get, until it's so insignificant that I can think of him without stopping my life." She turned her head toward Henry. "But he'll always be in there. Sometimes I'll have a bad day because of what happened. Can you handle that?"

Henry lowered his hands and leaned in toward her. "I can't understand exactly how you feel, as I've never been in your shoes... but I can be empathetic. Tell me what I can do to help you, and I'll do it. Your happiness is my happiness."

The terrible thing was that Monica didn't know what she needed. The good thing was that she at least believed him.

"Just like you'll always be healing, I'll always be fighting to earn your trust more and more." Henry pulled her toward him, their lips nearly touching. "I want to take over your heart, my Princess."

"You already have."

They kissed, the hot leather of the car heating up between them as Henry buried his face in her hair and held his hand securely around her neck. *I didn't think it was this possible to feel so safe with a man.* Henry may have been boring to the outside world, but to Monica he was enough mystery to keep her guessing – and enough security to help her trust him for the rest of her life. He was the perfect Dom. No, the perfect *boyfriend.* Well, for Monica, those two things went hand-in-hand.

"Monica." Henry took her hand, kissed it, and then held it to his freshly shaven cheek. "Marry me."

"Henry..."

"I'm already the happiest man alive. If you married me, I would never know sadness again."

She wanted to cry, but all she could do was giggle.

"What?' Henry sat back, his cheeks so pink that Monica could hardly believe he was embarrassed.

"You are seriously asking me to marry you *here?* Of all places!" Before Henry could open his mouth, she continued. "When I last left this property, I was full of fear and hurt. I didn't know if I would survive the next few days, let alone the next year. I didn't trust anyone... not even the people who helped me escape. I was nobody, both inside and out. My memories of this place are so bad that..."

"I know, love." Henry took her hand between their seats. "I want you to have at least one good memory of this place. You'll always be driving by it, remembering it, and hearing references to it. Let it be the place that I proposed to you and nothing else."

Monica squeezed his hand. *Marry Henry...* Was she ready for that? She could say yes, and then put off a wedding until she was ready. That could take another year. Or ten. Who knew? *I could be Monica Warren.* A girlish thought sprouted from her heart. *I could truly be his.* Not even Jackson had ever asked her to marry him in their ten years together. He never intended to make her his wife.

"I'm not going to say yes..." When Henry looked as if he were about to die, Monica smiled at him. "You need to re-do this proposal first. Somewhere else."

"I'll propose to you on the fucking Eiffel Tower if that's what you want."

"Oh, you can start at home. Tonight. When you make love to me."

"I'll ask you to marry me when I'm having the best pleasure of my life."

"Then you can ask me at that beautiful restaurant downtown. In front of everyone."

"All right!"

"And then on that beach on your private island. Propose to me in that hammock."

"How many times do I need to propose to you?"

Monica glanced at him, smirking. "Until I say yes."

"Who the hell is the Dom in this relationship again?"

That was the point. Monica wanted her Dom to keep pursuing her until the end of their days. Oh, she would say yes eventually. Probably on his second attempt, although she would encourage him to keep asking. After that? She would find ways to keep him after her. She would always submit, but Henry had to work to keep her.

Finally, he started the car. "The things I do for you…"

Monica rubbed his arm. "Because you love me, Mr. Warren."

His face softened, and eventually Henry relaxed in his seat. "That I do. Damn me for it."

This time she was prepared for his kiss as it came for her. Monica wrapped her hand around his head, savoring every moment their lips touched. When Henry pulled away, he did so with another kiss to her hand.

"Yes, Henry," she said, softly. "I'll marry you."

His smile against her cheek was so boyish that Monica had to laugh in joviality. "I didn't think you could make me any happier, but you have."

"I'm happy as well. Now please, take me away from this place. I want to go home."

"Our home?"

"Indeed."

They kissed one last time before returning to their seats. Henry pulled out of the driveway and cruised down the road and back to the highway that would take them *home*. Not a new prison, but a home for Monica to roam and have her fill of.

With sweet people who wanted her to be comfortable.

And family, as strange as they could be.

And so many friends who respected her that she didn't know who to invite first to a party.

And of course, love.

Euphoria bloomed throughout her body as Henry gassed the car down the highway, the wind whipping her in the face and caressing her body in a way only Henry knew how.

She rode to a better future, the past left in the dust behind her. For once, Monica didn't have to brave what lay ahead alone. She could do as she pleased – outside of the bedroom, anyway.

It felt good to trust again. Monica touched the leather collar around her neck and felt a sense of security wash over her. She was her own woman, but with the freedom to serve and submit to whomever she chose.

She chose Henry.

His was the type of domination she respected and felt most comfortable with. He treated her like a queen... a human being full of dreams and desires. No, Henry wasn't perfect. He was a man, a human like anyone else. For the faults she had seen so far, however, Monica was still confident that she could be happy with him. Moving in together... marriage... maybe children one day. The possibilities with Henry were endless. Really, all Monica cared about was moving on and exploring this happiness at her fingertips.

Maybe she could heal after all.

His Domination

Cynthia Dane spends most of her time writing in the great Pacific Northwest. And when she's not writing, she's dreaming up her next big plot and meeting all sorts of new characters in her head.

She loves stories that are sexy, fun, and cut right to the chase. You can always count on explosive romances - both in and out of the bedroom - when you read a Cynthia Dane story.

Falling in love. Making love. Love in all shades and shapes and sizes. Cynthia loves it all!

Connect with Cynthia on any of the following:

Website: http://www.cynthiadane.com
Twitter: http://twitter.com/cynthia_dane
Facebook: http://facebook.com/authorcynthiadane

Printed in Great Britain
by Amazon